兰州大学教材建设基金资助

兰州大学中央高校基本科研业务费专项资金项目"多模态《山海经》翻译数据库建设与研究"阶段性成果（2023lzujbkyjh003）

甘肃省大学外语教学研究会"大学外语教学与研究文库"丛书

中希神话赏析

主　编：张　敏　柴　櫧
副主编：赵燕凤　黄江娜　魏晨曦
参　编：龙　惠　朱文睿

中国社会科学出版社

图书在版编目（CIP）数据

中希神话赏析／张敏，柴櫹主编．—北京：中国社会科学出版社，2023.10
ISBN 978-7-5227-2455-3

Ⅰ.①中⋯　Ⅱ.①张⋯②柴⋯　Ⅲ.①神话—文学欣赏—中国②神话—文学欣赏—古希腊　Ⅳ.①I207.7②I545.077

中国国家版本馆 CIP 数据核字（2023）第 155664 号

出 版 人	赵剑英
责任编辑	张　浤
责任校对	姜志菊
责任印制	李寡寡

出　　版	中国社会科学出版社
社　　址	北京鼓楼西大街甲 158 号
邮　　编	100720
网　　址	http://www.csspw.cn
发 行 部	010-84083685
门 市 部	010-84029450
经　　销	新华书店及其他书店
印　　刷	北京明恒达印务有限公司
装　　订	廊坊市广阳区广增装订厂
版　　次	2023 年 10 月第 1 版
印　　次	2023 年 10 月第 1 次印刷
开　　本	710×1000　1/16
印　　张	20.25
字　　数	311 千字
定　　价	98.00 元

凡购买中国社会科学出版社图书，如有质量问题请与本社营销中心联系调换
电话：010-84083683
版权所有　侵权必究

甘肃省大学外语教学研究会
"大学外语教学与研究文库"丛书

中希神话赏析

Appreciation of Chinese and Greek Mythology

主　编：张　敏　柴　楠

副主编：赵燕凤　黄江娜　魏晨曦

参　编：龙　惠　朱文睿

中文序言

神话是上古先民通过幻想，以一种不自觉的艺术方式对自然现象和社会生活所作的形象描述和解释。它用虚幻的想象表现了先民征服自然、战胜自然的强烈愿望、乐观主义与英雄主义精神，是人类早期不自觉的浪漫主义艺术创作。神话可谓人们最早的哲学和人文思想来源，在不同程度上影响着人类的进步和发展。

在党的二十大会议上，习近平总书记强调："坚守中华文化立场，提炼展示中华文明的精神标识和文化精髓，加快构建中国话语和中国叙事体系，讲好中国故事、传播好中国声音，展现可信、可爱、可敬的中国形象。"[1] 作为中国文化中极为绚烂多彩且极具神秘色彩的一支，中国神话故事代表了中国古代人对大自然的无限崇拜以及中国古典文化中天人合一的思想观念，是中国文化中的瑰宝。即使在高科技发达的今天，中国神话依然具有不可替代的价值。

与中国神话相较，西方神话体系庞大，主要有希腊神话、凯尔特神话、北欧神话、希伯来神话与斯拉夫神话等，其中希腊神话和希伯来神话对西方文明的影响尤为重大。古希腊人在其生存和发展过程中创建了璀璨多彩的文化，传下丰富的遗产，神话传说就是其中之一。希腊神话内容集中完整，系统化程度非常高，是世界上现存的最完整、最庞大的神话体

---

[1] 习近平：《高举中国特色社会主义伟大旗帜　为全面建设社会主义现代化国家而团结奋斗——在中国共产党第二十次全国代表大会上的报告》，人民出版社2022年版，第45—46页。

系，对西方语言、文学、艺术与思想的发展影响深远。希伯来神话对西方文化的影响也不容忽视。希伯来神话蕴含丰富的内容，其中所有洞天万象都深切地表达着人类的情感，人与人之间的关系，善与恶的秘密，人的精神信仰，且不容忽视普遍存在的超越现象。

随着世界一体化的发展，中西方文化交流也逐渐深入。在中西方跨文化交际中，不仅需要学会对方的语言，了解对方的文化背景、文化认知是更加行之有效的交际手段。这就给我们提出了新的要求，即一方面我们需要了解西方文化背景，"以海纳百川的宽阔胸襟借鉴吸收人类一切优秀文明成果"①；另一方面，我们也需要敞开大门，推进中国传统文化"走出去"。因此，作为中国与西方文化发展的源泉，神话在中西方文化交流过程中所起的作用不容忽视。

有鉴于此，本书编者以通识选修课教学实践为基础，编辑了《中希神话赏析》。本教材的编写对象为具备中级水平英语阅读能力且对中西方神话有浓厚兴趣的学生。就内容而言，本教材仅收录了中国神话与希腊神话，原因如下：第一、尽管中国神话和希腊神话体现了不同的价值观念，但两者具有颇多相似之处，如都产生于社会发展的最原始阶段，神话内容结构均相对简单，具有很强的主观性和情感性，都是对人与自然、人与社会关系的思考且都体现了民族精神。第二、与中国神话和希腊神话不同，希伯来神话注重的是宗教精神，但这一方面似乎已经不再处于西方社会生活的核心，其文学性反倒备受关注。因此，编辑者仅收录了中国神话与希腊神话，以不同的神话主题为基础构建了教材篇章内容，包括中希宇宙起源神话、人类起源神话、洪水神话、水神神话、动物神话、惩罚神话、冥界神话、爱神神话、英雄神话以及神话中的女性形象等内容，基本涵盖中西方文明中脍炙人口的神话故事。编者依据了可靠的资源精心编撰。有些故事，尤其是中国神话故事较为零散，因此，编者对之进行了整合，进而

---

① 习近平：《高举中国特色社会主义伟大旗帜　为全面建设社会主义现代化国家而团结奋斗——在中国共产党第二十次全国代表大会上的报告》，第21页。

完整地将故事呈现在读者视野。而对于一些背景知识，编者也以脚注的形式进行了说明，这可以加深读者对中西文学与文化的认知。

教材各单元的编排大致如下：

1. 导读。该部分为对本单元的神话主题及相关故事的概括性介绍。

2. 中希神话阅读。该部分以生动优美的语言，引人入胜的情节对比呈现了同主题的中希神话故事。为加深读者对内容的掌握与理解，编者做了丰富、详实的脚注，每个故事结尾都设有原创的讨论问题。

3. 读后反思。该部分，针对"神话阅读"部分设计了巩固与拓展性练习，包括以下内容：

1）词汇扩展。萃选若干个与本节神话故事有关的词汇，拓展读者的相关词汇积累。

2）作品鉴赏。提供与中希神话相关的文学作品节选，提升读者对神话故事的鉴赏力。

3）对比赏析。以提问的形式对中希同主题神话进行对比，引导学生思考其所反映的中西方文化差异，并进一步探讨差异产生的原因。

历时三年，值此教材付梓之际，我想向致力于神话研究的中外学者致以最崇高的敬意。其次，我想对参与本教材的编写以及校订的所有人表示衷心的感谢，特别是兰州大学外国语学院柴橚副教授、华中科技大学外国语学院2023级博士生赵燕凤和兰州文理学院外语学院黄江娜老师。最后，将这本神话教材送给我两个可爱而又调皮的儿子，希望他们能够健康茁壮成长，通过阅读神话故事，插上想象的翅膀，体验神奇而多姿多彩的世界。

张　敏

兰州大学

Preface

Myths are descriptions and explanations of inexplicable natural phenomena and social life by ancient ancestors through imagination. As a kind of unconscious artistic creation, myths show the strong desire, optimism and heroism of early human beings when conquering nature. It is no exaggeration to say that they have become the earliest sources of philosophical and humanistic thoughts, influencing human progress and development to varying degrees.

At the 20th National Congress of the Communist Party of China, General Secretary Xi Jinping emphasized the importance of Chinese culture, stating that

> We will stay firmly rooted in Chinese culture. We will collect and refine the defining symbols and best elements of Chinese culture and showcase them to the world. We will accelerate the development of China's discourse and narrative systems, better tell China's stories, make China's voice heard, and present a China that is credible, appealing, and respectable.[①]

Among these invaluable cultural treasures are Chinese mythological stories,

---

[①] Xi Jinping, *Hold High the Great Banner of Socialism with Chinese Characteristics and Strive in Unity to Build a Modern Socialist Country in All Respects: Report to the 20th National Congress of the Communist Party of China*, Beijing: Foreign Languages Press, 2023, p. 61.

which represent the worship of nature by ancient Chinese people and the concept of harmony between heaven and man in classical Chinese culture, and they still have irreplaceable value even today.

Compared with Chinese mythology, western mythology system is huge, mainly including Celtic mythology, Greek mythology, Hebrew mythology, Nordic mythology and Slavic mythology, among which Greek and Hebrew myths have the greatest impact upon western culture. Greek mythology is the rich heritage left by ancient Greeks who created a brilliant and colorful culture in the process of survival and development. With its centralized, complete and systematic content, Greek mythology has the most comprehensive and the largest mythological system in existence, and exerts a profound influence on the development of western language, literature, art and thought. The influence of Hebrew mythology on western culture cannot be ignored either. Being rich in content, Hebrew mythology explores the intimate relationship between all things in the universe and human emotions, interpersonal relationships, secrets of good and evil, spiritual beliefs as well as universal phenomenon of transcendence.

As our world becomes increasingly globalized, cultural exchanges between China and the West is expanding. In cross-cultural communication, it is not only necessary to learn languages, but also to understand their cultural background and cognitive patterns. This puts forward new requirements. On the one hand, "with an open mind, we should draw inspiration from all of human civilization's outstanding achievements and work to build an even better world."[1] On the other hand, we also need to open the door and implement "going global" strategy for Chinese culture development. Therefore, myths, as the sources of Chinese and western cultures, cannot be disregarded.

---

[1] Xi Jinping, *Hold High the Great Banner of Socialism with Chinese Characteristics and Strive in Unity to Build a Modern Socialist Country in All Respects: Report to the 20th National Congress of the Communist Party of China*, pp. 27–28.

The editors have compiled this textbook *Appreciation of Chinese and Greek Mythology* based on the teaching practice of general education elective course. It is designed for students with intermediate language proficiency of English and strong interest in Chinese and western myths. In terms of content, only Chinese and Greek mythology are included in this textbook for the reason that although Chinese and Greek mythology embody different values, they have many similarities. For example, both mythologies are created at the most primitive stage of social development; the narrative structure of the two is relatively simple; both reflect the relationship between man and nature, man and society, as well as national spirit. Hebrew mythology differs from the two in that it places more emphasis on religious spirit, which seems to be no longer at the core of western social life, and its literary nature has attracted much more attention instead.

Therefore, editors focus on the most popular mythological stories in Chinese and Greek mythology and design the textbook according to mythological themes, namely the origin of cosmos, the origin of human beings, flood myths, water deities, myths of plants and animals, punishment myths, myths of the underworld, myths of gods of love, heroes and women in myths. The work has been compiled with care from reliable sources. Some stories, especially Chinese mythological stories, have been integrated as they are relatively scattered. Background knowledge and explanations for related literature works and culture are also given in the form of footnotes, helping the reader deepen their understanding of Chinese and Western literature and culture. The following is the general structure of each unit:

1. Introduction. This section provides a general introduction to the mythological themes and related stories in each unit.

2. Reading Material. This part presents Chinese and Greek mythological stories with the same theme. Detailed annotations are available to the reader to have a deeper understanding of the story, and questions for discussion are set at

the end of each story.

3. Reflections. Including supplementary vocabulary and excerpts from classic works, this part is for the reader to review and further study Chinese and Greek mythology. Discussion tasks related to myths are designed to promote critical thinking and encourage exploration of the commonplaces and differences in Chinese and western culture.

The work now completed is offered to the public in the hope that it may render the subject of mythology more popular in universities. Among the authors to whom the editors have been particularly indebted, I may mention Anne Birrell, E. M. Berens, Edward. T. C. Werner, Emilie Kip Baker, Thomas Bulfinch, Tao Jie, Yang Lihui, Yuan Ke and Wang Lei. In addition, I would like to express my heartfelt thanks to all those who participated in the compilation and revision, especially Dr. Chai Su, Zhao Yanfeng (HUST) and Huang Jiangna (LUAS). Furthermore, I want to give this textbook to my two lovely and naughty sons, hoping that they can thrive and experience the magical and colorful world by reading mythological stories.

Zhang Min

January 3rd 2023, at Lanzhou University

Contents

Introduction ··· (1)
    What is Myth? ·· (1)
    Sources of Chinese and Greek Mythology ···························· (4)
    Categories of Myths ·· (8)

Unit 1 Myths of Cosmogony ·· (10)
    Part 1 Chinese Myths of Cosmogony ································· (12)
    Part 2 Greek Myths of Cosmogony ···································· (16)
    Part 3 Reflections ·· (23)

Unit 2 Emergence of Human Beings ······································ (26)
    Part 1 Emergence of Human Beings in Chinese Mythology ······ (27)
    Part 2 Emergence of Human Beings in Greek Mythology ······ (31)
    Part 3 Reflections ·· (37)

Unit 3 Flood Myths ··· (39)
    Part 1 Flood Myths in Chinese Mythology ························· (41)
    Part 2 The Deluge in Greek Mythology ····························· (43)

　　　　Part 3　Reflections ·· (48)

Unit 4　Water Deities ·· (51)
　　　　Part 1　Water Deities in Chinese Mythology ·················· (52)
　　　　Part 2　Water Deities in Greek Mythology ····················· (63)
　　　　Part 3　Reflections ·· (72)

Unit 5　Vegetal Myths ·· (76)
　　　　Part 1　Plants in Chinese Mythology ···························· (77)
　　　　Part 2　Plants in Greek Mythology ······························· (86)
　　　　Part 3　Reflections ·· (99)

Unit 6　Animal Myths ·· (102)
　　　　Part 1　Animals in Chinese Mythology ························ (104)
　　　　Part 2　Animals in Greek Mythology ·························· (117)
　　　　Part 3　Reflections ·· (127)

Unit 7　Myths of Punishment ······································ (131)
　　　　Part 1　Punishment Stories in Chinese Mythology ·········· (133)
　　　　Part 2　Punishment Stories in Greek Mythology ············ (142)
　　　　Part 3　Reflections ·· (156)

Unit 8　Myths about the Underworld ····························· (159)
　　　　Part 1　The Underworld in Chinese Mythology ············· (160)
　　　　Part 2　The Underworld in Greek Mythology ················ (170)

Part 3　Reflections ………………………………………………… (186)

Unit 9　Gods of Love ……………………………………………… (190)
　Part 1　Gods of Love in Chinese Mythology ………………… (192)
　Part 2　Gods of Love in Greek Mythology …………………… (202)
　Part 3　Reflections ………………………………………………… (216)

Unit 10　Myths about Heroes …………………………………… (220)
　Part 1　Heroes in Chinese Mythology ………………………… (222)
　Part 2　Heroes in Greek Mythology …………………………… (242)
　Part 3　Reflections ………………………………………………… (266)

Unit 11　Myths about Women …………………………………… (269)
　Part 1　Women in Chinese Mythology ………………………… (271)
　Part 2　Women in Greek Mythology …………………………… (286)
　Part 3　Reflections ………………………………………………… (304)

Bibliography ………………………………………………………… (307)

Introduction

What is Myth?

The word "myth" derives from Greek "mythos," referring to an allegory or fable of certain important moral or religious truth, or some operation of nature. Mythology is a collective name, covering a series of historical myths and narratives of gods, demigods and heroes, which were current among the heathen in ancient times.[1] Scholars at home and abroad have, by this definition, divergent views on this term. In the preface of *A Contribution to the Critique of Political Economy*, Karl Marx holds that "all mythology masters and dominates and shapes the forces of nature in and through the imagination; hence it disappears as soon as man gains mastery over the forces of nature."[2] Northrop Frye defines myth as "a narrative in which some characters are superhuman beings who do things that 'happen only in stories'; hence, a conventionalized or stylized narrative not fully adapted to plausibility or 'realism'."[3] While Lewis

---

[1] Catherine A. White, *The Student's Mythology*, New York: A. C. Armstrong & Son, 1890, p. 15.

[2] Karl Marx, *A Contribution to the Critique of Political Economy*, trans. by N. I. Stone, Chicago: Charles H. Kerr & Company, 1904, pp. 310 – 311.

[3] Northrop Frye, *Anatomy of Criticism : Four Essays*, Princeton and Oxford: Princeton University Press, 2000, p. 366.

Spence's definition of myth is as follows:

> A myth is an account of the deeds of a god or supernatural being, usually expressed in terms of primitive thought. It is an attempt to explain the relations of man to the universe, and it has for those who recount it a predominantly religious value; or it may have arisen to "explain" the existence of some social organization, a custom, or the peculiarities of an environment.[①]

Robert A. Segal's proposition, nevertheless, seems utterly distant from the above scholars and challenges traditional definitions of myths. He holds that a myth should not be confined to a story, but be taken more broadly as a conviction or credo like the American "rags to riches myth" and the "myths of the frontier." Myths include not only stories that happened in the past, but also those in the present or the future.[②]

Similarly, there are differences among Chinese scholars on the matter. In *A Brief History of Chinese Fiction*, Lu Hsun thinks that when primitive men observed natural phenomena and changes which could not be accomplished by any human power, they made up stories to explain them, and these explanations became myths.[③] In his further interpretation of the content of myths and their relation to culture, Lu Hsun believes that myths usually centered around a group of gods worshipped by men through descriptions of them and their feats, hymns in praise of their divine power, and offerings in their shrines. Such a belief

---

① Lewis Spence, *An Introduction to Mythology*, New York: Moffat Yard and Company, 1921, pp. 11 – 12.
② Robert A. Segal, *Myth: A Very Short Introduction*, Oxford: Oxford University Press, 2004, p. 4.
③ Lu Hsun, *A Brief History of Chinese Fiction*, trans. by Yang Xianyi and Gladys Yang, Beijing: Foreign Languages Press, 2009, p. 9.

brings with it gradual progress in culture. For not only are myths the beginning of religion and art but the fountain-head of literature.① Another famous Chinese scholar Mao Dun regards myths as a kind of folk tales in ancient times which record the narration of gods' actions. These gods did not spring out of thin air, but were the inevitable product of the living and mental conditions of the primitive people.② Moreover, as one of the most distinguished modern mythologists, Yuan Ke's scope of myth is in the broadest sense, in which fables, legends and mythic novels all can be called as myths.③

Aforementioned opinions are of great help to our summary of the characteristics of myths. First of all, most scholars believe that myth is an application of primitive people for their explanation of natural phenomena and changes beyond their understanding though some hold that it can also refer to happenings in the present and future. Secondly, myths show a feature of collectiveness. That means they were not created by one person, but were processed by different narrators who passed them down from generation to generation. Thus, these mythological stories, as a projection of the collective spirit in ancient times, usually have no specific author. The Homeric epics constitute one example, in which the stories had already existed long before the books were written. Thirdly, myths, normally carrying a message of ethics, religion or nature, embody the characteristic of holiness. Lastly, myths are always metaphorical. It is incarnated on the one hand in the mind-set of mythmaking and, on the other hand, its great influence upon language. Ancient people believed that the unexplainable natural phenomena such as thunder and lightning, wind and rain, human death, were controlled by corresponding gods

---

① Lu Hsun, *A Brief History of Chinese Fiction*, p. 9.
② 茅盾:《中国神话研究初探》,江苏文艺出版社 2009 年版,第 3 页。
③ Yang Lihui, An Deming and Jessica Anderson Turner, *Handbook of Chinese Mythology*, Santa Barbara: ABC-CLIO, Inc., 2005, p. 1.

in their imagination. Our daily language is also deeply imprinted with mythological metaphors. For example, Chinese tend to describe a pathbreaker with sheer will-power and persistence as "someone with the spirit of Yu who tamed the flood"; while in English, "Adonis" is code for a handsome man; "Pandora's box" symbolizes the root of disasters; and "Achilles' heel" indicates one's fatal weakness.

Sources of Chinese and Greek Mythology

How do myths then, the evident product of ancient times, end up with what they are in the contemporary world?

No reference to an introduction of all Greek myths' characters and stories appears in any literature. Indeed, the earliest Greek myths were part of an oral tradition originating in the Bronze Age, and their plots and themes unfolded gradually in the written literature of the archaic and classical periods of the ancient Mediterranean world. *The Iliad* and *The Odyssey*, the eighth century B. C. epics by Homer, tell the story of the Trojan War as a divine conflict as well as a human one. They do not, however, bother to introduce the gods and goddesses, whom readers and listeners would already have been familiar with.

Around the seventh century B. C., the poet Hesiod's *Theogony* offered the first written cosmogony, or creation story of Greek mythology. *Theogony* sketches how the universe evolves from nothingness (Chaos, a primeval void) into being, and details an elaborate family tree of elements, gods and goddesses that developed from Chaos as descendants of Gaia (the Earth), Uranus (the Sky), Pontus (the Sea) and Tartarus (the Underworld). Hesiod's *Works and Days* systematically records the knowledge of farming and production at that time, showing a peaceful and beautiful scene of rural life. It also represents

Prometheus, Pandora, and the five ages of man, namely the Golden Age, the Silver Age, the Bronze Age, the Age of Heroes and the Iron Age.

These achievements laid the groundwork for later Greek writers and artists. Mythological figures and events appear in the 5th-century plays of Aeschylus, Sophocles and Euripides and the lyric poems of Pindar. A large quantity of plays and lyric poems have drawn their materials from the stories of Prometheus, Agamemnon, Oedipus, Antigone, Medea, Andromache, Helen, Apollo, Dionysus, etc. Greek mythographer Apollodorus of Athens in the second century B. C. and the Roman historian Gaius Julius Hyginus in the first century B. C. compiled the ancient myths and legends for contemporary audiences.

At the center of Greek mythology is the pantheon of gods and goddesses who were alleged to live on Mount Olympus, the highest mountain in Greece. From their lofty perch, they ruled every aspect of human life. Olympian deities had incarnations as human beings (though they could also change themselves into animals and other things) and were—as many myths recounted—vulnerable to human foibles and passions.

However, gods and goddesses are not the sole theme of Greek mythology. Human heroes—Heracles (aka Hercules), the adventurer who performed 12 impossible labors for King Eurystheus and was subsequently worshipped as a god for his accomplishments; Pandora, the first woman, whose curiosity brought evil to mankind; Pygmalion, the king who fell in love with an ivory statue; Arachne, the weaver who was turned into a spider for her arrogance; handsome Trojan prince Ganymede who became the cupbearer for the gods; Midas, the king with the golden touch; and Narcissus, the young man who fell in love with his own reflection—are just as significant.

Monsters and "hybrids" (creatures with human-animal forms) also feature prominently in the tales: the winged horse Pegasus, the horse-man Centaur, the lion-woman Sphinx, the bird-woman Harpies, the one-eyed giant Cyclops, automatons (metal creatures given life by Hephaestus), manticores, unicorns, Gorgons, pygmies, minotaur, satyrs and dragons of all sorts. Many of these creatures have become almost as well known as the gods, goddesses and heroes who share their stories.

For thousands of years, the characters, plots, themes and lessons of Greek mythology have made their projection in art and literature. They appear in Renaissance paintings as Sandro Botticelli's *The Birth of Venus* and Raffaello's *The Triumph of Galatea*, sculptures as Gian Lorenzo Bernini's *Apollo and Daphne* and Antonio Canova's *Daedalus and Icarus* and *Psyche Revived by Cupid's Kiss*, writings as Dante Alighieri's *Inferno* and William Shakespeare's *Venus and Adonis*, Romantic poetry, libretti, and scores of more recent novels, plays and movies.

Chinese mythology covers the body of not only ancient but also the currently transmitted myths within the territory of China, including the legend by the Han nationality and other fifty-five ethnic minorities. Due to their distinction from each other, no systematic, homogeneous integration of "Chinese mythology" shared by all the Chinese people has come into being.[①]

In China, there is no sacred canon recording myths, beliefs, or sacred history like the Bible or the Koran nor were there any literati, troubadours, or shamans who collected myths from oral tradition and compiled them into a systematic and integrated mythology.[②] The fact is that myths in ancient China were usually scattered in various writings, among which *Shanhaijing* (*The Classic of Mountains and Seas*), *Chuci* (*The Songs of Chu*), and *Huainanzi* are regarded as the major repositories.

As an encyclopedia, *The Classic of Mountains and Seas* gives a general

---

① Yang Lihui, An Deming and Jessica Anderson Turner, *Handbook of Chinese Mythology*, p. 4.
② Yang Lihui, An Deming and Jessica Anderson Turner, *Handbook of Chinese Mythology*, p. 6.

description of diversified landscapes, living beings, history, customs as well as myths, witchcraft, nations and religion of ancient China. The existing edition of this book contains eighteen chapters which can be divided into two parts, five chapters of *The Classic of Mountains* and thirteen chapters of *The Classic of Seas*. There is no consensus of opinions among people as to the author of this book. But most scholars agree that it was written by many authors in different times, dating back to the period from the middle of the Warring States (475/476 B. C. -221 B. C.) to the beginning of the Western Han Dynasty (206 B. C. - 24 A. D.). In an exalted position of Chinese mythology, *The Classic of Mountains and Seas* provides many famed mythological figures and images: Nüwa, Xiwangmu (the Queen Mother of the West), Gun, Yu, Jingwei (Shennong's youngest daughter), Huangdi (the Yellow Emperor), Chiyou (god of weapon), fusang (Leaning Mulberry, one species of mysterious tree), roumu, and the sky ladder (also known as jianmu), the pillars of which are supposed to hold up the sky and many others. Among those most have no complete plots apart from several pithy stories.

Another important source of Chinese mythology is *The Songs of Chu* by Qu Yuan (ca. 340 B. C. -278 B. C.), the earliest celebrated poet born in Chu of ancient China (now Hubei and Hunan provinces in southern China). He learned from folk sacrificial songs and adopted a large quantity of Chu myths and legends in his poems. The most known "Tianwen" ("Questions to Heaven") has been a classic example. The poem demonstrates 172 questions correlative of household myths, legends and history such as Yu taming the flood, Yi the archer, Gonggong (god of water) butting into the Buzhou Mountain, and many mystical images like Kunlun Mountain and Zhulong (Torch Dragon). But the form of questions makes the stories in it appear to be fragmentary.

Huainanzi was written and compiled at the beginning of the Western Han Dynasty by Liu An, the king of Huainan, and many of his aides. This book preserves many ancient myths, legends and historical accounts, capturing the fable of Chang'e, who steals the elixir of immortality and flees to the moon; the Cowherd and the Weaving Maiden and other aforementioned tales. Compared with *The Classic of Mountains and Seas* and "Tianwen," *Huainanzi* is more complete in documentation. Therefore, many of its records are cited in studies of Chinese mythology.

Other literary sources of Chinese myths include *Liezi*, *Zhuangzi*, *Shiyiji* (*Researches into Lost Records*), *Soushenji* (*Anecdotes about Spirits and Immortals*), *Shuyiji* (*A Record of Accounts of Marvels*), *Shiji* (*Records of the Grand Historian*) and *Biography of Mu Tianzi* (*The Chronicle of Emperor Mu*).

The Chinese mythic narratives have remained well-preserved in their original contexts of miscellaneous works on history, philosophy, literature, political theory and treaties for over two millennia, making readers today able to evaluate them in their earliest form among various versions. [1]

Categories of Myths

Scholars divide myths into different categories on the basis of their themes. Anne Birrell introduces a classification system of cosmogonic myths, creation myths, etiological myths, myths of divine birth, mythic metamorphoses, myths of strange places, peoples, plants, birds and animals, myths of the primeval and the lesser gods, mythical figures, myths of the semidivine heroes who founded their tribe, city, or dynasty at the dawn of history. [2] Another writer Lewis Spence, in his *An Introduction to Mythology*, classifies myths into 21

---

[1] Anne Birrell, *Chinese Mythology: An Introduction*, Baltimore and London: The Johns Hopkins University Press, 1993, p. 17.

[2] Anne Birrell, *Chinese Mythology: An Introduction*, p. 1.

categories, namely creation myths (creation of the earth and man), myths of the origin of man, flood myths, myths of a place of reward, myths of a place of punishment, sun myths, moon myths, hero myths, beast myths, myths to account for customs or rites, myths of journeys or adventures through the Underworld or place of the dead, myths regarding the birth of gods, fire myth, star myths, myths of death, food of the dead formula, myths regarding taboo, "dismemberment" myths (in which a god is dismembered), dualistic myths (the good god fighting the bad), myths of the origin of the arts of life and soul mythos.[①]

However, repetition occurs when myths are strictly consistent with the categories above. As in Birrell's mythic metamorphoses and plants, birds and animals, the former overlap with the latter. To be specific, Chiyou's fetters turned into maple trees after his death, and Kuafu's walking stick transformed into peach trees. So are Ovid's *Metamorphoses*, in which many people or gods transform into plants or animals. For instance, the nymph Daphne became the laurel; Clytie, being infatuated with Apollo, turned into a sunflower; the weaver Arachne offended Athena and was consequently transformed into a spider. Moreover, myths of the underworld and of death are also bewilderingly similar.

Based on the previous efforts, the editors have arranged this textbook in eleven chapters: myths of cosmogony, emergence of human beings, flood myths, myths of water deities, plants, animals, myths of punishment, myths of the underworld, myths of love gods, heroes, and women in myths, hopefully crystallizing the motifs per se, sorting out stories of the same motif in Chinese and Greek myths and serving as a great carrier of Chinese culture to aliens and beyond.

---

① Lewis Spence, *An Introduction to Mythology*, p. 138.

Unit 1

Myths of Cosmogony

Introduction

The emergence of the universe is recorded in both Greek and Chinese myths. Chinese etiological myths of **cosmogony**① are symbolic narratives about the origins of the universe and life in it. They fundamentally differ from **monolithic**② traditions with one authorized version, such as the Judeo-Christian Genesis creation myth. Chinese classics record numerous, sometimes contradictory, origin myths which demonstrate ways of conceptualizing the universe when it was created, or "in the beginning" of mythological time. The basic principle of Chinese cosmology is a **primeval**③ vapor, "qi," which was believed to embody cosmic energy governing matter, time, and space. This energy, according to Chinese mythic narratives, had undergone a transformation at the moment of creation so that the **nebulous**④ elements of vapor were differentiated into dual elements of male and female, Yin and Yang, hard and soft matter, and other binary elements. Chinese cosmogonic myths are recorded in ancient books: "Tianwen," one section of *Chu Ci*, asks questions about creation myths; *Dao De Jing* suggests a less mythical Chinese cosmogony and has

---

① cosmogony [kɒz'mɒgəni] n. 宇宙的产生
② monolithic [ˌmɒnə'lɪθɪk] adj. 完全统一的
③ primeval [praɪ'miːvl] adj. 原始的
④ nebulous ['nebjələs] adj. 朦胧的

some of the earliest allusions to creation; *Huainanzi*, an eclectic text compiled by Han prince Liu An, contains two cosmogonic myths that develop the dualistic concept of Yin and Yang. However, one of the most popular creation myths, describing the firstborn semidivine human Pangu separating the egglike "primordial chaos" into Heaven and Earth, is not included in any of the ancient Chinese classics until as late as the Three Kingdoms period (220 A. D. – 280 A. D.).

The beginning of the universe in Greek mythology is recorded in Hesiod's ***Theogony***①, which is also the generally accepted notion of the genesis. It is said that before this world came into existence, there was in its place a confused mass of shapeless elements called **Chaos**②. Then, either all by themselves or out of the formless void, sprang forth three more primordial deities: **Gaia**③ (Earth), **Tartarus**④ (the Underworld), and **Eros**⑤ (Love). Once Love was there, Gaia and Chaos—two female deities—were able to **procreate**⑥ and shape everything known and unknown in the universe. Chaos gave birth to **Erebus**⑦ (Darkness) and **Nyx**⑧ (Night). Erebus slept with his sister Nyx, and out of this union, **Aether**⑨, the bright upper air, and **Hemera**⑩, the Day, emerged. Afterward, feared by everyone but her brother, Nyx fashioned a family of haunting forces all by herself. Among others, her children included the hateful Moros (Fate), the black Ker (Doom), Thanatos (Death), Hypnos (Sleep), Oneiroi (Dream), Geras (Old Age), Oizys (Pain), Nemesis

---

① 《神谱》，古希腊诗人赫西俄德著，描写宇宙和神的诞生，讲述从地母盖亚诞生直到奥林匹亚诸神统治世界的历史。编者注。
② Chaos ['keɪɒs] n. 卡俄斯（希腊神话中的混沌之神）
③ Gaia (or Gaea) ['gaɪə] n. 盖亚（希腊神话中的大地女神，众神之母）
④ Tartarus ['tɑːtərəs] n. 塔耳塔洛斯（希腊神话中地狱的化身）
⑤ Eros ['ɪərɒs] n. 厄洛斯（希腊神话中的爱神）
⑥ procreate ['prəʊkrieɪt] vt. 生育
⑦ Erebus ['erəbəs] n. 厄瑞玻斯（混沌之子，永久黑暗的化身，代表冥土的黑暗）
⑧ Nyx ['nɪks] n. 尼克斯（司夜女神，夜的化身）
⑨ Aether ['iːθə] n. 埃忒耳（太空神，在希腊神话中是"太空"的拟人化神）
⑩ Hemera ['hɛmərə] n. 赫墨拉（白昼之神）

(Revenge), Eris (Strife), Apate (Deceit), Philotes (Sexual Pleasure), Momos (Blame), and the Hesperides (the daughters of the Evening). With the birth of gods, the universe came into being.

Part 1　Chinese Myths of Cosmogony

The recognized creator of the universe in Chinese mythology is Pangu. Before Pangu, some gods related to cosmogony are marked down in ancient books as well, one of whom is called Dijiang or Hundun. It's described in *The Classic of Mountains and Seas* as follows:

> 350 li further west is a mountain called Tianshan, which is rich in gold, jade, **azurite**① blue and red **orpiment**②. The Yingshui River flows out of this mountain and runs to the southwest before it empties itself into Tanggu. There is a god called Dijiang who looks like a yellow bag and can send off red light. He has six feet and four wings. Though he has neither face nor eyes, he knows how to sing and dance.③

Later, Zhuangzi portrays Dijiang in "Ying Di Wang," or "The Normal Course for Rulers and Kings" like this:

> The ruler of the Southern Sea is called Change; the ruler of the

---

① azurite [ˈæʒʊˌraɪt] n. 石青
② orpiment [ˈɔːpɪmənt] n. 雌黄
③ *The Classic of Mountains and Seas*, translated into Modern Chinese by Chen Cheng, translated into English by Wang Hong and Zhao Zheng, Changsha: Hunan People's Publishing House, 2010, p. 55.

Northern Sea is called Uncertainty, and the ruler of the Centre is called Primitivity. Change and Uncertainty often met on the territory of Primitivity, and being always well treated by him, determined to repay his kindness. They said: "All Men all have seven holes for seeing, hearing, eating, and breathing. Primitivity alone has none of these. Let us try to bore some for him." So every day they bored one hole; but on the seventh day Primitivity died. [1]

Both Dijiang and Primitivity (Hundun) metaphorically refer to the chaotic state of the universe before it was born. The death of Primitivity indicates the end of the chaotic state and the world thus came into being.

Another god related to cosmogony is Torch Dragon. Being able to manage the alternation of day and night and weather, Torch Dragon thus shows the divine power of the creator. It is depicted in *The Classic of Mountains and Seas* as follows:

Beyond the Northwest Sea and north of the Chishui River there is Mount Zhangwei. There is a god with a human face and a snake's body. He is red all over. He has vertical eyes which are in a straight seam. When he closes his eyes, there is darkness. When he opens his eyes, there is light. He neither eats, nor sleeps, nor breathes. He can get the rain and wind in and can light up all the dark places. He is called Torch Dragon. [2]

While *Shuyiji*, or *A Record of Accounts of Marvels*, recounts the story of

---

[1] Zhuangzi, *Chuang-tzu*, trans. by Feng Youlan, Beijing: Foreign Language Teaching and Research Press, 2012, pp. 99 – 100.

[2] *The Classic of Mountains and Seas*, p. 311.

Ghost Mother, who inhabited in Xiaoyu Mountain in South China Sea and had similar remarkable ability that gave birth to days, land and ghosts.

However, it is Pangu who has become the recognized creator of universe. Pangu's stories are recorded in *Sanwu Liji* (*Historical Records of the Three Sovereign Divinities and Five Emperors*) and *Wuyun Linian Ji* (*A Chronicle of the Five Circles of Time*), both of which were compiled in the third century C. E. by Xu Zheng. The stories about Pangu go like this: At the very beginning, heaven and earth were in chaos like a chicken's egg, and within this chaos Pangu was born. After eighteen thousand years the egg somehow opened and unfolded. The **limpid**[①] and light part of it, called as Yang, rose and then became the heavens, the **turbid**[②] and heavy part, called as Yin, sank down and became the earth. Pangu lived within them, and in one day he went through nine transformations, becoming more divine than Heaven and more sacred than earth. Each day the heavens rose ten feet higher, each day the earth grew ten feet thicker, and each day Pangu grew ten feet taller. And so it was that in eighteen thousand years the heavens reached their fullest height, earth reached its lowest depth, and Pangu became fully grown. Afterward, there were the Three Sovereign Divinities, who were the earliest divine lords in Chinese mythical history. Numbers began with one, were established with three, perfected by five, multiplied with seven, and fixed with nine. That is why the heavens are ninety thousand leagues from earth.

Another great deed of Pangu is that his body transformed into the universe after his death. It is said that when the firstborn, Pangu, was approaching death, his breath became the winds and clouds; his voice became **peals**[③] of thunder. His left eye became the sun; his right eye became the moon. His four

---

① limpid ['lɪmpɪd] adj. 透明的
② turbid ['tɜːbɪd] adj. 浑浊的
③ peal [piːl] n. 鸣响

limbs and trunk became the four extremes of the earth and the Five Mountains. His blood became the rivers; his veins became the earth's arteries. His flesh became fields and soil. His hair and beard became the stars; his skin and body hair became plants. His teeth and bones became various metals and rocks. His semen and **marrow**① became pearls and jade. His sweat became the rain and the dew. All the mites on his body were touched by the wind and were turned into the black-haired people.②

As creator of the universe, Pangu receives a high status in Chinese beliefs. Several temples were built for him in Henan, Guangdong, Jiangxi, and Zhejiang provinces, and in the Guangxi Zhuang Autonomous Region. Many of them were founded before Tang or Song Dynasties. In these regions, Pangu continues to be worshiped by people today.

Questions for Discussion:

1. Fill in the following table and draw a conclusion of the features of antediluvian gods.

Antediluvian Gods	Power	Deficiencies
Dijiang or Primitivity		
Torch Dragon		
Ghost Mother		

2. Why did Pangu become the recognized creation god in Chinese mythology instead of other antediluvian gods?

---

① marrow ['mærəʊ] n. 骨髓
② Anne Birrell, *Chinese Mythology: An Introduction*, pp. 32 – 33.

Part 2　Greek Myths of Cosmogony

The generally accepted notion in ancient Greece was that before this world, there was Chaos, that is, a mass of shapeless elements that later split into two substances and respectively formed the firmament and the solid mass beneath. Thus came into being the first two great primeval deities of the Greeks, **Uranus**① and Gaia.

As a more refined deity, Uranus represented the light and air of heaven, possessing the distinguishing qualities of light, heat, purity, and omnipresence. While Gaia, the firm, flat, life-sustaining earth, was worshipped as the great all-nourishing mother, which has been reflected more or less in her many titles. She appeared to be universally revered among the Greeks, because there was scarcely a city in Greece which did not contain a temple erected in her honor. Indeed, Gaia was held in such **veneration**② that her name was always invoked whenever the gods took a solemn oath, made an emphatic declaration, or implored assistance.

Uranus, the heaven, was believed to have united himself in marriage with Gaia, the earth; and a moment's reflection will show what a truly poetical, and also what a logical idea this was; for, taken in a figurative sense, this union actually did exist. The smiles of heaven produced the flowers of earth, whereas his long-continued frowns exercised so depressing an influence upon his loving partner, that she no longer decked herself in bright and festive robes, but responded with ready sympathy to his melancholy mood.

The first-born child of Uranus and Gaia was **Oceanus**③, the ocean stream,

---

① Uranus [juˈreɪnəs] n. 乌拉诺斯（古希腊神话中的第一代神王）
② veneration [ˌvenəˈreɪʃn] n. 尊敬
③ Oceanus [oʊˈsiənəs] n. 俄亥阿诺斯神（海洋之神，泰坦神族的一员）

that vast expanse of ever-flowing water which encircled the earth. Here we meet with another logical though fanciful conclusion, which a very slight knowledge of the workings of nature proves to have been just and true. The ocean was formed from the rain which descended from heaven and the streams which flowed from earth. By making Oceanus therefore the offspring of Uranus and Gaia, the ancients, if we take this notion in its literal sense, merely asserts that the ocean was produced by the combined influence of heaven and earth, meanwhile it was their fervid and poetical imagination that led them to see in this, as in all manifestations of the powers of nature, an actual, tangible divinity.

But Uranus, the heaven, the embodiment of light, heat, and the breath of life, produced offspring who were of a much less material nature than his son Oceanus. It is believed that these children were supposed to occupy the intermediate space which divided Uranus from Gaia. Nearest to Uranus, and just beneath him, came Aether (Ether), a bright creation representing a highly rarified atmosphere which immortals alone could breathe. Then followed **Aër**① (Air), which was in close proximity to Gaia, and represented, as its name implies, the grosser atmosphere surrounding the earth which mortals could freely breathe, and without which they would perish. Aether and Aër were separated from each other by divinities called **Nephelae**②, their restless and wandering sisters who existed in the form of clouds, ever floating between them. Gaia also produced the mountains and **Pontus**③ (the sea) and then united herself with the latter. Their offspring were the sea-deities **Nereus**④, **Thaumas**⑤, **Phorcys**⑥, **Keto**⑦, and **Eurybia**⑧.

---

① Aër (Air) [eə] n. 埃尔（大气神）
② Nephelae ['nefəli] n. 涅斐勒（云女神）
③ Pontus ['pʌntəs] n. 蓬托斯（海洋之神）
④ Nereus ['niəriəs] n. 涅柔斯（海洋之神）
⑤ Thaumas ['θɔːməs] n. 陶玛斯（海洋之神）
⑥ Phorcys ['fɔːrsɪs] n. 福耳库斯（海洋之神）
⑦ Keto ['kitəu] n. 刻托（半蛇半鱼的海怪，是叵测的大海给人类带来的危险的化身）
⑧ Eurybia [juə'ribiə] n. 欧律比亚（女海神，蓬托斯与盖亚之女）

At that time, the co-existent with Uranus and Gaia were two mighty powers who were also the offspring of Chaos—Erebus (Darkness) and Nyx (Night), who formed a striking contrast to the cheerful light of heaven and the bright smiles of earth. Erebus reigned in that mysterious world below where no ray of sunshine, no gleam of daylight, nor vestige of health-giving terrestrial life ever appeared. Nyx, the sister of Erebus, represented Night, and was worshiped by the ancients with the greatest solemnity.

Uranus was supposed to be united to Nyx as well, but only in his capacity as god of light, he was considered as the source and fountain of all light, and their children were **Eos**① (Aurora), the Dawn, and Hemera, the Daylight. Nyx again, on her side was also doubly united, having been married at some indefinite period to Erebus.

In addition to those children of heaven and earth already enumerated, Uranus and Gaia produced two distinctly different races of beings called Giants and Titans. The Giants personified brute strength alone, but the Titans combined their great physical power with intellectual qualifications variously developed. **Briareus**②, **Cottus**③, and **Gyges**④ were three Giants who each possessed a hundred hands and fifty heads, and were known collectively by the name of the **Hecatoncheires**⑤, which signified hundred-handed. These mighty Giants could shake the universe and produce earthquakes; it is therefore evident that they represented those active subterranean forces. The Titans were twelve in number; their names were: Oceanus, **Coeus**⑥, **Crios**⑦, **Hyperion**⑧,

---

① Eos [ˈiːɔs] n. 厄俄斯（黎明女神）
② Briareus [braiˈɛəriəs] n. 布里亚柔斯（百手三巨人之一）
③ Cottus [ˈkɔtəs] n. 科托斯（百手三巨人之一）
④ Gyges [ˈdʒaidʒiːz] n. 古阿斯（百手三巨人之一）
⑤ Hecatoncheires [ˈhɛkəˌtɒŋkəris] n. 赫卡同克瑞斯（希腊神话中的百臂巨人）
⑥ Coeus [ˈsiːəs] n. 科俄斯（泰坦神族的一员）
⑦ Crios (or Krios in ancient Greek) [ˈkraiəus] n. 克利俄斯（泰坦神族的一员）
⑧ Hyperion [haɪˈpiəriən] n. 亥伯龙神（泰坦神族的一员）

Iapetus①, **Cronus**②, **Theia**③, **Rhea**④, **Themis**⑤, **Mnemosyne**⑥, **Phoebe**⑦, and **Tethys**⑧.

Now Uranus, the chaste light of heaven, the essence of all that is bright and pleasing, held in **abhorrence**⑨ his crude, rough, and turbulent offspring, the Giants, and moreover feared that their great power might eventually prove hurtful to himself. He therefore hurled them into Tartarus, that portion of the lower world which served as the subterranean dungeon of the gods. In order to avenge the oppression of her children, the Giants, Gaia instigated a conspiracy on the part of the Titans against Uranus, which was carried to a successful issue by her son Cronus. He wounded his father, and from the blood of the wound which fell upon the earth sprang a race of monstrous beings also called Giants. Assisted by his brother-Titans, Cronus succeeded in **dethroning**⑩ his father, who, enraged at his defeat, cursed his rebellious son, and foretold to him a similar fate. Cronus now became invested with supreme power, and assigned to his brothers offices of distinction, subordinate only to himself. Subsequently, however, once secure of his position, he no longer needed their assistance. In return, he basely repaid their former services with treachery, making war upon his brothers and faithful allies. With assistance of the Giants, Cronus completely defeated his brothers, sending those who resisted his all-conquering arm down into the lowest depths of Tartarus.

---

① Iapetus [aɪˈæpətəs] n. 伊阿佩托斯（希腊神话中十二提坦之一）
② Cronus [ˈkroʊnəs] n. 克罗诺斯（泰坦巨人之一，天神乌拉诺斯和地神盖亚的儿子，他夺取了父亲的王位，后王位又被其儿子宙斯夺走）
③ Theia [ˈθaɪə] n. 忒伊亚（Hyperion 之妻，太阳神 Helios 之母，泰坦巨人之一）
④ Rhea [ˈriːə] n. 瑞亚（众神之母，泰坦巨人之一，掌握时光流逝的女神）
⑤ Themis [ˈθiːmɪs] n. 西弥斯女神（正义和秩序女神，泰坦巨人之一）
⑥ Mnemosyne [niːˈmɔzini] n. 摩涅莫辛涅（记忆女神，泰坦巨人之一）
⑦ Phoebe [ˈfiːbɪ] n. 福柏（希腊神话中的月亮女神）
⑧ Tethys [ˈtiːθɪs] n. 泰西丝（女大力十，大海女神）
⑨ abhorrence [əbˈhɒrəns] n. 痛恨
⑩ dethrone [diːˈθroʊn] vt. 废黜

Cronus was the god of time in its sense of eternal duration. He married Rhea, daughter of Uranus and Gaia, an all-important divinity. Their children were three sons, **Hades**①, **Poseidon**②, **Zeus**③, and three daughters, **Hestia**④, **Demeter**⑤, and **Hera**⑥. With an uneasy conscience, Cronus was afraid that his children might one day rise up against his authority, and thus verify the prediction of his father Uranus. Therefore, in order to render the prophecy impossible of fulfilment, Cronus swallowed each child the moment it was born, greatly to the sorrow and indignation of his wife Rhea. When it came to Zeus, the sixth and last, Rhea resolved to save this one child at least, to love and cherish, and appealed to her parents, Uranus and Gaia, for counsel and assistance. By their advice she wrapped a stone in baby-clothes, and Cronus, in eager haste, swallowed it without noticing the deception.

Anxious to preserve the secret of his existence from Cronus, Rhea sent the infant Zeus to **Crete**⑦ on the sly, where he was nourished, protected, and educated. A sacred goat, called **Amalthea**⑧, supplied the place of his mother, by providing him with milk; nymphs, called Melissae, fed him with honey; eagles and doves brought him **nectar**⑨ and **ambrosia**⑩. He was kept concealed in a cave in the heart of Mount Ida, and the Curetes, or priests of Rhea, by beating their shields together, kept up a constant noise at the entrance, which drowned the cries of the child and frightened away all intruders. Under the

---

① Hades ['heɪdiːz] n. 哈得斯（宙斯与波塞冬的兄弟，希腊神话中的冥王）
② Poseidon [pɒ'saɪdən] n. 波塞冬（海神）
③ Zeus [zjuːs] n. 宙斯（希腊最高神，众神和众生的主宰）
④ Hestia ['hɛstɪə] n. 赫斯提（司炉灶的女神）
⑤ Demeter [dɪ'miːtə] n. 得墨忒耳（司农业、丰饶、婚姻之女神）
⑥ Hera ['hɪərə] n. 赫拉（婚姻与生育女神，古希腊神话中的第三代天后，宙斯之妻）
⑦ Crete [kriːt] n.（希腊）克里特岛
⑧ Amalthea [ˌæmæl'θiːə] n. 阿玛耳忒亚（用山羊奶喂养婴儿宙斯的仙女）
⑨ nectar ['nektə] n. [植] 花蜜
⑩ ambrosia [æm'brəʊzɪə] n.（希腊罗马神话）神仙的食物

watchful care of the Nymphs, the infant Zeus throve rapidly, developing great physical powers, combined with extraordinary wisdom and intelligence. Grown to manhood, he determined to compel his father to restore his brothers and sisters to the light of day. It is said that Zeus was assisted in this difficult task by the goddess **Metis**①, who artfully persuaded Cronus to drink a potion, which caused him to give back the children he had swallowed. The stone which had counterfeited Zeus was placed at Delphi, where it was long exhibited as a sacred relic.

Cronus was so enraged at being **circumvented**② that the war between the father and son became inevitable. The rival forces ranged separate high mountains in Thessaly; Zeus, with his brothers and sisters, took his stand on Mount Olympus, where he was joined by Oceanus, and others of the Titans, who had forsaken Cronus on account of his oppressions. Cronus along with his brother-Titans took possession of Mount Othrys to prepare for battle. The struggle was long and fierce, and at length Zeus, finding that he was no nearer victory than before, bethought himself of the existence of the imprisoned Giants. Knowing that they would be able to render him most powerful assistance, he hastened to liberate them. Additionally, Zeus also called to his aid the **Cyclops**③ (sons of Poseidon and Amphitrite), who had only one eye each in the middle of their foreheads and were called **Brontes**④ (Thunder), **Steropes**⑤ (Lightning), and **Pyracmon**⑥ (Fire anvil). They promptly responded to his summons for help, and brought with them tremendous thunderbolts which the Hecatoncheires, with their hundred hands, hurled down upon the enemy.

---

① Metis [miːtis] n. 墨提斯（聪慧女神）
② circumvent [ˌsɜːkəmˈvent] vt. <古>欺骗
③ Cyclops [ˈsaɪklɒps] n. 复数形式（Cyclopes），库克罗普斯（古希腊神话中的独眼巨人）
④ Brontes [ˈbrɒntəs] n. 布戎忒斯（独眼巨人，雷神）
⑤ Steropes [ˈsterəʊps] n. 斯忒罗佩斯（电神）
⑥ Pyracmon [ˈpirikmən] n. 派拉刻蒙（霹雳神）

Concurrently, mighty earthquakes were raised to swallow up and destroy all who opposed them. Aided by these new and powerful allies, Zeus now made a furious onslaught on his enemies, which was so tremendous that all nature is said to throb in accord with this mighty effort of the celestial deities: the sea rose mountains high, and its angry billows hissed and foamed; the earth shook to its foundations, the heavens sent forth rolling thunder, and flash after flash of death-bringing lightning, whilst a blinding mist enveloped Cronus and his allies.

Now the fortunes of war began to turn, and victory smiled on Zeus. Cronus and his armies were completely overthrown, his brothers **dispatched**① to the gloomy depths of the lower world, and Cronus himself was banished from his kingdom and deprived forever of the supreme power, which now became vested in his son Zeus. This war was called the **Titanomachia**②, and is most graphically described by the old classic poets.

With the defeat of Cronus and his banishment from his dominions, his career as a ruling Greek divinity entirely ceased. But being, like all the gods, immortal, he was supposed to be still in existence, though possessing no longer either influence or authority, and his place was filled to a certain extent by his descendant and successor, Zeus. ③

Questions for Discussion:

1. Familiarize yourself with gods and goddesses by filling in the following table.

---

① dispatch [dɪˈspætʃ] vt. 派遣
② Titanomachia [ˌtaɪtəˈnɔməkɪ] n. 泰坦之战（指希腊神话中泰坦神族与奥林匹斯神族为争夺宇宙霸主地位而展开的战争）
③ E. M. Berens, *The Myths and Legends of Ancient Greece and Rome*, London: Blackie & Son, 1880, pp. 11 – 17.

Gods/Goddesses	Role in mythology
Chaos	
Gaia	
Uranus	
Pontus	
Cyclops	
Zeus	

2. Where did Erebus reign?

3. Which two different races of beings were produced by Uranus and Gaia?

4. How was Uranus overthrown?

5. What did Cronus do to his children?

6. How did Rhea preserve the secret of Zeus's existence from Cronus?

7. How did Zeus win the war against Cronus?

8. How is the birth of gods related to the emergence of the universe in Greek mythology?

Part 3 Reflections

1. Vocabulary Expansion

1) cosmogony: _____

2) Dijiang: _____

3) Torch Dragon: _____

4) Pangu: _____

5) *Theogony*: _____

6) Olympus: _____

7) Titans: _____

8) Chaos: _____

9) Aether and Aër：_____

10) Titanomachia：_____

11) Hecatoncheires：_____

2. **Appreciation**

1) 曰：遂古之初，谁传道之？
   上下未形，何由考之？
   冥昭瞢暗，谁能极之？
   冯翼惟象，何以识之？
   明明暗暗，惟时何为？
   阴阳三合，何本何化？
   圜则九重，孰营度之？
   惟兹何功，孰初作之？
   斡维焉系，天极焉加？
   八柱何当，东南何亏？
   九天之际，安放安属？
   隅隈多有，谁知其数？
   天何所沓？十二焉分？
   日月安属？列星安陈？
   出自汤谷，次于蒙汜。
   自明及晦，所行几里？
   夜光何德，死则又育？
   厥利维何，而顾菟在腹？

   《楚辞·天问》

2)   Chasm it was, in truth, who was the very first; she soon
   Was followed by broad-breasted Earth, the eternal ground of all
   The deathless ones, who on Olympos's snowy summits dwell,
   And murky Tartaros hidden deep from Earth's wide-open roads,
   And Eros, the most beautiful among the deathless gods—

Limb-loosener he is of all the gods and of all men;
Thought in the breast he overwhelms and prudent planning; then
Out of Chasm Erebos and black Night both were born,
And then from Night came Ether and came Day as well in turn;
For Night conceived them, having joined with Erebos in love.
Now Earth first brought forth Ouranos, the starry Sky above,
An equal to herself, so he could cover her around,
And she might serve the deathless gods as firm, eternal ground.
She bore the hills, the gracious haunts of mountain goddesses then—
The Nymphs, who range the wooded hills and up and down each glen;
And without sweet desiring love, she bore the barren Sea,
Pontos, the raging salt-sea swell; and when she had lain with Sky,
She bore deep-eddying Ocean and Koios and Kreios too,
Hyperion, father of the Sun, Iapetos also,
And Thea and Rhea and Themis and, in turn, Mnemosyne,
Phoebe the golden-crowned one, Tethys lovely to see;
And after these the youngest came, Kronos, crooked and sly,
The cleverest of all her children and his father's enemy.

Hesiod's *Theogony*

3. Discussion

1) Compare Chinese and Greek etiological myths of cosmogony. What kind of creation myth do they belong to?

2) What kind of world views are revealed in Chinese and Greek etiological myths of cosmogony?

Unit 2

Emergence of Human Beings

Introduction

Every culture has its own explanations about the origin of mankind. Chinese mythology generally holds two descriptions in this regard. Myths about Pangu suggest that human beings originally derived from mites on his corpse. While according to some other versions of early narratives, humans were but clay sculptures fashioned by the goddess Nüwa from yellow earth and mud. Whereas some later accounts claim human beings as descendants of her and her brother/ husband Fuxi. References about Nüwa creating human beings could be traced back to as early as "Tianwen" by Qu Yuan:

> When Snake-Queen mounted the throne,
> Who said it was well done?
> Who made her body change
> Into seventy shapes strange?[①]

Huainanzi makes a record of Nüwa mythology two centuries later. On top of that, Ying Shao's **Fengsu Tongyi**[②] (*Comprehensive Meaning of Customs and Habits*)

---

① Qu Yuan, *Elegies of the South*, trans. by Xu Yuan-zhong, Beijing: China Translation & Publishing Corporation, 2009, pp. 97 - 99.
② 《风俗通义》,东汉泰山太守应劭辑录的民俗著作。原书三十卷、附录一卷,今仅存十卷。该作考论典礼类《白虎通》,纠正流俗类《论衡》,记录了大量神话异闻,并加上作者自己的评议,是研究汉以前风俗和鬼神崇拜的重要文献,编者注。

gives a description of the customs and worship of the primeval gods before the Han Dynasty.

Various Greek myths, for example, narrate that human beings were made from dragons' teeth, as in the story of **Cadmus**①, or from a "mother's bones," or from stones, or the ashes of Titans destroyed by Zeus. The most complete one is told in *Theogony* by Hesiod. In describing human society, Hesiod named different periods of human history as Golden, Silver, Bronze, Heroic and Iron ages. The two great events happened in the Golden Age are **Prometheus**② stealing fire for human beings and Zeus giving Pandora to **Epimetheus**③ as his wife. With fire, people bid farewell to a primitive form of life, thus embracing the process of civilization. Driven by curiosity, Pandora unleashed endless sufferings upon human beings. Irritated by the fall of the human race, the gods sent a flood to expiate their sins. However, the survival of **Deucalion**④ and **Pyrrha**⑤ offered new hope for the renewal of humanity.

Part 1　Emergence of Human Beings in Chinese Mythology

The world was indeed a sparkling jewel. **Sturdy**⑥ pine trees dotted the mountains, and weeping willows lined the streams. Apple, quince, and plum blossoms burst into bloom and later yielded ripe, heavy fruit. Birds **flitted**⑦

---

① Cadmus [ˈkædməs] n. 卡德摩斯
② Prometheus [prəˈmiːθɪəs] n. 普罗米修斯
③ Epimetheus [ˌepɪˈmiːθəs] n. 厄庇墨透斯
④ Deucalion [djuːˈkeɪljən] n. 丢卡利翁（普罗米修斯之子）
⑤ Pyrrha [ˈpɪrə] n. 皮拉（潘多拉之女，与丈夫丢卡利翁躲过了宙斯降下的洪水）
⑥ sturdy [ˈstɜːdi] adj. 挺拔的
⑦ flit [flɪt] vi. 轻快地飞过

about in the azure sky, leaving their black, crimson, and **iridescent**① green feathers drifting in the wind. Silver fish and carp splashed gleefully in the waterways. Fierce beasts like tigers and gentle creatures like deer roamed with equal abandon across the rocky hills.

Nüwa, a goddess, stumbled accidently upon this **vibrant**② world during her travels. The earth was humming and teeming with life. She marveled at its assorted wondrous creatures. These bewildering living beings kept coming into her sight wherever she set eyes upon. She saw every type of fur and fin, feather and scale, horn, hoof, and stinger. They lumbered, crawled, and slithered upon the earth; they jumped, darted, and roiled in the sea. Scented flowers like jasmine, hyacinth, and narcissus cradled the entire world in their warm, heavy perfume.

But as Nüwa explored its niches and crannies, intense dissatisfaction towards the budding world crawled into her mind: what an enchanting but empty place! Deeply touched by the strong loneliness it **exuded**③, Nüwa sat by a river to ponder her feelings. She gazed at her reflection in the water, and suddenly she knew what was missing: she wanted the world to be filled with thinking, laughing creatures like herself.

The river stretched out before her, its waves slapping the shore. The cloudy green waters left a rim of thick yellow earth along its banks. Nüwa felt its slippery texture with her finger tips and **scooped**④ out a ball of clay. The cool, sticky earth deposited by the river was perfect for her task, and she rolled the damp clay into a doll, giving it a head, shoulders, chest, and arms like her own. While the doll's lower body rendered her a little hesitation. Nüwa

---

① iridescent [ˌɪrɪˈdesnt] adj. 色彩斑斓的
② vibrant [ˈvaɪbrənt] adj. 充满活力的
③ exude [ɪɡˈzjuːd] vt. 散发
④ scoop [skuːp] (scoop out) vi. 挖出

considered giving it scales and claws modeling on a lizard, or fins and tails modeling on a fish. Both shapes were quite useful, since the goddess frequently changed the shape of her own lower body to secure a quick bypass around the oceans and the heavens. Finally, she decided to attach legs to the new creature so it could both walk on land and paddle about in the sea.

From the variable shades of yellow earth, Nüwa made tall dolls and short dolls and straight-haired dolls. She made some with eyes as round and large as cherries, or as long and narrow as a mosquito's wings. She made some with eyes so dark they looked like the midnight sky, others so light they looked like liquid honey. Each creature was different, so the goddess could recognize her creations. Then, as she breathed on each doll, it sprang to life, giggling and hopping about.

Nüwa was so delighted with her **handiwork**[①] that she wanted to make more. But she craved more efficiency. Along the riverbanks, slender reeds arched their graceful stems over the water. Nüwa rolled up her sleeves, cut a reed, and dipped it into the river mud like a spoon. Expertly, she flicked her wrist and dropped blobs of mud on the ground. When they dried, she breathed a huge puff of air into each blob, and instantly they became round, smiling creatures. The cheerful laughter of her creatures filled the goddess with happiness and pride.

However, Nüwa was tired. As much as she loved her new creations, she knew she could not watch over these humans all the time. What would happen to these creatures when they grew old and died? Nüwa did not relish making repairs, nor did she wish to repeat the tiring task of making new people. She thought it over and over. How could these creatures reproduce themselves without her aid?

---

① handiwork ['hændiwɜːk] n. 此处指女娲手工捏成的泥人

With a twist and a poke, she made some of the clay creatures male and some of them female. Then she gathered up all the noisy creatures who were slipping and falling in the mud. In the **hubbub**①, she began to deliver her most important instructions; and then the clamor died down to a silent hush. The humans listened solemnly to her words. She spoke of the importance of marriage and a couple's obligations to each other. She told them how to make children and how to raise them. She wished them a long and joyful existence on their earth. As the goddess left, she expressed her fervent hope that they would make new people and live happily without her. Then she ascended to the sky seated in a thundering chariot pulled by six winged dragons.

To this day, people continue to marry and have children who brighten the world with their joyous laughter, just as the dancing mud dolls did in the days of Nüwa. ②

Another widely spread type of myth explaining the origin of today's humans maintains that they were re-created by a sibling couple after their elder generations were annihilated in a calamity. In China, this brother-sister marriage myth can be found in more than forty ethnic groups, including the Han. This myth basically states that in remote antiquity, the world suffered such a great disaster (flood, fire mixed with oil, uncommon snow, etc.) that all humans in the world were destroyed except for a brother and his sister. They wanted to marry each other in order to repopulate the earth but wondered whether this was proper. They agreed that if certain things happened in a test, they should get married. The test in some myth versions was to roll two pieces of a millstone down different sides of a mountain. If the stones touched at the bottom of the mountain, the siblings should tie the knot. In other versions the brother

---

① hubbub [ˈhʌbʌb] n. 喧嚷
② Irene Dea Collier, *Chinese Mythology*, Aldershot: Enslow Publishers, Inc., 2001, pp. 25 – 28.

and sister each lit a fire from a different place, and if the two lines of smoke joined each other instead of dispersing, they should marry. These things all went on in a smooth manner, and the two got hitched naturally. After their marriage, some myths state that the sister gave birth to normal children. ①

Questions for Discussion:

1. Why was Nüwa dissatisfied with the beautiful world?

2. What were the two ways Nüwa applied to create human beings?

3. Why was it important to the goddess to make each mud doll different?

4. Why did she want her creations to multiply their offspring?

5. What feelings did people share with the gods of old in the creation process?

Part 2 Emergence of Human Beings in Greek Mythology

In the days of long, long ago when men built altars, burned sacrifices and worshiped their gods in temples of pure white marble, Zeus, the greatest of the gods, sat upon his throne on high Olympus and looked down upon the doings of men. The topmost peak of Mount Olympus was covered with clouds, so high it was above all the hills of Greece, and its slopes were thickly wooded. The real height of the mountain could only be guessed, for no man had enough courage to ascend even as high as the first cloud line; though the story goes that once upon a time a wandering shepherd, looking for a strayed lamb, had ventured far up the mountain side and had soon lost his way. He groped about blindly, as the

---

① Yang Lihui, An Deming and Jessica Anderson Turner, *Handbook of Chinese Mythology*, p. 68.

mists began to thicken all around him, and the sound of his own footsteps terrified him in the dreadful silence that seemed to be suddenly creeping over him. Then mighty tempest broke over his head, and the mountain shook to its very base. From the hand of wrathful Zeus fierce thunderbolts were hurled, while the lightning flashed and gleamed through the darkness of the forest, searching out the guilty mortal who had dared to climb too high.

No human eye had ever seen the glories of Olympus, no human foot had ever stepped within its sacred halls, where the ceiling was of gold and the pavement of pearl and the thrones of the gods shone with a thousand glittering jewels. Of the life that was lived among the dwellers on Olympus, not even the poets could claim to know; but sometimes a tired soldier dozing by his camp fire dreamed dreams of this wonderful country where the immortal gods walked by night and day; and sometimes a lonely fisherman, looking across the blue waters of the Mediterranean to the crimsoning sunset, saw visions of youth, beauty and life that lasted for ever and ever.

It was long before the memory of man that the gods first came to live on Mount Olympus, and it was still longer ago that all the great powers of the universe pitted against each other for the rulership over the world. In this mighty war, which rent the very heavens with the crash of battle, Zeus at last conquered all his jealous enemies, and made himself ruler of both gods and the world. On that day he established his dwelling place on Mount Olympus, and set the earth below him for a footstool. From his throne in the high heavens he looked down upon the kingdoms that he had portioned out to each of his brothers; and he saw Poseidon, sea-king's beard and on his crown of shells and seaweed. The other kingdom was so far away that even the all-seeing eyes of Zeus were strained to catch any glimpse of the shapes that moved noiselessly there, for this was the realm of Hades, god of the underworld, that dread country of darkness and unending gloom, where no ray of sunlight ever came, and where the sad spirits of the dead wept for the lost world of love, light and laughter.

Sometimes the great **billows**① of clouds that rolled at the foot of the red-gold throne shut out for a moment all sight of the earth at his feet; but however thickly the mists gathered, Zeus could always see old Atlas standing on the shore of Africa with the heavens resting on his bent shoulders. This giant had stood so long that forests of huge trees had sprung up around his feet, and they had grown so tall during the past long ages, that their topmost branches reached to the giant's waist and almost hid him from the sight of men. No one offered to relieve him of his burden, not even his two brothers, Prometheus and Epimetheus, to whom had been given the less difficult task of creating man and placing him in the rich gardens of the earth. There was every kind of plant and animal life in the gardens, and all things were very beautiful in this morning of the world—so beautiful that the gods, who must forever dwell in Olympus, felt sad that no eyes like their own could enjoy the treat of the green meadows and flower-covered hillsides. So they bade Prometheus and Epimetheus fashion a being which should be like and yet unlike themselves. There was nothing but clay out of which to make this new creature called man, but the brothers spent much time over their task, and when it was finished, Zeus saw that the work was good, for they had given to man all the qualities that the gods themselves possessed—youth, beauty, health, strength—everything but **immortality**②.

Then Prometheus grew ambitious to add even more to the list of the blessings; and one day, as he sat brooding by the seashore, he remembered that there was as yet no fire on the earth; for the only flame that burned in all the world was glowing in the sacred halls of Zeus. For a long time he sat on the seashore, and before night fell he had formed the daring plan of stealing some of

---

① billow ['bɪləʊ] n. 翻滚的云团
② immortality [ˌɪmɔː'tæləti] n. 永生

the divine fire that burned for always and always on Mount Olympus, and carrying it to the earth that men might revel in its warmth and light.

It was a bold thing to dream of doing, but Prometheus forgot the fear of Zeus's wrath, so determined was he to carry out his plan; and one night, when the gods were in council, seated around the great red-gold throne, he crept softly into the hall, unseen and unheard. The sacred fire was burning brightly on a hearth of polished silver. Some of it Prometheus secreted in a hollow reed and hurried with it back to the earth. Then he waited, with terror at his heart, for he knew that sooner or later the vengeance of Zeus would search him out, even though he fled to the uttermost parts of the earth.

When the council of the gods was over, Zeus looked down through the clouds and saw a strange light on the earth. For a while he did not realize that it was man, building himself a fire; but when he learned the truth, his wrath became so terrifying that even the gods trembled and turned away in fear. In a moment Prometheus was seized and carried off to the Caucasus Mountains, where he was securely chained to a rock, and a hungry vulture was sent to torture him, his liver being torn out and eaten by the vulture as soon as the sun rose. This terrible punishment kept on for years and years. Although Zeus heard the cries of Prometheus, and many tales were told of his sufferings, the ruler of the gods never forgave the theft of the sacred fire, nor would he set Prometheus free. But the story tells us that at last there came an end to this cruel vengeance, for Heracles, son of Zeus, went wandering one day among the mountains, found the tortured Prometheus, and broke his chains after killing the vulture that had been enjoying this hateful feast.

Though the gods were rejoiced at his freedom, the name of Prometheus was never spoken on Mount Olympus for fear of Zeus's all-hearing ears; but on the earth men uttered his name in their prayers and taught their children to honor the

Fire-giver as one of the greatest among heroes.①

Another story about the origin of human beings is related to Cadmus. After the **abduction**② of his daughter Europa by Zeus, Agenor, king of Phenicia, unable to reconcile himself to her loss, dispatched his son Cadmus in search of her, demanding him not to return without his sister.

For many years Cadmus pursued his search through various countries, but his efforts were to no avail. Not daring to return home without her, he consulted the oracle of Apollo at Delphi; and the reply was that he must **desist**③ from his task, and take upon himself a new duty, i.e., that of founding a city, the site of which would be indicated to him by a **heifer**④ which had never borne the yoke, and which would lie down on the spot whereon the city was to be built.

Scarcely had Cadmus left the sacred **fane**⑤, when he observed a heifer who bore no marks of servitude on her neck, walking slowly in front of him. He followed the animal for a considerable distance, until at length, on the site where Thebes afterwards stood, she looked towards heaven and, gently lowing, lay down in the long grass. Grateful for this mark of divine favor, Cadmus resolved to offer up the animal as a sacrifice, and accordingly sent his followers to fetch water for the **libation**⑥ from a neighboring spring. This spring, which was sacred to Ares, was situated in a wood, and guarded by a fierce dragon, who, at the approach of the retainers of Cadmus, suddenly pounced upon them and killed them.

After waiting some time for the return of his servants, Cadmus grew

---

① Emilie Kip Baker, *Stories of Old Greece and Rome*, New York: The Macmillan Company, 1913, pp. 1-6.
② abduction [æb'dʌkʃn] n. 诱拐
③ desist [dɪ'zɪst] vi. 停止
④ heifer ['hefə] n. 小母牛
⑤ fane [feɪn] n. 神庙
⑥ libation [laɪ'beɪʃn] n. 奠酒祭神仪式

impatient, and hastily arming himself with his lance and spear, set out to seek them. On reaching the spot, the **mangled**① remains of his unfortunate followers met his view, and near them he beheld the frightful monster, dripping with the blood of his victims. Seizing a huge rock, the hero hurled it with all his might upon the dragon; but protected by his tough black skin and steely scales as by a coat of mail, he remained unhurt. Cadmus now tried his lance, and with more success, for it pierced the side of the beast, who, furious with pain, sprang at his adversary, when Cadmus, leaping aside, succeeded in fixing the point of his spear within his jaws, which final stroke put an end to the encounter.

While Cadmus stood surveying his vanquished foe, Pallas-Athene appeared to him, and commanded him to sow the teeth of the dead dragon in the ground. He obeyed; and out of the **furrows**② there arose a band of armed men, who at once commenced to fight with each other, until all except five were killed. These last surviving warriors made peace with each other, and it was with their assistance that Cadmus now built the famous city of Thebes. In later times the noblest Theban families proudly claimed their descent from these mighty earth-born warriors. ③

Questions for Discussion:

1. What did the gods on Mount Olympus bid Prometheus and Epimetheus to do?

2. What qualities did Zeus bestow on human beings?

3. What did Prometheus add to the list of the blessings?

4. What punishment did Prometheus receive after he stole fire from Zeus?

5. What did Agenor send Cadmus to do?

---

① mangle [ˈmæŋgl] vt. 损坏
② furrow [ˈfʌrəʊ] n. 犁沟
③ E. M. Berens, *The Myths and Legends of Ancient Greece and Rome*, pp. 203 - 204.

6. What new task did Cadmus take upon after consulting the oracle of Apollo at Delphi?

7. How did Cadmus create human beings?

Part 3　Reflections

1. **Vocabulary Expansion**

1）Nüwa：_____

2）Prometheus：_____

3）Epimetheus：_____

4）Delphi：_____

5）Cadmus：_____

6）Deucalion and Pyrrha：_____

7）earth-born warriors：_____

2. **Appreciation**

1）有神十人，名曰女娲之肠，化为神，处栗广之野，横道而处。

《山海经·大荒西经》

2）黄帝生阴阳，上骈生耳目，桑林生臂手，此女娲所以七十化也。

《淮南子·说林训》

3）俗说天地开辟，未有人民，女娲抟黄土作人。剧务，力不暇供，乃引绳于泥中，举以为人。故富贵者，黄土人也；贫贱凡庸者，縆人也。

《太平御览·风俗通》

4）首生盘古，垂死化身，

　　气成风云，声为雷霆，

　　左眼为日，右眼为月，

　　四肢五体为四极五岳，

　　血液为江河，筋脉为地里，

肌肉为田土，发髭为星辰，

皮毛为草木，齿骨为金石，

精髓为珠玉，汗流为雨泽，

身之诸虫，因风所感，化为黎氓。

《五运历年记》

5) But Zeus, being angered in his heart, hid it away from us,

Having been crookedly deceived by sly Prometheus.

He, on account of this, devised for humans pain and dole,

Concealed the fire, which the noble son of Iapetos stole

In a hollow stalk of fennel back for mankind's use,

Unheeded by the wise counselor, thunder-delighting Zeus.

Then the Cloud-Gatherer in rage addressed the Titan thus:

"Your schemes surpass all other schemes, son of Iapetos;

Now you rejoice at having stolen fire, outwitting me:

Much misery both for yourself, yourself and men to be.

To them in recompense for fire, I shall bequeath a woe,

Which they will cherish in their hearts, although it lays them low."

Hesiod's *Works and Days*

3. Discussion

1) Draw a conclusion of the myths about emergence of human beings.

	Chinese Myth	Greek Myth
The creator		
The archetype		
Raw material		
Method		
Quantity		

2) How are the Chinese and Greek myths about the emergence of human beings related to views on body and soul?

Unit 3

Flood Myths

Introduction

The story of flood plays a dramatic role in Chinese mythology, and its various versions① provide abundant sources for the motif of deluge in the world. A mass of Chinese flood narratives, somewhat lacking in internal consistency, incorporating various magical transformations and interventions of divine and semi-divine beings, share certain common features. On the one hand, a certain emphasis on the flood as a result of natural causes rather than punishment for human sins has been made. On the other hand, the alleviation of the flooding normally lies in the construction of dikes, dams, canals and the widening or deepening of the existing ones, which is to be imparted to others as a skill, as in the tales of Nüwa, Gun, and Yu. Therefore, one of the distinct themes in the Great Flood myths of China is in its stress on heroism and mettle in their struggle against the disaster. Another salient theme is the progress of civilization in spite of human beings' sufferings. The fighting, surviving, and eventual victory over the **inundation**② stimulate much progress in terms of land management, beast control, and agricultural techniques. As an integral part of the developments of civilization, flood narratives exemplify a wider approach to human health and

---

① 《山海经》《史记》和《孟子》都记载了洪水神话故事。编者注。
② inundation [ˌɪnʌnˈdeɪʃn] n. 洪水

societal well-being rather than just dealing with flood emergency and its immediate effects.

Greek mythology knows four floods: the flood of **Ogyges**①, the sinking of **Atlantis**②, the flood of Deucalion, and the flood of **Dardanus**③, among which the Ogygian Deluge terminated the Silver Age, and the flood of Deucalion the First Bronze Age. The Deucalion legend, as told by Apollodorus in ***The Library***④, bears some resemblance to other deluge myths like the story of Noah's Ark in Hebrew mythology. In the story, Prometheus warned his son, Deucalion of the upcoming flood, who was made to build a chest as a shelter. When the holocaust started, all other men perished except for a few who escaped to high mountains. Then the mountains in **Thessaly**⑤ were parted, and all the world beyond the Isthmus and Peloponnese was overwhelmed. Deucalion and his wife Pyrrha, after floating in the chest for nine days and nights, landed on Parnassus. While an older version of the story told by **Hellanicus**⑥ has Deucalion's "ark" landing on Mount Othrys in Thessaly, and some others on a peak, probably Phouka in Argolis (later called **Nemea**⑦). When the rains

---

① 俄古革斯，原为玻俄提亚地方早期居民的国王，在位期间发生洪水，故命名为俄古革斯洪水，编者注。

② 亚特兰蒂斯，又译阿特兰蒂斯，又称大西洲、大西国，位于欧洲到直布罗陀海峡附近的大西洋之岛，传说中拥有高度文明发展的古老大陆、国家或城邦之名。柏拉图的著作《克里特阿斯》(Critas) 和《提迈奥斯》(Timaeus) 均有提及，据称其在公元前一万年被史前大洪水毁灭，编者注。

③ 达尔达努斯，宙斯和厄勒克特拉之子，厄勒克特拉是阿特拉斯之女，也是特鲁阿德的伊达山达尔达尼亚城的建立者。达尔达努斯娶了雅典娜的女儿克丽丝，育有两子：伊代乌斯 (Idaeus) 和戴马斯 (Dymas)。当发生大洪水时，幸存者分成了两组：一组留下来并继承戴马斯为王，另一组乘船离开，最终定居在萨莫色雷斯岛，编者注。

④ 译为《书库》或是《万卷书》。据说是一位名叫阿波罗多罗斯的希腊人所著，被誉为"从古代流传下来的最有价值的神话作品"。该书共有三卷，记录了希腊神话和英雄传说。后来由公元九世纪君士坦丁堡的族长兼学者弗提乌斯编撰而成，编者注。

⑤ Thessaly ['θesəli] n. 塞萨利（希腊地名）

⑥ 赫拉尼库斯是出生于列士波斯岛的希腊散文作家，平生著作极为丰富，他的作品包括史诗英雄的谱系，诸多地区的方志，第一部雅典史等，编者注。

⑦ Nemea ['ni:miə] n. 尼米亚（希腊河谷）

ceased, Deucalion sacrificed to Zeus. Then, at the bidding of the god, the husband and wife threw stones behind themselves. Those thrown by Deucalion became men, and by Pyrrha became women. Hence an etymology for Greek *Laos* "people" as derived from *laas* "stone" by Apollodorus at a later date.

Part 1　Flood Myths in Chinese Mythology

Gun-Yu taming the flood is one of the most popular flood myths that found their way in Chinese mythology through ages.

It was during the reign of Emperor Yao that the Great Flood began, a flood so vast as even to strike the Yellow River and the Yangtze River basin, leaving no part of Yao's territory spared. According to both historical and mythological sources, the flooding continued relentlessly. Emperor Yao, seeking to find someone to regulate the disorder, turned for advice to his special adviser, or advisers, the Four Mountains, who, after deliberation, gave Yao some advice which he did not especially appreciate. Yao eventually consented to promote Gun, the Prince of Chong, who was a distant relative of Yao through shared lineage from the Yellow Emperor, to office after hesitating at the Four Mountains' persuasion.

According to mythological tradition, Gun's plan was through the use of the Supreme Divinity's autogenetic and everlasting soil, known as **Xirang**①, to keep out the flood. But he stole the soil to dam the floodwater without waiting for the god's official permission. Year in and year out, hard work had been carried on to block and **barricade**② the floodwaters with the help of the magic soil, but in

---

① 息壤，"息"为生长之意；息壤，指能自己生长、膨胀的土壤。郭璞注《海内经》："息壤者，言土自长息无限，故可以塞洪水也"，编者注。
② barricade ['bærɪkeɪd] vt. 堵住

vain. Whether Gun's failure to **abate**① the flood was due to the divine wrath or to the defects in his approach to **hydrological**② engineering remains an unanswered question. He was killed afterwards by the fire god Zhurong at the outer edge of Yushan (which literally means "feather mountain"). However, Gun's corpse did not rot for three years. Later, when his belly was opened with a sword under the command of the Yellow Emperor, his son Yu was born.

Yu continued the great enterprise of his father. Taking an approach of dredging, he deepened the seas and lakes, and dug mountains, channeling the overflowing water to the East China Sea. Eventually the **demigod**③ Yu beat off the evil and turned the miserable world into a habitable place for humankind. He then became the founder of the first civilized state in Chinese history, Xia. Allegedly, in the flooding time, Yu was thirteen years away from his home, and though he passed his house three times, he did not enter. In another version, Yu, for the water affair, had changed into a bear to dig a mountain when his pregnant wife came to bring him food. Feeling embarrassed at what she saw, the wife ran away. When Yu found her, she **metamorphosed**④ into a stone. Then Yu shouted, "Give back my son!" The stone opened up and out came Qi (literally meaning "open up"), the first ruler of Xia.

The notable myth about "Nüwa mending the broken sky" is at times incorporated in the scope of flood myth as well. In some versions, this calamity was caused by the collapse of the four poles supporting heaven; while in others, it was caused by the breakdown of one of them, namely Mount Buzhou (literally means "not full"). As the story goes, Gonggong battled with Zhuanxu (one of the Five Emperors, whose names differ in various texts) for the title of the

---

① abate [ə'beɪt] vt. 减退
② hydrological [ˌhaɪdrə'lɒdʒɪkəl] adj. 水文学的
③ demigod ['demigɒd] n. 半神半人（此处指禹）
④ metamorphose [ˌmetə'mɔːfəʊz] vi. 变形

supreme god but fell short. So large was his rage that he butted into Buzhou Mountain, leading to disasters in all its manifestations. **Unquenchable**① flames burned; water flowed without abating; ferocious birds and beasts pressed upon men. Under such circumstances, the goddess Nüwa melted the stones of five different colors to patch heaven, and cut the legs of a huge tortoise, setting them up to support the four extremities of the sky. On the heels of that she defeated the savage Black Dragon and collected luhui (ashes of reeds) to block the flood. Her arduous work cleared up the terrible mess, putting the world in order again. In some versions collected in the twentieth century, Nüwa not only mended the broken sky but also healed the earth in tatters. Her mythical actions often serve as an explanation for the existence of colorful clouds in heaven (the goddess mended heaven with colorful stones), and China's terrain features with the western land falling away sharply towards the east (she used the longer legs of the tortoise for the west and the shorter ones for the east).②

Questions for Discussion:

1. What led to the flood in Chinese myths?
2. What methods were applied to control the flood by Gun, Yu and Nüwa?
3. What lessons can we learn from Gun-Yu myth?

Part 2　The Deluge in Greek Mythology

Legend has it that the children of Epimetheus and Pandora wandered in the gardens of the earth just as their parents had done; and the generations that

---

① unquenchable [ʌnˈkwentʃəbl] adj. 不灭的
② Yang Lihui, An Deming and Jessica Anderson Turner, *Handbook of Chinese Mythology*, pp. 73–75.

followed them lived in the haven of peace and tranquility, in spite of the brown-winged **sprites**① that went about doing **mischief**②. Men helped each other to cultivate the fruitful soil, and offered sacrifices to the gods in return for a bountiful harvest.

This Golden age might have lasted forever if men had continued their **reverence**③ for the gods; but after a time they ceased to offer prayers for health and safety and boasted proudly of their own strength. They looked no more to high Olympus for help, and each man trusted to his own right arm. Then **strife**④ and **discord**⑤ arose, triggering off pitched battles all over the land. Brother killed brother, and fathers strove with their own sons. Every man's hand was against his fellow, and he knew no law but that of his own will. Seldom now were the fires kindled on the neglected altars, and the smell of burnt offerings dear to the gods no longer mingled with the smoke that rose up to the white clouds around Olympus. Sacred **vessels**⑥ **moldered**⑦ in forsaken temples; around the **shrines**⑧ of the gods the snakes crawled lazily; and the bat and owl dwelt undisturbed among the pillars of the temples.

For a time the gods sat patient, believing that this state of things could not last; but seeing mankind was growing worse instead of better, they determined to put an end to this godlessness destroying the whole race of man. Then Zeus called a council of the gods to decide on the most effective way of wiping out every **vestige**⑨ of human life that not one soul would be left to tell to his children

---

① sprite [spraɪt] n. 妖精
② mischief [ˈmɪstʃɪf] n. 恶作剧
③ reverence [ˈrevərəns] n. 崇敬
④ strife [straɪf] n. 冲突
⑤ discord [ˈdɪskɔːd] n. 分歧
⑥ vessel [ˈvesl] n. 圣器
⑦ molder [ˈməʊldə] vi. 腐朽
⑧ shrine [ʃraɪn] n. 神殿
⑨ vestige [ˈvestɪdʒ] n. 遗迹

the story of those evil days, when men neglected to worship the immortal gods and allowed their temples to decay.

The most horrific punishment to visit upon man would be to set the whole world on fire, to make of it one great **sacrificial**① altar on which human victims, rather than **garlanded**② ox, would burn night and day, and from which the smoke would rise up into the heavens so thickly that it would shut out the sight of a blackened and smouldering earth. One objection to carrying out this plan was from the fear lest the flames would leap so high that they would reach even to lofty Olympus, endangering the sacred throne of Zeus. Though the fire might not strike a fatal blow to it, the gods could not bear to think of its burnished red-gold base being touched by the slightest flame from earth's unholy fires.

What was then left with the deities was water, which they decided to employ. Therefore, on a certain day when men were everywhere feasting, singing songs and boasting of their victories in battle, Zeus rent the heavens with a mighty thunderbolt, whose crashing drowned all sounds of merriment and made men turn pale with fear. The skies opened and the rain poured down in torrents; the rivers became swollen and flooded their banks; the waves of the sea in the wake of the winds were let loose to work a **havoc**③ on the earth. Soon all the lowland was covered with water; not a dry spot remained anywhere but on the hills. Terrified people rushed hither and thither in the vain hope that the flood would **subside**④ before the mountains were **submerged**⑤. But the waves surged higher and higher; and the winds, rejoicing in their freedom, beat up the water until it almost touched the clouds. The **frail**⑥ boats to which men had at first

---

① sacrificial [ˌsækrɪˈfɪʃl] adj. 献祭的
② garland [ˈɡɑːlənd] vt. 戴花环
③ havoc [ˈhævək] n. 灾难
④ subside [səbˈsaɪd] vi. 平息
⑤ submerge [səbˈmɜːdʒ] vt. 浸没
⑥ frail [freɪl] adj. 脆弱的

desperately clung were shattered to pieces in the fury of the storm, and on the crest of the waves the bodies of the dead were tossed like playthings. There was not a lull until the mountain tops were at length drowned out, making dry land a complete goner. So were the gods avenged.

There was one spot, however, that was not yet hidden under the waters, and this was the top of Mount Parnassus, the highest hill of Greece. To this place of refuge had fled Deucalion and his wife Pyrrha, two virtuous souls who alone, of all the people on the earth, had lived uprightly and worshiped the gods. When Zeus saw them standing on the top of Mount Parnassus and weeping over the universal destruction, he remembered their **piety**① and decreed that their lives should be spared. So he gave commands that the rains and the floods and the winds should cease, and the dry land reappear. Then Aeolus brought the winds back from their mad wanderings and bound them again in the cave. Poseidon blew upon his **conch**② shell, summoning the angry waves back to the sea. Little by little the treetops showed above the water, and the green earth smiled again under the warm rays of the sun.

But it was upon a **desolate**③ and unpeopled world that the eyes of Deucalion and Pyrrha rested, and in their utter loneliness they almost wished that they had **perished**④ with their friends. They went slowly down the mountain-side, not knowing where to go, being led blindly by the will of the gods to the temple of Delphi—the only building that was not destroyed. To this sacred spot men had been **wont**⑤ to come in the old, god-fearing days to consult the wishes of the gods and to learn their own destinies. Here lies the divine oracle that not even the most daring mortal would refuse to obey.

---

① piety ['paɪəti] n. 虔诚
② conch [kɒntʃ] n. 海螺壳
③ desolate ['desələt] adj. 荒无人烟的
④ perish ['perɪʃ] vi. 死去
⑤ wont [wəʊnt] adj. 惯常的

When Deucalion and Pyrrha found themselves at the temple of Delphi, they made haste to consult the oracle, for they wished to repeople the land before another morning's sun could look down upon a lifeless earth. To their surprise the oracle returned them this answer: "Depart from here with veiled heads and throw your mother's bones behind you."

This command seemed impossible to obey; for they could never hope to find any grave, when all **landmarks**① had been washed away; and, even could they do so, it was an unheard-of sacrilege to disturb the bones of the dead. Deucalion sought, therefore, to explain the strange words of the oracle in some other way; and at length he guessed the meaning of the god's answer. It was no human remains that he was commanded to **desecrate**②; the bones referred to were those of Mother Earth. So husband and wife left the temple with veiled heads; and as they went they gathered up the stones at their feet and threw those behind them.

Thus it was through the kindness and wisdom of the immortals that the earth was repeopled with a new race of men with fear of evil and reverenced piety, who walked humbly before the gods. Never again was Zeus forced to unleash a deluge on the earth, for men no longer let the altar-fires burn low, nor did they neglect to offer sacrifices because of forgotten prayers. ③

Questions for Discussion:

1. What led to the flood in Greek mythology?
2. How did Zeus respond to man's blasphemy?
3. What was Zeus's original plan? Why did he quit it?
4. What did Zeus do at last?

---

① landmark ['lændmɑːk] n. 地标
② desecrate ['desɪkreɪt] vt. 亵渎
③ Emilie Kip Baker, *Stories of Old Greece and Rome*, pp. 16 – 21.

5. How long did the flood last?

6. How were humans recreated?

Part 3　Reflections

1. **Vocabulary Expansion**

   1）Xirang：_____

   2）Gun：_____

   3）Yu：_____

   4）Mount Parnassus：_____

   5）Deucalion：_____

2. **Appreciation**

   1）禹、鲧是始布土，均定九州。炎帝之妻，赤水之子听訞生炎居。炎居生节并，节并生戏器，戏器生祝融，祝融降处于江水，生共工。共工生术器，术器首方颠，是复土壤，以处江水。共工生后土，后土生噎鸣，噎鸣生岁十有二。洪水滔天，鲧窃帝之息壤以堙洪水，不待帝命。帝令祝融杀鲧于羽郊。鲧复生禹，帝乃命禹卒布土以定九州。

   《山海经·海内经》

   2）共工之臣名曰相繇，九首蛇身，自环，食于九土。其所歍所尼，即为源泽，不辛乃苦，百兽莫能处。禹湮洪水，杀相繇，其血腥臭，不可生谷，其地多水，不可居也。禹湮之，三仞三沮，乃以为池，群帝因是以为台。在昆仑之北。

   《山海经·大荒北经》

   3）当其末年也，诸侯有共工氏，任智刑以强，霸而不王，以水乘木，乃与祝融战，不胜而怒，乃头触不周，山崩，天柱折，地维缺。

   《史记·补三皇本纪》

   4）当尧之时，天下犹未平，洪水横流，泛滥于天下，草木畅茂，禽兽繁殖，五谷不登，禽兽逼人，兽蹄鸟迹之道交于中国。尧独忧之，举舜而敷治焉。舜使益掌火，益烈山泽而焚之，禽兽逃匿。禹疏九河，瀹济、漯而注诸海；决汝、汉，排淮、泗而注之江，然后中国可得而食也。当是时也，禹八年于外，三过其门而不入，虽欲耕，得乎？

《孟子·滕文公上》

5）龙门未辟，吕梁未凿，河出孟门之上，大溢逆流，无有丘陵、高阜灭之，名曰洪水。大禹疏通，谓之孟门。

《淮南子》

6)   I wish that I were not among this last, fifth race of men,
But either dead already or had afterwards been born;
For this race now is iron indeed, and never, night or morn,
Will leave off from their suffering, worn down by toil and woe.
The gods will give them harsh and grievous cares, but even so,
They too shall have a share of good, mixed though it be with pain—
Also, Zeus will eradicate this race of mortal men:
In such a time when at their birth babies turn out to be
Gray at the temples; when fathers and sons have lost all harmony;
When the relation of comrade to comrade fails, and of host to guest;
When brother no longer is friend to brother, as formerly in the past.
They'll treat their parents with disdain as soon as they are old,
Heartlessly finding fault with them in accents harsh and cold;
And ignorant of the punishment the gods mete, as they are,
They'll not be likely to repay their parents for their care.
Taking the law into their hands, they'll pillage and destroy
Each other's cities; gratitude shall no man then enjoy
Who righteously serves justice and who keeps his oath, but him
Who's wicked and does violence—that man they will esteem.
Might shall make right: the evil man his better will subdue

By speaking crooked words and swearing oaths upon them too;

And shrieking Envy that delights in harming wretched men,

With foul-mouthed, hate-filled face shall be each man's companion then.

Forsaking humankind to be among the deathless gods,

Leaving the earth's broad pathways for the Olympian abodes,

Their lovely bodies mantled in white cloaks without a stain,

Restraint and Censure will depart—sad sufferings remain

For death-born men, and no defense from evil will avail.

Hesiod's *Works and Days*

3. Discussion

1) Compare flood myths of Chinese and Greek mythology and finish the following table.

Types	Cause	Process	Results	Survivors
Chinese flood myth				
Greek flood myth				

2) Discuss the conception of nature in Chinese and western culture by referring to flood myths.

Unit 4

Water Deities

Introduction

A water deity is a mythological figure presiding over the watery element, such as oceans, rivers, springs or even wells, who usually possesses the power to control the rain and water. Water deities are attached more significance to among civilizations in which the sea or a great river occupies an important place. They are frequently recorded in Chinese ancient books such as *The Classic of Mountains and Seas*, *Zhuangzi*, *Huainanzi*, and *The Songs of Chu*, etc. The water deities in record are Gonggong and Tianwu, Xuanming and Yujiang (sea gods), and Hebo (god of the Yellow River), Xiangfei (goddesses of the Xiangjiang River) and Fufei (goddess of the Luo River), etc. However, since the introduction and subsequent popularity of Buddhist sutras after the Tang Dynasty, the legends of the Dragon Kings began to prevail in the Central Plains, leaving ancient water deities like He Bo rarely mentioned.

While in the introduction to the creation myth of Greek mythology, we get to know that there is existence of water deities in every generation of Greek gods. Gaia gave birth to Uranus the sky, Ourea the mountains and Pontus the sea. Then Pontus united with Gaia and bore numerous progeny with various attributes of the sea: Nereus representing the kindness, Eurybia the strength, Thaumas the wonder, Phorcys the anger, and Ceto, the danger. Poseidon, god of the sea, was an important Olympian power as the chief patron of Corinth, a host of cities in **Magna Graecia**①, and also of Plato's legendary Atlantis. He remained in control of the oceans and the seas, and was the creator of horses as well. As such, he was intimately connected with the pre-historic office of king—whose chief emblem of power and primary sacrificial animal was the horse. Several types of sea gods conformed to a single version, that of Homer's **Halios Geron**② or Old Man of the Sea: Nereus, Proteus, Glaucus and Phorcys. Being the minor gods, they were not as powerful as Poseidon, the main god of the oceans and seas, and thus were subject to him. Each one was a **shape-shifter**③, a prophet, and the father of either radiantly beautiful nymphs or hideous monsters (or both, in the case of Phorcys).

Part 1 Water Deities in Chinese Mythology

Gods of Sea

Yuqiang

In *The Classic of Mountains and Seas*, Yuqiang is identified as the son of Yuhao, who was born by Huang Di, the Yellow Emperor. Yuhao lived in the East Sea, and his son Yuqiang lived in the North Sea. They both were sea gods. Being described as "a god who has a human face and a bird's body," and "hangs two green snakes on his ears and treads two red snakes (or green snakes) underfoot,"④ Yuqiang is regarded as a god who took charge of affairs both about the sea and the wind by some scholars. This may be substantiated by various

---

① 大希腊，古希腊殖民地，编者注。
② 荷马的"海洋老人"（Halios Geron）涅柔斯、普罗透斯、格劳刻和福耳库斯，他们都是变身者、预言家、美艳的宁芙或丑恶的怪兽之父，编者注。
③ shape-shifter [ˈʃeɪp ʃɪftə] n. 变形人
④ *The Classic of Mountains and Seas*, p. 237.

accounts in *Huainanzi*, *Lüshi Chunqiu* (*The Spring and Autumn Annals of Master Lü*) and *Zhuangzi*. They all mention that the northwest wind came from Yuqiang. In Zhuangzi's *A Happy Excursion*, the fish Kun was de facto the sea god Yuqiang for both of them lived in the sea called Beiming, and although Yuqiang was a sea god in the North Sea, he transformed into a bird and as a wind god when going to the South Sea.

Regardless of the wide assortment of descriptions of Yuqiang, he is securely recognized as sea god in Chinese mythology, with the miraculous turtles which are said to be his **envoys**[1]. In *Liezi*, a story tells how Yuqiang helped the God of Heaven rearrange the natural order. In the remote area east of the Bohai Sea, there was a bottomless deep into which all water from every river and other source flowed. In this deep there stood the five highest mountains. Each mountain was 30,000 li (about 10,000 miles) in height and circumference, and the distance between two mountains was 70,000 li (about 23,000 miles). On the top of these mountains were fantastic scenery and many mythical animals and fruits. Many gods and demigods lived there. They could fly from one mountain to another in one day and night. However, because these mountains did not have roots, they often floated with the waves and were never still. The gods and demigods living there worried about this and complained to the God of Heaven. Yuqiang was in turn asked to deal with the situation. He arranged for fifteen huge sea turtles to carry the mountains on their heads. The turtles were divided into three groups. Each group should take a turn in carrying the mountains for 60,000 years. From then on, the mountains were fixed.[2]

Here is the passage quoted from *Liezi*:

---

[1] envoy ['envɔɪ] n. 使者
[2] Yang Lihui, An Deming and Jessica Anderson Turner, *Handbook of Chinese Mythology*, p. 244.

However, the five mountains were baseless and thus were forever kept rising and falling with the waves, and shifting here and there with the tides. It proved vexing to the inhabitants, who appealed to the Heavenly Emperor. For fear the mountains should be drifted to the remotest west, the Emperor issued an order for Yuqiang, god of the North Pole, to send fifteen huge tortoises to carry the mountains on their backs, on three shifts relaid at an interval of sixty thousand years. And then they became rock-firm.[①]

Questions for Discussion:

1. What did Yuqiang look like according to *The Classic of Mountains and Seas*?

2. Why was Yuqiang regarded as sea god and wind god?

3. How did Yuqiang help to fix the five mountains?

Mazu

Another widely worshipped sea god is Mazu, the patron goddess of sailors, fishermen and travelers. Unlike many Chinese mythological figures, Mazu was believed to have been a real girl named Lin Mo who lived off the coast of Fujian on Meizhou Island during the tenth century. When she was born, she didn't cry or shed a single tear. Therefore, she was nicknamed "Mo Niang" or "Silent Girl." Despite being mute when born, Lin Mo was blessed with a number of amazing gifts. She could accurately predict the weather, fall into deep **trances**[②] and experience divine visions. With a vast knowledge of astronomy and Chinese

---

① Lieh Tzu, *Liezi*, translated into Modern Chinese by Li Jianguo, translated into English by Liang Xiaopeng, Beijing: Zhonghua Book Company, 2005, pp. 109 – 111.

② trance [trɑːns] n. 出神

medicine, she was also well-known for outstanding swimming skills and **prowess**①. Throughout her life, Mazu helped coastal residents and local seafarers by making medicines, curing patients as well as forecasting the weather, planning safe routes and saving lives from shipwrecks.

There are several legends about her death and how she turned into the goddess. One version of the story is that one day when her father and four brothers were fishing off the coast of Meizhou Island, dark, ominous clouds suddenly blocked out the sun and fierce winds began to blow off the coast. Her father and brothers' boat was rocked by the storm's huge waves and **capsized**②. At the same time, when weaving at her loom, Lin Mo fell into a deep trance. In her pure spiritual form, she projected herself to her father and brothers' boat, saw what had happened, and managed to get her brothers to land. Her mother didn't know what the young girl was trying to do and shook Lin Mo awake before she was able to save her father. In her grief, Lin Mo climbed to the top of a high cliff and threw herself into the sea. Before she hit the water, her body transformed into a pure beam of celestial light and ascended to Heaven where she became the goddess Mazu.

Another oft-told version goes that Lin Mo sacrificed herself at the age of 28 while trying to rescue the survivors of a shipwreck. Her fellow townspeople then built a temple in memory of the virtuous and kind woman and to worship her as the goddess, representing mercy, kindness and compassion.

Today, many Chinese, especially those living in coastal China, still strongly believe that Mazu will always look out for the brave sailors and fishermen. As maritime activities flourished, Mazu temples were established in various port cities all over the world, following in footprints of Chinese

---

① prowess ['praʊəs] n. 英勇
② capsize ['kæpsaɪz] vi. 倾覆

immigrants. Mazu belief and customs have spread over 20 countries and regions. There are more than 200 million devotees worldwide and over 5,000 temples dedicated to her.①

Questions for Discussion:

1. Why was Li Mo nickramed "Mo Niang"?

2. What special ability did she have?

3. How did she die and become a goddess?

The Sea-dragon Kings

Though the dragon showed up very early in Chinese history and culture, and sea-dragons kings have become popular gods in Chinese belief nowadays, the figures of dragon kings did not appear until the Eastern Han Dynasty when Buddhism was imported to China.

Worshipped by Chinese for good weather, bountiful harvest all year round, the Sea-dragon Kings were considered the rulers of weather and water. There were four of these divinities (in some other versions five), namely Ao Guang, Ao Qin, Ao Shun and Ao Run, occupying the East, the South, the North, and the West China Sea respectively. Each divinity was a **league**② in length, and so **bulky**③ that in shifting its posture it **tossed**④ one mountain against another. It had five feet, one of them being in the middle of its belly, and every foot was armed with five sharp claws. It could reach into the heavens, and stretch itself into all quarters of the sea. It also had a glowing **armour**⑤ of yellow

---

① https://mythopedia.com/topics/mazu
② league [liːg] n. 里格（旧时长度单位，约等于5公里）
③ bulky [ˈbʌlki] adj. 庞大的
④ toss [tɒs] vt. （使）摇摆
⑤ armour [ˈɑːmə] n. 盔甲

scales, a beard under its long **snout**①, a hairy tail, and shaggy legs. The forehead of every sea-dragon king projected over its blazing eyes, the ears were small and thick, the mouth gaping, the tongue long, and the teeth sharp. Fish were boiled by the blast of its breath, and roasted by the fiery **exhalations**② of its body. When it rose to the surface the whole ocean surged, **waterspouts**③ foamed, and typhoons raged. When it flew, wingless, through the air, the winds howled, torrents of rain descended, houses were unroofed, the **firmament**④ was filled with a **din**⑤, and whatever lay along its route was swept away with a roar in the hurricane created by the speed of its passage.

The four Sea-dragon Kings were all immortal. They could read each other's mind without intercommunication. Like all the other gods they made their presence once a year to the superior Heavens, for an annual report to the Supreme Ruler; their arrival was in the third month, at which time none of the other gods dared appear, but their stay above was but brief. They generally possessed royal residences in the depths of the ocean, where inhabited their **progeny**⑥, dependents, and attendants, and also where their presence was required at the council of the gods and **genii**⑦. Their palaces, of diverse colored transparent stones, with crystal doors, are said to have been seen in the early morning by people gazing into the deep waters. ⑧

Questions for Discussion:

1 Why did people worship the Sea-dragon Kings?

---

① snout [snaʊt] n. 鼻子
② exhalation [ˌekshəˈleɪʃn] n. 呼气（龙身喷出的火焰）
③ waterspout [ˈwɔːtəspaʊt] n. 海龙卷
④ firmament [ˈfɜːməmənt] n. 天空
⑤ din [dɪn] n. 喧嚣声
⑥ progeny [ˈprɒdʒəni] n. 后裔
⑦ genii [ˈdʒiːnɪˌaɪ] n. 守护神
⑧ Edward T. C. Werner, *Myths and Legends of China*, London: George G. Harrap & Co. Ltd., 1922, pp. 210–211.

2. What were the names of the Sea-dragon Kings?

3. What did they look like?

4. Why did they make their presence to the superior Heavens?

Gods of River

He Bo

Gods of river and their stories are also on record in ancient books, among which god He Bo, goddesses Xiangfei and goddess of the Luo river have developed a wide reputation in China.

He Bo ("He" literally means "river" and "Bo" means "master" or "god"), a household name in China, is believed to be the god of the Yellow River in ancient Chinese mythology. It was said that He Bo used to be a human being named Fengyi (sometimes Pingyi or Bingyi; the names differ with versions). He was drowned while ferrying the Yellow River. The Supreme Divinity had compassion for him, so he appointed Fengyi to be the god of the river. When Yu started his mission of flood control with an investigation of the situation at the Yellow River, a god with a white human face and a fish trunk emerged from the water. He informed Yu of his identity as He Bo, and handed him a map of the locations of rivers. Then he dove into the river again. With this map, Yu grasped the broad situation of world flooding so that the land had been saved from the catastrophe through the application of a proper strategy. [1]

Questions for Discussion:

1. How did He Bo become the god of the Yellow River?

2. What did He Bo look like?

---

[1] Yang Lihui, An Deming and Jessica Anderson Turner, *Handbook of Chinese Mythology*, p. 131.

3. How did he help Yu?

Goddess of the Luo River

Goddess of the Luo River is another famous water deity in Chinese mythology. Originally called "Fu Fei," she is said to be the daughter of Fu Xi. Qu Yuan's "Tianwen" keeps a record of her: When playing in the Luo River, Fu Fei's beauty drew the attention of He Bo, the god of the Yellow River. Therefore, He Bo tried to make Fu Fei get drown so as to take the opportunity to seize her. At this time, the monarch from the Youqiong clan named Hou Yi in Xia Dynasty (not Houyi the archer who married Chang'e) developed an irresistible attraction for Fu Fei. Getting to know this, He Bo started a flood in the Luo River, bringing disaster in this area. So outraged was Hou Yi that he injured He Bo and finally married Fu Fei. He Bo complained about it to the Emperor of Heaven, but was ridiculed instead. Finally, the Emperor of Heaven offered help to Hou Yi and Fu Fei, making Hou Yi **the God of Zongbu**[①] and Fu Fei the Goddess of the Luo River.

The mythology of an earlier time cultivated the image of Fu Fei as a beautiful, loving sex incarnated spouse God. She appeared in ancient Chinese literature works frequently, such as Zhang Heng's *Sixuan Fu*, and Cao Zhi's *Ode to the Goddess of the Luo River*, the most well-known one in which her beauty is vividly described.[②]

Questions for Discussion:

1. What did He Bo intend to do with Fu Fei?
2. Who saved Fu Fei?

---

① 宗布神，最早记载于《淮南子·氾论训》，"羿除天下之害，死而为宗布"，编者注。
② http://chinaknowledge.de/History/Myth/personsluoshen.html

3. How did the Emperor of Heaven help Hou Yi and Fu Fei?

Ehuang and Nüying

Stories about Shun and his two wives, Ehuang and Nüying abound in the early texts of Chinese literature. Ehuang and Nüying were begot by King Yao, and were promised to Shun as a result of Yao's appreciation for Shun's virtues and abilities. By marrying his daughters to him, Yao wanted to further test Shun's capacity for family affairs, which was regarded as a basic and vital ability for a person to govern a country. Shun proved his exceeding competence in managing family affairs. With two virtuous wives, the family got along very well.

When assisting Shun in administering the country, Ehuang and Nüying also showed their intelligence and divine abilities to deal with all types of intractable problems. One of the most renowned examples is that they helped Shun survive several murders plotted by his father and stepbrother before his succession to Yao. Shun's father **Gu Sou**①, a blind man, remarried a pretty woman after the death of Shun's mother. He soon had a second son, Xiang, who grew to be a very arrogant man. The father only loved his second wife and child. The father and stepmother were jealousy of Shun's family possessions, and the half-brother Xiang **coveted**② his two wives. Therefore, they often **conspired**③ to kill Shun. One day the father asked Shun to repair the roof of a barn. Before going out, Shun told this to his two wives. The wives said, "They are going to kill you. Please take off your clothes and put on the coat with the bird pattern before you go." When Shun climbed up to the roof of the barn, his father took away the ladder and set the barn on fire. But Shun flew out of the fire with his magic coat. Days later, the father asked Shun to dredge a well. This time the wives told

---

① 瞽瞍，古帝虞舜之父，编者注。
② covet ['kʌvət] vt. 觊觎
③ conspire [kən'spaɪə] vi. 密谋

Shun to wear a coat with a dragon pattern. As soon as Shun went down into the well, Xiang and his father blocked the mouth of it. However, Shun swam out of the well under the protection of his magic dragon-patterned coat. Another attempt was to kill Shun after he was drunk. Again, the trap was seen through by Shun's wives. They let Shun go after giving him a bath in water with dissolved magic medicine. As expected, the magical medicine kept Shun sober throughout the whole day of drinking.

The topic of Shun surviving his parents' and stepbrother's murders is familiar in stories spread by word of mouth in many places, including Sichuan, Henan, Anhui, and Shanxi provinces. Diverse versions of this story exist. In each the trick of Shun's father and stepbrother tends to be different from that described in others. Most of them do not mention Ehuang and Nüying's help for Shun in pulling through all the traps set by his father and stepbrother. For example, a story based on Chengdu, Sichuan Province describes several traps Shun's parents and Xiang made in order to kill Shun. At first, they planned to kill Shun when he was dredging the well. What makes the difference is that Shun was rescued out of the well by the God of the Earth. Then they wanted to burn him as he was asked to repair the barn roof as told by the abovementioned edition. But Shun was saved by the God of Fire. At last, they invited Shun to dinner and let him sit on a specifically prepared chair, which was put on a piece of bamboo mat that covered the mouth of a well. They assumed that Shun would drop down into the well and die as soon as he sat on that chair. However, when Shun sat on the chair, it was very steady. Xiang felt so curious that he lifted a corner of the mat and looked into the well stealthily. Under the mat he found that a dragon was supporting the mat with its head. The scene scared Xiang, and afterwards he and the parents never dared to do harm to Shun again.

Before Yao's appreciation, Shun was a farmer cultivating in the Li Mountains. He was so virtuous and filial, even to his parents and stepbrother who treated him badly, that many people recommended him to King Yao. Through further examination of Shun both in virtue and in ability to rule the country, King Yao recognized that Shun was worthy of receiving the throne, thus he passed it to Shun. When Shun went back home as a king, he treated his father as respectfully and cautiously as before. As for his stepbrother Xiang, he conferred on him the title of duke.

It was said that after Shun took power, his wives contributed numerous ideas for keeping the country in perfect order. This was one of the main reasons why Shun became a great king.

There is a **poignant**[①] story that describes King Shun and his wives' undying love, which can be commonly found in both early records and oral transmission. King Shun died when he made an inspection trip to the south. Upon the arrival of the news of Shun's death, Ehuang and Nüying were plunged into deep sorrow. They cried in an uncontrolled, hopeless way day in and day out, hair thinning, and tears spattered and **speckled**[②] the bamboo trees. From then on, a sort of spotted bamboo tree appeared, called **Xiangfei's Bamboo**[③]. Xiangfei literally means "Xiang Madams." According to another account, when Shun's two wives hastened to where Shun died, they both joined their husband in the journey to heaven in overwhelming sadness and weariness beside the Xiang River. Observing this, the God of Heaven was touched, and then decreed that Shun should be the god of Xiang and his two wives the madams of the river.[④]

Questions for Discussion:

1. Why did King Yao marry his two daughters to Shun?

---

① poignant [ˈpɔɪnjənt] adj. 悲惨的
② speckle [ˈspekl] vt. 弄上斑点
③ "斑竹",也称湘妃竹。晋张华《博物志·史补》云:"舜崩,二妃啼,以涕挥竹,竹尽斑。"今江南有"斑竹""湘妃竹"之说,盖出于此也,编者注。
④ Yang Lihui, An Deming and Jessica Anderson Turner, *Handbook of Chinese Mythology*, pp. 202 – 204.

2. How did Ehuang and Nüying help Shun to escape from the dangers?

3. What did Ehuang and Nüying do upon the news of Shun's death?

4. What did the God of Heaven do after the death of Shun and his two wives?

Part 2　Water Deities in Greek Mythology

Poseidon

In the days when the Titans ruled the universe, Oceanus, with his wife Tethys, controlled all the lakes, rivers, and seas; but after the Titans were overthrown, Poseidon took possession of this great kingdom, and old Oceanus reluctantly gave up his dominion over the waters of the earth. Though anxious to assert his supreme authority, Poseidon allowed some of the descendants of the Titans to keep their small kingdoms, on condition that they own **allegiance**① to him as their sovereign ruler. Among these was Nereus, son of Oceanus, who was celebrated for his vast knowledge, his gift of prophecy, and his love of truth and justice. With his wife **Doris**② (also an heir of Oceanus), he fathered fifty daughters called **Nereids**③, and they were so beautiful that Poseidon chose one of them, named Amphitrite, as his wife. There were two others of the Nereids who became famous: **Galatea**④, beloved by the Cyclops Polyphemus, and **Thetis**⑤, the mother of Achilles; but none of them equaled Amphitrite in beauty.

---

① allegiance [əˈliːdʒəns] n. 忠诚
② Doris [ˈdɒrɪs] n. 多丽斯（希腊神话中的海洋女神）
③ Nereids [ˈnɪərɪɪdz] n. 涅瑞伊得斯（涅柔斯和多丽斯的五十个可爱女儿，是古希腊神话中的海洋女神）
④ Galatea [ˌgæləˈtɪə] n. 海中女神伽拉忒亚
⑤ Thetis [ˈθitɪs] n. 忒提斯（希腊神话中的海洋女神，佩琉斯的妻子）

When Poseidon first went wooing the Nereid, she was frightened by his formidable appearance, for he drove in an elegant chariot drawn by huge sea-horses with brazen hoofs and golden manes; and the god himself carried his mighty trident, or **three-pronged**① spear, by means of which he shattered rocks, commanded the storms, and shook the shores of earth. None knew better than Amphitrite the extent of Poseidon's power, for she had often watched him, when a storm was at its height, raise his all-compelling trident, and immediately the angry waves would cease raging, and there would be a great calm. Sometimes she saw a ship, doomed by the sea-god to disaster, now gliding confidently in quiet waters, when all at once a fierce storm would break over its head; and the hapless sailors, as they breasted the angry waves, would pray vainly to Poseidon for the help that would never come.

When Amphitrite saw this imposing-looking god driving toward her, she was frightened by so much splendor, though she could not help admiring Poseidon with his curling sea-green beard, and his long flowing hair crowned with shells and seaweed. Since the enamored god could never come near enough to plead his suit, he sent one of his dolphins to do the wooing, which was so successful that the fair Nereid was persuaded to become Poseidon's wife, sharing his golden throne in the heart of the sea. To reward the dolphin for its skill in having won for him his much-desired bride, Poseidon changed it into an immortal constellation in the sky, where it formed the well-known Delphinus.

Though Poseidon held indisputable dominion over all the waters of the earth and all that moves through the paths of the sea, he once aspired to greater power, and even plotted to dethrone Zeus. But the great ruler of Olympus discovered his wicked plans, and administered the punishment of forgoing his dominion over the sea for some years, during which time he was obliged to

---

① three-pronged [θriːprɔŋd] adj. 三叉的

submit to the humiliation of serving **Laomedon**①, king of Troy. It was while he was in service here that he, in conjunction with Apollo, built the wall of Troy, whose stones fell place under the spell of the sun-god's music. Laomedon had promised Poseidon a large reward if the wall was built within a certain time; but when it was finished, he refused to pay the sum agreed upon. Though angered at this treachery, Poseidon had to endure the king's injustice until his years of service were over; but upon his restoration to the former power, he created a hideous sea-monster, which spread terror and death over all the land. Not knowing how to meet this calamity, the Trojans consulted an oracle, and were advised to sacrifice to the monster a beautiful maiden each year to prevent the wrath of Poseidon from overwhelming the whole country in disaster.

Reluctantly the sorrowing people prepared to obey the oracle; and a victim was chosen by lot, and led by the priest to a large rock on the seashore, where she was securely chained. Then the hideous sea-beast glided out of its cave in the slimy rocks to devour her. This obnoxious ceremony was repeated year by year, and at last the lot fell upon **Hesione**②, the king's only daughter. Laomedon tried in vain to save her, for the lot was cast, and nothing could avert the appointed sacrifice. In despair, the wretched father saw the fatal hour approaching; and when the day drew near when Hesione was to be led down to the sea, he forgot his avarice and proclaimed throughout the land that a great reward would be given to anyone who could slay the monster. Heracles appeared just in time to save the doomed maiden, and killed the monster with his oaken club as it was dragging Hesione to its cave. The king was overjoyed at his daughter's rescue and told Heracles that he might claim the reward; but even when he saw the hero come with the beast's head as a proof that he had slain it,

---

① Laomedon [lei'ɔmidən] n. 拉俄墨冬（希腊神话中特洛伊的创建人）
② Hesione [hɪ'saɪəni] n. 赫西俄涅（特洛伊公主，特洛伊国王拉俄墨冬之女，普里阿摩斯的妹妹，萨拉米斯国王忒拉蒙的第二位妻子）

he refused to part with his much-loved gold. So Heracles returned home, but he did not forget Laomedon's **perfidy**①.

Poseidon had other famous deeds as well, among which his battling with Athena for the city of Athens was one of the most notable. In the reign of **Cecrops**②, the first king of Athens, the two deities had contended for the possession of the city. The gods decreed that it should be awarded to the one who produced the gift most useful to mortals. Poseidon gave a horse; Athena produced the olive. The gods returned a verdict of awarding the city to the goddess, and after her Greek appellation, Athena, it was named. Next, he made other vain attempts to contest Corinth with Helios, Argos with Hera, Aegina with Zeus, Naxos with Dionysus, and Delphi with Apollo.

Poseidon, like all the immortals, loved more than once; and among those who shared his affections was a maiden named **Theophane**③, who had so many suitors that it kept the jealous sea-god in constant fear lest she should prefer some earthly lover. So he took her to the island of Crumissa, and there changed her into a sheep, while he carried on his wooing in the form of a ram. The offspring of this marriage was the famous golden-fleeced ram, whose **pelt**④ was the object of that ill-fated expedition made by Jason and his fellow Argonauts.

Poseidon also once fell in love with the goddess **Demeter**⑤ (Ceres in Roman mythology), following her during the long time that she spent in search of her daughter Persephone. Demeter was angered by the sea-god's persistent courtship. Hoping to escape from him, she took the form of a mare; but

---

① perfidy [ˈpɜːfədi] n. 背信弃义
② Cecrops [ˈsiːkrɔps] n. 刻克洛普斯（雅典创建者，阿提卡第一任国王）
③ 提奥芬尼，比萨尔特斯的女儿，由于非凡的美貌，她被恋人围困，后被波塞冬带到克里尼萨岛。爱侣们一直跟着她，波塞冬把少女变成了绵羊，把自己变成了公羊，把岛上所有的居民都变成了动物，编者注。
④ pelt [pelt] n. (动物的) 皮毛
⑤ Demeter [diˈmiːtə] n. 得墨忒耳（司掌农业，结婚，丰饶之女神）

Poseidon was not so easily discouraged, for he changed himself into a horse and contentedly trotted after her. The child of this strange pair was Arion, a wonderful winged steed that had the power of speech, and was of such incredible swiftness that nothing could ever equal.

The most noted children of Poseidon and Amphitrite were **Triton**① and **Proteus**②. Triton acted as his father's trumpeter, and at Poseidon's command he would blow upon his conch-shell to calm the restless sea. He is normally represented as half man and half fish, who gave the name of Tritons to all his male descendants, who, with the Nereids and **Oceanides**③ (daughters of Oceanus), followed the chariot of Poseidon when he went abroad to view his kingdom. Proteus was put in charge of the great flock of sea-calves which fed on the soft seaweed and basked in the warm sands near his cave. He was renowned for his wisdom and for the truth of the answers that he gave to those fortunate enough to make him speak. Homer calls him "the Ancient of the Deep whose words are ever true"; but his knowledge was far from available, for he had the extraordinary power of assuming any shape he pleased, and only those mortals gained his advice who persistently clung to him through his many bewildering changes. ④

Questions for Discussion:

1. What was the weapon of Poseidon? What could he do with it?

2. Who was the wife of Poseidon? How did Poseidon succeed as one of the suitors?

3. What did Poseidon once plot to do? What punishment befell him?

---

① Triton ['traɪtn] n. 特里同（人身鱼尾的海神）
② Proteus ['prəʊtɪəs] n. 普罗透斯（希腊海神）
③ Oceanid [əʊ'si:ənɪd] n. 海洋的女神
④ Emilie Kip Baker, *Stories of Old Greece and Rome*, pp. 152–157.

4. What did Poseidon do when Laomedon refused to pay the reward?

5. What did the Trojans do to prevent the wrath of Poseidon?

6. Who killed the monster in the rescue for Hesione in the end?

7. Who was the offspring of the marriage between Poseidon and Theophane?

8. Who was the child of Poseidon and Demeter? What kind of power did he have?

9. Who were the children of Poseidon and Amphitrite?

Proteus

Aristaeus[①] was the son of Apollo and the water-nymph, Cyrene. Besides tending his flocks and herds, he took care of the olive trees and vineyards, and also was familiarly known as a keeper of bees. He was very proud of his hives, and the swarm of bees increased each year under the guidance of his skillful hands; but one day he found hundreds of the bees lying lifeless beside the hives, and on the **morrow**[②] the next day he suffered more casualties. At a loss how to account for this disaster, Aristaeus hurried to his mother to ask for help in saving the few bees that remained. Cyrene lived under a mountain stream; and, hearing that her son wished to speak to her, she commanded the river to divide and form a wall on either side, so that Aristaeus might walk in dry places. When the youth told her of the tragedy befalling his hives, she could not help him, but bade him go to old Proteus, for he alone could tell what the trouble was and find a remedy. She warned Aristaeus of the difficulty in holding the Ancient of the Deep when he tried to bewilder and terrify the stranger by rapidly assuming different forms; and she had it drummed into him that he must keep the

---

① Aristaeus [ˌæriˈstiːəs] n. 阿里斯泰俄斯（太阳神阿波罗与女神库瑞涅之子，兽群与牧场的保护神）

② morrow [ˈmɒrəʊ] n. 晨间

sea-god fast bound if he would receive the wished-for answers. Then she led him to the cave of Proteus and hid him there, exhorting him to be bold and fearless.

At noon the Wizard of the Deep came up out of the sea, followed by his herd of sea-calves; and while they lay stretched out on the warm sands, the god sought the retreat of his cave and soon was in a deep **slumber**①. When Aristaeus saw Proteus fast asleep, he stepped cautiously up to him and bound him with strong fetters. The god woke with a start, and tried to shake himself free of his chains; but on finding that he was a prisoner, he resorted to all the trickery that he could command. He became a fire, a flood, a wild beast, a horrible serpent, and many other forms calculated to terrify the beholder. But Aristaeus was not afraid, and informed him of the death of his bees, begging for some remedy. Then Proteus reminded him of how he had been the real cause of Eurydice's death, by making her flee from him in such haste that she did not see the snake at her feet. The wood-nymphs, who were Eurydice's companions, had therefore wished to punish Aristaeus, thus sending this destruction to his hives. So, it was of great necessity to appease the wrath of the nymphs; and for that purpose Proteus bade the youth build four altars, and sacrifice on them four bulls and four cows of perfect form and size. This burnt-offering was to **placate**② the nymphs, and when it was made, he must pay funeral honors to Orpheus and Eurydice to pacify their anger against him. At the end of nine days, he was to return to the grove where he had made the sacrifices.

Aristaeus thanked the Ancient of the Deep for his wise words, and after releasing him from the fetters, hurried away to do as Proteus had advised. The sacrifices were made, and suitable honors paid to the dead; and then, after waiting impatiently for nine days, Aristaeus went back to the grove. To his great

---

① slumber ['slʌmbə] n. 睡眠
② placate [plə'keɪt] vt. 抚慰

joy he found that a swarm of bees had taken possession of the **carcasses**①, and that he was now the owner of a much larger number than he had ever had before.②

Questions for Discussion:

1. What did Aristaeus do?

2. How did Proteus bewilder and terrify Aristaeus?

3. According to Proteus, what led to the death of Aristaeus's bees?

4. How could Aristaeus appease the wrath of the nymphs?

Glaucus③

One of the many sea-divinities who ruled under Poseidon was Glaucus, who was once a poor fisherman, earning his living by angling. One morning he had an extra-large haul; and when he threw the fish on the ground beside him, he noticed that they were eagerly **nibbling**④ the grass that grew very thickly in the spot where he had flung his net. As he stood watching them, the fish suddenly leaped up from the ground; and having **flopped**⑤ back into the water, swam away. Curious to see whether it was the grass that gave them this extraordinary power, Glaucus proceeded to gratify it by chewing a bit of it himself. Hardly was this done when he felt an irresistible impulse to **precipitate**⑥ himself into the sea. Fearlessly he dived beneath the waves, and soon found no difficulty in keeping under water, for the ocean seemed now to be his native element. He

---

① carcass ['kɑːkəs] n. 动物尸体
② Emilie Kip Baker, *Stories of Old Greece and Rome*, pp. 158 – 161.
③ Glaucus ['glɔkəs] n. 格劳克斯（希腊神话中的海神，善做预言）
④ nibble ['nɪbl] vt. 小口咬
⑤ flop [flɒp] vi. 扑通跳进
⑥ precipitate [prɪ'sɪpɪteɪt] vt. 使沉入

saw his beard turning a lovely sea-green; and his hair, growing suddenly long and green, was trailing out behind him. His arms turned azure-colored, and his legs became a fish's tail; but he felt no regrets over losing his human form, and stayed contentedly in the ocean. In time Poseidon made him one of the lesser gods, and took him into the friendly fraternity of the sea.

As Glaucus was swimming one day near the shore, he saw a beautiful maiden named Scylla. He was completely infatuated with her that he forgot he was half fish, and begged her to be his wife. Scylla stared at his green hair and blue skin, but not in shock, nor did she wonder at his fish's tail; for she had often played with the sea-nymphs, and was accustomed to their strange appearance. Encouraged by her behavior, Glaucus begged her to listen to the story of his life. He told her how he had suffered a sea change, and now occupied the lofty position of a god. The maiden was interested in this recital, but she had no desire to marry a merman, even if he were a god; so when Glaucus ventured to come nearer to her, she turned and fled. Discouraged but still determined, the young god sought **Circe**① and asked for a dose of potion to make Scylla fall in love with him, but unexpectedly Circe fell in love with him instead. She tried to win his heart with her most passionate and loving words, urging him to accept her love, and forget the maiden who scorned him; but Glaucus would not yield to the persuasions of the **enchantress**②, and kept pleading for the desired love potion.

Seeing that she could not gain his affections, Circe determined that at least no one else should enjoy his love; so she refused to make the potion, and sent Glaucus angrily away. When she saw him go sorrowfully from her palace, mixed a magic liquid, brewed from poisonous plants and deadly weeds, and this she

---

① Circe [ˈsəːsi] n. 喀耳刻（或瑟茜，希腊神话中的巫术女神）
② enchantress [ɪnˈtʃɑːntrəs] n. 女巫

poured over the waters where Scylla was wont to bathe. The maiden, suspecting no treachery, sought the ocean at her accustomed hour, and as soon as the poisoned waves touched her body, she was metamorphosed into a monster of horrible aspect, with six heads—each having three rows of sharp teeth. She saw all around her serpents and bark dogs, which had suddenly become rooted to the spot where she stood. She never regained her human form, but stayed in this place forever to terrify all mariners, and to devour the hapless sailors that came within her reach. Opposite her was the den of **Charybdis**[①], who thrice a day swallowed the waters of the sea, and thrice threw them up again. On the rock above the den was an immense fir-tree, and all ships that passed that way watched eagerly for this signal of danger, and prayed that they might safely steer between the double horrors of Scylla and Charybdis.[②]

Questions for Discussion:

1. What kind of changes took place on Glaucus after he chewed the grass?

2. Whom did Glaucus fall in love with?

3. What did Circe do to Scylla?

4. What did Scylla become in the end?

Part 3　Reflections

1. Vocabulary Expansion

1) Yuqiang: _____

2) He Bo: _____

---

① Charybdis [kəˈrɪbdɪs] n. 卡律布迪斯（希腊神话中该亚与波塞冬的女儿，荷马史诗中的女妖，为坐落在女海妖斯库拉隔壁的大漩涡怪，会吞噬所有经过的东西，包括船只）

② Emilie Kip Baker, *Stories of Old Greece and Rome*, pp. 161 – 163.

3) Goddess of the Luo River: _____
4) Xiangfei: _____
5) Amphitrite: _____
6) Triton: _____
7) Proteus: _____
8) Glaucus: _____

2. Appreciation

1) 东海之渚中有神，人面鸟身，珥两黄蛇，践两黄蛇，名曰禺䝞。黄帝生禺䝞，禺䝞生禺京。禺京处北海，禺䝞处东海，是为海神。

《山海经·大荒东经》

2) 其中有五山焉：一曰岱舆，二曰员峤，三曰方壶，四曰瀛洲，五曰蓬莱。其山高下周旋三万里，其顶平处九千里。山之中间相去七万里，以为邻居焉。其上台观皆金玉，其上禽兽皆纯缟。珠玕之树皆丛生，华实皆有滋味，食之皆不老不死。所居之人皆仙圣之种，一日一夕飞相往来者，不可数焉。而五山之根无所连箸，常随潮波上下往还，不得暂峙焉。仙圣毒之，诉之于帝。帝恐流于西极，失群仙圣之居，乃命禺强使巨鳌十五举首而戴之。迭为三番，六万岁一交焉。五山始峙而不动。

《列子·汤问》

3) 与女游兮九河，
　　冲风起兮横波。
　　乘水车兮荷盖，
　　驾两龙兮骖螭。
　　登昆仑兮四望，
　　心飞扬兮浩荡。
　　日将暮兮怅忘归，
　　惟极浦兮寤怀。
　　鱼鳞屋兮龙堂，
　　紫贝阙兮朱宫。

灵何为兮水中?
乘白鼋兮逐文鱼,
与女游兮河之渚,
流澌纷兮将来下。
子交手兮东行,
送美人兮南浦。
波滔滔兮来迎,
鱼邻邻兮媵予。

《九歌·河伯》

4) 翩若惊鸿,婉若游龙。
   荣曜秋菊,华茂春松。
   髣髴兮若轻云之蔽月,
   飘飖兮若流风之回雪。
   远而望之,皎若太阳升朝霞;
   迫而察之,灼若芙蕖出渌波。

《洛神赋》

5)   And then from Amphitrite and the loud Earth-Shaker came
Great Triton, mighty far and wide, who occupies the sea:
Beside his lordly father and beloved mother, he
Dwells in a golden house, a fearsome god. To Ares, who
Can pierce the skin inside a shield, Kytherea bore the two
Ferocious gods, Terror and Fear, who drive the ordered ranks
To chaos in the chilling battle—with Ares, he who sacks
Cities; and she bore Harmony, whom Kadmos took as spouse.

Hesiod's *Theogony*

6)   Just to the cavern's mouth, There Scylla dwells.
And fills the air with fearful yells; her voice
The cry of whelps just littered, but herself

A frightful prodigy—a sight which none
Would care to look on, though he were a god.
Twelve feet are hers, all shapeless, six long necks,
A hideous head on each, and triple rows
Of teeth, close-set and many, threatening death.
And half her form is in the cavern's womb.
And forth from the dark gulf her heads are thrust,
To look abroad upon the rocks for prey, —
Dolphin, or dogfish, or the mightier whale,
Such as the murmuring Amphitrite breeds
In multitudes. No mariner can boast
That he has passed by Scylla with a crew
Unharmed;...

Homer's *The Odyssey*

3. **Discussion**

Fill in the following table and draw a conclusion of the features of water deities in Chinese and Greek mythology.

	Name	Birth	Image	Duty
Water Deities in Greek Mythology				
Water Deities in Chinese Mythology				

Unit 5

Vegetal Myths

Introduction

In mythology, nature usually manifests itself as a god-haunted world under the sway of supernatural beings; it is subordinated to gods who are **immanent**① in sacred mountains, streams, rocks, and trees. In turn, nature reveals the **potency**② of gods for they are elemental, controlling light, heat, wind, and rain; and they are generative, producing irrigated fields, fertile soil, and abundant crops. Closely related to the mythic nature are the vegetal myths which include stories about different plants with real or imaginary characteristics, conveying concepts of primitive allegory. Various trees, shrubs, herbs, grains, flowers, and fruit appear in myths and legends as general symbols of rebirth, decay, immortality, etc. Some plants have acquired much more specific meaning or special power.

In both Chinese and Greek mythology, plants come to be connected with certain deities as well, such as **millet**③ with **Hou Ji**④, maple with Chiyou, peaches with the Queen Mother of the West, oak with Zeus, pine with Rhea,

---

① immanent [ˈɪmənənt] adj. 内在的
② potency [ˈpəʊtnsi] n. (人、行动或思想的) 影响力
③ millet [ˈmɪlɪt] n. 黍类
④ 后稷,姬姓,名弃,黄帝的玄孙,帝喾嫡长子,出生于稷山(今山西省稷山县)。其母亲名曰姜嫄,是帝喾元妃,编者注。

white **poplar**① with Hades. This sort of symbolism, however, is not as well-developed in Chinese mythology as it was in the Greco-Roman tradition, with most of the gods having their emblem or attribute drawn from nature. The sources for these vegetal myths constitute an early form of "unnatural natural history."

The records pertaining to vegetal myths in Chinese mythology is for the most part fragmentary. The source **par excellence**② is *The Classic of Mountains and Seas*; other early texts, such as *Zhuangzi*, *Xun Zi*, and *Huainanzi*, also retain a great many scattered narratives relating to vegetal myths. Stories about plants in Greek mythology are relatively systematic. The earliest documents, *The Iliad* and *The Odyssey*, mainly telling stories of gods and heroes, also reflect interpretations of nature. The most vivid descriptions of vegetal myths are given in Ovid's *The Metamorphoses*, in which many plants are associated with gods and heroes and are named after them, some of whom are metamorphosized gods or people, such as laurel, narcissus, and hyacinth. It is a common belief that the vegetal myths present the Greeks' observation of nature and their explanation of the changes in the natural world.

Part 1 Plants in Chinese Mythology

The Sky Ladder

The motif of the sky ladder exists in many ethnic groups in China, such as the Han, Buyi, Miao, Yao, Qiang, Naxi, Dulong, and Kazak. The sky ladder can assume the form of a high mountain or mythical tree, and it is

---

① poplar ['pɒplə] n. 杨树（white poplar：银白杨）
② par excellence [ˌpɑːrˈeksəlɑːns] adj. 出类拔萃的

sometimes depicted as a rainbow, sky rope, sky tower, or cobweb. But it is widely accepted that the sky ladder is situated at the center of the land of ancient China, and it usually acts as the **axis mundi**① where Heaven and earth meet.

In myths recorded in ancient Chinese writings, the most distinguished sky ladder is Kunlun Mountain, one of the most remarkable mythical mountains in Chinese mythology. Being the earthly residence of the Supreme Divinity and the paradise of deities and immortals, Kunlun Mountain is said to be one of the pillars of the sky that keeps heaven from collapsing, and a sky ladder that links the earth to heaven. A text from *Huainanzi* (chapter 4) clearly shows the nature of Kunlun as the sky ladder and even describes the process of climbing it to heaven. It maintains that the first tier of Kunlun Mountain was Liangfeng (Cool Wind Mountain). Anyone who climbed it would receive immortality. The second tier was called Xuanpu. Anyone who climbed this tier would acquire spiritual power and control the wind and rain. And if one climbed further, one would arrive at heaven, the residence of the Supreme Divinity, and become a spirit.

In some other versions, the sky ladder is a huge tree. The most noted tree sky ladder in ancient writings is Jianmu (literally meaning "Building Tree"). According to an account in *Huainanzi* (chapter 4), Jianmu grew in Mount Duguang. Along that tree, the gods went up and down between heaven and earth. At midday it had no shadow; shouting to it, there was no echo. Some suggest that perhaps it was the center of the world.② In another text in *The Classic of Mountains and Seas* (chapter 18), Jianmu was an enormous tree with a height of 800 feet. It had no branches in the middle, only twigs curled on the top and roots twisted and **gnarled**③. Its fruit was like the seeds of **hemp**④, and its

---

① 世界之轴，地球的运转轴心或地球中心，传说中众多神灵由此地来、往此地去，编者注。
② Liu An, *Huainanzi*, translated into modern Chinese by Zhai Jiangyue, translated into English by Zhai Jiangyue and Mou Aipeng, Guilin: Guangxi Normal University Press, 2010, p. 231.
③ gnarled [nɑːl] vi. 形成木节
④ hemp [hemp] n. 麻类植物

leaves were like those of the Mang tree.

Another well-known ancient myth relating to the sky ladder states that the Supreme Divinity had the connection between the sky and the earth cut off. Though it does not clearly mention "sky ladder," it actually tells a story about why and how the sky ladder was destroyed. A text from *Shangshu* (*Book of History*) states that Chiyou started a revolt and brought disaster to the common people. Influenced by him, people on the earth gradually degenerated. They began to cheat and steal. However, the Miao people did not obey him at first. Chiyou thus applied five brutal punishments against them. Then, little by little, the Miao people also became corrupt. They began to cheat each other within their own group, mistreat people from other groups, disobey their faith, and violate the oath between them and the Supreme Divinity. Many innocent people complained against them to the Supreme Divinity. The Supreme Divinity thus ordered two of his subordinates, the deities **Zhong**[①] and **Li**[②], to cut off the link between heaven and the earth. From then on, the Miao people could never ascend to heaven again, but at the same time, the deities could no longer descend to the earth.

In the oral traditions of many ethnic groups, such as the Han, Miao, Qiang, Buyi, and Tujia, the tree of the sky ladder is commonly said to be **Coriaria Sinica maxim**[③]. In the remote past, the tree was so high that it reached heaven. One year, twelve suns showed up together in the sky. The world became so hot that the earth almost burned. At this time, a hero on the earth climbed to the sky through the tree and smashed the surplus suns with a stick, leaving only one to serve humankind. Though the world order was restored to normal again, the God of Heaven worried that humans would ascend

---

① 重，祝融直系后代，为南正，司上天之火，编者注。
② 黎，祝融直系后代，为火正，司人间之火，编者注。
③ 马桑，落叶灌木。高 2–6 米，根呈圆柱形，略弯曲，有分枝，长短不等，编者注。

to the sky in the future and intervene with heavenly affairs again, so he cursed,

> The Coriaria Sinica maxim tree,
> Will no longer grow so high any more.
> It will bend down at its waist,
> Before it reaches the height of three feet.

Since that time, the tree has grown low and curved, and human beings can never again use it to ascend to heaven as a result.[①]

Questions for Discussion:

1. Where is the sky ladder situated?

2. How is the sky ladder related to Kunlun Mountain?

3. How is the sky ladder described in *Huainanzi* and *The Classic of Mountains and Seas*?

4. According to *Shangshu*, why was the sky ladder cut off by the Supreme Divinity?

5. According to the oral traditions of many ethnic groups, why was the sky ladder made low and curved?

The Giant Peach Tree

Among the ranks of divine trees is also the giant peach tree in Chinese mythology. Like Jianmu, it grows in a **convoluted**[②] tangle against the sky barrier it cannot pierce. In common with other world-tree myths, the peach tree

---

① Yang Lihui, An Deming and Jessica Anderson Turner, *Handbook of Chinese Mythology*, pp. 207–208.

② convoluted [ˈkɒnvəluːtɪd] adj. 旋绕的

creates a passage to the sky beyond the human world, and carries at its **crest**① celestial gates presided over by two **punitive**② gods, **Shen Shu**③ and **Yü Lü**④, the guardian gods of the gates to Heaven. The legend is linked to the Yellow Emperor, who issued a ritual which enacts the punitive role of the gods in order to **exorcize**⑤ evil from the home.

The reading is authored by **Wang Chong**⑥ of the first century A. D. , who states in his text that he is citing *The Classic of Mountains and Seas*. Although this citation does not in fact appear in extant editions of the *Classic*, it reveals how valuable Wang Chong's **eclectic**⑦ essays are for their preservation of otherwise lost material.

The excerpt from Wang Chong's *Lun Heng* is as follows:

In Cang Sea there is the Dushuo Mountain. On its summit is a huge peach tree. It twists and turns over three thousand leagues. Among its branches on the northeast side are what is called **Goblin**⑧ Gates through which myriad goblins pass. On top there are two gods. One is called Shen Shu; the other is called Yü Lü. These lords supervise and control the myriad goblins. Whenever a goblin does evil, they bind him with a reed rope and feed him to tigers. Then the

---

① crest [krest] n. (山)顶
② punitive ['pjuːnətɪv] adj. 惩罚性的
③ 神荼（"shēn shū"），门神，位于左边门扇上，身着斑斓战甲，面容威严，姿态神武，手执金色战戟，编者注。
④ 郁垒（"yù lù"），门神，位于右边门扇上，一袭黑色战袍，神情显得安闲自适，两手并无神兵或利器，只是探出一掌，轻抚着坐立在他身旁巨大的金眼白虎，编者注。
⑤ exorcize ['eksɔːsaɪz] vt. 陈怪
⑥ 王充（公元27年—约公元97年），字仲任，东汉思想家、文学批评家，出生于会稽上虞（今属浙江绍兴）。王充的代表作品《论衡》，共计八十五篇，二十余万字；该书以小见大，辨析万物之理，开释世俗之疑，是中国历史上一部重要的思想著作，编者注。
⑦ eclectic [ɪ'klektɪk] adj. 兼收并蓄的
⑧ goblin ['gɒblɪn] n. 小妖精

Yellow Emperor devised a ritual ceremony so that they could expel the evildoer in due season. They set up large peach wood **figurines**① and painted images of Shen Shu and Yü Lü and a tiger on gates and doors, and hung reed ropes from them so as to harness the evil. (*Lun Heng*, *Ding Gui*, citing a non-extant passage from *The Classic of Mountains and Seas*)②

Questions for Discussion:
1. According to the excerpt from *Lun Heng*, where is the giant peach tree?
2. Who guard the celestial gates?
3. How do the two gods exorcize the evildoers?

Fusang

Fusang (literally meaning "Leaning Mulberry") is a world-tree in the east where the ten suns stay, bathe, and rise. It is also known as Fumu (Leaning Tree).

Fusang is usually described in various mythologies as a huge divine tree that links earth with heaven and communicates the human and profane condition to the divine and sacred realm. Among its many parallels in Europe, Australia, North America, and other areas, Fusang is one of the most famous Chinese world-trees. According to texts from *The Classic of Mountains and Seas*, Fusang grew in a valley called Tanggu. It grew to a height of 300 li and its leaves looked like the mustard plant. The ten suns stayed on the tree and bathed in the valley. Nine of them stayed on the lower branches of Fusang while the sun that was going

---

① figurine [ˌfɪɡəˈriːn] n. 小雕像
② Anne Birrell, *Chinese Mythology: An Introduction*, pp. 233 – 234.

to rise stayed on its top branch. The ten suns rose from the Fusang tree one by one. As soon as one sun came back from crossing the sky, another sun went up. Each sun was carried by a crow. In an account from *Huainanzi*, the sun is said to rise from the Yang Valley (the same as the Tang Valley) and be bathed in the Xian Pool.① When the sun swept past Fusang it was called First Dawn. When it climbed up Fusang and was prepared to begin its journey, it was called Daybreak.

In some later versions, Fusang is described as a large tree in the east. Its top reached heaven while its trunk curved down and reached the Three Springs of the earth. However, according to **Shizhouji**② (*A Record of Ten Mythic Islets*), Fusang seemed to be not only a kind of tree but also a mythical place that was located in the middle of the Blue Sea. It was thousands of miles in **circumference**③ with a palace for an immortal built on it. Fusang trees grew here. Their leaves were like those of the mulberry, and they also produced the same fruit. The biggest one of them was more than 100,000 feet high and 2,000 wei wide (one wei is equal to the diameter of a circle created by a person's arms). Since the trees grew in pairs, every pair of them shared the same root and their trunks leaned toward each other; therefore, they received the name "Leaning Mulberry." Though the trees were extremely large, their fruits were rare, because the trees produced fruit only once every 9,000 years. The fruit was red, and it tasted sweet and savory. When the immortals ate the fruit, their bodies would turn a golden color, and they were able to fly and float in the air.

Other legends state that there were Heaven Chickens on the Fusang tree. The chickens nested in the top of the mythical tree and crowed at midnight each night. Every time they crowed, the crows inside the suns followed them. And

---

① 《淮南子》："日出扶桑，入于咸池"，编辑注。
② 《十洲记》，又称《海内十洲记》，古代志怪小说集，旧本题汉东方朔撰，编辑注。
③ circumference [sə'kʌmfərəns] n. 周长

then all the chickens in the world would follow and crow loudly.①

Questions for Discussion:

1. What is Fusang like according to *The Classic of Mountains and Seas*?

2. How is Fusang described in *Shizhouji*?

3. What do the myths of Fusang reveal about the worship of ancient Chinese?

Ming-jia②, Sha-pu③, and Ning-zhi④

Yao, the first of the demigods in the Golden Age, was viewed as an exemplar of the wise and benign ruler who embodied humanitarian principles, the sociopolitical principle of **meritocracy**⑤ in particular, advocated by the early Confucian school. Compared with stories about Shun and Yu, there are very few myths specifically about Yao. Nevertheless, he is mentioned in numerous accounts. The main body of myths about Yao is contained in *The Classic of History* edited in the Han Dynasty, a book consisting of selected passages dating from the late Zhou Dynasty (1046 B.C. -256 B.C.) to the Han Dynasty (202 B.C. -220 A.D.), which reconstructs Chinese history since the time of Yao. Compared with other late Zhou mythic narratives and political theory, a proportion of mythological materials have been largely rewritten and reinterpreted in this book.

---

① Yang Lihui, An Deming and Jessica Anderson Turner, *Handbook of Chinese Mythology*, pp. 117 - 118.

② 蓂荚，帝尧时期一种神草。一名历荚，象征祥瑞。每月从初一至十五，每日结一荚；从十六至月终，每日落一荚。因此可以从荚数多少推知时日，编者注。

③ 萐莆，《说文解字》曰："萐莆，瑞艸也。尧时生於庖厨，扇暑而凉"，编者注。

④ 佞草，又名佞枝。《博物志》曰："尧时有屈佚草，生于庭，佞人入朝，则屈而指之。一名指佞草"，编者注。

⑤ meritocracy [ˌmerɪˈtɒkrəsi] n. 精英领导体制

Other fragmented texts about Yao, unlike *The Classic of History*, are not politicized or historicized, but are recognizable as the authentic accounts of mythology. **Zhu Shu Ji Nian**①, a chronicle written by historians of Jin State in the Spring and Autumn Period and Wei State in the Warring States Period, relates that a miraculous plant, the Ming-jia, alias the Calendar Petal or the **Portent**② Plant, grew in Yao's garden, serving him as a natural calendar: it grew one petal a day from the beginning of each month until the fifteenth day, and then shed one petal a day until the end of the month until it was bare again. The second plant related to Yao is Sha-pu plant, described in Xu Shen's *Shuo Wen Jie Zi*, the first Chinese dictionary in China. According to its account, sha-pu had the roots that were as fine as silk thread and large prolific leaves. It whirled about like the wind so that it could drive away insects and cool food and drink in hot kitchens. **Bo Wu Zhi**③, a collection of strange stories written by Zhang Hua (232 A. D. – 300 A. D.) in the Western Jin Dynasty, tells of Ning-zhi, the plant of omen which grew in Yao's courtyard. Whenever the crafty **sycophants**④ came to court, the grass would bend and point at him. ⑤

Questions for Discussion:

1. Why was Ming-jia regarded as a natural calendar?

2. What supernatural power did Sha-pu have?

3. How did Ning-zhi get its name?

---

① 《竹书纪年》，共十三篇，是春秋时期晋国史官和战国时期魏国史官所作的一部编年体史书，叙述夏、商、西周和春秋战国的历史，按年编次。《今本竹书纪年》有"五帝纪"，记录黄帝、颛顼、帝喾、帝尧、帝舜之事，编者注。

② portent [ˈpɔːtent] n. 前兆

③ 《博物志》，西晋博物学家张华（公元232年—公元300年）著作的志怪小说集，记载异境奇物、琐闻杂事、神仙方术、地理知识、人物传说，内容包罗万象，编者注。

④ sycophant [ˈsɪkəfænt] n. 谄媚者

⑤ Anne Birrell, *Chinese Mythology: An Introduction*, pp. 238 – 240.

Part 2 Plants in Greek Mythology

Echo and Narcissus

Echo was a beautiful nymph, fond of the woods and hills, where she devoted herself to woodland sports. She was a favorite of **Artemis**①, and attended her in the chase. But one failing of Echo is that she was a great talker, and whether in chat or argument, would have the last word. The myth concerning Echo's failing is as follows.

One day Hera was seeking her husband, who, she had reason to fear, was amusing himself among the nymphs. Echo by her talk **contrived**② to **detain**③ the goddess till the nymphs made their escape. When Hera discovered it, she passed sentence upon Echo: "You shall **forfeit**④ the use of that tongue with which you have cheated me, except for that one purpose you are so fond of—reply. You shall still have the last word, but no power to speak first."

Later this nymph saw Narcissus, a youth with striking good looks, as he pursued the chase upon the mountains. Captivated by him, she followed his footsteps. O how she longed to address him in the softest accents, and win him to converse! But it was not in her power.

In increasingly accumulated impatience for him to speak first, Echo had her answer ready. One day the youth, being separated from his companions, shouted aloud, "Who's here?" Echo replied, "Here." Narcissus looked

---

① Artemis ['ɑːtəmɪs] n. 阿尔忒弥斯（希腊神话中手持弓与箭的狩猎女神，十二主神之一）
② contrive [kən'traɪv] vi. 谋划
③ detain [dɪ'teɪn] vt. 留住
④ forfeit ['fɔːfɪt] vt. 丧失

around, but seeing no one, called out, "Come." Echo answered, "Come." As no one came, Narcissus called again, "Why do you **shun**① me?" Echo replied with the same question. "Let us join one another," said the youth.

The maid answered with all her heart in the same words, and hastened to the spot, ready to throw her arms about his neck. But he started back, exclaiming, "Hands off! I would rather die than you should have me!" "Have me," said she; but it was all in vain. He left her, and she went to hide her blushes in the recesses of the woods.

From that time forth she lived in caves and among mountain cliffs. Her form faded with grief, till at last all her flesh shrank away. Her bones were changed into rocks and there was nothing left of her but her voice. With that she is still ready to reply to anyone who calls her, and keeps up her old habit of having the last word.

Narcissus's cruelty in this case was not the only instance. He shunned all the rest of the nymphs, as he had done poor Echo. Until one day a maiden who had in vain endeavored to attract him uttered a prayer that he might some time or other feel what it was to love and meet no return of affection, which was heard and granted by avenging goddess.

There was a clear fountain, with water like silver, to which the shepherds never drove their flocks, nor the mountain goats resorted, nor any of the beasts of the forests; neither was it **defaced**② with fallen leaves or branches; the grass grew fresh around it, and the rocks sheltered it from the sun. Hither came one day the youth, fatigued with hunting, heated and thirsty.

He stooped down to drink, catching a sight of his own image reflected in the water, which he thought was some beautiful water-spirit living in the fountain.

---

① shun [ʃʌn] vt. 避开
② deface [dɪˈfeɪs] vt. 毁坏

He stood gazing with admiration at those bright eyes, the locks curled like those of **Dionysus**① or Apollo, the rounded cheeks, the ivory neck, the parted lips, and the glow of health and exercise over all. He fell in love with himself. He brought his lips near to take a kiss; he plunged his arms in to embrace the beloved object. It fled at the touch, but returned again after a moment and renewed the fascination.

He could not tear himself away; he lost all thought of food or rest, while he hovered over the brink of the fountain gazing upon his own image. He talked with the supposed spirit: "Why, beautiful being, do you shun me? Surely my face is not one to repel you. The nymphs love me, and you yourself look not indifferent upon me. When I stretch forth my arms you do the same; and you smile upon me and answer my **beckonings**② with the like."

His tears fell into the water and disturbed the image. As he saw it depart, he exclaimed, "Stay, I entreat you! Let me at least gaze upon you, if I may not touch you." With this, and much more of the same kind, he cherished the flame that consumed him, so that by degrees he lost his color, his vigor, and the beauty which formerly had so charmed the nymph Echo.

She kept near him though, and when he exclaimed, "Alas! alas!" she answered him with the same words. He pined away and died; and when his shade passed the Stygian River, it leaned over the boat to catch a look of itself in the waters. The nymphs mourned for him, especially the water-nymphs; and when they smote their chest Echo smote hers also. They prepared a funeral pile and would have burned the body, but it was nowhere to be found; but in its place a flower, purple within, and surrounded with white leaves, which bears

---

① Dionysus [ˌdaɪəˈnaɪsəs] n. 狄俄倪索斯（希腊神话中的酒神，十二主神之一）
② beckoning [ˈbekənɪŋ] n. 召唤

the name and preserves the memory of Narcissus. ①

Questions for Discussion:

1. How did Echo offend Hera?
2. What kind of punishment did Echo suffer?
3. What led to Narcissus's falling into love with himself?
4. How did Narcissus die? What did he transform into after his death?

Daphne and Laurel

Daphne was Apollo's first love. It was not brought about by accident, but by the **malice**② of Cupid. Apollo saw the boy playing with his bow and arrows, and being himself **elated**③ with his recent victory over **Python**④, he said to him, "What have you to do with warlike weapons, **saucy**⑤ boy? Leave them for hands worthy of them. Behold the conquest I have won by means of them over the vast serpent who stretched his poisonous body over acres of the plain! Be content with your torch, child, and kindle up your flames, as you call them, where you will, but presume not to **meddle**⑥ with my weapons."

Aphrodite's boy heard these words, rejoining "Your arrows may strike all things else, Apollo, but mine shall strike you." So saying, he took his stand on a rock of Parnassus and drew from his **quiver**⑦ two arrows of different workmanship, one to excite love, the other to repel it. The former was of gold

---

① 王磊:《希腊罗马神话赏析》,上海外语教育出版社 2008 年版,第 91—93 页。
② malice ['mælɪs] n. 恶意
③ elated [ɪ'leɪtɪd] adj. 兴高采烈的
④ Python ['paɪθən] n. 皮同(阿波罗神所杀死的巨蟒)
⑤ saucy ['sɔːsi] adj. 调皮的
⑥ meddle ['medl] vi. (meddle with) 乱弄
⑦ quiver ['kwɪvə] n. 箭袋

and sharp pointed, the latter blunt and tipped with lead. With the leaden **shaft**① he struck the nymph Daphne, the daughter of the river-god Peneus, and with the golden one Apollo, the god of the sun through the heart. Forthwith the god was seized with love for the maiden, whose delight, however, was in woodland sports and in the spoils of the chase, **abhorring**② the thought of loving. Many lovers sought her, but she drove them all away, ranging the woods, and taking no thought of Cupid nor of Hymen. Her father often said to her, "Daughter, you owe me a son-in-law; you owe me grandchildren." She, hating the thought of marriage as a crime, with her beautiful face tinged all over with blushes, threw her arms around her father's neck and said, "Dearest father, grant me this favor, that I may always remain unmarried, like Diana." He consented, but at the same time with a sense of misgiving, "Your own face will forbid it."

Apollo loved her and longed to obtain her; the god who gives oracles to all the world was not wise enough to look into his own fortunes. He saw her hair flung loose over her shoulders and said, "If so charming in disorder, what would it be if arranged?" He saw her eyes bright as stars; he saw her lips, and was not satisfied with only seeing them. He admired her hands and arms, naked to the shoulder, and whatever was hidden from the view he imagined more beautiful still. He followed her; she fled, swifter than the wind, and delayed not a moment at his entreaties. "Stay," said he, "daughter of Peneus; I am not a foe. Do not fly me as a lamb flies the wolf, or a dove the hawk. It is for love I pursue you. I am no clown, no rude peasant. Zeus is my father, and I am the god of song and the lyre. My arrows fly true to the mark; but alas! An arrow more fatal than mine has pierced my heart! I am the god of medicine, and know

---

① shaft [ʃɑːft] n. 杆
② abhor [əb'hɔː] vt. 痛恨

the virtues of all healing plants. Alas! I suffer a malady that no balm can cure!"

The nymph continued her flight and left his plea half uttered. And even as she fled, she charmed him. The wind blew her garments, with her unbound hair streaming loose behind her. The god grew impatient to find his wooing thrown away; and, sped by Cupid, gained upon her in the race. It was like a **hound**① pursuing a hare, with open jaws ready to seize, while the feebler animal darted forward, slipping from the very grasp. So flew the god and the virgin he on the wings of love and she on those of fear. The pursuer was the more rapid, however, and caught hold of her in the end, with his panting breath blowing upon her hair. Her strength began to fail, and, ready to sink, she called upon her father, the river-god, "Help me, Peneus! Open the earth to enclose me, or change my form, which has brought me into this danger!" Scarcely had she spoken, when a **stuffiness**② seized all her limbs; her bosom began to be enclosed in a tender bark; her hair became leaves; her arms became branches; her foot stuck fast in the ground, as a root; her face became a treetop, retaining nothing of its former self but its beauty. Apollo stood amazed. He touched the stem, and felt the flesh tremble under the new bark. He embraced the branches and **lavished**③ kisses on the wood. The branches shrank from his lips. "Since you cannot be my wife," said he, "You shall assuredly be my tree. I will wear you for my crown. I will decorate with you my harp and my quiver; and when the great Roman conquerors lead up the triumphal pomp to the Capitol, you shall be woven into wreaths for their brows. And, as eternal youth is mine, you also shall be always green, and your leaf know no decay." The nymph, now changed into a laurel tree, bowed its head in

---

① hound [haʊnd] n. 猎犬
② stuffiness ['stʌfinəs] n. 闷热
③ lavish ['lævɪʃ] vt. 慷慨给予

grateful acknowledgment.①

Questions for Discussion:

1. What did Cupid do to Apollo and Daphne?

2. After being shot by Cupid, what took place on Apollo and Daphne?

3. What did Daphne change into at last?

4. What did Apollo do with the tree?

Apollo and Hyacinthus②

Apollo was passionately fond of a youth named Hyacinthus. He accompanied him in his sports, carried the nets when he went fishing, led the dogs when he went to hunt, followed him in his **excursions**③ in the mountains, and neglected for him his lyre and his arrows. One day they played a game of **quoits**④ together, and Apollo, heaving aloft the discus, with strength mingled with skill, sent it high and far. Hyacinthus watched it as it flew, and excited with the sport ran forward to seize it, eager to make his throw, when the quoit bounded from the earth and struck him in the forehead. He fainted and fell. The god, as pale as himself, raised him and tried all his art to **stanch**⑤ the wound and retain the flitting life, but all in vain; the hurt was past the power of medicine. As when one has broken the stem of a lily in the garden it hangs its head and turns its flowers to the earth, so the head of the dying boy, as if too

---

① Thomas Bulfinch, *The Illustrated Age of Fable: Myths of Greece and Rome*, London: Frances Lincoln, 1998, pp. 22-25.
② Hyacinthus [ˌhaɪəˈsɪnθəs] n. (希腊神话人物) 雅辛托斯
③ excursion [ɪkˈskɜːʃn] n. 远足
④ quoit [kɔɪt] n. 铁饼
⑤ stanch [stɑːntʃ] vt. 止血

heavy for his neck, fell over on his shoulder. "Thou diest, Hyacinth," so spoke **Phoebus**①, "robbed of thy youth by me. Thine is the suffering, mine the crime. Would that I could die for thee! But since that may not be, thou shalt live with me in memory and in song. My lyre shall celebrate thee, my song shall tell thy fate, and thou shalt become a flower inscribed with my regrets." While Apollo spoke, behold the blood which had flowed on the ground and stained the **herbage**② ceased to be blood; but a flower of hue more beautiful than the Tyrian sprang up, resembling the lily, if it were not that this is purple and that silvery white. And this was not enough for Phoebus; but to confer still greater honor, he marked the petals with his sorrow, and inscribed "Ah! ah!" upon them, as we see to this day. The flower bears the name of Hyacinthus, and with every returning spring revives the memory of his fate.

It was said that Zephyrus (the West wind), who was also fond of Hyacinthus and jealous of his preference of Apollo, blew the quoit out of its course to make it strike Hyacinthus.③

Questions for Discussion:

1. What did Apollo and Hyacinthus usually do?
2. How was Hyacinthus injured?
3. What kind of flower did Hyacinthus change into?

Apollo and Sunflower

Apollo, the son of Zeus who fathered all gods and human, is called "sun-

---

① Phoebus ['fi:bəs] n. 福玻斯（希腊神化中的太阳神）
② herbage ['hɜ:bɪdʒ] n. 草
③ Thomas Bulfinch, *The Illustrated Age of Fable: Myths of Greece and Rome*, p.57.

god." During the day Apollo drove his carriage of gold and ivory across the sky to spread light, life and love to the great world below. At dust he finished his journey in the far western sea and returned to his eastern home in his golden boat.

There was once a nymph named **Clytie**①, who gazed ever at Apollo as he drove his sun-chariot through the heavens. Apollo saw not Clytie. He had no thought for her, but shed his brightest beam upon her sister the white Nymph **Leucothoe**②. When Clytie perceived this she was filled with envy and grief.

Night and day she sat on the bare ground weeping. For nine days and nine nights she never raised herself from the earth, nor did she take food or drink — but ever she turned her weeping eyes toward the sun god as he moved through the sky.

And her limbs became rooted to the ground. Green leaves enfolded her body. Her beautiful face was concealed by tiny flowers, violet-colored and sweet with perfume. Thus, was she changed into a flower, roots holding her fast to the ground, but ever she turned her blossom-covered face toward the sun. In vain were her sorrow and tears, for Apollo regarded her not.

And so through the ages has the Nymph turned her dew-washed face toward the heavens, and men no longer call her Clytie, but by name of the sunflower, **heliotrope**③.④

Questions for Discussion:

1. Whom did Apollo shed his brightest beam on?

---

① Clytie [ˈkliti] n. 克吕提厄（古希腊神话中的海仙女、大洋神女、向日葵女神；河流海洋之神俄亥阿洛斯和沧海女神泰西斯之女）

② Leucothoe [luːˈkəʊθiː] n. 琉科忒亚（巴比伦国王之女，因与阿波罗相爱遭到克吕提厄的嫉妒，告发于其父，被其父活埋，后被阿波罗挖出，但无法死而复生，只能将其变成乳香树）

③ heliotrope [ˈhiːliətrəʊp] n. 向阳植物

④ https://www.psdl.org/cms/lib/WA01001055/Centricity/Domain/36/ES_Clytie.pdf

2. How did Clytie feel?

3. What kind of change took place on Clytie?

Adonis and Wind Flower

Venus, playing one day with her boy Cupid, wounded her bosom with one of his arrows. She pushed him away, but the wound was deeper than she thought. Before it healed she beheld Adonis, and was **captivated**① with him. She no longer took any interest in her favorite resorts—Paphos, and Cnidos, and Amathos, rich in metals. She absented herself even from heaven, for Adonis was dearer to her than heaven. Him she followed and bore him company. She who used to love to recline in the shade, with no care but to cultivate her charms, then **rambled**② through the woods and over the hills, and was dressed like the huntress Artemis; she called her dogs, and chased hares and stags, or other game that it was safe to hunt, but kept clear of the wolves and bears, **reeking**③ with the slaughter of the herd. She charged Adonis, too, to beware of such dangerous animals. "Be brave towards the timid," said she, "courage against the courageous is not safe. Beware how you expose yourself to danger and put my happiness to risk. Attack not the beasts that Nature has armed with weapons. I do not value your glory so high as to consent to purchase it by such exposure. Your youth, and the beauty that charms Aphrodite, will not touch the hearts of lions and **bristly**④ boars. Think of their terrible claws and **prodigious**⑤ strength! I hate the whole race of them. Do you ask me why?" Then she told

---

① captivate ['kæptɪveɪt] vt. 迷住
② ramble ['ræmbl] vi. 漫步
③ reek [riːk] vi. 散发出（强烈难闻的气味）
④ bristly ['brɪsli] adj. 毛发粗硬的
⑤ prodigious [prə'dɪdʒəs] adj. 巨大的

him the story of Atalanta and Hippomenes, who were changed into lions for their ingratitude to her.

Having given him this warning, she mounted her chariot drawn by swans and drove away through the air. But Adonis was too noble to **heed**① such counsels. The dogs had roused a wild boar from his **lair**②, and the youth threw his spear and wounded the animal with a **sidelong**③ stroke. The beast drew out the weapon with his jaws and rushed after Adonis, who turned and ran; but the boar overtook him, and buried his tusks in his side, and stretched him dying upon the plain.

Venus, in her swan-drawn chariot, had not yet reached Cyprus, when she heard coming up through mid-air the groans of her beloved, and turned her white-winged coursers back to earth. As she drew near and saw from on high his lifeless body bathed in blood, she **alighted**④, and bending over it beat her breast and tore her hair. Reproaching the Fates, she said, "Yet theirs shall be but a partial triumph; memorials of my grief shall endure, and the spectacle of your death, my Adonis, and of my lamentation shall be annually renewed. Your blood shall be changed into a flower; that consolation none can envy me." Thus speaking, she sprinkled nectar on the blood; and as they mingled, bubbles rose as in a pool, on which raindrops fell, and in an hour's time there sprang up a flower of bloody hue like that of the pomegranate. But it is short-lived. It is said the wind blows the blossoms open, and afterwards blows the petals away; so it is called **Anemone**⑤, or Wind Flower, from the cause which assists equally in its

---

① heed [hiːd] vt. 留意
② lair [leə] n. 巢穴
③ sidelong [ˈsaɪdlɒŋ] adj. 侧面的
④ alight [əˈlaɪt] vi. 飞落
⑤ anemone [əˈneməni] n. 银莲花

production and its decay.①

Questions for Discussion:

1. How did Aphrodite fall in love with Adonis?
2. What did Aphrodite warn Adonis not to do?
3. How did Adonis die?
4. What did Aphrodite do after Adonis's death?

Pan and Reed

Pan, god of woods and fields, of the flocks and herds, and the special patron of all shepherds and huntsmen, was alleged to be the son of **Hermes**②. Who his mother was remained unknown according to the common belief. But it's certain that she has had some **sylvan**③ blood in her veins, for the youthful Pan showed every evidence of having been born of woodland creatures, as he had the pointed ears of the **fauns**④, and the horns sprouting from his forehead and goat's legs of the **satyrs**⑤. The story goes that his mother—whichever nymph it was of the many reputed to have borne him—was so disgusted with his absurd appearance that she refused to own him for her child, fleeing in dismay; but Hermes was delighted with his son's **grotesque**⑥ figure, and took him to Olympus to amuse the gods.

Pan's favorite haunt was **Arcadia**⑦, where he wandered over the hills and

---

① 陶洁等:《希腊罗马神话》,中国对外翻译公司2007年版,第126—128页。
② Hermes [ˈhɜːmiːz] n. 赫耳墨斯（希腊神话中的商业、旅者、小偷和畜牧之神）
③ sylvan [ˈsɪlvən] adj. 森林的
④ faun [fɔːn] n. 半人半羊的农牧神
⑤ satyr [ˈsætə] n. 希腊神话中的半人半兽
⑥ grotesque [grəʊˈtesk] adj. 怪诞的
⑦ Arcadia [ɑːrˈkeɪdɪə] n. 阿卡狄亚（古希腊一山区，人情淳朴，生活愉快）

among the rocks, or roamed through the fertile valleys. Not only did he take delight in hunting, but also in various **pastimes**①—his especial pleasure being lead in the dances with the nymphs. Devoted to music, he was usually seen playing on the **syrinx**②, or shepherd's pipes, which he himself invented and named after a nymph whom he unsuccessfully wooed. The maiden Syrinx was a follower of Artemis; and one day, as she was returning from the chase, she met Pan, who became enamored with her beauty immediately. Pan begged her to be his wife, but the nymph had always scorned to listen to any lover, and Pan's repulsive appearance did not tend to soften her objections; so while he was praising her unparalleled charms to plead for her love, she turned and ran away. The woodland god was not to be put off so lightly, however; and he promptly gave chase to the fleeing maiden, who, finding her pursuer near approach, called wildly on the river nymphs for assistance. She had by this time reached the water's edge; and just as Pan's arms were about to **enfold**③ her, the kindly nymphs, in answer to her prayer, transformed her into a cluster of reeds. The god was much **chagrined**④ at the failure of his hopes; but since he could not have the living maiden, he determined to take whatever remained of the beautiful thing that had charmed him. So he gathered a bunch of the reeds, and after cutting them into unequal lengths, bound them together into a sort of shepherd's pipes. When he put the reeds to his lips, they gave forth the softest, most **plaintive**⑤ tones, which Pan called the syrinx, in honor of the nymph. ⑥

---

① pastime [ˈpɑːstaɪm] n. 消遣
② syrinx [ˈsɪrɪŋks] n. 潘神箫（形似笙的古乐器）
③ enfold [ɪnˈfəuld] vt. 拥抱
④ chagrined [ˈʃægrɪnd] adj. 苦恼的
⑤ plaintive [ˈpleɪntɪv] adj. 哀伤的
⑥ Emilie Kip Baker, *Stories of Old Greece and Rome*, pp. 183 – 185.

Questions for Discussion:

1. What did Pan look like?

2. What did Pan usually do?

3. How did Syrinx react to Pan's Courtship?

4. How did Syrinx change into reeds?

Part 3　Reflections

1. **Vocabulary Expansion**

   1）Fusang：_____

   2）The Sky Ladder：_____

   3）Ming-jia：_____

   4）Sha-pu：_____

   5）Ning-zhi：_____

   6）Narcissus：_____

   7）Daphne：_____

   8）Hyacinthus：_____

   9）Sunflower：_____

2. **Appreciation**

   1）下有汤谷。汤谷上有扶桑，十日所浴，在黑齿北。居水中，有大木，九日居下枝，一日居上枝。

   《山海经·海外东经》

   2）三桑无枝，在欧丝东，其木长百仞，无枝。

   《山海经·海外北经》

   3）多生林木，叶如桑。又有椹，树长者二千丈，大二千余围。树两两同根偶生，更相依倚，是以名为扶桑也。

《海内十洲记》

4）时有丹雀衔九穗禾，其坠地者，帝乃拾之，以植于田，食者老而不死。

《拾遗记》卷一《炎帝神农》

5）沧海之中，有度朔之山，上有大桃木，其屈蟠三千里，其枝间东北曰鬼门，万鬼所出入也。上有二神人，一曰神荼，一曰郁垒，主阅领万鬼。恶害之鬼，执以苇索，而以食虎。于是黄帝乃作礼以时驱之，立大桃人，门户画神荼、郁垒与虎，悬苇索以御凶魅。

《论衡·订鬼篇》

6）　　　　　As Daphne ran

Phoebus had more to say, and she, distracted,

In flight, in fear, wind flowing through her dress

And her wild hair—she grew more beautiful

The more he followed her and saw wind tear

Her dress and the short tunic that she wore,

The girl a naked wraith in wilderness.

And as they ran young Phoebus saved his breath

For greater speed to close the race, to circle

The spent girl in an open field, to harry

The chase as greyhound races hare,

His teeth, his black jaws glancing at her heels.

The god by grace of hope, the girl, despair,

Still kept their increasing pace until his lips

Breathed at her shoulder and almost spent,

The girl saw waves of a familiar river,

Her father's home, and in a trembling voice

Called, "Father, if your waters still hold charms

To save your daughter, cover with green earth

This body I wear too well," and as she spoke

A soaring drowsiness possessed her; growing

In earth she stood, white thighs embraced by climbing

Bark, her white arms branches, her fair head swaying

In a cloud of leaves; all that was Daphne bowed

In the stirring of the wind, the glittering green

Leaf twined within her hair and she was laurel.

Ovid's *The Metamorphoses*

3. Discussion

1) Draw a conclusion of the commonplaces and differences of vegetal myths in Chinese and Greek mythdogy.

2) What philosophical thoughts are revealed through the vegetal myths?

Unit 6

Animal Myths

Introduction

Since the dawn of human history, people have lived in close contact with animals—usually as hunters and farmers—and have developed assorted myths and legends about them. All kinds of creatures, from ferocious leopards to tiny spiders, play important roles in mythology without exception. A myth can infuse special meaning or extraordinary qualities into common animals such as frogs and bears. However, other creatures found in myths—multi-headed monsters, dragons, unicorns, etc.—never have existence in the real world. Animals may serve as **stand-ins**① for humans or human characteristics, as in the African and Native American trickster tales or the fables of the Greek storyteller Aesop. In some legends, animals perform heroic deeds or act as mediators between heaven and earth. They may also be the source of the wisdom and power of a **shaman**②. Meanwhile, they can be harmful to human beings by bringing various kinds of disasters. The dualistic quality possessed by animals symbolically represent the mystery and power of the natural world. Therefore, to some extent, bestiary myths help readers understand the ancient ecological environment and also provide an opportunity for them to get a glimpse of the ancients' understanding

---

① stand-in ['stænd ɪn] n. 替身
② shaman ['ʃeɪmən] n. 巫师

and imagination of the unknowns.

A variety of animals can be found in ancient Chinese mythology. When the gods manifest themselves, they appear as half-human, half-animal beings, or as hybrid creatures. For instance, Nüwa and Fuxi take on half-human, half-serpentine form. And the animals' characteristics, whether real or imagined, are attached to moral significance. The ram of the mythical judge Gao Yao is a case in point. Some animals are endowed with special powers, such as the Beast of White Marsh's ability to decipher the enigmatic workings of the universe. A few birds and beasts come to be emblematic of deities, the bluebirds and hybrid **panthers**① of the Queen Mother of the West, the bear with Yu, and the toad with Chang'e are typical examples.

Greek myths and legends are filled with a wide variety of monsters and creatures ranging from dragons, giants, demons and ghosts, to multi-formed beings such as the Sphinx, Minotaur, **Centaurs**②, **Manticores**③ and **Griffins**④. There are also many fabulous animals such as the Nemean Lion, golden-fleeced Ram and winged horse Pegasus, not to mention the creatures of legend such as the Phoenix, Unicorns (Monocerata). Even amongst the tribes of man, myths speak of strange peoples inhabiting the far reaches of the earth such as the one-eyed **Arimaspians**⑤, the Dog-Headed men, and the puny **Pygmies**⑥.

---

① panther ['pænθə] n. 豹子
② Centaur ['sentɔː] n. 半人半马的怪物
③ Manticore ['mæntɪkɔː] n. 人头狮身蝎尾怪
④ Griffin ['ɡrɪfɪn] n. 半狮半鹰的怪兽
⑤ Arimaspians [ˌærɪməs'piən] n. 阿里马斯皮人（传说中的独眼类人种族，居于伊塞多涅斯人和许佩耳玻瑞人之间，善骑马。他们附近有一条含金的河流，一说有一金窟，由半狮半鹰的怪物格里芬看守，因此阿里马斯皮人一直在同格里芬斗争）
⑥ Pygmy ['pɪɡmi] n. 俾格米人（希腊神话中一种身高不足五英尺的矮小人种）

Part 1　Animals in Chinese Mythology

Kaiming

Various kinds of animals are depicted in *The Classic of Mountains and Seas*, including the rare fish Luoyu, Ranyi, the rare birds Qitu, Guanguan, and the rare beasts, Huan, sky dog, Qiongqi, and the divine beast Kaiming (literally meaning "enlightened"), etc. Kaiming is the beast that faces east and guards Mount Kunlun, which leads to the heavens. It has the body of a tiger and nine heads with human-like faces. The following is an excerpt about it:

Mount Kunlun lies northwest of the capital of the mortal world under the rule of the God of Heaven. It covers an area of 800 square li and rises to a height of 80,000 feet. On its top there are rice shoots which are forty feet high and five spans wide. On each side of the mountain there are nine wells and their **railings**[①] are made of jade. Each side of the mountain has nine gates and at each of these gates there is a kaiming animal acting as the guard. This is the place where a hundred gods live. They stay on the cliffs of the eight mountains adjacent to the Chishui River. No one can climb up these steep cliffs except Renren and Yi.

The Chishui River flows out of the southeast corner of Mount Kunlun and runs to the northeast.

The river flows out of the northeast corner of Mount Kunlun, runs

---

① railing ['reɪlɪŋ] n. 围栏

to the north and turns to the southwest before it empties itself into the Bohai Sea. Later it flows overseas, turns to the west and then runs northwards to Mount Jishi which Yu has dredged.

The Xiangshui and Heishui rivers flow out of the northwest corner of Mount Kunlun. They run southeast and then northeast before turning southwards to enter the sea in the south of the kingdom of Yumin.

The Ruoshui and Qingshui rivers flow out of the southwest corner of Mount Kunlun. They run northeast and then southwest before passing through the east land of **bifang**① birds.

South of Mount Kunlun is a pool which is 2,400 feet deep. The kaiming animal has a body as big as that of a tiger. It has nine heads, each of which has a human face. It stands on Mount Kunlun, facing eastwards.

West of where kaiming lives there are phoenixes and wonder birds. They hang snakes on their heads and tread snakes underfoot. They also hang a red snake on their breasts.

North of where kaiming lives there are shirou, the pearl tree, the patterned jade tree, the red jade tree and the never-die tree. Both phoenix and wonder bird wear a shield-like thing on their heads. There are also red birds, rice shoots, cypress trees, sweet springs, wisdom trees and thorn trees. Some people say that the thorn trees are thrust trees or crossed-tooth trees.

East of where kaiming lives there are many wizards and witches such as Wupeng, Wudi, Wuyang, Wulu, Wufan, and Wuxiang.

---

① 毕方，形状像鹤，只有一只脚，青色的羽毛之上有红色的斑纹，长着白色的嘴巴，编者注。

Surrounding the corpse of Yayu, they all hold the never-die medicine to pray to gods to seek his survival. Yayu, a god with a human face and a snake's body, was killed by an official of Er'fu.

On the top of fuchang, a legendary tree, there are people with three heads. They are guarding langgan, another legendary tree, nearby.

South of where kaiming lives there are tree birds, alligators with six heads, serpents, snakes, long-tailed apes, and leopards. There are also trees called niaozhi which surround the surface of the pool. And there are humming birds, hawks and shirou. ①

Questions for Discussion:

1. What is the duty of kaming?
2. What does kaming look like?
3. What kind of animals live west of kaiming? What do they look like?
4. What can be found north of kaiming?
5. Who live east of kaiming?
6. What can be found south of kaiming?

The Beast of White Marsh②

This account falls into the didactic category of bestial myths. It is taken from **Xuan Yuan Ben Ji**③ (or *Basic Annals of Xuan Yuan*), a fanciful biography of the Yellow Emperor, compiled by **Wang Guan**④ in the Tang

---

① *The Classic of Mountains and Seas*, pp. 251 - 253.
② 白泽，中国古代神话中的瑞兽。能言语，通万物之情，知鬼神之事，"王者有德"时才出现，能辟除人间一切邪气，编者注。
③ 《轩辕本纪》是宋朝道家经典《云笈七签（笺）》中的一篇，记述了黄帝一生的重要事迹与其对人民的贡献，也是唯一将少典记载为伏羲之子，轩辕为伏羲之孙的古籍，编者注。
④ 王瓘，唐代医家，生平履贯欠详。所撰《广黄帝本行纪》是现存最全面的一部记载黄帝修道成仙的传记文献，此书收录于《道藏》。又《云笈七签》卷100《纪传部》收录的《轩辕本纪》即系转录此文，略有变动，编者注。

Dynasty, who was of the Taoist persuasion. It will be recalled that the Yellow Emperor was adopted as the supreme deity of the Taoist **pantheon**① in the Latter Han era. In this narrative he is known by the name Xuan Yuan, which originally belonged to a shadowy primeval god but later became attached to the more **illustrious**② god, the Yellow Emperor. The format of Wang's account is modeled on the official biography of emperors and kings to be found in traditional histories since the Han period. Like many earthly rulers, the Yellow Emperor conducts a royal tour of his realm according to this episode from the biography. And in the manner of sage-rulers, he seeks wisdom from others, in this case, from a god known as the Beast of White Marsh. This god in bestial form knows the **infinitesimal**③ number of metamorphosed beings as well as the mystery of the cosmos. The quest of the Yellow Emperor for divine knowledge is cast in the heroic mold, and his success is crowned with the reward of the chart of the cosmos, for knowledge is power. His portrayal as a god who prays to a lesser god in the traditional pantheon exemplifies the **desacralization**④ of deities in later **mythography**⑤.

> The Emperor went on a tour of inspection. In the east he came to the sea. He went up Mount Huan. On the seashore he found the Holy Beast of White Marsh which could speak and understand the natures of all living creatures. There were a total of 11,520 kinds of wandering souls that had undergone a metamorphosis. While White Marsh was talking about them, the Emperor ordered someone to write them down on a chart to show them to the whole world. Then the

---

① pantheon [ˈpænθiɔn] n. 众神
② illustrious [ɪˈlʌstriəs] adj. 著名的
③ infinitesimal [ˌɪnfɪnɪˈtesɪml] adj. 极小的
④ desacralization [diːˈseɪkrəlaɪzeɪʃn] n. 自然的非神圣化
⑤ mythography [mɪˈθɒɡrəfi] n. 神话艺术

Emperor ordered someone to compose a written prayer to pray to him. (*Yun Ji Qi Qian*, *Xuan Yuan Ben Ji*)①

Questions for Discussion:

1. What does the Yellow Emperor do with the Beast of White Marsh?
2. What kind of magic power does the Beast of White Marsh possess?

Fabled Horses of King Mu②

An inscription on an early Zhou bronze wine vessel in the shape of a **foal**③ reveals the king's interest in horse breeding; it says that King Mu handled a foal and gave its owner two **colts**④. His legendary association with horses is confirmed by the fourth-century B. C. text "Tianwen," which relates the brief mythic narrative: "King Mu was a breeder of horses" (*Chuci*, "Tianwen"). The following reading is taken from **Shi Yi Ji**⑤ or *Researches into Lost Records*, from the fourth to sixth century.

When King Mu had been on the throne for thirty-two years, he went on a royal tour of the empire…The king drove a fleet of eight horses swift as dragons. One horse was called Beyond Earth, whose hooves did not touch the ground. The second was called Windswept

---

① Anne Birrell, *Chinese Mythology: An Introduction*, pp. 235 – 236.
② 周穆王姬满（约公元前1026年—公元前922年），姬姓，名满，又称"穆天子"，周昭王之子，西周第五位统治者。在位55年，是西周在位时间最长的君主。周穆王的一生非常富有传奇色彩，在位期间，曾征犬戎（一作畎戎）、伐徐戎、甫刑（亦称《吕刑》）。此外，史料还有关于穆王西游见西王母的记载，其中尤以《穆天子传》最为详细，编者注。
③ foal [fəʊl] n. 马驹
④ colt [kəʊlt] n. 雄马驹
⑤ 《拾遗记》是东晋时期王嘉编写的古代中国神话志怪小说集，共10卷。前9卷记载上古时起至东晋各代的历史异闻，末1卷记昆仑等8座仙山，编者注。

Plumes, which went faster than any winged bird. The third was called Rush-by-Night, which covered ten thousand leagues in the night. The fourth was called Faster-than-Shadow, which could keep up with the journeying sun. The fifth was called Finer-than-Flashing-Light, whose coat was the **sheen**① of dazzling light. The sixth was called Faster-than-Light, whose single bound cast ten shadows. The seventh was called Rising Mist, which rushed along on the crest of the clouds. The eighth was called Wing Bearer, whose body had fleshy plumes. (*Shi Yi Ji*)②

Questions for Discussion:
1. What was King Mu of Zhou fond of doing?
2. How many horses did King Mu drive?
3. What were the names of the horses? And what extraordinary abilities did they have?

The Many-Splendored Bird③

The account of the Many-Splendored Bird, a mythical bird of evil **omen**④, is excerpted from the same classical source attributed to Wang Jia (fourth century A. D.) and edited by **Xiao Qi**⑤, of the sixth century. Like Wang Chong's

---

① sheen [ʃiːn] n. 光泽
② Anne Birrell, *Chinese Mythology: An Introduction*, pp. 236 – 237.
③ 重明鸟是中国古代神话传说中的神鸟。其形似鸡，鸣声如凤，双目各生双瞳，所以叫作重明鸟，亦称重睛鸟。它气力很大，能够搏逐猛兽、降妖除邪。中国民间过春节素有在门窗上帖画鸡的习俗，实则在敬奉重明鸟的化身。编者注。
④ omen [ˈəʊmən] n. 征兆
⑤ 萧绮（生卒年不详），南朝梁小说家，兰陵（今江苏省常州市）人。曾将前秦王嘉所著而当时已散佚的《拾遗记》重新整理成十卷，并在某些篇章后加有批评性文字。编者注。

account of Shen Shu and Yü Lü on the giant peach tree, this passage provides an explanation of the popular custom of exorcism through mimetic ritual. In this case it is the post-Han custom of exposing images of the ill-omened bird, the Many-Splendored Bird, outside homes in the New Year to ward off evil. Again the ritual derives from a myth. The myth narrative **purports**① to date from the era of Yao, but it does not even occur in any pre-Han source, and it probably belongs to the oral myth tradition of a minority tribe which became incorporated into the canon of mythological writings. The bird's features include double **pupils**②, signifying great wisdom, as with the demigod Shun. The bird is a hybrid, rolling the characteristics of many aggressive birds into one, such as the eagle and rooster, and the bird of Heaven, the phoenix. It should be noted that although the Chinese mythical bird "feng" is rendered as "phoenix," it does not possess the phoenix's symbolic meaning of **resurrection**③. The "qilin" (or Kylin), mentioned in the reading is a hybrid mythical creature that resembles a deer; it was believed to appear on earth when the ruler was a sage and governed well. Qilin is usually, while erroneously, translated as "the unicorn." The excerpt about the Many-Splendored Bird goes as follows:

While Yao was on the throne for seventy years, every year young male phoenix flocked to him, the qilin roamed through the lush marshes, and eagle-owls fled to the farthest desert. There was a country called Di Zhi, which brought the Many-Splendored Bird to him in **tribute**④. It was also known as the Double-Pupil Bird, which

---

① purport [pə'pɔːt] vi. 声称
② pupil ['pjuːpl] n. 瞳孔
③ resurrection [ˌrezə'rekʃn] n. 复活
④ tribute ['trɪbjuːt] n. 礼物

means that its eyes had double pupils. In appearance it was like a rooster, and its call was like that of the phoenix. It would often shed its down and feathers, flap its fleshy wings, and fly off. It could **swoop**① down on wild beasts like a tiger or wolf and could cause unnatural disasters and all kinds of evil, but it could not be harmed itself. Sometimes, if it was offered the essence of rare red jade, it might appear several times in one year, but otherwise it would fail to appear for several years. All the people in the land swept and sprinkled their gateways and doorways hoping to make the Many-Splendored Bird come to **roost**②. When it did not appear, the people in the land carved the likeness of the bird in wood or cast its image in metal and fixed it between their gates and doors, so that if there were any goblins or **trolls**③, they would be repelled or vanquished. Nowadays, every New Year's morning, when people make an image of the bird carved out of wood, or cast in metal, or else painted in a picture, and then place it over the window, this is a vestige of the custom in olden days of making the bird's image. (*Shi Yi Ji*)④

Questions for Discussion:

1. When does the myth about the Many-Splendored Bird date back to?
2. What did this bird look like?
3. What magical power did the bird own?
4. How was it related to the New Year ceremony?

---

① swoop [swu:p] vi 猛扑
② roost [ru:st] vi. 栖息
③ troll [trɒl] n. 巨怪
④ Anne Birrell, *Chinese Mythology : An Introduction*, pp. 237 – 238.

Gao Yao[①] Honors His Ram

Mythological material relating to the figure of Gao Yao is similar to the case of myths about Yao, in the sense that much of it is to be found in ***Shang Shu***[②], or *The Classic of History*. The earliest reference to Gao Yao occurs in poem 299 of *Shijing* (*The Classic of Poetry*), where he is a judge commended for his treatment of prisoners of war. In the chapter of *Shang Shu* entitled "**Canon of Yao**,"[③] Gao Yao is depicted as the supreme judge who is responsible for administering punishment as a minister in the government of Yao. In another chapter of *Shang Shu*, "**The Speeches of Gao Yao**,"[④] the wisdom of the judge is manifested in formal discourse.

The **tendentious**[⑤] rationalizing impulse of the anonymous political theorist who authored *Shang Shu* in the late Zhou or Han period did not permit the inclusion of more recognizably mythological material about Gao Yao. Several colorful details have survived in other texts, although they are fragmentary and some are of late **provenance**[⑥]. The first of the readings that follow is from ***Shuo Yuan***[⑦] (*A Garden of Anecdotes*) of the first century B.C. The second is taken from the third-century B.C. Confucian philosopher **Xun Zi**[⑧], who refers to Gao

---

① 皋陶（公元前2220年—公元前2113年），偃姓（一说为嬴姓），皋氏，名繇，字庭坚。上古时期华夏部落首领，伟大的政治家、思想家、教育家，"上古四圣"（尧、舜、禹、皋陶）之一，被后世尊为"中国司法始祖"，编者注。

② 《尚书》，最早书名为《书》，一部追述古代事迹著作的汇编。分为《虞书》《夏书》《商书》《周书》。因是儒家五经之一，又称《书经》，编者注。

③ 《尚书·大禹谟》记载皋陶在处理刑狱的基本原则，编者注。

④ 《皋陶谟》讲的是舜、禹、皋陶等人在一次会议上的讨论。主要发言人是舜的大臣皋陶，讨论的中心问题是如何继承尧的光荣传统，把国家治理得更好，编者注。

⑤ tendentious [tenˈdenʃəs] adj. 有偏见的

⑥ provenance [ˈprɒvənəns] n. 出处

⑦ 《说苑》又名《新苑》，古代杂史小说集，西汉刘向编，成书于鸿嘉四年（公元前17年）。按各类记述春秋战国至汉代的遗闻轶事，编者注。

⑧ 荀子（约公元前313年—公元前238年），名况，字卿，战国末期赵国人思想家、哲学家、教育家，儒家学派的代表人物，先秦时代百家争鸣的集大成者。《荀子·非相》中有载"皋陶之状，色如削瓜"，编者注。

Yao in his essay "Fei Xiang" ("Against **Physiognomy**①") as a man whose complexion resembles a peeled melon. Another detail is given in the third passage, which draws on physiognomical correlations. It is from ***Bai Hu Tong Yi***② or *Debates in the White Tiger Hall*, attributed to the Han historian Ban Gu (32 A.D. – 92 A.D.). The last reading narrates a bestiary myth about Gao Yao's **percipient**③ ram. It appears in an essay by Wang Chong in which he explains the juridical custom in the Han of painting images of Gao Yao and his divine one-horned ram in the courtroom.

In the era of Yao... Gao Yao became grand controller. (*Shuo Yuan*)

In appearance Gao Yao's complexion was like a peeled melon. (*Xun zi*)

Gao Yao's horse muzzle means that he was perfectly truthful and the sentences he passed were clear, for he penetrated the mind and heart of humans. (*Bai Hu Tong Yi*)

The **Xie Zhi**④ creature has one ram's horn, and it has the ability to know who is a criminal. When Gao Yao was conducting a trial and was in doubt about who the guilty person was, he would order the

---

① physiognomy [ˌfɪzɪˈɒnəmɪ] n. 面相
② 《白虎通义》，中国汉代讲论五经同异、统一今文经义的一部重要著作。班固等人根据汉章帝建初四年（公元79年）经学辩论的结果撰集而成。因辩论地点在白虎观而得名。编者注。
③ percipient [pəˈsɪpɪənt] adj. 目光敏锐的
④ 獬豸又称獬廌、解豸（xiè zhì），中国古代神话传说中的神兽，体形大者如牛，小者如羊，类似麒麟，全身长着浓密黝黑的毛，双目明亮有神，额上通常长有一角。编者注。

ram to **butt**① the criminal. It would butt the guilty one, but it would not butt the innocent. Now this is a case of a sage beast born in Heaven who helped provide evidence in a trial. That is why Gao Yao honored his ram, even rising from the bench to look after its needs. (*Lun heng*)②

Questions for Discussion:
1. According to *Xun Zi*, what did Gao Yao's complexion resemble?
2. According to *Lun Heng*, how did Gao Yao conduct a trial?
3. What would the ram do to the criminal?

Dragon

In Chinese mythology and belief, the dragon often appears as a most powerful and divine creature. People believe that the dragon can fly in the sky and make clouds with its breath. Among its many miraculous abilities, the power of controlling rain and the river is the most well-known. Whenever there is a drought in any area, residents would pray to a dragon to get rain.

Although the dragon is a mythological creature, there are abundant descriptions about its figure in classical documents and in oral tradition. Some versions state that there are several varieties of dragons. The dragons that have scales are called Jiao Long, those that have horns Qiu Long, and those that do not have horns are called Chi Long. In many texts, the dragon's figure is depicted in a very detailed way. Some say that dragons had hang-scales one chi (one third of one meter) in diameter below their jaw. Some say that dragons

---

① butt [bʌt] vt. 用头（或角）顶
② Anne Birrell, *Chinese Mythology: An Introduction*, pp. 240–241.

appear with a horse's head and snake's tail. And in another version a dragon appears with a deer's horns, an ox's ears, a camel's head, a rabbit's eyes, a snake's neck, a clam's **abdomen**①, a fish's scales, a tiger's paws, and an eagle's claws. Some documents note that dragons have a body part on their heads shaped like overlapping hills. This part is called **Chimu**②, without which dragons cannot fly into the sky. It is also said that below a dragon's jaw grows the most valuable pearl.

Another famous attribute regarding the dragon is that dragons may give birth to nine varieties of offspring that are quite different from the dragon's species. Each kind of offspring has a specific name, and they are very dissimilar in appearance, nature, and ability. However, though this belief is well-known, there are no conclusive findings about the names of the dragon's nine varieties of offspring. According to the semantic features in traditional Chinese language, some scholars assert that in early history the Chinese word for "nine" did not mean a certain amount. It was just a word that generally referred to "many" or "a lot." In later times, people considered it to be an exact figure and tried to give names to the nine varying offspring of the dragon. Therefore, several stories about these nine offspring appeared. One of the most popular versions identifies the dragon's offspring and their abilities. Because of these abilities, they were used, and continue to be used, as decorations, and thus show people's belief in these mythical creatures. The nine offspring are the following: Bixi, which is good at bearing heavy things, and thus its figure is often sculpted as the foundation of stone monuments; Chiwen, keen on looking long distances so that its figure is often painted or sculpted on eaves; Taotie, which is good at drinking water, thus its figure is usually carved on bridges to prevent flood; Yazi, which

---

① abdomen ['æbdəmən] n. 腹部
② 尺木，古人谓龙升天时所凭依的短小树木。王充《论衡·龙虚》："短书言龙无尺木，无以升天。"宋尝赠诗云："昔日曾为尺木阶，今朝真是青云友"，编者注。

is fond of fighting, thus its figure is often used to decorate the handles of knives and swords; Bi'an, which hates criminals and therefore its figure often ornaments the gates of prisons; Suanni, keen on smoke and fire so that its figure often appears on the lid of incense burners; Gongfu, which likes water very much so that its figure is usually carved on the guardrails of bridges; Jiaotu, which dislikes others to enter its house, thus its figure often appears on the gates of houses; and Pulao, which likes music and roaring, therefore its figure often decorates bells.①

In *The Classic of Mountains and Seas*, numerous gods or demigods are associated with dragons. Most of these divine creatures are described as having a dragon's or snake's appearance. Some of them had a dragon's trunk and a human head, such as Pangu, Fuxi, Nüwa, Huang Di, Yan Di, the Thunder God living in the Thunder Marsh, and gods living in areas from Tianyu Mountain to Nanyu Mountain, from Chanhu Mountain to Qi Mountain, and from Guanling Mountain to Dunti Mountain. Some of them had a bird's head and a dragon's trunk, such as the gods living in the area from Gui Mountain to Qiwu Mountain, and from Zhaoyao Mountain to Qiwei Mountain.②

One of the most famous dragons in Chinese mythology is Ying Long, or Responding Dragon. Ying Long appears in the myths of the deaths of Kua Fu and Chiyou as a god in control of the element of water.③ In many places people pray to him in order to receive rain. The story of "Ying Long Assisting Yu in Controlling water" is recorded in Wang Jia's *Shi Yi Ji* as follows:

---

① 龙之九子分别为赑屃（bì xì）、螭吻（chī wěn）、饕餮（tāo tiè）、睚眦（yá zì）、狴犴（bì àn）、狻猊（suān ní）、蚣蝮（gōng fù）、椒图（jiāo tú）和蒲牢（pú láo），编者注。
② Yang Lihui, An Deming and Jessica Anderson Turner, *Handbook of Chinese Mythology*, pp. 101-104.
③ 《山海经·大荒北经》："应龙已杀蚩尤，又杀夸父，乃去南方处之，故南方多雨"，编者注。

Yu exhausted his strength in cutting dikes and ditches and in conducting the courses of rivers and leveling mounds. The yellow dragon dragged its tail in front of him, while the dark tortoise carried green mud on its back behind him. (*Shi Yi Ji*)①

Questions for Discussion:

1. What magical powers do dragons have?

2. How are dragons described in classical documents and in oral tradition?

3. Who are the nine offspring of the dragon? What abilities do they possess?

4. According to *Shi Yi Ji*, what kind of assistance did Ying Long offer to Yu?

Part 2　Animals in Greek Mythology

The Gorgons②

The Gorgons, **Stheno**③, **Euryale**④, and **Medusa**⑤, were the three daughters of Phorcys and Ceto, and were the personification of those benumbing, and, as it were, petrifying sensations, which result from sudden and extreme fear.

They were frightful winged monsters, whose bodies were covered with **scales**⑥; hissing, wriggling snakes clustered round their heads instead of hair;

---

①　Anne Birrell, *Chinese Mythology: An Introduction*, p. 242.
②　Gorgons [ˈgɔːrgən] n. 蛇发女怪（希腊神话中三个长有尖牙，头生毒蛇的恐怖女妖）
③　Stheno [ˈsθeno] n. 蛇发女怪之一斯忒诺
④　Euryale [juəˈraiəli] n. 蛇发女怪之一欧律阿勒
⑤　Medusa [mɪˈdjuːzə] n. 蛇发女怪之一美杜莎
⑥　scales [skeɪlz] n. 鳞屑

their hands were of **brass**①; their teeth resembled the **tusks**② of a wild boar; and their whole aspect was so appalling, that they are said to have turned into stone all who beheld them.

These scary sisters were supposed to dwell in that remote and mysterious region in the far West, beyond the sacred stream of Oceanus.

The Gorgons were the servants of Hades, who took advantage of them to terrify and **overawe**③ those shades, doomed to be kept in a constant state of unrest as a punishment for their misdeeds, whilst the **Furies**④, on their part, **scourged**⑤ them with their whips and tortured them incessantly.

The most celebrated of the three sisters was Medusa, who alone was mortal. She was originally a golden-haired and gorgeous maiden, who, as a priestess of Athene, was devoted to a life of **celibacy**⑥; but being wooed by Poseidon, she fell in love with him in return.

She forgot her vows, and tied the knot with him. For this offence she was punished by the goddess in a most appalling manner. Each wavy lock of the beautiful hair which had so charmed her husband, was changed into a **venomous**⑦ snake; her once gentle, love-inspiring eyes now became blood-shot, furious orbs, which excited fear and disgust in the mind of the beholder; whilst her former **roseate**⑧ hue and milk-white skin assumed a loathsome greenish tinge. Seeing herself thus transformed into so **repulsive**⑨ an object, Medusa fled

---

① brass [brɑːs] n. 黄铜
② tusk [tʌsk] n. 尖牙
③ overawe [ˌəʊvərˈɔː] vt. 使敬畏
④ 复仇女神，不安女神阿勒克图（Alecto）、妒嫉女神墨纪拉（Megaera）和报仇女神提希丰（Tisiphone）的总称，任务是追捕并惩罚那些犯下严重罪行的人，无论罪人在哪里，她们总会跟着他，使他的良心受到痛悔的煎熬。编者注。
⑤ scourge [skɜːdʒ] vt. 鞭打
⑥ celibacy [ˈselɪbəsi] n. 独身
⑦ venomous [ˈvenəməs] adj. 有毒的
⑧ roseate [ˈrəʊziət] adj. 容光焕发的
⑨ repulsive [rɪˈpʌlsɪv] adj. 令人厌恶的

from her home, never to return. Wandering about, abhorred, dreaded, and shunned by all the world, she now developed into a character, worthy of her outward appearance. In despair she fled to Africa, where, as she passed restlessly from place to place, infant snakes dropped from her hair, and thus, according to the belief of the ancients, that country became the hotbed of these venomous reptiles. Haunted by the curse of Athene, she turned into stone whomsoever she gazed upon, till at last, after a life of unimaginable misery, deliverance came to her in the shape of death, at the hands of **Perseus**[①].

It is noteworthy that when the Gorgons are spoken of in the singular, it is Medusa who is alluded to. [②]

Questions for Discussion:

1. What did the Gorgons look like?
2. What was their duty?
3. What was Medusa used to be?
4. Why was she turned into a monster?
5. Who killed her at last?

Pegasus[③]

Pegasus was a beautiful winged horse who sprang from the body of Medusa when she was slain by the hero Perseus, the son of Zeus and **Danae**[④]. Spreading out his wings he immediately summited the top of Mount Olympus, where he was received with delight and admiration by all the immortals. A place

---

① Perseus ['pəːsjuːs] n. 珀尔修斯（宙斯之子）
② E. M. Berens, *The Myths and Legends of Ancient Greece and Rome*, pp. 144 – 145.
③ Pegasus ['pegəsəs] n. 珀加索斯（希腊神话中的双翼神马）
④ Danae ['dæneɪi] n. 达娜厄（阿哥斯国王之女）

in his palace was assigned to him by Zeus, who employed him to carry his thunder and lightning. Pegasus permitted none but the gods to mount him, except in the case of **Bellerophon**①, whom, at the command of Athene, he carried aloft, to aid him in slaying the Chimera with his arrows.

The later poets represent Pegasus as being at the service of the Muses, and for this reason he is more celebrated in modern times than in **antiquity**②. He would appear to symbolize that poetical inspiration, which tends to develop man's higher nature, and causes the mind to soar heavenwards. The only mention by the ancients of Pegasus in connection with the Muses, is the story of his having produced with his hoofs, the famous fountain **Hippocrene**③.

It is said that during their contest with the **Pierides**④, the Muses played and sang on the summit of Mount Helicon with such extraordinary strength and appeal, that heaven and earth stood still to listen, whilst the mountain raised itself in ecstasy towards the abode of the celestial gods. Poseidon, beholding his special function thus interfered with, sent Pegasus to check the boldness of the mountain, in daring to move without his permission. When Pegasus reached the summit, he stamped the ground with his hoofs, and out gushed the waters of Hippocrene, afterwards so renowned as the sacred **fount**⑤, whence the Muses **quaffed**⑥ their richest draughts of inspiration.⑦

Questions for Discussion:

1. How was Pegasus born?

---

① Bellerophon [beˈlerəfən] n. 柏勒罗丰（科林斯英雄，在有翼神马珀加索斯的帮助下常有善举，较为杰出的贡献之一是杀死吐火怪兽）
② antiquity [ænˈtɪkwəti] n. 古代（尤指古埃及、古希腊和古罗马时期）
③ Hippocrene [ˌhɪpəʊˈkriːniː] n.（赫利孔山上的）灵泉
④ Pierides [paɪˈɪərɪdiːz] n. 皮厄里得斯（即缪斯）
⑤ fount [faʊnt] n. 泉
⑥ quaff [kwɒf] vt. 痛饮
⑦ E. M. Berens, *The Myths and Legends of Ancient Greece and Rome*, p.162.

2. What did he do for Zeus?

3. What did Pegasus do on Mount Helicon?

Sirens

The Sirens would appear to have been personifications of those numerous rocks and underlying dangers, which abound on the South West coast of Italy. They are sea-nymphs with wings attached to their shoulders. The upper part of the body resembles a maiden and the lower a sea-bird. Being endowed with such alluring voices, their magical songs are said to have lured mariners to destroy themselves.

On the homeward voyage, Odysseus and his companions were put to sea and had to pass the island of the Sirens. Now Circe had warned Odysseus on no account to listen to the **seductive**① melodies of these **treacherous**② nymphs; for that all who gave ear to their enticing strains felt an unconquerable desire to leap overboard and join them. As consequences, they either perished at their hands, or were **engulfed**③ by the waves.

In order that his crew should not hear the song of the Sirens, Odysseus had filled their ears with melted wax; but the hero himself was so indulged in adventure that he could not resist the temptation of braving this new challenge. By his own desire, therefore, he was lashed to the **mast**④, and his comrades took strict orders on no account to release him until the island was out of sight, no matter how intensely he might implore them to set him free.

As they neared the fatal shore, they beheld the Sirens seated side by side on

---

① seductive [sɪˈdʌktɪv] adj. 有魅力的
② treacherous [ˈtretʃərəs] adj. 奸诈的
③ engulf [ɪnˈgʌlf] vt. 吞没
④ mast [mɑːst] n. 桅杆

the **verdant**① slopes of their island; and as their sweet and alluring strains fell upon his ear the hero became so profoundly affected by them, that, forgetful of all danger, he entreated his comrades to release him; but the sailors, sticking to their orders, refused to unbind him until the enchanted island had disappeared from view. Being helped out of the crisis, the hero gratefully acknowledged the firmness of his followers, which had been the means of saving his life.②

Questions for Discussion:

1. What did the Sirens symbolize?

2. What did the Sirens look like?

3. How did Odysseus manage to hear the song of the Sirens and survive?

The Halcyon Birds

Ceyx was king of Thessaly. His wife Halcyone, the daughter of Aeolus, was devotedly attached to him. At present Ceyx was in deep **affliction**③ for the loss of his brother. He thought best to make a voyage to Claros in Ionia, to consult the oracle of Apollo. But as soon as he disclosed his intention to Halcyone, a shudder ran through her frame, and her face grew deadly pale. She said, "Dear husband, let me go with you, otherwise I shall suffer, not only the real evils which you must encounter, but those also which my fears suggest."

These words weighed heavily upon the mind of King Ceyx, but he could not bear to expose her to the dangers of the sea. He answered, therefore, with these words, "I promise, by the rays of my father the Day-star, that if fate

---

① verdant ['vɜːdnt] adj. 青翠的

② E. M. Berens, *The Myths and Legends of Ancient Greece and Rome*, p. 315.

③ affliction [ə'flɪkʃn] n. 苦恼

permits, I will return before the moon shall have twice rounded her orb." When he had thus spoken, he ordered the vessel to be drawn out of the ship-house and the oars and sails to be put aboard. When Halcyone saw these preparations, she shivered, as if with a **presentiment**① of evil. With tears and sobs, she bid her husband farewell, and then fell senseless to the ground.

Meanwhile they **glided**② out of the harbor, and the breeze played among the ropes. The seamen drew in their oars and **hoisted**③ their sails. When half or less of their course was passed, as night drew on, the sea began to whiten with swelling waves, and the east wind to blow a gale.

Rain fell in **torrents**④, as if the skies were coming down to unite with the sea. Skill failed, courage sank, and death seemed to loom up with every wave. The men were **stupefied**⑤ with terror. Presently the mast was shattered by a stroke of lightning, the rudder broken, and the triumphant surge curling over dominated the wreck, then fell, and crushed it to fragments. Ceyx held fast to a **plank**⑥, calling for help in vain, upon his father and his father-in-law. But oftenest on his lips was the name of Halcyone. He prayed that the waves may bear his body to her sight and that it may receive burial at her hands. At length the waters overwhelmed him, and he sank.

In the meanwhile, Halcyone, ignorant of all these horrors, counted the days till her husband's promised return. To all the gods she offered frequent incense, but more than all to Hera. For her husband, who was no longer in the world of the living, she prayed incessantly. The goddess, at length, could not bear any longer to be pleaded with for one already dead, and to have hands

---

① presentiment [prɪˈzentɪmənt] n. 预感
② glided [glaɪd] vi. 滑行
③ hoist [hɔɪst] vt. 升起
④ torrent [ˈtɒrənt] n. 奔流
⑤ stupefy [ˈstjuːpɪfaɪ] vt. 使惊呆
⑥ plank [plæŋk] n. 厚木板

raised to her altars that ought rather to be offering funeral rites. So, calling **Iris**①, she said, "Iris, tell **Somnus**② to send a vision to Halcyone, in the form of Ceyx, to make known to her the event." Thereupon Somnus sent one of his numerous sons, **Morpheus**③—the most expert in **counterfeiting**④ forms of men, to perform the command of Iris.

Morpheus soon came to the Haemonian city, where he assumed the form of Ceyx. Pale like a dead man, naked, he stood before the couch of the wretched wife. Leaning over the bed, tears streaming from his eyes, he said, "Do you recognize your Ceyx, unhappy wife? Your prayers, Halcyone, availed me nothing. I am dead. No more deceive yourself with vain hopes of my return."

Halcyone groaned and stretched out her arms in her sleep, striving to embrace his body, but grasping only the air "Stay!" she cried. Her own voice awakened her. Starting up, she gazed eagerly around, to see if he was still present. When she found him not, she smote her breast and rent her garments. Her nurse asked what was the cause of her grief. "Halcyone is gone," she answered, "she perished with her Ceyx. He died in the shipwreck."

It was now morning. She went to the seashore and sought the spot where she last saw him, on his departure. Looking out over the sea, she spotted an indistinct object floating in the water. It was her husband! Stretching out her trembling hands towards it, she exclaimed, "O, dearest husband, is it thus you return to me?" She leaped upon the **mole**⑤ built out from the shore and she flew, striking the air with wings produced on the instant. As she flew, her throat poured forth sounds overflowed with grief, like the voice of one lamenting. When she touched that mute and bloodless body, she enfolded its beloved limbs

---

① Iris [ˈaɪrɪs] n. (沿着彩虹来到地球为诸神报信的) 彩虹女神
② Somnus [ˈsɒmnəs] n. 索莫纳斯 (睡眠之神)
③ Morpheus [ˈmɔːfiəs] n. 墨菲斯 (梦神)
④ counterfeit [ˈkaʊntəfɪt] vt. 佯装
⑤ mole [məʊl] n. 海堤港

with her new-formed wings and tried to give kisses with her horny beak. By the merciful gods both of them were changed into birds.①

Questions for Discussion:

1. Where was Ceyx's destination?
2. What was Ceyx's promise to Halcyone?
3. What did Ceyx encounter on the sea?
4. What did Halcyone do when anticipating the return of Ceyx?
5. How did Hera help Halcyone?
6. How did Morpheus perform Iris's command?
7. What did Halcyone do the next morning on the seashore?
8. What change took place on her?

Nightingale, Swallow and Hoopoe②

Tereus③, a son of Ares, having acted as a **mediator**④ in a boundary dispute for **Pandion**, King of Athens, married his daughter **Procne**⑤, who bore him a son, Itys.

Unfortunately, Tereus, enchanted by the voice of Pandion's younger daughter Philomela, had fallen in love with her; and, a year later, concealing Procne in a **rustic**⑥ cabin near his palace at Daulis, he reported her death to Pandion. Pandion, **condoling**⑦ with Tereus, generously offered him Philomela

---

① 陶洁等.《希腊罗马神话》, 第 204—209 页。
② hoopoe [ˈhuːpəu] n. 戴胜鸟
③ Tereus [ˈtiərjuːs] n. 忒雷俄斯（色雷斯国王）
④ mediator [ˈmiːdieɪtə] n. 调停者
⑤ Procne [ˈpraːkni] n. 普洛克涅（希腊神话中雅典国王潘狄翁之女，色雷斯国王忒雷俄斯之妻）
⑥ rustic [ˈrʌstɪk] adj. 乡村的
⑦ condole [kənˈdəʊl] vi. 慰问

in Procne's place, and dispatched Athenian guards to escort her when she headed for Daulis to attend the wedding. Tereus murdered these guards, and then when Philomela reached the palace, he had already forced her to lie with him. Procne soon heard the news but, as a measure of precaution, Tereus cut out her tongue and confined her to the slaves' quarters, where she could communicate with Philomela only by weaving a secret message into the pattern of a bridal robe intended for her: "Procne is among the slaves."

Meanwhile, an oracle had warned Tereus that Itys would die by the hand of a blood relative. Suspecting his brother Dryas of a murderous plot to usurp the throne, Tereus struck him down unexpectedly with an axe. The same day, Philomela read the message woven into the robe. She hurried to the slaves' quarters, found one of the rooms **bolted**①, broke in and released Procne, who was chattering **unintelligibly**② and rushing around in circles.

"Oh, to be revenged on Tereus, who pretended that you were dead, and seduced me!" Wailed Philomela, **aghast**③.

Procne, being tongueless, could not reply, but flew out and, seizing her son Itys, killed and **gutted**④ him, then boiled his body in a copper **cauldron**⑤ for Tereus to partake on his return.

When Tereus realized what flesh he had been tasting, he grasped the axe with which he had killed Dryas and pursued the sisters as they fled from the palace. He soon overtook them and was on the point of committing a double murder when the gods changed all three into birds: Procne became a swallow; Philomela, a nightingale; Tereus, a hoopoe. And the Phocians say that no swallow dares nest in Daulis or its environs, and no nightingale sings, for fear of

---

① bolt [bəʊlt] vt. (把门、窗等) 闩上
② unintelligibly [ˌʌnɪnˈtelɪdʒəbli] adv. 难以理解地
③ aghast [əˈɡɑːst] adj. 吓呆的
④ gut [ɡʌt] vt. 取出内脏
⑤ cauldron [ˈkɔːldrən] n. 大锅

Tereus. But the swallow, having no tongue, screams and flies around in circles; while the hoopoe flutters in pursuit of her, crying "Pou? Pou?" (where? where?) Meanwhile, the nightingale retreats to Athens, where she mourns without cease for Itys, whose death she **inadvertently**[①] prompted, singing "Itu! Itu!"[②]

Questions for Discussion:

1. Why did Pandion, king of Athens, let Tereus marry his daughter Procne?

2. How did Pandion condole with Tereus when the death of Procne was reported?

3. What did Tereus do to Prcone when Philomela arrived at the palace?

4. How did Prcone communicate with Philomela?

5. What did Tereus do to his brother Dryas?

6. What did Procne do to her son Itys?

7. What did Procne, Philomela and Tereus transform into?

Part 3 Reflections

1. **Vocabulary Expansion**

1) kaiming: _____

2) the Beast of White Marsh: _____

3) the Many-Splendored Bird: _____

4) Gao Yao and his Ram: _____

---

① inadvertently [ˌɪnədˈvɜːtntli] adv. 无意地
② 陶洁等：《希腊罗马神话》，第 302—305 页。

5）Ying Long：_____

6）the nine offspring of the dragon：_____

7）Gorgons：_____

8）Pegasus：_____

9）Sirens：_____

2. Appreciation

1）（穆）王驭八龙之骏：一名绝地，足不践土；二名翻羽，行越飞禽；三名奔霄，夜行万里；四名超影，逐日而行；五名逾辉，毛色炳耀；六名超光，一形十影；七名腾雾，乘云而奔；八名挟翼，身有肉翅。递而驾焉，按辔徐行，以匝天地之域。王神智远谋，使迹毂遍于四海，故绝异之物，不期而自服焉。

《拾遗记》

2）东五百里，曰祷过之山，其上多金、玉，其下多犀、兕，多象。有鸟焉，其状如鵁，而白首、三足、人面，其名曰瞿如，其鸣自号也。浪水出焉，而南流注于海。其中有虎蛟，其状鱼身而蛇经尾，其音如鸳鸯，食者不肿，可以已痔。

《山海经·南次三经》

3）龙门山，在河东界。禹凿山断门一里余，黄河自中流下，两岸不通车马。每岁季春，有黄鲤鱼，自海及渚川，争来赴之。一岁中，登龙门者，不过七十二。初登龙门，即有云雨随之，天火自后烧其尾，乃化为龙矣。

《太平广记》

4）又东五百里，曰丹穴之山，其上多金、玉。丹水出焉，而南流注于渤海。有鸟焉，其状如鸡，五采而文，名曰凤皇，首文曰德，翼文曰义，背文曰礼，膺文曰仁，腹文曰信。是鸟也，饮食自然，自歌自舞，见则天下安宁。

《山海经·南次三经》

5）帝巡狩，东至海，登桓山，于海滨得白泽神兽。能言，达于万物之情。因问天下鬼神之事，自古精气为物、游魂为变者凡万一千五百二十种。白泽言之，帝令以图写之，以示天下。

《云笈七签》

6)   In the land of the Arimoi, beneath the earth, she stayed—
Baleful Echidna—all her days an ageless, deathless maid.
But Typhon mingled with her in love—or so it has been said,
The terrible, unruly one with her of the glancing eye;
So she conceived and she gave birth to dauntless progeny.
Orthos, a dog for Geryon this was the first she bore;
Then one that was impossible, unspeakable, the cur
Kerberos of Hades, fifty-headed, with great power:
Shameless, he had a brazen voice and raw flesh would devour.
The baleful-hearted Hydra was the one that she bore third—
Hydra of Lerna, whom the white-armed goddess Hera reared
To wreak her wrath on Herakles—but Herakles, the son
Of both Amphitryon and Zeus, slaughtered that monstrous one
With help from Iolaus who loves Ares (it was planned
By Athena who rules the war hosts and was at her high command).

    But she bore the fierce Chimaera, who breathes overwhelming fire;
Huge, mighty, and fleet footed, she is terrible and dire.
She had three heads, the Chimaera: first a lion that would glower,
Then the second was a she-goat, last a serpent of great power.
Bellerophon and Pegasus despatched her; even so,
She bore the Sphinx (who brought the house of Kadmos death and woe)
When Orthos had subdued her, the Nemean lion too,
Which Hera, Zeus's glorious mate, nurtured until it grew,
Then settled in the Nemean hills—for humankind a bane:
So, living there it brought destruction to the tribes of men,

Ruling Nemean Tretos and the Apesas ruling too;
But the sheer force of Heraklean power laid it low.

Hesiod's *Theogony*

3. Discussion

Make a comparison between myths about the dragon in Chinese and Greek mythology and discuss its meanings in Chinese and western culture.

Unit 7

Myths of Punishment

Introduction

In *An Introduction to Mythology*, Lewis Spence divides mythology into 21 categories, "myths of a place of punishment"[①] being one of them. Punishment, as a sort of self-restraint of human beings, is reflected in many myths. The primitive ancestors integrated their opinions on immoral behaviors into myths of punishment and spread these stories so as to give people **admonishments**[②].

In Chinese mythology, people are condemned to divine punishment for their immorality, such as Gun who stole Xirang from the Supreme Divinity, Wei (a god having a bird's head and a human body with wooden crutches) who slew **Yayu**[③] (a human-eating beast), the daughter of Zhenmeng, one of the tribe chiefs in ancient times, who stole the black pearl of the Yellow Emperor, Chang'e who stole the elixir of immortality from the Queen Mother of the West, and **Emperor Wang of Shu**[④] who ravished his prime minister's wife. Besides, the divine punishment would also fall on people who neglect their duty, such as

---

① Lewis Spence, *An Introduction to Mythology*, p. 138.
② admonishment [əd'mɒnɪʃmənt] n. 训诫
③ 窫窳，古代神话传说中的神祇。原为人首蛇身，后被危与贰负所害，化为龙首猫身。《山海经·海内南经》云："窫窳龙首，居弱水中，在狌狌知人名之西，其状如龙首，食人"，编者注。
④ 《说文·隹部》云："……蜀王淫其相妻，惭，亡去为子规鸟，故蜀人闻子规鸣。皆起曰，是望帝也"，编者注。

Mr. and Mrs. Pufu, the giant couple who were commanded to dredge the waters since the birth of the firmament. Those who fought against or offended gods suffered from god's punishment as well, such as Xingtian who was beheaded for vying with Emperor Yan, Chiyou who was executed after fighting against the Yellow Emperor, Wugang who was sent to the moon to cut down the immortal laurel tree, and Yi Yin's mother who disobeyed the command of a spirit in her dream not to look back on her flooded city[①]. Another thing that merits attention is that the theme of punishment frequently occurs in Chinese myths of metamorphosis.

As one of the main themes of Greek myths, the punishment of mortals for their crimes from gods reflects the perspectives of ancient people on matters of justice. Most cases are connected to disrespectful conduct and the lack of obedience. For example, Prometheus stole fire from Zeus and was locked on the Caucasus mountain, suffering the endless pain caused by the vulture; Sisyphus was tortured for his **inveterate**[②] trickery and twice cheating death; Tantalus was dislodged from Olympus and was sentenced to suffer for eternity after his death, with fruits and water receding when he reached for them; Ixion was condemned to eternal punishment on a fiery wheel to pay for his insult to Hera; Erysichthon offended Demeter for he ordered to cut down the tree from the goddess's sacred grove; Arachne, the weaver, challenged Athena and was consequently transformed into a spider. In this way, the principal conflict is conditional upon the uneven distribution of power. While the representations of sins vary with authors, they still share a row of common characteristics, allowing them to form

---

① 《水经注疏·卷十五·伊水篇》："昔有莘氏女，采桑于伊川，得婴儿于空桑中，言其母孕于伊水之滨，梦神告之曰，臼水出而东走。母明视而见臼水出焉，告其邻居而走，顾望其邑，咸为水矣。其母化为空桑，子在其中矣。撒女取而献之，命养于庖，长而有贤德，殷以为尹，曰伊尹也"，编者注。

② inveterate [ɪnˈvetərət] adj. 成癖的

an opinion on their roles in the process and the **proportionality**① of the punishment.

Part 1 Punishment Stories in Chinese Mythology

Crimes of the Gods

The two excerpts below, from *The Classic of Mountains and Seas*, narrate myths of crimes committed by lesser gods and their corresponding punishments.

The first one is about **Gu**②, the son of Mount Zhongshan, and **Qinpi**③, a lesser god whose identity is uncertain. They suffered ritual execution for the murder of a sky god, **Baojiang**④. Their evil lived on after their change into monster birds, bringing war and drought.

The second reading gives a graphic account of the punishment by ritual exposure on a mountaintop for the crime of murder committed by the lesser god **Erfu**⑤, or Double Loads, and his officer, Wei. Their victim was Yayu, whose identity remained unknown. But in other passages of *The Classic of Mountains and Seas*, it is described as "looks like an ox and has a red body, a human face and hoofs of a horse"⑥ or "has a dragon's head"⑦. The two readings are as follows:

---

① proportionality [prəˌpɔːʃəˈnæləti] n. 相称
② 鼓，中国古代神话中的形象，钟山神的儿子，编者注。
③ 钦䲹（pī），神话人物，被天帝所杀，化而为大鹗，形状像雕，有黑花纹，白头，红嘴，爪像虎足。传说中这种凶鸟的出现预示战争，编者注。
④ 葆江，《山海经》中一位著名的神，掌管不死仙药，又名祖江，编者注。
⑤ 贰负，古代神话传说中的神祇，人而蛇身，是人蛇合体的图腾，古代跑得最快的神人，喜杀戮，后成为武官的象征，编者注。
⑥ *The Classic of Mountains and Seas*, pp. 75–77.
⑦ *The Classic of Mountains and Seas*, p. 247.

420 li further northwest is a mountain called Zhongshan. The son of Mount Zhongshan is called Gu who has a human face and a dragon's body. Together with Qinpi, he kills Baojiang at a place south of Mount Kunlun. Feeling wrathful, the God of Heaven kills Gu and Qinpi at a cliff east of Mount Zhongshan. As a result, Qinpi turns into a big **cormorant**①. He looks like an eagle, but he has black markings, a white head, a red beak and a tiger's paws. He makes a sound like a swan. Wherever it appears, there will be a major war. Gu also turns into a bird called junniao, which looks like a sparrow hawk and has red claws and a straight beak. Singing like a swan, it has yellow markings and a white head. Wherever it appears, there will be a severe drought in that place. ②

Wei was an official under the rule of Erfu, a god with a human face and a snake's body. They jointly killed Yayu, another god. Feeling wrathful, the God of Heaven tied them up on Mount Shushu. He fettered their right feet, bound their hands behind them with their own hair and then chained them to a tree on the mountain. This place lies northwest of Kaiti. ③

Questions for Discussion:

1. What did Gu look like?
2. What did Gu and Qinpi do?
3. What punishment did they get?
4. What would happen when cormorant and junniao appear?

---

① cormorant [ˈkɔːmərənt] n. 鸬鹚
② *The Classic of Mountains and Seas*, p. 45.
③ *The Classic of Mountains and Seas*, p. 249.

5. What did Wei and Erfu do?

6. How were they punished?

The Story of Xingtian

Xingtian is a notable deity who continued to fight against the Supreme God even after he was beheaded. In some early texts he is also said to have served as a minister of Emperor Yan, or Shennong.

According to *The Classic of Mountains and Seas*, Xingtian fought with the Supreme God to become the Supreme Divinity, but he lost the battle. The god cut off Xingtian's head and buried it on Changyang Mountain. However, Xingtian persevered. Head lost, he used his nipples as eyes and his **navel**① as mouth, continuing to **brandish**② his shield and battle-ax, which was a testament to his will-power and persistence. The reading from *The Classic of Mountains and Seas* is as follows:

> Xingtian and the God of Heaven came to this place and **vied**③ with each other for the leadership. As a result, the God of Heaven beheaded him and buried him on Mount Changyang. Using his nipples as eyes and navel as mouth, Xingtian still wielded his battleax and shield, dancing wildly. ④

The solemn and stirring spirit reflected in this story has been an attraction and a spur of Chinese people for a long time. The hero Xingtian has become a

---

① navel ['neɪvl] n. 肚脐
② brandish ['brændɪʃ] vt. 挥舞
③ vie [vaɪ] vi. 争夺
④ *The Classic of Mountains and Seas*, p. 225.

symbol for Chinese people to express their will to resist whatever pressures and difficulties confronting them. Many writers in different eras have composed poetry and prose to express praise and admiration for Xingtian. One of the most noteworthy examples is a poem written by Tao Yuanming (365 A. D. – 427 A. D.), a distinguished poet in the Jin Dynasty (266 A. D. – 420 A. D.). This poem states that "Xingtian brandished his shield and battle-ax, and his fortitude would live on."①

In an account from **Lushi**②, a book of history compiled by Luo Mi, a scholar in the Southern Song Dynasty, another of Xingtian's great deeds is mentioned. He was one of the ministers of Emperor Yan. In accordance with Emperor Yan's command, Xingtian composed music to complement the work of plowing and the harvest. The Chinese character of "xing" in this "Xingtian" is different from that in *The Classic of Mountains and Seas*. However, many scholars argue that they are the same figure.③

Questions for Discussion:

1. Why did Xingtian fight with the God of Heaven?
2. What punishment did he get after his failure?
3. What does Xingtian symbolize for Chinese people?

The Yellow Emperor Loses the Black Pearl

Zhuangzi, the earliest **verifiable**④ work of philosophical Taoism, is a

---

① 陶渊明《读山海经十三首·其十》:"精卫衔微木,将以填沧海。刑天舞干戚,猛志固常在。同物既无虑,化去不复悔。徒设在昔心,良辰讵可待",编者注。

② 《路史》是南宋罗泌所撰杂史,共47卷,前记9卷,后记14卷,国名记8卷,发挥6卷,余论10卷。《路史》取材繁博庞杂,是神话历史集大成的作品,编者注。

③ Yang Lihui, An Deming and Jessica Anderson Turner, *Handbook of Chinese Mythology*, pp. 217 – 218.

④ verifiable [ˈverɪfaɪəbl] adj. 可证实的

valuable source of primal myth, but it suffered a degree of distortion from the practice of its author, Zhuangzi, or Master Zhuang, through his improper utilization of these myths for the purpose of illustrating his philosophical beliefs. This tendency is exemplified by Zhuangzi's treatment of the mythical figure of the Yellow Emperor. The only reference to the god as a warrior occurs in a negative critique of his battle with Chiyou①. Most of the other references to the Yellow Emperor in *Zhuangzi* are ambiguous or negative, since he casts him in the role of a lesser god and as a demythologized figure who **subserviently**② seeks the Truth from wiser Taoists or innocents③. Therefore, while Zhuangzi subverts the classical mythological tradition for **polemical**④ and satirical purposes, he embarks on a new **mythopoeic**⑤ course, creating his own myths. In *Zhuangzi*, the philosopher argues that knowledge, sensory excellence, and **elocution**⑥ are the marks of civilized behavior, which have to be learned, whereas inborn nature or instinct, characterized as Shapeless, belongs to a higher order of human existence. This idea is reflected in the story "The Yellow Emperor Loses the Black Pearl" in *Zhuangzi*, which story is recorded in *Yun Ji Qi Qian*, or *Seven Tomes from the Cloudy Shelf*, a Taoist text compiled in the Tang Dynasty, and ***Shu Tao Wu***⑦, an account from the Song Dynasty as well. The story is as follows:

The Yellow Emperor was traveling north of Scarlet River. He climbed up the Mount of Kunlun and gazed south. On his way back

---

① Zhuangzi, *The Complete Works of Chuang Tzu*, trans. by Burton Waston, New York: Columbia University Press, 1968, p. 327.
② subserviently [səbˈsɜːviəntli] adv. 恭顺地
③ Zhuangzi, *The Complete Works of Chuang Tzu*, trans. by Burton Waston, p. 266.
④ polemical [pəˈlemɪkl] adj. 好辩的
⑤ mythopoeic [ˌmɪθəʊˈpiːɪk] adj. 创作神话的
⑥ elocution [ˌeləˈkjuːʃn] n. 雄辩术
⑦ 《蜀梼杌·二卷》（浙江吴玉墀家藏本），一名《外史梼杌》，宋张唐英撰，编者注。

he dropped his black pearl. He told Zhi (Knowledge) to look for it, but he could not find it. He told **Chigou**① (Wrangling Debate) to look for it, but he could not find it. So he told **Xiangwang**② (Shapeless) to do so, and Xiangwang found it. The Yellow Emperor said, "That's amazing! How was Xiangwang the one who was able to find it?" Later, the daughter of the Meng clan, the Lady Qixiang, stole the black pearl. In his chagrin, the Yellow Emperor investigated the matter and sent one god to hunt down the daughter of Zhen Meng's clan. Afraid of being punished, Zhen Meng's daughter swallowed the black pearl and sank into Wenchuan (the Mingjiang river in present Sichuan province) and became a monster called Qixiang, with a horse's head and dragon's body. Since then, she became the water god of Wenchuan. It is said that she helped Yu a lot when he tamed the flood. ③

Questions for Discussion:

1. What philosophical thought did Zhuangzi convey in the story "The Yellow Emperor Loses the Black Pearl"?

2. Who did the Yellow Emperor ask to look for the black pearl?

3. Who found it at last?

4. Who stole the black pearl from Xiangwang? What punishment did she get?

Chang'e's Escape to the Moon

The myths about Hou Yi include several other mythical figures—Di Jun, the

---

① 吃诟，传说中的大力士或是善言力诤者，编者注。
② 象罔，《庄子》寓言中的人物。含无心、无形迹之意，编者注。
③ Anne Birrell, *Chinese Mythology: An Introduction*, pp. 136–137.

six monsters, the Lord of the River, **Luo Pin**①, his wife (identified possibly mistakenly as Fu Fei, goddess of the Luo River, who in turn is wrongly identified as Fu Xi's daughter), God in Heaven, and Feng Meng. But the best-known myths centers on Chang'e, formerly known as Heng'e, who was Hou Yi's wife. She stole the **elixir**② of immortality given to her husband by the Queen Mother of the West and was metamorphosed into a toad on the moon. She is not the moon goddess as such but is said to be the "essence of the moon." Her lunar role is parallel in some respects to that of Chang Xi, the mother of the twelve moons and consort of Di Jun. Although there is a myth that explains the disappearance of the nine suns, leaving just one, through the heroism of Yi the Archer, no myth exists for the eventual vanishment of the eleven moons to leave one. The demigod Hou Yi is linked, however, to a major solar myth and a major lunar myth in the classical narratives, just as Di Jun is through somewhat different narratives.

The earliest account of Chang'e introduces the motif of a toad, the creature she metamorphosed into on the moon. This motif denotes immortality because of the toad's shedding its skin and its apparent rebirth. The wax and wane of the moon has the same **denotation**③. The motif of the cycle of eternal return have parallels worldwide. In Han iconography the toad on the moon is often depicted dancing on its hind legs while pounding the drug of immortality in a mortar.

Another worldwide motif that occurs in the Chang'e moon myth is the theft of a gift of the gods and the punishment of the thief. This motif has already been discussed with reference to Gun. Chang'e fits this pattern of the **trickster**④ in several respects: she stole the gift of the drug of immortality from Yi the Archer,

---

① 雒嫔 (luò pín), 又名宓妃。《天问》:"帝降夷羿, 革孽夏民。胡欵大河伯, 而妻彼雒嫔", 编者注。
② elixir [ɪˈlɪksə] n. 长生不老药
③ denotation [diːnəʊˈteɪʃn] n. 指称意义
④ trickster [ˈtrɪkstə] n. 骗子

who had received it from the Queen Mother of the West; she metamorphased into an ugly creature with the saving grace of immortality. The readings about Chang'e are as follows:

> Yi got some elixir from the Queen Mother of the West, but his wife Chang'e stole it and flew away with it to the moon. Thereafter she lived on the moon in the form of a toad, and was called the Moon Spirit. ①

> This is somewhat the same as Yi's getting the pill ensuring immortality from the Queen Mother of the West (Xiwangmu), after Chang'e—Lord Yi's wife **pilfered**② and took the pill and then flew to the moon. Yi was so disappointed and could not obtain such a pill again. Why? Because he did not know how such pills were produced. Hence, borrowing kindling is not as good as looking for a **flint**③ stone yourself, and going to another family to fetch water is not as convenient as digging a well at your own home. ④

Although her punishment is not specified but only surmised from the context of the myth, the theme of punishment is clearly expressed in the final reading, which concerns another mythical figure on the moon, Wu Gang. The text is from **You Yang Za Zu**⑤, or *A Miscellany from You Yang*, by Duan Chengshi (803

---

① 丁往道:《中国神话及志怪小说一百篇》,商务印书馆1991年版,第49页。
② pilfer ['pɪlfə] vt. 偷窃
③ flint [flɪnt] n. 燧石
④ Liu An, *Huainanzi*, translated into modern Chinese by Zhai Jiangyue, translated into English by Zhai Jiangyue and Mou Aipeng, p. 389.
⑤ 《酉阳杂俎》为唐代段成式创作的笔记小说集。该作品有前卷20卷,续集10卷。据作者自序,"固役不耻者,抑志怪小说之书也"。所记有仙佛鬼怪、人事以至动物、植物、酒食、寺庙等等,分类编录,一类属志怪传奇,另一类记载珍异之物,与晋张华《博物志》相类,编者注。

A. D. -863 A. D.), a work which contains a wealth of early material. It relates the fate of Wu Gang, an alchemist seeking the elixir of immortality, who was punished for making an error against the unseen world of the spirits. He was condemned to chop down a tree on the moon which would restore upon being cut. The sustainability of his punishment is implied in the name of the tree: "gui" (Cassia), a pun homophonic with "gui" (to return), signifying his eternal cycle in an act of **atonement**①. Sarcastically, the brilliant red of the cassia perhaps reflects the color of **cinnabar**②, the alchemist's stone. In contrast to the sun, which in some versions has only a single bird in it, the moon is cluttered with mythical figures: Chang'e, the toad, a hare, the **mortar**③ and **pestle**④, Wu Gang with his ax, and the cassia tree. In later iconography, the moon was furnished with a jade tree, a jade palace, and other **accouterments**⑤ denoting neo-Taoist symbolism. The reading about Wu Gang is as follows:

> In those days people said that there was a cassia on the moon and the striped toad, Chan-chu. That is why books on marvels say that the cassia on the moon is five thousand feet high, and there is someone under it who is always chopping the tree but the **gash**⑥ in the tree soon becomes whole. This man's family name is Wu, and his given name is Gang, and he is from the West River area. They say that because he made a mistake in his quest for immortality, he was exiled and forced to chop the tree. (*You Yang Za Zu*)⑦

---

① atonement [əˈtəʊnmənt] n. 赎罪
② cinnabar [ˈsɪnəbɑː] n. [矿物][中医] 辰砂
③ mortar [ˈmɔːtə] n. 研钵
④ pestle [ˈpesl] n. 杵槌
⑤ accouterment [əˈkuːtəmənt] n. 饰物
⑥ gash [ɡæʃ] n. 很深的裂缝
⑦ Anne Birrell, *Chinese Mythology: An Introduction*, pp. 144-145.

Questions for Discussion:

1. What did Chang'e do? What punishment did she get?

2. What did Wu Gang do? How was he punished?

3. How are the stories of Chang'e and Wu Gang related to the collective consciousness of the Chinese?

Part 2　Punishment Stories in Greek Mythology

The Story of Sisyphus①

Sisyphus, son of Aeolus, married Atlas's daughter Merope, one of the Pleiades, and owned a fine herd of cattle on the Isthmus of Corinth.

Near him lived **Autolycus**②, who was a past master in theft, to whom Hermes had given the power of **metamorphosing**③ whatever beasts he stole, from **horned**④ to unhorned, black to white, and **contrariwise**⑤. Thus, although Sisyphus noticed that his own herds grew steadily smaller, while those of Autolycus increased, he was unable at first to convict him of theft; and therefore, one day, engraved the inside of all his cattle's hooves with the **monogram**⑥ "SS." That night Autolycus helped himself as usual, and at dawn

---

① sisyphus ['sɪsəfəs] n. 西绪福斯（科林斯的建立者和国王，因绑架死神而触怒众神后受到惩罚）

② Autolycus [ɔːˈtɒlɪkəs] n. 奥托吕科斯（希腊神话中著名的窃贼和骗子，奥德修斯的外祖父）

③ metamorphose [ˌmetəˈmɔːfəʊz] vt. 变形

④ horned [hɔːnd] adj. 家养的

⑤ contrariwise [kənˈtreərɪwaɪz] adv. 反之

⑥ monogram [ˈmɒnəɡræm] n. 由姓名首字母组合而成的图案（此处指刻上姓名首字母"SS"）

hoof-prints along the road provided Sisyphus with sufficient evidence to summon neighbors in witness of the theft. He visited Autolycus's stable, recognized his stolen beasts by their marked hooves and, leaving his witnesses to **remonstrate**① with the thief, hurried around the house, entered by the **portal**②, and while the argument was in progress outside seduced Autolycus's daughter Anticleia, who bore him Odysseus.

After Zeus's **abduction**③ of Aegina, her father the River-god **Asopus**④ came to Corinth in search of her. Sisyphus knew well what had happened to Aegina but would not reveal anything unless Asopus undertook to supply the **citadel**⑤ of Corinth with a **perennial**⑥ spring. Asopus accordingly made the spring **Peirene**⑦ rise behind Aphrodite's temple. Then Sisyphus told him all he knew.

Zeus, who had narrowly escaped Asopus's **vengeance**⑧, ordered his brother Hades to fetch Sisyphus down to Tartarus and punish him everlastingly for his betrayal of divine secrets. Yet Sisyphus would not be **daunted**⑨: he cunningly put Hades himself in handcuffs by persuading him to demonstrate their use, and then quickly locking them. Thus, Hades was kept a prisoner in Sisyphus's house for some days—an impossible situation, because nobody could die, even men who had been beheaded or cut in pieces; until at last Ares, whose interests were threatened, came hurrying up, set him free, and delivered Sisyphus into his clutches.

---

① remonstrate ['remənstreɪt] vi. 责备
② portal ['pɔːtl] n. 大门
③ abduction [æb'dʌkʃn] n. 诱拐
④ Asopus [ə'səupəs] n. 阿索普斯（希腊神话中的河神，一说为波塞冬和佩洛之子，另一说为俄刻阿诺斯与忒堤斯之子）
⑤ citadel ['sɪtədəl] n. 城堡
⑥ perennial [pə'renɪəl] adj. 常年的
⑦ Peirene [pi'raɪni] n. 希腊南部科林索斯市的佩瑞涅泉
⑧ vengeance ['vendʒəns] n. 复仇
⑨ daunted [dɔːntɪd] adj. 胆怯的

Sisyphus, however, kept another trick in reserve. Before descending to Tartarus, he instructed his wife Merope not to bury him; and, on reaching the Palace of Hades went straight to Persephone, and told her that, as an unburied person, he had no right to be there but should have been left on the far side of the river Styx. "Let me return to the upper world," he pleaded, "arrange for my burial, and avenge the neglect shown to me. I will be back within three days." Persephone was deceived and granted his request; but as soon as Sisyphus found himself once again under the light of the sun, he **repudiated**① his promise to Persephone. Finally, Hermes was called upon to **hale**② him back by force.

It may have been because he had betrayed Zeus's secret, or because he had always lived by robbery and often murdered unsuspecting travelers; at any rate, Sisyphus was given an exemplary punishment. The Judges of the Dead showed him a huge block of stone which he was ordered to roll up the brow of a hill and **topple**③ down the farther slope. He had never yet succeeded in doing so, for as soon as he had almost reached the summit, he was forced back by the weight of the shameless stone, which bounced to the very bottom once more; where he wearily **retrieved**④ it and must begin all over again. ⑤

Questions for Discussion:

1. How did Sisyphus manage to catch Autolycus?

2. What deal did Sisyphus make with the River-god Asopus?

3. What did Zeus order Hades to do?

4. What did Sisyphus do to Hades?

---

① repudiate [rɪ'pjuːdieɪt] vt. 否定
② hale [heɪl] vt. <古>用力拖(或拉)
③ topple ['tɒpl] vi. (使) 不稳而倒下
④ retrieve [rɪ'triːv] vt. 找回
⑤ 陶洁等:《希腊罗马神话》, 第278—282页。

5. How did Sisyphus cheat Persephone?
6. What kind of punishment did Sisyphus get at last?

The Story of Tantalus①

Tantalus, the spoiled son of Zeus, by dint of his noble lineage, enjoyed profound fondness from the gods, and was even bestowed upon the privilege to share the same table of the gods during the banquets of nectar and ambrosia at the Olympus. From his privileged position, he had a peculiar access to the gods' private conversations and gossip. Tantalus, despite being welcome with **full-fledged**② hospitality by the other deities in his visits to the Olympus, was sometimes disrespectful to his hosts. After returning from the Olympus, he spread the secrets of the gods, which he had heard during the banquets. On another occasion, he stole a bit of nectar and ambrosia from the table of the gods, which **conceded**③ immortality and were confined to the gods. In the know about Tantalus' **perpetration**④, the omniscient gods ignored the situation and did not punish him since they enjoyed his presence.

Tantalus was king of Lydia, and would care to repay the gods' hospitality by offering them a feast in his palace. Zeus, Hermes and Demeter accepted the invitation and confirmed their presence. The King was at great pains to ready the feast's preparations. He wanted the event to be perfect in order to be bestowed with even more benefits from the gods. He called his son **Pelops**⑤, saying, "My son, today you will have the honor to share the table with no one else but the gods of the Olympus." "Thank you, my beloved father, at last I will have

---

① Tantalus ['tæntələs] n. 坦塔罗斯（希腊神话中阿耳戈斯或科林斯的国王，宙斯之子）
② full-fledged [ˌfʊl 'fledʒd] adj 彻底的
③ concede [kən'si:d] vt. 授予
④ perpetration [ˌpɜ:pə'treɪʃn] n. 犯罪
⑤ Pelops ['pi:ˌlɑ:ps] n. 珀罗普斯（坦塔罗斯之子）

the privilege, as you do to be at the table in the presence of my glorious grandfather." Pelops said. Being amazed, he went to his room to get ready for the banquet. Tantalus called the cook and said, "Today you will prepare the most splendorous meal of all types." The king whispered something in the cook's ear who could not conceal his concern.

The gods arrived at the palace and were promptly greeted with total **reverence**①. The banquet started and the **attendees**② talked about the most different matters. Then Zeus asked, "Where is my grandson, you said he would join us." "Don't worry, he is preparing a surprise for you, sir," answered Tantalus. It was time for the main dish. The chef brought a beautiful stew with an unmatched flavor. Either to test Zeus's omniscience, or merely to demonstrate his good will, Tantalus cut up his son Pelops, and added the pieces to the **stew**③ prepared for them. None of the gods failed to notice what was on their **trenchers**④, or to recoil in horror, except Demeter, who, still mourning over her daughter's **detention**⑤ in Hades, did not realize what was happening and bit off some of the lad's shoulder. When the gods restored Pelops to life, Demeter was very sorry for her carelessness and gave him a shoulder of ivory.

For these crimes Tantalus was punished with the ruin of his kingdom and, after his death by Zeus's own hand, with eternal torment in the company of **Ixion**⑥, Sisyphus, Tityus, the Danaids, and others. The inhuman Tantalus was condemned to the torments of Tartarus, where he stood up to his chin in a clear stream. Though **frenzied**⑦ with thirst he could never drink of the water,

---

① reverence ['revərəns] n. 崇敬
② attendee [ˌætenˈdiː] n. 出席者
③ stew [stjuː] n. 炖煮的菜肴
④ trencher ['trentʃə] n. (尤指旧时) 木制食盘
⑤ detention [dɪˈtenʃn] n. 关押
⑥ Ixion [ɪkˈsaɪən] n. 伊克西翁 (原特萨利国王)
⑦ frenzied ['frenzid] adj. 疯狂的

for whenever he bent his head the stream **receded**① from his parched lips. Above him hung a branch of delicious fruit; but when, tormented with hunger, he strived to grasp it, the branch eluded his eager fingers. Thus he stayed, always "tantalized" by the sight of food and drink he never could secure. ②

Questions for Discussion:
1. What kind of privilege did Tantalus have among the gods?
2. What did Tantalus do to his son Pelops?
3. Why didn't Demeter notice the deeds of Tantalus?
4. What kind of punishment did Tantalus get?

The Story of Arachne③

Arachne lived in a hamlet on the shores of the Mediterranean. Her family was poverty-stricken. While her mother was busy cooking the simple meals for the family, or working in the fields, Arachne used to spin all day long.

Her wheel made a steady whirring like the buzzing of some insect. She grew so skillful from constant practice that the threads she drew out were almost as fine as the mists that rose from the sea nearby. However, the neighbors used to hint, at times, that such fine-spun threads were rather useless, and that it might be better if Arachne would help her mother more and spin less.

One day Arachne's father, who was a fisherman, came home with his baskets full of little shellfish, which were of a bright crimson or purple color. He thought the color of the little fish so pretty that he tried the experiment of dyeing Arachne's wools with them. The result was the most vivid hue that had ever been

---

① recede [rɪˈsiːd] vi. 后退
② Emilie Kip Baker, *Stories of Old Greece and Rome*, p. 146.
③ Arachne [əˈrækni] n. 阿拉克妮（吕狄亚少女，善织绣）

seen in any kind of woven fabric. This was the color which was afterward called **Tyrian**① purple, or royal purple, which had long been favored by the kings.

After the surprising discovery, Arachne's **tapestries**② always showed some touch of the new color. They now found a ready sale, and, in fact, soon became famous.

Arachne's family changed their little cottage for a much larger house. Her mother did not have to work in the fields any more, nor was her father any longer obliged to go out in his boat to catch fish.

Arachne herself became as celebrated as her tapestries. She heard admiring words on every side and her head was a little turned by them. When, as often happened, people praised the beautiful color that had been produced by the little shellfish, she did not tell how her father had helped her, but took all the credit to herself.

While she was weaving, a group of people often stood behind her loom, watching the pictures grow. One day she overheard someone say that even the great goddess, Athena, the patron goddess of spinning and weaving, could not weave more beautiful tapestries than this plain fisherman's daughter. This was a very foolish thing to say, but Arachne thought it was true. She heard another say that Arachne wove so beautifully that she must have been taught by Athena herself.

Now, the truth is, that Athena did teach Arachne. It was Athena who had sent the little shellfish to those coasts; and, although never allowing herself to be seen, she often stood behind the girl and guided her **shuttle**③.

But Arachne, never having seen the goddess, thought she owed everything to herself alone, and began to boast of her skill. One day she said, "It has

---

① Tyrian [ˈtiriən] adj. 提尔紫的
② tapestry [ˈtæpəstri] n. 织锦
③ shuttle [ˈʃʌtl] n. 梭子

been said that I can weave quite as well, if not better, than the goddess, Athena. I should like to have a weaving match with her, and then it would be seen which could do best."

These wicked words had hardly left Arachne's mouth when she heard the sound of a **crutch**① on the floor. Turning to look behind her, she saw a feeble old woman in a rusty gray cloak. The woman's eyes were as gray as her cloak, and strangely bright and clear for one so old. She leaned heavily on her crutch, and when she spoke, her voice was cracked and weak.

"I am many years older than you," she said. "Take my advice. Ask Athena's pardon for your ungrateful words. If you are truly sorry, she will forgive you."

Now Arachne had never been very respectful to old persons, particularly when they wore rusty cloaks, and she was very angry at being **reproved**② by this one.

"Don't advise me," she said, "go and advise your own children. I shall say and do what I please."

At this an angry light came into the old woman's gray eyes; her crutch suddenly changed to a shining **lance**③; she dropped her cloak; and there stood the goddess herself.

Arachne's face grew very red, and then very white, but she would not ask Athena's pardon even then. Instead, she said that she was ready for the weaving match.

So two weaving frames were brought in, and attached to one of the beams overhead. Then Athena and foolish Arachne stood side by side, and each began to weave a piece of tapestry.

---

① crutch [krʌtʃ] n. 拐杖
② reprove [rɪˈpruːv] vt. 责骂
③ lance [lɑːns] n. 长矛

As Athena wove, her tapestry began to show pictures of mortals who had been **foolhardy**① and boastful, like Arachne, and who had been punished by the gods. It was meant for a kindly warning to Arachne.

But Arachne would not heed the warning. She wove into her tapestry pictures representing certain foolish things that the gods of Olympus had done. The act was of great profaneness. It was no wonder Athena gathered her wrath, and when Arachne's tapestry was finished, she tore it to pieces wrathfully.

Arachne was frightened now, but it was too late. Athena suddenly struck her on the forehead with her shuttle. Then Arachne shrank to a little creature no larger than one's thumb.

"Since you think yourself so very skillful in spinning and weaving," said Athena, "you shall do nothing else but spin and weave all your life."

Upon this Arachne, in her new shape, ran quickly into the first dark corner she could find. She was now obliged to earn her living by spinning webs of exceeding fineness, in which she caught many flies, just as her father had caught fish in his nets. She was called the Spinner.

The descendants of this first little spinner have been in large number; but their old name of spinner has been changed to that of spider. Their delicate webs, which are as mist-like as any of Arachne's weaving, often cover the grass on a morning when the day is to be fine.②

Questions for Discussion:

1. What was Arachne good at?

2. Who taught Arachne the skill of spinning?

3. What did Arachne want to do after hearing the praise of other people?

---

① foolhardy [ˈfuːlhɑːdi] adj. 有勇无谋的

② LiLian Stoughton Hyde, *Favorite Greek Myths*, Boston: D. C. Heath and Company, 1904, pp. 79 - 83.

4. What did the old woman ask Arachne to do?

5. Who did the old woman turn out to be?

6. What did Arachne weave into her tapestry?

7. How did Athena punish Arachne?

The Story of Erysichthon①

This section tells the story of Erysichthon, who dared to defy the goddess Demeter, recklessly destroying her beloved tree, and thus receiving a fitting punishment. There was a certain grove of trees sacred to Demeter, where grew a lofty oak on which **votive**② tablets were often hung, and around which the nymphs and **Dryads**③ danced hand in hand. Erysichthon ordered his servants to cut down this **venerable**④ oak; and when they hesitated, telling him that it was a tree endeared by Demeter and should not suffer such a **sacrilege**⑤, he seized the ax himself and made a deep **gash**⑥ in the trunk. He lifted his ax for a mighty stroke, and as the servant again sought to stay his arm, he turned fiercely and killed the man with one swift blow. Then he proceeded to destruct the tree, and soon it was lying, bruised and bleeding on the ground.

The nymphs rushed to Demeter, and begged her to punish the man who committed this wicked **violation**⑦ of her grove. The goddess promised that Erysichthon would not get away with it, and sent an **Oread**⑧ to the remote part

---

① Erysichthon [ˌeriˈθikθən] n. 厄律西克同（希腊神话中忒萨利亚王子）
② votive [ˈvəʊtɪv] adj. 诚心祈求的
③ Dryad [ˈdraɪæd] n. 德律阿得斯（希腊神话中的树神）
④ venerable [ˈvenərəbl] adj. 珍贵的
⑤ sacrilege [ˈsækrəlɪdʒ] n. (对圣物或圣地的) 亵渎
⑥ gash [gæʃ] n. 很深的裂缝
⑦ violation [ˌvaɪəˈleɪʃn] n. 破坏
⑧ Oread [ˈɔːrɪæd] n. 俄瑞阿得（山岳女神）

of **Scythia**①, where the ice lay thick on the dreary soil in the land that was always desolate and bleak. "Here dwell drowsy Cold and Paleness and Shuddering and dreadful Famine." When the Oread drew near this barren country, she saw far off the **gaunt**② form of Famine pulling up with her teeth and claws the **scant**③ bits of vegetation that could be found here and there in the frozen earth. The nymph did not want to linger near the dreadful form of Famine, lest the **hag**④ should reach out her lean finger and touch the maiden's robes; so she hurriedly delivered the message of Demeter, and sped quickly back to her own fair land of Thessaly.

Not daring to disobey the goddess's command, Famine left her dreary country and sought out the home of Erysichthon. She found him, and as he slept she enfolded him with her wings, and breathed into his nostrils her deadly breath. Then she returned to her frantic digging in the unyielding soil. When Erysichthon awoke, he was at once consumed with a fierce desire for food; but no matter how much he ate, the desperate **craving**⑤ never ceased. All day long he devoured things with **voracity**⑥, but at night his hunger was still unsatisfied. His servants piled up food in enormous quantities before him, but the gnawing pangs of hunger never left him. He spent all his wealth in a vain attempt to buy enough food to **appease**⑦ the **insatiable**⑧ monster within him; but, though he at last sold all that he had, even his house and his clothing, it was not enough to buy him the food he craved. There was nothing left him now but his daughter; and frenzied by his hunger, he offered to sell her to a slave-dealer.

---

① Scythia ['siθiə] n. 塞西亚（或斯基泰，东欧和西亚之间的一个地区）
② gaunt [gɔːnt] adj. 憔悴的
③ scant [skænt] adj. 不足的
④ hag [hæg] n. 丑老太婆
⑤ craving ['kreɪvɪŋ] n. 渴望
⑥ voracity [vəˈræsəti] n. 贪婪
⑦ appease [əˈpiːz] vt. 使平息
⑧ insatiable [ɪnˈseɪʃəbl] adj. 贪得无厌的

The girl pitied her father's sufferings and would have done anything to help him; but she resented his **baseness**① in selling her, for she came of a noble race. While her purchaser was disputing with her father over the price, the maiden, who was standing on the seashore, a short distance away from her new master, implored Poseidon to save her from the disgrace of being sold as a slave. The kindly sea-god heard her cry, and changed her into an old fisherwoman. When the bargain between Erysichthon and the dealer was settled, the man looked around for his new purchase, but she was nowhere to be seen. The only person on the seashore, beside the brutal bargainers, was an old woman who sat mending her net. The **irate**② owner searched in vain for his slave and even asked the fisherwoman if she had seen a weeping maiden. Unable to find the girl, he at last went away, concluding that Erysichthon's daughter had tried to escape and so had been drowned in the sea. The maiden was rejoiced at her deliverance; but her cruel father, on seeing her regain her own form, decided that this was an easy way of making the money he desperately needed. So he sold his daughter again and again, and each time she sought the help of Poseidon, who obligingly turned her into a donkey, a butterfly to help her escape from her father and master. Without any income and still hungry, Erysichthon went back to the woods of Demeter and prayed for forgiveness. The goddess did not pay attention to him. The poor man, desperate by his hunger, sat beneath a tree and started to devour his own foot. Erysichthon spent the night eating himself. Nothing of him remained on earth in the following morning. So was Demeter avenged.③

Questions for Discussion:

1. Why did Erysichthon offend Demeter?

---

① baseness ['beɪsnəs] n. 卑鄙
② irate [aɪ'reɪt] adj. 生气的
③ Emilie Kip Baker, *Stories of Old Greece and Rome*, pp. 187-191.

2. How did Demeter punish Erysichthon?

3. How did Poseidon help Erysichthon's daughter?

4. How did Erysichthon die in the end?

The Story of the Danaides①

The story of the Danaides begins with the rivalry between the twin sons, Danaus and Aegyptus of Belus, the king of Egypt, who was believed to be a descendant of Io, a princess of Argos who lived most of her life in Egypt. When Belus died, he ordered Danaus king of Libya and Aegyptus, king of Arabia. The two brothers had regular rivalries over their kingdoms and were trying one to get the other's land.

The most interesting fact about these brothers is their **progeny**②. The myth says that Danaus had fifty daughters, known as the Danaides, from four different women, while Aegyptus had fifty sons. The intelligent Aegyptus intended to arrange marriages between his sons and the Danaides. For Aegyptus, these fifty marriages appeared as an easy route to acquire the properties of Danaus. But Danaus soon saw through the little game of his brother, and was unwilling to surrender his beautiful daughters to his nasty nephews. Guided by the gods and with no intention of provoking a war between them, he decided to give his kingdom to his brother and leave the country in search for another life. Then Danaus built a ship with fifty oars and fled to Greece with his fifty daughters.

They first made a stop in Rhodes, where they founded Lindos town and built a temple to goddess Athena Lindia. Then, Danaus and his daughters reached Argos, the birthplace of his great-grand-mother, the Argian princess Io. The

---

① Danaides [dəˈneidiz] n. 达那伊德斯姐妹（丹尼亚斯的五十个女儿）

② progeny [ˈprɒdʒəni] n. 子孙

minute he stepped off the ship, he went to Gelanoras, the king of the town, and demanded to be given the throne, for he was the rightful heir, as descendent of Io. When the people of Argos were about to choose their king, a wolf entered the city and tore a bull into pieces. The people of Argos took this as a sign of providence, choosing Danaus as their king.

Danaus ruled Argos for many years and was leading a quiet life till one day a foreign ship came. His brother, Aegyptus, had sent his fifty sons to find Danaus and attempted to take over his new kingdom. Soon the sons of Aegyptus presented themselves to the palace and asked once more to marry the Danaides. The climax of the story starts here. Danaus didn't want his beautiful and prosperous Argos to suffer from a war. Having no other option, he consented for the wedding and organized a **low-profile**① wedding party. He plotted to get rid of Aegyptus and his sons for good. Before the wedding, he presented each of his daughters a dagger and instructed them to kill their husbands in their wedding night.

All his daughters had to obey their father, for disobeying to parents was a great wrongdoing back then in the ancient world. They indeed killed their bridegrooms and buried their heads in Lerma, a region with lakes in southern Argos. Only one of the girls, **Hypermnestra**②, did not commit this brutal crime. She felt pity for her husband, **Lynceus**③, and chose to spare his life. Without doubt, Danaus brought her in front of the Argos court. However, Aphrodite, the goddess of love, intervened and saved her from punishment. Lynceus, the only survivor of the fifty sons of Aegyptus, later killed Danaus to revenge for his brothers. Afterwards, Lynceus and Hypermnestra started a new

---

① low-profile [ˌləʊ ˈprəʊfʊɪl] adj. 低调的
② Hypermnestra [ˌhaɪpəmˈnestrə] n. 许珀耳涅斯特拉（违抗父命，保全心爱的丈夫林叩斯的性命）
③ Lynceus [ˈlɪnsɪəs] n. 林叩斯

dynasty of Argive Kings, known as the Danaan Dynasty.

The story, however, does not stop here. The forty-nine brides who killed their husbands were punished for their crime. The myth says that when they died, the Danaides were forced to a torment for eternity, for they should carry jugs of water to fill a basin. It's said that they would be released from this punishment only if the basin was full of water. However, this torture would never stop because the basin had holes all over it and water would run out.①

Questions for Discussion:

1. Why did Aegyptus want to get his sons married to the Danaides?

2. How did Danaus become the king of Argos?

3. Why did Danaus consent the wedding?

4. What did Danaus ask his daughters to do in their wedding night?

5. What did Hypermnestra do?

6. What punishment did the other 49 daughters of Danaus get?

Part 3 Reflections

1. Vocabulary Expansion

1) Xingtian: _____

2) Chang'e: _____

3) Qixiang: _____

4) Yayu: _____

5) Wugang: _____

6) Arachne: _____

---

① https://www.greeka.com/greece-myths/danaides/

7) Tantalus: _____

8) Erysichthon: _____

9) Sisyphus: _____

10) the Danaides: _____

2. **Appreciation**

1) 东南隅大荒之中，有朴父焉。夫妇并高千里，腹围自辅。天初立时，使其夫妻导开百川，懒不用意。谪之，并立东南。男露其势，女露其牝。不饮不食，不畏寒暑，唯饮天露。须黄河清，当复使其夫妇导护百川。古者初立，此人开导河，河或深或浅，或隘或塞，故禹更治，使其水不壅。天责其夫妻倚而立之，若黄河清者，则河海绝流，水自清矣。

《神异经·东南荒经》

2) 黄帝游乎赤水之北，登乎昆仑之丘而南望。还归，遗其玄珠。使知索之而不得，使离朱索之而不得，使喫诟索之而不得也，乃使象罔，象罔得之。黄帝曰："异哉！象罔乃可以得之乎？"

《庄子·天地》

3) 嫦娥，羿妻也，窃西王母不死药服之，奔月。将往，枚占于有黄，有黄占之，曰："吉。翩翩归妹，独将西行，逢天晦芒，毋惊毋恐，后且大昌。"嫦娥遂托身于月，是为蟾蜍。

《绎史》卷十三引《灵宪》

4) 贰负之臣曰危，危与贰负杀窫窳。帝乃梏之疏属之山，桎其右足，反缚两手与发，系之山上木。在开题西北。

《山海经·海内西经》

5) So in this way the Thunderer set out for mortal men
   The woe that comes from women who conspire to bring men pain,
   And gave another evil that would countervail the good:
   If, fleeing from the baneful deeds of women, someone should
   Prefer not to be married, then to dread senectitude
   He'll come—without a soul to take care of his livelihood,

And when he's dead his kinsmen will divide his property.
Now, he who has a share in marriage as his destiny,
And has been joined together with a wise, devoted wife,
Even for him unwavering ill is measured all his life
Against the good; but should he be given the baneful sort,
Then unabating sorrow while he lives in his heart,
And in his mind and spirit, and his heartache can't be healed.
It isn't possible to evade or hide what Zeus has willed.
Prometheus, Iapetos's guileless son, could never
Escape from Zeus's darkened rage, although he was so clever,
But rather by Necessity the great chain binds him down.

Hesiod's *Theogony*

3. Discussion

1) Draw a conclusion of the reasons for various punishments in Chinese and Greek mythology. What philosophical thoughts are reflected in these stories?

2) What are the commonplaces of the stories about Sisyphus, Tantalus and the Danaides? What do they reveal about the early Greek people?

Unit 8

Myths about the Underworld

Introduction

The Underworld generally refers to the underground kingdom where the spirits of the dead live. Like many other pertinent concepts in Chinese mythology, the Underworld is a tangled mix of Taoism, Buddhism and traditional folk legend. For example, Diyu, a vast **subterranean**① maze of gloomy chambers, corridors and courts, whose entrance is housed in an enormous mountain on the other side of the **astral**② plane. Mortals may also sneak in via the ghostly town of **Fengdu**③. All legends incline to the view that it's a dark and sinister place like a prison with ample torture facilities. Buddhist and Taoist hold divided interpretations on how many levels there are in Diyu and on the associated deities. Some speak of "Ten Courts of Hell," each of which is ruled by a judge, and others speak of the "Eighteen Levels of Hell," but what they both agree on is that sinners who accumulate bad **karma**④ alive are doomed to atone for their sins after their death. Their souls are therefore taken into hell, a fiery place consisting of several layers, courts, or circles, each **doling**⑤ out a

---

① subterranean [ˌsʌbtəˈreɪniən] adj. 地下的
② astral [ˈæstrəl] adj. 星的
③ 酆都，又称酆都岁山，中国传说中的地府、地狱，编者注。
④ karma [ˈkɑːmə] n. 佛教和印度教用语，认为人的行为发生后将引起来世的善恶报应
⑤ dole [dəʊl] vt. 少量发放

different punishment for specific sins.

Much of what we know about how the Ancient Greeks and Romans imagined the Underworld is from Homer's *The Odyssey* and Virgil's *The Aeneid*, in which the Underworld is described as the kingdom of the dead, hidden deep within the bowels of the earth, and a sunless place under the reign of Hades and his wife Persephone. Watered by the streams of five rivers (Styx, Acheron, Cocytus, Phlegethon, and Lethe), the Underworld is divided into at least four regions: Tartarus (reserved for the worst **transgressors**①), the **Elysian**② Fields (where only the most excellent of men dwelled), the Fields of Mourning (for those who were hurt by love), and the **Asphodel**③ Meadows (for the souls of the majority of ordinary people). Various heroes and one heroine (Psyche) help lay claim to their heroic stature by making trips to the land of the dead, among which Heracles' bringing the watchdog **Cerberus**④ back from the Underworld is the most well-known. Another famous Greek Underworld myth is the tale of Hades' abduction of Demeter's young daughter, Persephone. In addition, the story of Orpheus may bear the same familiarity. As a wonderful **minstrel**⑤, Orpheus was so devoted to his wife that he attempted to win her back from the Underworld but in vain.

Part 1 The Underworld in Chinese Mythology

The Journey through Hell

Chinese myths about the Underworld are greatly influenced by Taoism,

---

① transgressor [trænz'gresə] n. 罪人
② Elysian [ɪ'lɪziən] adj. 极乐世界的
③ asphodel ['æsfədel] n. 水仙
④ Cerberus ['sɜːbərəs] n. 刻耳柏洛斯（希腊神话中的地狱看门犬）
⑤ minstrel ['mɪnstrəl] n. 吟游诗人

Buddhism and traditional folk legend. The Buddhist text ***Sutra on Questions about Hell***① mentioned 134 worlds of hell which were simplified to a total of 18 for convenience in the Tany Dynasty. Each of the 18 levels contains a specific method of torture for a specific sin. The souls of sinners are able to feel pain just like living humans, but cannot die again from their **ordeals**②. Similar to how Zeus appointed Hades as the guardian of the Underworld in Greek mythology, the Jade Emperor, the Supreme Deity of Taoism, put Yan Wang, or **Yama**③ in charge of hell. The period of time a soul spends in hell depends on the severity of their sins, and Yama makes the final call as to when they will pass from each stage, eventually being sent for **reincarnation**④ after being punished for long enough.

By tradition the deceased souls are firstly greeted by the two mythological creatures known as Ox-Head and Horse-Face, the guardians of the Underworld. As the name might suggest, they both have the bodies of men topped with the heads of an ox and a horse respectively. Apart from guarding the gates, the pair are also charged with the duty of capturing human souls that have reached the end of their earthly existence and bringing them before the courts of hell to be judged. There has been **hearsay**⑤ that the Chinese people who went through near-death experiences have claimed to glimpse Ox-Head and Horse-Face!

If a soul passes the stage of judgement and is deemed good enough not to be punished for their earthly deeds, they can head straight to being reincarnated again into the earthly cycle, or—in some rare cases—achieve enlightenment, exempt from human life cycles. The majority of souls normally have something to **repent**⑥ for, and so are sent down to the 18 levels of hell, where each sinner

---

① 《地狱经》，佛教典籍，东汉安世高翻译，主要由佛陀为众生讲述地狱中苦难。编者注。
② ordeal [ɔːˈdiːl] n. 磨难
③ Yama [ˈjɑmə] n. 阎罗王
④ reincarnation [ˌriːɪnkɑːˈneɪʃn] n. 转世
⑤ hearsay [ˈhɪəseɪ] n. 传闻
⑥ repent [rɪˈpent] vi. 忏悔

corresponds to a stage of their type or types before they are able to eventually leave and be reincarnated back into the upper world. A breakdown of the levels is as follows:

1) Hell of Tongue-ripping, where those who gossip and spread trouble with their words will repeatedly have their tongues ripped out.

2) Hell of Scissors, where those who destroy someone else's marriage will have their fingers repeatedly cut off.

3) Hell of Trees of Knives, where those who sow **discord**① amongst family members will be repeatedly hung from trees made of sharp knives.

4) Hell of Mirrors of **Retribution**②, where those who have managed to escape from punishment for their crimes while alive will be repeatedly shown their true horrific selves.

5) Hell of Steamers, where hypocrites and troublemakers will be repeatedly steamed "alive."

6) Hell of Copper Pillars, where **arsonists**③ will be repeatedly chained to red-hot pillars of copper.

7) Hell of the Mountain of Knives, where those who have killed for pleasure or without good reason will be repeatedly made to climb a mountain made of sharp blades sticking out of it.

8) Hell of the Mountain of Ice, where adulterers, deceivers of elders, and schemers will be repeatedly left out on a barren mountain of ice to freeze.

9) Hell of the **Cauldrons**④ of Oil, where rapists, thieves, abusers, and false accusers will be repeatedly fried in **vats**⑤ of boiling oil.

10) Hell of the Cattle **Pit**⑥, where those who have abused animals will be

---

① discord [ˈdɪskɔːd] n. 纷争
② retribution [ˌretrɪˈbjuːʃn] n. 报应
③ arsonist [ˈɑːsənɪst] n. 纵火犯人
④ cauldron [ˈkɔːldrən] n. 大锅
⑤ vat [væt] n. 大桶
⑥ pit [pɪt] n. 深渊

repeatedly hurt by animals in turn.

11) Hell of the Crushing **Boulder**①, where those who have abandoned or killed children will be repeatedly made to hold up heavy boulders, eventually being crushed by its weight.

12) Hell of Mortars and Pestles, where those who voluntarily waste food will be repeatedly force-fed hell fire by demons.

13) Hell of the Blood Pool, where those who disrespect others will be thrown in and submerged into a pool of blood.

14) Hell of the Wrongful Dead, where those who have committed suicide—considered deliberately going against the karmic course of the universe—will be forced to repeatedly wander the realm without a way out, while being pelted constantly by the Winds of Sorrow and the Rains of Pain.

15) Hell of **Dismemberment**②, where tomb raiders will have their bodies repeatedly torn into pieces.

16) Hell of the Mountain of Fire, where thieves, robbers, and the corrupt will be repeatedly thrown into the fiery pits of an active volcano.

17) Hell of Mills, where those who have misused their power to oppress the weak will be repeatedly crushed in a stone mill.

18) Hell of Saws, where those who have engaged in unethical or unfair business practices, or exploited loopholes in the legal system, will be repeatedly sawn in half by demons with saws.

Thus a popular Chinese saying was born: "上刀山、下油锅," which connotes an extreme suffering whose literal meaning is to "climb mountains of blades and be thrown into the boiling oil," a clear reference to two levels of the Underworld.③

---

① boulder ['bəʊldə] n. 巨石
② dismemberment [ˌdɪsˈmembəmənt] n. 肢解
③ https://www.localiiz.com/post/culture-local-stories-chinese-mythology-101-18-levels-hell

Questions for Discussion:

1. Who are sent to capture human souls in Chinese mythology?

2. What will take place to the soul that passes the stage of judgement and is deemed good enough not to be punished for their earthly deeds?

3. What kind of torture is there in each of the eighteen levels of hell?

Pan Guan① and Zhong Kui②

The Ministry of **Exorcism**③ is a Taoist invention composed of seven chief ministers, whose duty is to expel evil spirits from dwellings and generally to **counteract**④ the annoyances of infernal demons. The two gods usually referred to in the popular legends are Pan Guan and Zhong Kui. Pan Guan is the very Guardian of the Living and the Dead in the Otherworld, Fengdu, also known as the inferno. He was originally a scholar named Cui Jue, who held office as Magistrate of Luzhou, and later Minister of Ceremonies. After his death he was appointed to the spiritual post above mentioned. It's said that his best-known achievement is the prolongation of the life of **the Emperor Taizong**⑤ of the Tang Dynasty by twenty years by changing "one" into "three" in the life-register, or Register of the Living and the Dead, kept by the gods. The term Pan Guan is, however, more generally used as the designation of an officer or civil or military

---

① 判官，阴间官名。长相凶神恶煞，判处人的轮回生死，对坏人进行惩罚，对好人进行奖励。此处指判官崔珏，即崔府君，是中国民间信仰的神仙之一，编者注。

② 钟馗，道教俗神，专司打鬼驱邪。中国民间常挂钟馗神像辟邪除灾，从古至今都流传着"钟馗捉鬼"的典故，编者注。

③ exorcism [ˈeksɔːsɪzəm] n. 驱魔

④ counteract [ˌkaʊntərˈækt] vt. 抵抗

⑤ 唐太宗李世民（公元599年—公元649年），唐朝第二位皇帝（公元626年—公元649年在位），政治家、战略家、军事家、书法家、诗人。贞观二十三年五月二十六日（公元649年7月10日），李世民驾崩于含风殿，享年五十二岁，在位二十三年，庙号太宗，谥号文皇帝（后加谥文武大圣大广孝皇帝），葬于昭陵，编者注。

attendant upon a god than of any special individual. However, Pan Guan, "the Decider of Life in Diyu," has been gradually supplanted by Zhong Kui, "the Protector against Evil Spirits," a figure in the growing favor among people.

The Emperor Minghuang① of the Tang Dynasty, also known as Emperor Xuanzong in the Kaiyuan Reign Period (712 A. D. – 742 A. D.), was attacked by fever after an expedition to Li Mountains in Shensi (today's Shaanxi Province). During a nightmare he saw a small demon fantastically dressed in red trousers, with a shoe on one foot but none on the other, and a shoe hanging from his **girdle**②. Having broken through a bamboo gate, he took possession of Xuanzong's jade flute, and an **embroidered**③ box of Concubine Yang, and then began to make a tour of the palace, sporting and **gambolling**④. The Emperor grew angry and questioned him. "Your humble servant," replied the little demon, "is named **Xu Hao**⑤, 'Emptiness and Devastation,'" "I have never heard of such a person," said the Emperor. The demon rejoined, "Xu means to desire Emptiness, because in 'Emptiness' one can fly just as one wishes; Hao, 'Devastation,' changes people's joy to sadness." The Emperor, irritated by this **flippancy**⑥, was about to call his guard, when suddenly a great devil appeared, wearing a **tattered**⑦ head-covering and a blue robe, a horn clasp on his belt, and official boots on his feet. He went up to the **sprite**⑧, tore out one of his eyes, crushed it up, and ate it. The Emperor asked the newcomer who he was.

---

① 唐玄宗李隆基（公元685年—公元762年），唐高宗李治与武则天之孙，唐睿宗李旦第三子，故又称李三郎，母窦德妃。宝应元年四月甲寅日（公元762年5月3日），病逝于长安神龙殿，终年七十八岁，谥号至道大圣大明孝皇帝，庙号玄宗，葬于金粟山，名为泰陵，编者注。

② girdle [gɜːdl] n. 腰带

③ embroider [ɪmˈbrɔɪdə] vt. 刺绣

④ gambol [ˈɡæmbl] vi. 嬉戏

⑤ 虚耗，古代汉族民间传说中鬼怪之一，属恶鬼，是祸害的象征。传说虚耗身穿红色的袍服，长有牛鼻，一只脚穿鞋着地，另一只脚挂在腰间，腰里还插有一把铁扇子，编者注。

⑥ flippancy [ˈflɪpənsi] n. 轻率

⑦ tattered [ˈtætəd] adj. 衣衫褴褛的

⑧ sprite [spraɪt] n. 鬼怪

"Your humble servant," he replied, "is Zhong Kui, from Zhongnan Mountain in Shensi. In the Wu De Reign Period (618 A. D. – 627 A. D.) of **the Emperor Gaozu**① of the Tang Dynasty I was ignominiously rejected and unjustly **defrauded**② of a first class in the imperial examination. Overwhelmed with shame, I committed suicide on the steps of the imperial palace. The Emperor ordered me to be buried in a green robe (reserved for members of the imperial clan), and for that favor I swore to protect the sovereign in any part of the Empire against the evil **machinations**③ of the demon Xu Hao." At these words the Emperor awoke and found that the fever had left him. His Majesty called for **Wu Daozi**④ (one of the most celebrated Chinese artists at that time) to paint the portrait of the person he had seen in his dream. The work was done at such a level of verisimilitude that the Emperor recognized it as the actual demon he had seen in his sleep, and rewarded the artist with a hundred **taels**⑤ of gold. The portrait is said to have been still in the imperial palace during the Song Dynasty.

Another version of the legend says that Zhong Kui's essay was recognized by the examiners as equal to the writings of the best authors of **antiquity**⑥, but the Emperor rejected him on account of his extremely ugly features, whereupon he committed suicide in his presence, and was honored by the Emperor and **accorded**⑦ a funeral as if he had been the champion of the Examination. Meanwhile, he was **canonized**⑧ with the title of Great Spiritual Chaser of

---

① 唐高祖李渊（公元566年—公元635年），字叔德。中国唐朝开国皇帝（公元618年—公元626年在位），初唐政治家、军事统帅，唐太祖李虎之孙，唐世祖李昞之子。唐高祖李渊在位时期的年号为武德，编者注。
② defraud [dɪˈfrɔːd] vt. 欺骗
③ machination [ˌmæʃɪˈneɪʃn] n. 诡计
④ 吴道子（约公元680年—公元759年），又名道玄，唐代著名画家，有画圣之称，编者注。
⑤ tael [teɪl] n. 银两
⑥ antiquity [ænˈtɪkwəti] n. 古代
⑦ accord [əˈkɔːd] vt. 给予（某种待遇）
⑧ canonize [ˈkænənaɪz] vt. 褒扬

Demons for the Whole Empire. ①

Questions for Discussion:

1. What was the best-known achievement of Pan Guan?
2. How did Zhong Kui help Emperor Xuanzong of the Tang Dynasty?
3. What did Emperor Xuanzong do after he woke up?
4. What title did Zhong Kui get?

Miao Shan's② Visit to the Infernal Regions

King Miao Zhuang had three daughters, the youngest named Miao Shan. At the time of Miao Shan's birth, the earth trembled and a wonderful fragrance and flower blossoms sprang up around the land. Many of the local people were astounded, saying they saw the signs of a holy **incarnation**③ on her body.

Unfortunately, though amazed by this blessing, the king and queen were corrupt and saw little value in a child who appeared pure and kind. When Miao Shan got older, the king prepared to find her a husband. But she told her father she would only marry if by so doing she would be able to help **alleviate**④ the suffering of all mankind. The king became enraged when he heard of her devotion to helping others at cost of her own marriage, and forced her to slave away at **menial**⑤ tasks. Her mother, the queen, and her two sisters admonished her, but all to no avail.

In desperation, the king decided to let her pursue her religious calling at a monastery, but ordered the nuns there to treat her ill so that she would change

---

① Edward T. C. Werner, *Myths and Legends of China*, pp. 248–250.
② 妙善，南北朝时期，邢台朝平（今邢台南和县）人，妙庄王的第三个女儿，世人尊称为"三皇姑"，出家白雀庵，修炼成为千手观音，是观世音菩萨中国化和女性化的原型，编者注。
③ incarnation [ˌɪnkɑːˈneɪʃn] n. 化身
④ alleviate [əˈliːvieɪt] vt. 减轻
⑤ menial [ˈmiːniəl] adj. 卑微的

her mind. She was forced to fetch wood and water, and tend a garden for the kitchen. They thought these tasks would be impossible, since the land around the monastery was barren. However, to everyone's amazement, the garden flourished, even in winter, and a spring welled up out of nowhere next to the kitchen.

When hearing about these miracles, the King became extremely furious and issued the edict that Miao Shan should be executed. As soon as the King's warrant arrived, the sky suddenly became overcast and darkness fell upon the earth. A bright light surrounded Miao Shan, and when the sword of the executioner fell upon the neck of the victim it was broken in two. Then they thrusted at her with a spear, but the weapon fell to pieces. After that the King ordered that she be strangled with a silken cord and so she did. However, a few moments later a tiger leapt into the execution ground, dispersed the executioners, put the inanimate body of Miao Shan on his back, and disappeared into the pine-forest. Hu Pi-li rushed to the palace, recounted to the King full details of all that had occurred, and received a reward of two **ingots**[①] of gold.

Meantime, Miao Shan's soul, which remained unhurt, was borne on a cloud; when, waking as from a dream, she lifted her head and looked round, she could not see her body. "My father has just had me strangled," she sighed. "How is it that I find myself in this place? Here are no mountains, no trees or vegetation; no sun, no moon or stars; no habitation, no sound, and no cackling of a fowl or barking of a dog. How can I live in this desolate region?"

Suddenly a young man dressed in blue, shining with a brilliant light, and carrying a large banner, appeared and said to her: "At command of Yan Wang, the King of the Hells, I come to take you to the eighteen infernal regions."

"What is this cursed place where I am now?" asked Miao Shan.

---

① ingot ['ɪŋgət] n. 锭

"This is the lower world, Hell," he replied. "Your refusal to marry, and the **magnanimity**① with which you chose an **ignominious**② death rather than break your resolutions, deserve the recognition of Great Jade Emperor, and the ten gods of the lower regions, impressed and pleased at your eminent virtue, have sent me to you. Fear nothing and follow me."

Thus Miao Shan began her visit to all the infernal regions. The Gods of the Ten Hells came to congratulate her.

"Who am I," asked Miao Shan, "that you should **deign**③ to take the trouble to show me such respect?"

"We have heard," they replied, "that when you recite your prayers all evil disappears as if by magic. We should like to hear you pray."

"I consent," replied Miao Shan, "on condition that all the condemned ones in the ten infernal regions be released from their chains in order to listen to me." Thus the deal was made.

At the appointed time the condemned were led in by Ox-head and Horse-face, the two chief constables of Hell, and Miao Shan began her prayers. No sooner had she finished than Hell was suddenly transformed into a paradise of joy, and the instruments of torture into lotus-flowers.

Pan Guan, the keeper of the Register of the Living and the Dead, presented a memorial to Yan Wang stating that since Miao Shan's arrival there was no more pain in Hell; and all the condemned were beside themselves with happiness. "Since it has always been decreed," he added, "that, in justice, there must be both a Heaven and a Hell, if you do not send this saint back to earth, there will no longer be any Hell, but only a Heaven."

"Since that is so," said Yan Wang, "let forty-eight flag-bearers escort her across the Nai He Bridge (or the Bridge of Forgetfulness), that she may be

---

① magnanimity [ˌmæɡnəˈnɪməti] n. 宽宏大量
② ignominious [ˌɪɡnəˈmɪniəs] adj. 可耻的
③ deign [deɪn] vi. 屈尊

taken to the pine-forest to reenter her body, and resume her life in the upper world."

The King of the Hells having paid his respects to her, and the youth in blue conducted her soul back to her body, which she found lying under a pine-tree. Having reentered it, Miao Shan came to herself. A bitter sigh escaped from her lips. "I remember," she said, "all that I saw and heard in Hell. I sigh for the moment which will find me free of all impediments, and yet my soul has re-entered my body. Here, without any lonely mountain on which to give myself up to the pursuit of perfection, what will become of me?" Great tears welled from her eyes. ①

Questions for Discussion:

1. What happened when Miao Shan was born?

2. Why did the King want to kill Miao Shan?

3. What did the Gods of the Ten Hells ask Miao Shan to do?

4. What did the Hell transform into after Miao Shan's prayers?

5. Why did Yan Wang send Miao Shan back to the upper world?

Part 2　　The Underworld in Greek Mythology

Hades and the Underworld

In the beginning of the world, before the gods came to dwell in Olympus, all the universe was at the mercy of the Titans; and among these the greatest was Cronos—who wedded his sister Rhea (also called Cybele) and begot three sons, Zeus, Hades, and Poseidon, and three daughters, Demeter, Hestia, and

---

① Edward T. C. Werner, *Myths and Legends of China*, pp. 265 – 269.

Hera. Having subdued all the opposing Titans, Cronos and Rhea ruled over heaven and earth for many ages; but when the cruelty of Cronos drove his children into rebellion, there arose a mighty war in the universe, in which the sons and daughters of Cronos **leagued**① against their father, who had called upon the other Titans for aid. After years of combat the six brothers and sisters, helped by the Cyclops, defeated the allied Titans and imprisoned them in the black abyss of Tartarus—all except a few who had not joined in the war against the children of Cronos. Among those who were wise enough to accept the new sovereignty were Mnemosyne, goddess of memory and Themis, goddess of justice. Those descendants of the Titans who refused to acknowledge the supremacy of Zeus were **consigned**② to the center of Mount Etna, where the giants launched a great deal of revolt, making Hades fear for the safety of his realm. A few of the giants were spared though: Atlas, whose punishment was to hold the heavens on his shoulders for eternity, and Prometheus and Epimetheus who had **espoused**③ the cause of Zeus and so escaped the fate of the conquered Titans. When the offspring of Cronos found themselves masters of the world, they agreed to accept Zeus as their ruler, on condition that the two other brothers be given a share in the universe. So a division was made whereby Hades became king of the underworld; Poseidon took the dominion of the sea; and Zeus, having married his sister, Hera, established his dwelling in Olympus as lord of heaven and earth.

The kingdom of Hades was dreaded by all mortals, and its ruler inspired men with great fear. Though Hades was known to visit the earth at intervals, no one wished to see his face, and each man dreaded the moment when he should be obliged to appear before the grim monarch of Hades, and be assigned a place among the innumerable dead. No temples were dedicated to Hades, though

---

① league [liːg] vi. 组成联盟
② consign [kənˈsaɪn] vt. 交付
③ espouse [ɪˈspaʊz] vt. 支持

altars were sometimes erected on which men burned sacrifices to this **inexorable**① god, petitioning him to be merciful to the souls of the departed. The festivals held in his honor were celebrated only once in a hundred years, and on these occasions none but black animals were slaughtered for the sacrifice.

The underworld, over which Hades reigned, is deep in the heart of the earth; but there are several entrances to it, one being near **Avernus**②, where the mist rising from the waters is so foul that no bird could fly over it. The lake itself is in an extinct volcano near Vesuvius. It is very deep, surrounded by high banks covered with a thick forest. The first descent into Hades could be easily accomplished, says the poet Virgil, but no mortal is able to come back from it.

At the **portals**③ of Hades sits the fierce three-headed dog Cerberus, who keeps all living things from entering the gate, and allows no spirit that has once been admitted to pass out again. From here a long dark pathway leads deeper into the nether world, and is finally lost in the rivers that flow around Hades' throne. **Cocytus**④ is one of the five rivers in the infernal regions of the underworld, along with the rivers **Styx**⑤, **Lethe**⑥, **Phlegethon**⑦, and **Acheron**⑧. The waters of the river Cocytus are salt, as they are made of the tears that stream forever from the eyes of those **plaintive**⑨ souls who are condemned to labor in Tartarus, which part is the exclusive abode of the wicked. The Phlegethon River, a stream of fire, separates Tartarus from the rest of

---

① inexorable [ɪnˈeksərəbl] adj. 不可阻止的
② Avernus [əˈvɜːnəs] n. (Lake Avernus) 意大利阿佛纳斯湖（在神话中被描述为通往地下世界的入口）
③ portal [ˈpɔːtl] n. 壮观的大门
④ Cocytus [kəuˈsaitəs] n. 科赛特斯河（五条冥河中的痛泣之河）
⑤ Styx [ˈstɪks] n. 斯堤克斯（希腊神话中象征苦难、守誓、愤怒的冥河）
⑥ Lethe [ˈliːθi] n. 勒忒（五条冥河中的遗忘之河）
⑦ Phlegethon [ˈflegəθɒn] n. 佛勒革同河（五条冥河中的火河）
⑧ Acheron [ˈækəˌrɒn] n. 阿刻戎（五条冥河中的愁苦之河）
⑨ plaintive [ˈpleɪntɪv] adj. 哀伤的

Hades, and wretched indeed is the soul that is forced to cross its **seething**① waters. On the banks of the Acheron, the river of woe, black and turbid, stand the souls who come fresh from the sunlit earth; for all must pass this river and be brought before the judgment-throne of Hades. There is no bridge over the **murky**② stream, and the current is so swift that the boldest swimmer would not trust himself to its treacherous waters. The only way to cross is by the leaky, worm-eaten boat rowed by **Charon**③, an aged ferryman who has plied his oar ever since the day that the curse of death first came upon the earth.

No spirit is allowed to enter the leaky craft until he has first paid Charon the fee of a small coin called the **obolus**④ (the coin laid on the tongue of the dead before the body is committed for burial so that the soul may have no trouble in passing to the throne of Hades). If any spirits cannot furnish the necessary money, they are ruthlessly pushed aside by the **mercenary**⑤ boatman and are required to wait a hundred years. At the end of this time Charon grudgingly ferries them over the river free of charge. As the unstable boat can hold but few, there is always an eager group of spirits on the further bank, clamoring to be taken across the river; but Charon is never in a hurry.

There is also in Hades the river Styx, upon whose sacred waters the deities swear the most terrible oaths. On the other side of Hades's throne is the softly flowing Lethe, of which only those righteous and heroic souls can drink who would spend endless days of happiness in the Elysian Fields. As soon as they have tasted of the waters of Lethe, those blessed spirits would experience complete forgetfulness of all regrets, and joy and grief, and pleasure and pain of the life on earth. In the Elysian Fields there is no darkness which fills the rest of

---

① seething [ˈsiːðɪŋ] adj. 火热的
② murky [ˈmɜːki] adj. (尤指因浓雾而) 昏暗的
③ Charon [ˈkeərən] n. 卡戎 (希腊神话中的冥府渡神)
④ obolus [ˈɒbələs] n. 奥波勒斯 (圆货贝)
⑤ mercenary [ˈmɜːsənəri] adj. 唯利是图的

Hades with its thick gloom; but a soft light spreads over the meadows where the spirits of the thrice-blessed wander. There are willows here, and stately silver poplars, and the "meads of Asphodel" breathe out a faint perfume from their pale flowers. The sighs and groans that rise by night and day from the black abyss of Tartarus do not reach the ears of those who dwell at peace in the Elysian Fields, and the sight of its painful torments is hid forever from their eyes.

Beside Hades' throne sit the Three Fates or Moirai, the three sisters who hold the threads of life and death in their hands. **Clotho**①, the youngest, with huge shears in her hand, spins the thread of life, in which the bright and dark lines are intermingled; **Lachesis**② turns the wheel and measures its length; and **Atropos**③ cuts the string asunder when spun to a due length.

Hades and his queen Persephone are seated side by side on a **sable**④ throne, ruling over the myriad souls that compose the vast kingdom of the dead. Perched on the back of the throne is the blinking owl, who loves this eternal darkness, and the black-winged raven that was once a bird of snowy plumage and the favorite messenger of Apollo. The raven fell from his high estate on account of some unwelcome tidings that he once brought to Apollo when that god was an **ardent**⑤ lover of the fair-haired **Coronis**⑥. Believing that no one could supplant him in the maiden's affections, Apollo was happy in the thought of being beloved by so beautiful a mortal; but one day his snow-white raven flew in haste to Olympus, claiming that the maiden was listening to the wooing of another lover. Enraged at this duplicity, Apollo seized his bow and shot the faithless Coronis; but the moment that he saw her lying dead, he repented of his rash deed and banished the raven forever from his sight.

---

① Clotho [ˈkləʊθəʊ] n. 克洛索（命运之线的纺织者）
② Lachesis [ˈlækɪsɪs] n. 拉克西斯（主宰人类寿命）
③ Atropos [ˈætrəˌpɒs] n. 阿特罗波斯（负责剪断生命线）
④ sable [ˈseɪbl] adj. 黑色的
⑤ ardent [ˈɑːdnt] adj. 热心的
⑥ Coronis [ˈkɔrənis] n. 科洛尼斯（希腊神话中拉皮斯国王费烈基斯的女儿）

Near Hades' throne are seated the three judges of Hades, **Minos**①, **Rhadamanthus**②, and **Aeacus**③, who question all souls that are brought across the river. When they have learned every detail of the newcomer's past life, they deliver the cowering spirit into the judgment of **Themis**④, the blindfolded goddess of justice, who weighs impartially the good and bad deeds in her unerring scales. If the good outweighs the evil, the soul is led gently to the Elysian Fields; but if the bad overbalances the good, then the wretched spirit is driven to Tartarus, there to suffer for all its wrongdoings in the fires that burn permanently behind the brazen gates. To these gates the guilty one is urged by the three Furies, the **chthonic**⑤ goddesses of vengeance, whose snaky hair shakes hideously as they **ply**⑥ their lashes to **goad**⑦ the shrinking soul to its place of torment. Sometimes they are joined by Nemesis, goddess of revenge, who hurries the doomed spirit over the fiery waters of the Phlegethon with her merciless whip, and sees that it follows no path but the one leading to the brazen gates of Tartarus. ⑧

Questions for Discussion:

1. How did Hades become the king of the Underworld?

2. Who sits on guard before the gate of the Underworld?

3. How many rivers are there? What are they?

4. What do the spirits have to do if they cannot furnish the necessary money to Charon?

---

① Minos ['maɪnɒs] n. 迈诺斯（希腊神话中的克里特之王，冥府三判官之一）
② Rhadamanthus [ˌrædə'mænθəs] n. 拉达曼提斯（宙斯和欧罗巴之子，冥府三判官之一）
③ Aeacus ['iːəkəs] n. 爱考士（宙斯与埃癸娜之子，冥府三判官之一）
④ Themis ['θiːmis] n. 忒弥斯（希腊神话中十二提坦神之一，是象征法律和正义的规则女神）
⑤ chthonic ['θɒnɪk] adj. 神秘的
⑥ ply [plaɪ] vt. 使用
⑦ goad [ɡəʊd] vt. 用刺棒驱赶
⑧ Emilie Kip Baker, *Stories of Old Greece and Rome*, pp. 137 – 145.

5. What kind of place is Elysium?

6. What do the three Fates do?

7. Who are the three judges of Hades? What are their duties?

Hades and Persephone

When Zeus made himself the presiding deity of the universe, the ruler of heaven and earth, he imprisoned some of the warring giants under Mount Etna in Sicily, much to the disgust of Hades, who was always fearing that when the giants got restless and turned over and over underground (thus causing earthquakes) they would some day make such a large crack in the earth that daylight would be let into Hades. So Hades often went up out of his sunless land to look carefully over the island to be sure that no new fissure was being made in the earth's surface. One day, as he was driving his four coal-black horses through the vale of Enna, he saw a group of maidens gathering violets on the hillside; and among them was one so exquisitely fair that Hades determined to take her for his wife. This was Persephone, daughter of Demeter, the goddess of agriculture, a maiden who had ever **shunned**① the thought of marriage and preferred to spend her life playing games and dancing in the beautiful plain of Enna, where there was never any frost or snow, but springtime throughout the year.

Hades had often tried to chase his lady by gentle means, but no one would consent to share his grewsome home; so, knowing that this maiden he desired would never listen to honeyed words of love, he determined to take her by force. Driving his fiery horses at full speed, he rushed toward the group of laughing girls, who scattered and fled at his approach. Persephone alone stood still, and stared, frightened and wondering, at the grim figure confronting her, while the

---

① shun [ʃʌn] vt. (故意) 避开

flowers she had gathered dropped from her trembling hands. In a moment Hades had seized her in his strong arms; and, trampling all her violets under his ruthless feet, he sprang into the chariot and urged his horses to their full speed, hoping to reach Hades before the maiden's cries brought Demeter to the rescue.

As he neared the Cyane River, the waters, wishing to befriend Persephone, began to rise higher and higher, and with tossing waves opposing the madly-rushing **steeds**①. Fearing to risk the chariot in the angry waters, Hades struck the ground with his terrible two-pronged fork, and a great **chasm**② opened before him, into which the ruler of the inferno hurriedly plunged. Then the earth closed again over him and the captured maiden. During the dreadful moments when Persephone felt herself held a prisoner in the arms of this bold wooer, she called wildly to her mother for help; but soon she realized that her cries would never reach Demeter's ears, and that she must find some other way to let the goddess know of her tragical fate. So she summoned enough strength to struggle in her captor's embrace until she freed one arm from his hold, and with it loosened her girdle, which she flung into the Cyane River just before the yawning earth hid her completely, leaving no traces to tell where she had gone.

When Demeter came that evening into the vale of Enna and found that her daughter was not playing as usual with the other maidens, she questioned them, and learned their tearful story of the chariot with its four black horses. For days and days, she wandered, never stopping to rest except for a few hours at night when it was too dark for her to see her way. Rosy-fingered **Aurora**③, when she left her soft couch to open the gates of the morning, and **Hesperus**④, when he led out the stars at evening, saw her still searching for the lost Persephone. Sometimes she was so weary that she sank down by the roadside and let the night-

---

① steed [stiːd] n. 战马
② chasm [ˈkæzəm] n. 裂口
③ Aurora [ɔːˈrɔːrə] n. 奥罗拉（曙光女神）
④ Hesperus [ˈhespərəs] n. 赫斯珀洛斯（晚星之神）

dew **drench**① her aching limbs. Sometimes she rested under the trees when a storm broke over her head; but even here the rain beat down upon her, and the wind blew its cold breath in her face. Kindly people gave her food whenever she stopped to ask for it, and though none knew that she was a goddess, they sympathized with her grief when she told them that she was seeking her lost child. Only once did she meet with unkindness. She was sitting at a cottage door eating gruel from a bowl, and a lad—Stellio by name—laughed **insolently**② at her enjoyment of the meal. To punish him for his rudeness the goddess threw some of the gruel in his face, and immediately he was changed into a lizard.

One day Demeter found herself near the city of Eleusis, and to avoid being recognized as a goddess, she disguised herself as an old beggar woman. She sat for a long time on a stone by the roadside, mourning her lost Persephone, until a little girl came by, driving some goats. Seeing the old woman's tearful face, the child stopped to ask her trouble, but before Demeter could answer, the girl's father joined her and together they begged the stranger to come to their cottage for a rest. The goddess yielded at last to their kindly insistence, and as she walked beside the old man, whose name was Celeus, he told her that at home he had a sick boy who had lately grown so ill that today they believed he would surely die. Demeter listened to his pathetic story, and for a moment forgot her own grief. Seeing a chance to return the old man's kindness, she followed him into the cottage; but first stopped by the meadow to gather a handful of poppies. When the parents led her to the sick child's bedside, she stooped and kissed the pale little face which immediately became rosy with health. The boy sprang up well and strong again, to the great astonishment of his delighted family.

As they sat at the simple evening meal, the goddess put some poppy-juice in the glass of milk set out for the boy; and that night, when he was in a heavy

---

① drench [drentʃ] vt. 使湿透
② insolently [ˈɪnsəlntli] adv. 粗鲁地

sleep, she rubbed his body with oil, murmured over him a solemn charm, and was about to lay him on the red-hot ashes in the fire—that his mortal parts might be consumed and he himself be made immortal—when his mother chanced to enter the room, and springing forward with a cry of horror, snatched the boy from the fire. Before the excited mother could vent her wrath on the old woman, Demeter assumed her goddess form and quietly reproved the intruder; for her interference had not **averted**① a harm, but had prevented a great gift from being conferred upon the unconscious child.

When Demeter left the cottage of Celeus, she continued her wanderings over the earth, and finally returned, discouraged and heartbroken, to Sicily. Chancing to be near the river Cyane, she went down to the water's edge to drink, and accidentally discovered the girdle that Persephone had dropped there in her flight. This made her hopeful of finding further traces of her lost daughter, so she lingered by the river bank, eagerly scanning the overflowing stream. As she stood there some strange voice came; and soon she found that the soft tones proceeded from a fountain which was so close to her that its lightly-tossed spray fell on her hand. The murmur was often indistinct, but Demeter understood enough to realize that the words were addressed to her, and that the fountain was trying to tell her how Hades had come up from the Underworld and carried off Persephone to be his wife.

While the goddess was musing over this painful revelation, the fountain went on to say that it had not always been a stream in sunny Sicily, but was once a maiden named **Arethusa**② and a native of the country of Elis. As a follower of Diana she had roamed the wooded hills; and one day, being wearied from the chase, she sought refreshment in the forest stream. The drooping willows hung protectingly over the water, and here the nymph bathed fearlessly, believing

---

① avert [əˈvɜːt] vt. 防止
② Arethusa [ˌæriˈθjuːzə] n. 阿瑞图萨（希腊神话中的泉水女神）

herself alone. But **Alpheus**①, the river-god, heard the splashing of the water, and rose from his grassy bed to see who was disturbing his noon-day rest. At the sight of Arethusa, he was so delighted that he ventured to approach her but she fled terrified through the forest, calling on Diana for help. The goddess, hearing her cries, changed her into a fountain; and to further baffle the pursuing Alpheus, she wrapped it in a thick mist. As the river-god could no longer see the nymph, he was about to give up the chase, when Zephyrus maliciously blew away the cloud, and Alpheus saw the bubbling fountain. Suspecting that this was Arethusa, the god changed himself into a rushing torrent, and was preparing to mingle his impetuous waves with the waters of the fountain, when the nymph again prayed to Diana for protection. The goddess came to her rescue by opening a **crevice**② in the earth, and here the shivering waters of the fountain found a speedy refuge. To keep far out of the reach of Alpheus it continued to flow underground for many miles, and even crept beneath the sea until it reached Sicily, where Diana again cleft the earth and allowed the fountain to come up into the sunlight. During her journey through the dark underworld, Arethusa said that she had seen Persephone sitting, tearful and rueful, on a throne beside the grim ruler of the dead.

When she heard this story, Demeter was no longer in doubt where her daughter could be found; but the knowledge gave her little comfort, for she was aware how useless it would be to ask Hades to give up the wife he had so daringly won. Seeing no hope of regaining her child, Demeter retired to a cave in the hills, and paid no heed to the waiting earth that had suffered so long from her neglect. The land was drought-stricken: the crops were failing for want of water; the fruit trees were drying up; the flowers were withering on the parched hillsides. Everything cried out for the protecting care of Demeter, who,

---

① Alpheus [æl'fiːəs] n. 阿尔斐俄斯（希腊神话中的河神）
② crevice ['krevis] n. 裂缝

however, stayed her hand, and in the solitude of the cave mourned unceasingly for Persephone. Famine spread over the land immediately, but the people, in spite of their **dire**① need of food, burned sacrifices of sheep and oxen on the altars of Demeter, while they **importuned**② her with their prayers. Zeus heard their cries and besought the goddess to take the earth again under her wise care; but Demeter refused to listen, for she was indifferent now to the welfare of men, and no longer delighted in the ripening harvest.

When sickness and death followed hard upon the famine, Zeus saw that he must save the sorely-stricken land, so he promised the goddess that her daughter should be restored to her if she had eaten nothing during all her sojourn in Hades' realm. Hermes, the herald of the gods, was sent to lead Persephone out of the Underworld. When Hermes met Hades, the wily monarch consented; but, alas! the maiden had taken a pomegranate which Hades offered her, and had sucked the sweet pulp from a few of the seeds. This was enough to prevent her complete release. Demeter was about to shut herself up again in the cave, when Zeus, in behalf of the suffering earth, made a compromise with Hades whereby Persephone was to spend half her time with her mother in the land of sunshine and flowers, and the rest with her husband in cold and cheerless Hades. Each spring Hermes was sent to lead Persephone up from the underworld lest her eyes, grown accustomed only to shadows, should be dazzled by the blinding sunlight, and she herself should lose the way. All things awaited her coming; and as soon as her foot touched the winter-saddened earth the flowers bloomed to delight her eyes, the grass sprang up to carpet her way with greenness, the birds sang to cheer her long-depressed spirit, and above her the sun shone brilliantly in the blue Sicilian sky.

Demeter no longer mourned, nor did she again let the great famine cast a

---

① dire ['daɪə] adj. 紧急的
② importune [ˌɪmpɔː'tjuːn] vt. 再三要求

shadow over the land. The patient old earth smiled again on Persephone's return, for then her mother gave the **blighted**① vegetation a redoubled care. But happiness did not make the goddess forget the kindly old man who had given her food at Eleusis, for she returned there and taught the boy **Triptolemus**② all the secrets of agriculture. She also gave him her chariot, and bade him journey everywhere, teaching the people how to plow and sow and reap, and care for their harvests. Triptolemus carried out all her instructions; and as he traveled over the country he was eagerly welcomed alike by prince and peasant until he came to Scythia, where the cruel King Lyncus would have killed him, in a fit of jealous wrath, had not Demeter interfered with timely aid and changed the treacherous monarch into a **lynx**③. ④

Questions for Discussion:

1. What happened to the giants after being defeated?

2. How did Hades get Persephone?

3. What did Demeter do after losing her daughter?

4. How did Zeus deal with this matter?

5. What prevented Persephone's complete release from the Underworld?

6. Why and how did Demeter help Triptolemus?

7. What did Demeter do to Stellio?

8. How is the story of Persephone related to spring?

The Story of Orpheus and Eurydice

The most illustrious of all musicians, except the one who played in the

---

① blighted ['blaɪtɪd] adj. 枯萎的
② Triptolemus [trɪp'tɔlɪməs] n. 特里普托勒摩斯（希腊神话中得墨忒尔女神最早的祭司）
③ lynx [lɪŋks] n. 山猫
④ Emilie Kip Baker, *Stories of Old Greece and Rome*, pp. 127-136.

shining halls of Olympus, was Orpheus, son of Apollo and of the muse Calliope. When he was a mere child, his father gave him a lyre and taught him to play upon it; but Orpheus needed very little instruction, for he was endowed with the ability to charm all living things and even stones with his music. As soon as he laid his hand upon the strings the wild beasts crept out of their lairs to crouch beside him; even trees and rocks moved about him in dance.

When Orpheus sought the marriage to the golden-haired Eurydice, there were other suitors for her hand, but though they brought rich gifts gathered out of many lands, they could not win the maiden's love, and she turned from them to bestow her hand upon Orpheus, who had no way to woo her but with his music. On the wedding day there was the usual mirth and feasting, but one event occurred that cast a gloom over the happiness of the newly-married pair. When **Hymen**①, god of marriage, came with his torch to bless the nuptial feast, the light that should have burned clear and pure began to smoke ominously, as if predicting future disaster.

This evil omen was fulfilled all too soon, for one day when Eurydice was walking in the meadow, she met the youth Aristaeus, who was so charmed with her beauty that he insisted upon staying beside her to pour his ardent speeches into her unwilling ears. To escape from these troublesome attentions, Eurydice started to run away, and as she ran she stepped on a poisonous snake, which quickly turned and bit her. She had barely time to reach her home before the poison had done its work, and Orpheus heard the sad story from her dying lips. As soon as Hermes had led away the soul of Eurydice, the bereaved husband hastened to the shining halls of Olympus, and throwing himself down before Zeus's golden throne, he implored that great ruler of gods and men to give him back his wife. There was always pity in the hearts of the gods for those who

---

① Hymen ['haɪmən] n. 许门（希腊神话中的婚姻之神）

perish in flowering time, so Zeus gave permission to Orpheus to go down into the land of the dead, and beg of Hades the **boon**① he craved.

It was a steep and perilous journey to the kingdom of the dead, and the road was one that no mortal foot had ever trod; but through his love for Eurydice, Orpheus forgot the dangers of the way, and when he spoke her name, the terrors of the darkness vanished. In his hand he held his lyre, and when he arrived at the gate of Hades, where the fierce three-headed dog Cerberus refused to let him pass, Orpheus stood still in the uncertain darkness and began to play. And as he played the snarling of the dog ceased and the noise of its harsh breathing grew faint. Then Orpheus went on his way undisturbed, but still he played softly on his lyre, and the sounds floated far into the **dismal**② interior of Hades, where the souls of the condemned labored forever at their tasks. Upon hearing the music, Tantalus ceased to strive for a drop of the forbidden water; Ixion rested a moment beside his ever-revolving wheel; and Sisyphus stopped the eternal labor of rolling the rock which hereupon fell from his wearied arms; the daughters of Danaus laid down their urns beside the sieve into which they were forever pouring water. As the mournful wailing of Orpheus's lyre told the story of his lost love, they wept then for a sorrow not their own. So plaintive, indeed, was the music, that all the shadowy forms that flitted endlessly by shed tears of sympathy for the player's grief, and even the cheeks of the Furies were wet.

When Orpheus came before the throne of Hades, that relentless monarch repulsed him angrily as he attempted to plead his cause, and commanded him to depart. Then the son of Apollo began to play upon his lyre, and through his music he told the story of his loss, and besought the ruler of these myriad souls to give him back the single one he craved. So wonderfully did Orpheus play that

---

① boon [buːn] n. 福音
② dismal [ˈdɪzməl] adj. 阴沉的

the hard heart of Hades was touched with pity, and he granted Orpheus's plea but on one condition: upon leaving the Underworld, he must not turn around to see if Eurydice was following behind him. If he did, she would return to the land of the dead forever. Orpheus gladly promised obedience; so Eurydice was summoned from among the million shadow-shapes that thronged the silent halls of death. Hades told her the condition on which her freedom was to be won, and then bade her follow her husband.

During all the wearisome journey back to earth, Orpheus never forgot the promise he had made, though he often longed to give just a hurried glance at the face of Eurydice to see whether it had lost its sadness. As they neared the spot where the first faint glimmerings of light filtered down into the impenetrable darkness, Orpheus thought he heard his wife calling, and he looked quickly around to find whether she was still following him. In a twinkling the slight form close behind him began to fade away, and a mournful voice—seemingly far in the distance—called to him a sad farewell. Afterwards Charon, the grim ferryman, took him across the river. So he went forlornly back to earth and lived in a forest cave far from the companionship of men. At first there was only his lyre to share his solitude, but soon the forest creatures came to live beside him, and often sat listening to his music, looking exceedingly wise and sorrowful. Even in his sleepless hours, when he fancied he heard Eurydice calling, he was never quite alone, for the bat and owl and the things that love the darkness flitted about him, and he saw the glow-worms creep toward him out of the night-cold grass.

One day a party of **Bacchantes**[①] found him seated outside the cave, playing the mournful music that told of his lost love, and they bade him change the sad

---

① bacchante [bəˈkænti] n. 巴克坎特斯（酒神巴克斯的女祭司）

notes to something gay so that they might dance. But Orpheus, too wrapped up in his sorrow to play any strain of cheerful music, refused to do as they asked. The Bacchantes, who were half maddened by their festival days of drinking, became so enraged by the refusal that they fell upon the luckless musician and tore him to pieces. Then they threw his mangled body into the river, and as the head of Orpheus drifted down the stream, his lips murmured again and again "Eurydice," until the hills echoed the beloved name, and the rocks and trees and rivers repeated it in mournful chorus. Later on, the Muses gathered up his remains to give them honorable burial; and it is said that over Orpheus's grave the nightingale sings more sweetly than in any other spot in Greece. [1]

Questions for Discussion:

1. How did Orpheus woo Eurydice?

2. What happened to Eurydice?

3. Whom did Orpheus implore first?

4. How did Orpheus manage to meet Hades?

5. What promise did Orpheus make to Hades?

6. How did Orpheus die?

Part 3　Reflections

1. **Vocabulary Expansion**

1) the 18 levels of hell: _____

2) Zhong Kui: _____

---

[1] Emilie Kip Baker, *Stories of Old Greece and Rome*, pp. 109 – 114.

3）Pan Guan：_____

4）Ox-Head and Horse-Face：_____

5）Tartarus：_____

6）Acheron：_____

7）Styx：_____

8）Elysium：_____

9）Persephone：_____

2. **Appreciation**

1）北海之内，有山，名曰幽都之山，黑水出焉。其上有玄鸟、玄蛇、玄豹、玄虎、玄狐蓬尾。有大玄之山。有玄丘之民。有大幽之国。有赤胫之民。

《山海经·海内经》

2）魂兮归来，

君无下此幽都些！

土伯九约，

其角觺觺些。

敦脄血拇，

逐人驱驱些。

参目虎首，

其身若牛些。

此皆甘人。

归来兮，

恐自遗灾些。

《楚辞·招魂》

3）佛告比丘：此四天下有八千天下围绕其外。复有大海水、周匝围绕八千天下。复有大金刚山绕大海水。金刚出外复有第二大金刚山，二山中间窈窈冥冥；日月神天有大威力，不能以光照及于彼。彼有八大地狱，其一地狱有十六小地狱。第一大地狱名想。第二名黑绳。第三名堆压。第四名叫唤。第五名大叫唤。第六名烧炙。第七名大烧炙。第八名无间。

《长阿含经》

4）妙庄王有三女，长妙音，次妙缘，三妙善，妙善即观音大士。王令赘婿不从，逐之御花园，居之白雀寺，苦以搬运，极所不堪，旁役鬼力代之。王怒，命焚白雀寺，寺僧俱毁于焰，大士无恙如初。命斩之，刀三折；命缢以白练，忽黑风遮天，一白虎背之去。至尸多林，青衣童侍立，遂历地府，过奈河桥，救诸苦难。还魂再至尸多林，遇一耆硕，指香山修行。后，庄王病急，剜目断臂救之，尔时道成。空中现千手眼，故曰：南无大慈大悲救苦救难灵广大感观世音菩萨。

《搜神记》

5) And now with homeward footstep he had passed

　　All perils scathless, and, at length restored,

　　Eurydice to realms of upper air

　　Had well-nigh won, behind him following—

　　So Proserpine had ruled it—when his heart

　　A sudden mad desire surprised and seized—

　　Meet fault to be forgiven, might Hell forgive.

　　For at the very threshold of the day,

　　Heedless, alas! and vanquished of resolve,

　　He stopped, turned, looked upon Eurydice

　　His own once more. But even with the look,

　　Poured out was all his labor, broken the bond

　　Of that fell tyrant, and a crash was heard

　　Three times like thunder in the meres of hell.

　　"Orpheus! what ruin hath thy frenzy wrought

　　On me, alas! and thee? Lo! once again

The unpitying fates recall me, and dark sleep

Closes my swimming eyes. And now farewell:

Girt with enormous night I am borne away,

Outstretching toward thee, thine, alas! no more,

These helpless hands." She spake, and suddenly,

Like smoke dissolving into empty air,

Passed and was sundered from his sight; nor him

Clutching vain shadows, yearning sore to speak,

Thenceforth beheld she, nor no second time

Hell's boatman brooks he pass the watery bar.

Virgil's The Georgics

3. Discussion

1) Draw a conclusion of the differences and similarities between Chinese and Greek myths of the Underworld.

2) Make a comparison of the death views in Chinese and western culture.

Unit 9

Gods of Love

Introduction

Love is central to many ancient myths, as it is generally described as an extremely powerful force that can help gods and mortals to overcome various hardships, find peace of mind, settle down, and live happily with their loved ones. Beauty (or attractiveness), **procreation**①, mystery, and even death are marked **attributes**② associated with deities of love, who have been depicted in mythologies in almost every culture. These myths mirror different views on love, romance, marriage, beauty and sexuality in different cultures.

Stories related to gods and goddesses of love abound in Chinese mythology. For example, Fuxi and Nüwa are considered as gods of marriage and worshipped by people who long for a desired match. Using a red string, Yue Lao (literally the Old Man under the Moon), the god of marriage and love, binds together men and women who are predestined to be in wedlock. As his legend shows, attempts to deny or undo these bonds are futile and could only lead to tragedy. Chuang Mu, goddess of the bedchamber, looks after sleep, sex, love and childbirth. The legend of the Cowherd and the Weaving Maiden sets a holiday called the Double Seventh Festival, also known as the Chinese Valentine's Day,

---

① procreation [ˌprəʊkriˈeɪʃn] n. 生殖
② attribute [əˈtrɪbjuːt] n. 特质

on which single women would pray to the celestial couple in hopes to find a good spouse, and newly married women would wish to bear a baby. Another god of marriage was Chang'e, a goddess living in the moon, whose story of flying to the moon lends a romantic glamour to the ancient worship.

In Greek mythology, there are multiple gods that are meant to induce desire and cause the creation of other gods. The main two are Eros and Aphrodite. Eros appears in ancient Greek sources under several different guises. In the early records, he is a primeval deity who embodies not only the force of love but also the creative urge of ever-flowing nature, the firstborn Light for the coming into being and ordering of all things in the cosmos. In Hesiod's *Theogony*, Eros springs forth from the **primordial**① Chaos together with Gaia, the Earth, and Tartarus, the underworld. In some other sources, Eros is also one of Aphrodite's offspring. He is often a companion or intermediary for the goddess, but he doesn't always act with her blessing, and is frequently portrayed as a troublesome child. If Eros embodies mindless desire, or sex without passion or romance, Aphrodite, born from the white foam produced by the severed genitals of the primordial god Uranus, or the daughter of Zeus and a sea-nymph Dione, represents not only sexual desire, but also the concept of courtship, wherewith people would grow to adore each other based on more than simply their appearances. As well as intervening in the lives of mortals, Aphrodite has numerous affairs amongst the gods. She is married to **Hephaestus**②, the god of fire, blacksmiths and metalworking, but is famously caught in the act of adultery with Ares, the god of war. Other divine lovers of hers include Dionysus and Hermes, from whom she has given birth to the fertility deities **Priapus**③ and

---

① primordial [praɪˈmɔːdiəl] adj. 原始的
② Hephaestus [hiˈfiːstəs] n. 赫菲斯托斯（宙斯与赫拉之子，诸神中唯一丑陋者，但妻子却是爱与美之神阿佛洛狄忒，是火与锻造之神、铁匠和织布工的保护神）
③ Priapus [praɪˈeipəs] n. 普利阿普斯，男性生殖神（酒神和爱神之子）

Hermaphroditus[①], respectively.

Part 1　Gods of Love in Chinese Mythology

Nüwa's Wedlock with Her Brother in the First Marriage

Nüwa has been placed first in Chinese mythology because the goddess originally belonged to the pantheon of primeval deities as **creatrix**[②] and savior of the world. But in this text, which is late in the mythographic tradition, she does not appear in her earlier **emanation**[③]. The reading serves to show how a classical myth is reworked to convey new values and is thus subverted. The author **Li Rong**[④] in the Tang Dynasty (846 A. D. − 874 A. D.) has eliminated the two main functions of the goddess and has humanized her, **relegating**[⑤] her to a conventionally subordinate female role subject to a higher god with diminished divinity and mythic power.

In his mythopoeic passage, Li Rong presents an etiological myth of the institution of marriage. The sentence "there were two people, Nüwa, older brother and sister," is so **recondite**[⑥] that it deviates from the reworking of old mythic material. Some scholars interpret it to mean that "Nü" is the sister, "wa" the brother. The same odd construction occurs in the narrative of Woman Chou: "There are two people in the sea. Her name is Woman Chou." Leaving

---

① Hermaphroditus [həˌmæfrəˈdaɪtəs] n. 赫马佛洛狄忒斯（希腊神话中的阴阳神）
② creatrix [kriːˈeɪtrɪs] n. 女创作者（等于 creatress）
③ emanation [ˌeməˈneɪʃn] n. （神的）显灵
④ 李冗，又作李亢、李元、李尤，唐代作家，著有《独异志》，原书十卷，现存三卷，撰有从上古三皇五帝至隋唐时期的各种志人志怪故事，编者注。
⑤ relegate [ˈrelɪgeɪt] vt. 使降级
⑥ recondite [ˈrekəndaɪt] adj. 深奥的

aside the question of the name or names, the narrative relates how the brother and sister invoked God to **sanction**① their union and how permission was granted for what was the first marriage among humans.

There are various versions of the origin myth of Fuxi and Nüwa. One version states that they were the first two human beings who appeared when Pangu created the world, while another states that they were the two sole survivors after a great flood that destroyed humanity. In yet another account, Fuxi and Nüwa were the children of little-known goddess, **Huaxu**②, who became pregnant after stepping on the footprint of the thunder god. The most popular version records that Nüwa and Fuxi were children of the Jade Emperor and lived by themselves before any other men or gods were created. It was this lonely existence that led Nüwa to eventually create mankind. Although they were brother and sister, Nüwa and Fuxi began to develop feelings for one another. Fearing that such an attraction would not be allowed, they asked for a sign to determine whether or not they would be allowed to marry. Finally, their marriage was permitted because they were among the only beings in creation. Like Adam and Eve, the first couple, who covered their nakedness with a fig leaf, the brother and sister felt ashamed of their sexual difference after **carnal**③ knowledge of each other and hid behind a fan. Later, holding a fan in such a manner became a tradition for Chinese brides. The following is an excerpt from Li Rong's work:

> Long ago, when the world first began, there were two people, Nüwa and her older brother. They lived on Mount Kunlun. And there were not yet any ordinary people in the world. They talked about

---

① sanction ['sæŋkʃn] vt. 准许
② 华胥是中国上古时期母系氏族社会杰出的部落女首领，相传她踩雷神脚印，感应受孕，生伏羲和女娲，传嗣炎帝黄帝，从而成为中华民族的始祖母。编者注。
③ carnal ['kɑːnl] adj. 肉体的

becoming husband and wife, but they felt ashamed. So the brother at once went with his sister up Mount Kunlun and made this prayer: "Oh Heaven, if thou wouldst send us two forth to become man and wife, then make all the misty vapor gather; if not, then make all the misty vapor disperse." At this, the misty vapor immediately gathered. When the sister became intimate with her brother, they **plaited**[①] some grass to make a fan to screen their faces. Even today, when a man takes a wife, they hold a fan, which is a symbol of what happened long ago. (*Du Yi Zhi*)

Nüwa and Fuxi's marriage was the first of its kind in Chinese history. It not only established Nüwa as the goddess of marriage and brides, but also set the precedence that marriages were arranged by divine decree rather than personal preference.[②]

Questions for Discussion:

1. What mortification did Li Rong, the author in the Tang Dynasty, make to the story of Nüwa?

2. How did scholars explain the name of Nüwa?

3. How did Nüwa and Fuxi get to know the god's idea?

4. Why did Nüwa and Fuxi screen their faces?

God of Matchmaking and Marriage—Yue Lao

Depicted as an old, greying man in long and colorful robes, Yue Lao was

---

① plait [pleɪt] vt. 编织
② Anne Birrell, *Chinese Mythology: An Introduction*, pp. 203 – 204.

called "the Old Man under the Moon." According to the myth, he was believed to live either in the moon or in Yue Ming, the obscure regions associated with the underworld.

Whatever his dwelling place is, Yue Lao is immortal as a god should be, and his main focus is finding the perfect marriage matches for people. He is often found sitting on the ground in the moonlight, reading books and playing with his bag of silk threads.

The legend of Yue Lao takes shape during the Tang Dynasty between the 7th and 10th century A.D. In it, a young man by the name of Wei Gu encountered Yue Lao as he was sitting in the moonlight, reading a book. Wei Gu asked the old man what he was doing and the god told him: "I am reading a book of marriage listing for who is going to marry whom. In my pack are red cords for tying the lot of husband and wife." But Wei Gu doubted the old man's story. They then walked together, however, until they came to the local marketplace. When an old blind woman passed by with a three-year-old girl in her arms, Yue Lao pointed to the child and claimed that she was Wei Gu's future wife. Wei Gu still didn't believe that the old man was a god and refused to believe that he was fated to marry the child of a blind woman. Therefore, in an effort to **thwart**① the prophecy, he ordered his servant to stab the little girl with his knife.

Fourteen years later, Wei Gu was ready to marry. He made a good match with the daughter of Wang Tai, the governor of Xiangzhou, but could not understand why the young lady had not been promised to anyone before. The governor explained that his daughter was beautiful but had difficulties walking as well as a scar on her back. When Wei Gu asked her what had caused these injuries, he learned that his future bride had been stabbed by an unknown man when she was just three years old.

---

① thwart [θwɔːt] vt. 阻挠

Wei Gu married her nevertheless and the two lived a happy life and had three children. Knowing Yue Lao's power, Wei Gu sought him out to arrange suitable matches for his two sons and daughter years later. However, Yue Lao refused to make matches for his children because he still remembered the man's lack of faith and cruelty in his youth. Hence the man's bloodline ended as neither of his three children ever married.

Since then, people begin to worship Yue Lao as the God of Marriage. When Yue Lao ties a red string to a couple, regardless of them being **archenemies**[①], in times of riches, poverty or how far both are away from each other, they will by all means be husband and wife. Hence comes into being the Chinese saying, "marriage of a thousand miles bonded by a string."

Today, this red string legend still stands, tying lovestruck couples who hope to enjoy everlasting love and a meaningful marriage. As for married couples, they can also pray to Yue Lao for marital happiness. If a marriage is going through rough patches, praying to Yue Lao will bring fortune and **amicability**[②] to the family.[③]

Questions for Discussion:

1. How did Yue Lao arrange matches?

2. What did Wei Gu do to thwart the prophecy of Yue Lao?

3. What do people worship Yue Lao for?

The Cowherd and the Weaving Maiden

The story of the cowherd and the weaving maiden is narrated in *The Book of*

---

① archenemy [ˌɑːtʃˈenəmi] n. 死敌
② amicability [ˌæmɪkəˈbɪləti] n. 友善
③ https://mythologysource.com/yue-lao-chinese-god/

Songs, or *The Classic of Poetry*, poem 10 of the "Nineteen Ancient Poems" of the Han era and ***Er Ya Yi***① in the Song Dynasty. The story goes like this:

Once upon a time there lived a poor cowherd. His parents had died and he lived with his brother and sister-in-law, the only relatives that were left of him. But they were cruel to him and one day drove him out of the house. A farmer took pity on the homeless boy, and offered him a daily meal and a bed of straw in the **cowshed**②. In return, the boy would look after the farmer's old ox. From then on, the boy spent his days and nights with the animal. In fact, the beast was his only companion. Despite his great age, the ox was a handsome creature. His golden hair shone in the moonlight. The boy knew in his heart that his friend had something heavenly about him.

One day, when they were out on the hills, the Ox turned his great head to the boy and spoke to him clearly in an almost human voice.

"Boy," he **lowed**③, "You are my friend and have looked after me faithfully. Now I am old, and soon I will die. My time on earth is done. I will return to my place in the heavens where I am the chief star in the constellation of the Ox. Before I go, I wish to see you married."

The poor lad did not know how to reply. He knew not a single girl, let alone one that would marry him. The Ox saw how perplexed he looked, and said, "Listen carefully to me, for this is what you must do. Today is the seventh of the month. This very night, the seven weaving maidens of the skies will float down to the river to take a bath. You will see their clothes by the bank.

---

① 《尔雅翼》，南宋解释名物的训诂著作，宋罗愿著。共有三十二卷，成书于宋淳熙元年（公元1174年），但到咸淳六年（公元1270年）王应麟守徽州时，才得以刻版行世。元代延祐七年（公元1320年），歙人洪炎祖为作音释，附于每卷之后。此书仿《尔雅》，分释草、释木、释鸟、释兽、释虫与释鱼六类。作者观察实物细致，描写生动活泼又具有科学性，其体例严谨，考据精博，较有价值。有《学津讨原》《格致丛书》《丛书集成》等版本，编者注。

② cowshed ['kauʃed] n. 牛棚

③ low [ləu] vi. (牛) 哞哞叫

The seventh daughter wears robes of red. Sneak down quietly to the bank and steal her clothes. In this way, you will get to know her, for she will call out and demand the return of the robes."

The boy sighed, for the river was far away on the other side of the mountain. He would not be able to reach its banks before nightfall. The celestial Ox again saw that the boy was at a loss—but he had an answer for this problem too. He told the cowherd to climb on his back. Then off they flew through the skies to the river.

When they arrived, the boy stepped down from his friend's back, and swiftly hid behind a jade tree. Towards midnight, he heard splashing and giggling. So he peeped around the tree and saw the maidens swimming and playing in the water. While they were having fun, he crawled stealthily forward and **pinched**① the red robe of the seventh daughter of the skies.

When the weaving maidens had finished washing and frolicking, they came out onto the bank. But where were the red robes of the seventh daughter of the skies? They knew right away that somebody must have stolen them. The girl without clothes hid behind a bush to cover her modesty. Her sisters called, "Come out whoever you are. It is not wise to play **pranks**② on the immortals. Our father is the Great Jade Emperor, the ruler of all Heaven. He knows how to punish naughty human folk."

The boy saw the funny side of the situation and felt bold. He stepped forward, holding the red robes before his eyes. He called out, "Lovely maiden, Seventh Daughter of the Skies, promise to be my wife and I will return these clothes to you."

It was such a **cheeky**③ proposal that the weaving maidens could not help but

---

① pinch [pɪntʃ] vt. <非正式> 偷窃
② prank [præŋk] n. 恶作剧
③ cheeky [ˈtʃiːki] adj. 厚脸皮的

laugh. The seventh daughter who was hiding behind the bush was furious—but in a way, she was impressed too by this brazen boy. She had to admit, he was not bad looking, for a human. There was something about him.

Her eldest sister said, "Listen to the lad. You are not able to fly away without your robes. If you do not agree to his demand, we must leave you here."

"Throw the robes over here and I will think about it," said the maiden from behind the bush.

The boy threw the robes. "Now will you marry me?" He demanded.

"I'll let you know," she replied.

Her sisters gasped and giggled. "Don't miss your chance," said the eldest. "I bet a good-looking lad like him has plenty of offers. It's not every day that a maiden of the skies gets a proposal. Think about it. How often does a man want to marry a cloud?" So the maiden, now fully clothed in her red robes, stepped out from the bush. She held out her lovely hand. The boy knelt and kissed it. She agreed to be his wife.

Her sisters flew away to the skies where they continued as usual to **flit**[①] across the heavens in the form of fluffy clouds. By contrast, the lovely seventh maiden lived on earth with the cowherd. She took the shape of a most beautiful woman. On her arrival, the boy's fortunes prospered. The farmer adopted him as his son and gave him a wedding gift of land and livestock. His mean brother and sister-in-law could only look on enviously at his prosperity. The cowherd lived happily with his heavenly wife, and three years later they had twins—a beautiful boy and girl. The only sadness in their lives was that the dear old Ox had passed away. They had a comfort in that they could look up at the sky and see him twinkling in the sky at night.

---

① flit [flɪt] vi. 轻快地飞

Up in the heavens, the passing of three years is like three days to the gods. The heavenly mother began to notice that the dawn and the evening clouds had lost their rosy tint. She realized that the seventh weaving maiden of the red robes had gone missing. She scanned the earth with her all-seeing eye, and spotted the happy couple living in a humble **hovel**①.

"That is not fit for a divine maiden!" She shouted. The whole sky was then filled with a terrible thunder storm. Mad with fury, she sent her heavenly soldiers to the farmhouse. They delivered the queen's message to her daughter. She must return to the skies, or would face the destruction of her family and children. With great sadness, she had no choice but to go back to heaven. The soldiers escorted her, leaving her wailing children and husband behind.

For the first time since the night at the river, the cowherd was in despair and did not know what to do. He looked up into the heavens and saw the twinkling star of his friend the ox. Then he remembered that when the mortal form of the ox had died, he had kept his hide. He took the ox skin down from the wall, and spread it out on the floor like a carpet. When he sat down on it, the hide began to fly, lifting him up to the heavens and sweeping him away to the palace of the Great Jade Emperor who dominated all heaven and earth. There he found himself in front of the throne of the heavenly mother.

The cowherd fell down on his knees and prayed, "Oh, Queen of heaven, I have come to **reclaim**② my wife. I married her lawfully and she must live with me as long as she loves me as I love her."

But the queen flew into a fury. "How dare you, a mere mortal, a cowherd to boot, marry my daughter through trickery, and then follow us up to heaven and make your **insolent**③ demand!"

---

① hovel ['hɒvl] n. 茅舍
② reclaim [rɪ'kleɪm] vt. 要求归还
③ insolent ['ɪnsələnt] adj. 无礼的

The boy trembled, thinking that his last moment had come. The queen reached up to her headdress, and pulled out a silver hairpin. She cast it across the heavens. It scattered silver across the skies, spreading **stardust**① in its wake, forming the Silver River, or the Milky Way. Now the cowherd and the seventh weaving maiden stood on either side of the river and gazed all year long at each other. The hard heart of the queen of heaven **relented**② and she agreed to let them reunite on the Milky Way on the seventh day of the seventh lunar month (the Double Seventh Festival) once a year. On that day, the magpies gathered to build a bridge, stretching over the Milky Way, where the Cowherd family could enjoy the transient reunion time. ③

In the course of time, July the seventh day of lunar calendar has evolved into the Chinese Valentine's Day, becoming the most romantic traditional festival in China. On that day single women would pray to the celestial couple in hopes to find a good spouse, and newly married women would wish to bear a baby.

Questions for Discussion:

1. What was the identity of the ox?

2. What did the ox ask the cowherd to do?

3. How was the life of the cowherd and the weaving maiden as a couple?

4. How did the heavenly mother find that the weaving maiden had gone missing?

5. How did the heavenly mother separate the cowherd and the weaving maiden?

6. How could the cowherd and the weaving maiden reunite?

---

① stardust ['stɑːdʌst] n. 星尘
② relent [rɪ'lent] vi. 变温和
③ https://www.storynory.com/the-cowherd-and-the-weaving-maid/

Part 2　Gods of Love in Greek Mythology

The Story of Aphrodite

In Greek mythology, Aphrodite is worshipped as goddess of fertility, love, and beauty. Referring to aphrós (ἀφρός) (meaning "sea-foam") as the etymology of "Aphrodite," Hesiod depicts in *Theogony* that she was born off the coast of **Cythera**① from the foam where Uranus' genitals had fallen after he had been mutilated by Cronus. Homer regarded her as the daughter of Zeus and **Dione**②. Dione, being a sea-nymph, gave birth to her daughter beneath the waves; but the child of the heaven-inhabiting Zeus was forced to ascend from the ocean-depths and mount to the snow-capped summits of Olympus for that **ethereal**③ and most **refined**④ atmosphere which **pertains**⑤ to the celestial gods.

Aphrodite was the mother of Eros (Cupid), the god of Love, and also of Aeneas, the great Trojan hero and the head of that Greek colony which settled in Italy, and from which arose the city of Rome. As a mother Aphrodite claims our sympathy for the tenderness she exhibited towards her children. Homer in *The Iliad* relates how, when Aeneas was wounded in battle, she came to his assistance disregarding her personal safety, and was herself severely wounded in attempting to save his life.

Aphrodite possessed a magic **girdle**⑥ which she frequently lent to unhappy

---

① Cythera [sə'θɪrə] n. 塞西拉岛（希腊南部岛屿）
② Dione [daɪ'əuni] n. 狄俄涅（提坦女神之一，掌管洋流）
③ ethereal [ɪ'θɪərɪəl] adj. 超凡的
④ refined [rɪ'faɪnd] adj. 纯净的的
⑤ pertain [pə'teɪn] vi. (pertain to) 从属于
⑥ girdle ['ɡɜːdl] n. 腰带

maidens suffering from the pangs of **unrequited**① love, as it was endowed with the power of inspiring affection for the wearer, whom it invested with every attribute of grace, beauty, and fascination.

Her usual attendants were the Graces (Euphrosyne, Aglaia, and Thalia), who were represented **undraped**② and intertwined in a loving embrace.

In Hesiod's *Theogony* Aphrodite is supposed to belong to the more ancient divinities, and, whilst those of later date are represented as having descended one from another, and all more or less from Zeus, Aphrodite has a variously-accounted-for, yet independent origin. The most poetical version of her birth is that when Uranus was wounded by his son Cronus, his blood mingled with the foam of the sea, whereupon the bubbling waters at once assumed a rosy tint, and from their depths arose, in all the surpassing glory of her loveliness, Aphrodite, goddess of love and beauty! As she shook her long, fair tresses, the water-drops rolled down into the beautiful sea-shell in which she stood, and became transformed into pure glistening pearls. **Wafted**③ by the soft and **balmy**④ breezes, she floated on to Cythera, and was thence transported to the island of Cyprus. Lightly she stepped on shore, and under the gentle pressure of her delicate feet the dry and rigid sand converted into a verdant meadow, where every varied shade of color and every sweet odor charmed the senses. The whole island of Cyprus became clothed with **verdure**⑤, and greeted this fairest of all created beings with a glad smile of friendly welcome. Here she was received by the Seasons, who decked her with garments of immortal fabric, encircling her fair brow with a wreath of purest gold, whilst from her ears swayed costly rings, and a glittering necklace embraced her swan-like throat. And now, arrayed in

---

① unrequited [ˌʌnrɪˈkwaɪtɪd] adj. 无回报的
② undraped [ʌnˈdreɪpt] adj. 裸体的
③ waft [wɒft] vt. 吹拂
④ balmy [ˈbɑːmi] adj. 温和的
⑤ verdure [ˈvɜːdʒə] n. 青翠植物

all the **panoply**① of her irresistible charms, the nymphs escorted her to the dazzling halls of Olympus, where she was received with ecstatic enthusiasm by the admiring gods and goddesses. Aphrodite was also frequently represented in the act of confining her dripping locks in a knot, while her attendant nymphs enveloped her in a gauzy veil. Of the many animals sacred to her were the dove, swan, swallow, and sparrow. Her favorite plants were the myrtle, apple-tree, rose, and **poppy**②.③

Endowed with beauty unmatched, Aphrodite became all gods' desire. The gods vied with each other in aspiring to the honor of her hand, but Hephaestus became the envied possessor of this lovely being, who, however, proved as faithless as she was beautiful, and caused her husband Hephaestus much unhappiness, owing to the preference she showed at various times for some of the other gods and also for mortal men.

Originally a deity of Asia Minor and the adjoining islands (in particular Lemnos), Hephaestus, the god of fire, was worshiped primarily at the Lycian Olympus. His cult reached Athens not later than about 600 B. C. (although it scarcely touched Greece proper) and arrived in Campania not long afterward. His Roman counterpart was Vulcan.

According to myth, Hephaestus was born lame and was cast from heaven in disgust by his mother, Hera, and again by his father, Zeus, after a family quarrel. He was brought back to Olympus by Dionysus, the God of wine, and was one of the only gods to have returned after exile. Being a blacksmith and craftsman, Hephaestus made weapons and military equipment for the gods and certain mortals, including a winged helmet and sandals for Hermes and

---

① panoply ['pænəpli] n. 华丽服饰
② poppy ['pɒpi] n. 罂粟花
③ E. M. Berens, *The Myths and Legends of Ancient Greece and Rome*, pp. 59 – 61.

armour① for Achilles. He also built an extremely beautiful throne which he put quietly where Hera had to go. The vain Hera immediately took the bait in her fondness for the charming throne. Once seated on the throne, the goddess found her joints locked by the mechanism of the chair, unable to move. The gods asked Hephaestus to return to Olympus and release Hera, but Hephaestus repeatedly refused until Dionysus got him drunk, put him on the back of a mule and took him to Mount Olympus.

Hephaestus agreed to release Hera only if his three demands were met: first, Hera's admitting the mistake of abandoning him; second, acceptance of his identity as the god of Olympus; third, marriage to Aphrodite, the God of love. Hera gave consent to all demands of Hephaestus in order to save herself. While another version is that the marriage between Hephaestus and Aphrodite was **facilitated**② by Zeus, because Hephaestus was the most single-minded of all gods. Betrothing Aphrodite to him can avoid the discord between the gods caused by her. So after marrying Aphrodite, Hephaestus finally released Hera.

Aphrodite had been given in marriage to Hephaestus; but the true father of the three children with whom she presented him—the twin sons Phobus and Deimus, and the daughter Harmonia—was Ares, the good-looking, **impetuous**③, drunken, and quarrelsome god of war who had a weakness for goddesses and women. Hephaestus knew nothing of the deception until, one night, the lovers stayed too long together in bed at Ares's Thracian palace; then Helios, as he rose, saw them at their sport and told tales to Hephaestus.

Hephaestus angrily retired to his forge, and hammered out a bronze hunting-net, as fine as **gossamer**④ but quite unbreakable, which he secretly attached to

---

① armour ['ɑːmə] n. 盔甲
② facilitate [fə'sɪlɪteɪt] vt. 促进
③ impetuous [ɪm'petʃuəs] adj. 鲁莽的
④ gossamer ['gɒsəmə] n. 蛛丝

the posts and sides of his marriage-bed. He told Aphrodite who returned from Thrace, all smiles, explaining that she had been away on business at Corinth, "Please excuse me, dear wife, I am taking a short holiday on Lemnos, my favorite island." Aphrodite did not offer to accompany him and, when he was out of sight, sent hurriedly for Ares, who soon arrived. The two went merrily to bed but, at dawn, found themselves entangled in the net, naked and unable to escape. Hephaestus, turning back from his journey, surprised them there, and summoned all the gods to witness his dishonor. He then announced that he would not release his wife until the valuable marriage-gifts which he had paid Zeus, were restored to him.

Up ran the gods, to watch Aphrodite's embarrassment; but the goddesses, from a sense of **delicacy**①, stayed in their houses. Apollo, **nudging**② Hermes, asked: "You would not mind being in Ares's position, would you, net and all?"

Hermes swore by his own head, that he would not, even if there were three times as many nets, and all the goddesses were looking on with disapproval. At this, both gods laughed **uproariously**③, but Zeus was so disgusted that he refused to hand back the marriage-gifts, or to interfere in a vulgar dispute between a husband and wife, declaring that Hephaestus was a fool to have made the affair public. Poseidon who, at sight of Aphrodite's naked body, had fallen in love with her, concealed his jealousy of Ares, and pretended to sympathize with Hephaestus. "Since Zeus refuses to help," he said, "I will undertake that Ares, as a fee for his release, pays the equivalent of the marriage gifts in question."

---

① delicacy [ˈdelɪkəsi] n. 体谅
② nudge [nʌdʒ] vt. (用肘) 轻推
③ uproariously [ʌpˈrɔːriəsli] adv. 喧嚣地

"That is all very well," Hephaestus replied gloomily. "But if Ares **defaults**①, you will have to take his place under the net."

"In Aphrodite's company?" Apollo asked, laughing.

"I cannot think that Ares will default," Poseidon said nobly. "But if he should do so, I am ready to pay the debt and marry Aphrodite myself."

So Ares was set at liberty, and returned to Thrace; and Aphrodite went to Paphos, where she renewed her virginity in the sacred sea.

Flattered by Hermes's frank confession of his love for her, Aphrodite presently spent a night with him, the fruit of which was Hermaphroditus, a double-sexed being; and, equally pleased by Poseidon's intervention on her behalf, she bore him two sons, Rhodus and Herophilus. Needless to say, Ares defaulted, pleading that if Zeus would not pay, why should he? In the end, nobody paid, because Hephaestus was madly in love with Aphrodite and had no real intention of divorcing her. ②

Questions for Discussion:

1. What are the two versions of Aphrodite's birth?

2. What kind of magic power was Aphrodite's girde endowed with?

3. Who were her attendants?

4. What animals were sacred to her? What were her favorite plants?

5. Who was the husband of Aphrodite? How did they get married?

6. Who was the father of Phobus, Deimus, and Harmonia?

7. How was Hermaphroditus born?

8. What can we get to know about Aphrodite through her love stories?

---

① default [dɪˈfɔːlt] vi. 不履行
② 陶洁等：《希腊罗马神话》，第58—62页。

The Story of Eros

According to Hesiod's *Theogony*, Eros, the divine spirit of Love, sprang forth from Chaos, while all was still in confusion, and by his **beneficent**① power reduced to order and harmony the shapeless, conflicting elements, which, under his influence, began to assume distinct forms. In the earliest account, Eros is represented as a full-grown and mesmerizing youth, crowned with flowers, and leaning on a shepherd's **crook**②.

In the course of time, nevertheless, the image of Eros as one of the primordial gods gradually faded away, and though occasional mention still continues to be made of the Eros of Chaos, he is replaced by the identity as the son of Aphrodite, the popular, mischief-loving little god of Love who intervenes the affairs of gods and mortals, so familiar to us all. In later sources, Eros is depicted as a lovely boy, with rounded limbs, and a merry, **roguish**③ expression. He has golden wings, and a quiver slung over his shoulder, which contains his magical and unerring arrows; in one hand he bears his golden bow, and in the other a torch.

He is also frequently depicted riding on a lion, dolphin, or eagle, or seated in a chariot drawn by stags or wild boars, undoubtedly emblematical of the power of love as the subduer of all nature, even of the wild animals.

In one of the myths concerning Eros, Aphrodite is alleged to complain to **Themis**④, that her son, though so beautiful, did not appear to increase in stature; whereupon Themis suggested that his small proportions were probably attributable to the fact of his being always alone, and advised his mother to let

---

① beneficent [bɪˈnefɪsnt] adj. 善行的
② crook [krʊk] n. (主教在宗教仪式上所用的或牧羊人使用的) 曲柄手杖
③ roguish [ˈrəʊgɪʃ] adj. 恶作剧的
④ Themis [ˈθiːmɪs] n. 忒弥斯 (正义和秩序女神)

him have a companion. Aphrodite accordingly arranged for him, as a **playfellow**①, his younger brother **Anteros**②, the god of requited love (literally "love returned" or "counter-love"), and soon had the gratification of seeing the little Eros begin to grow and thrive; but, curious to relate, this desirable result only continued as long as the brothers remained together, and for the moment they were separated, Eros shrank once more to his original size.

By degrees the conception of Eros becomes multiplied and we hear of little love-gods Amors, who appear under the most charming and diversified forms. These love-gods, who afforded to artists inexhaustible subjects for the exercise of their imagination, are narrated as being engaged in various occupations, including hunting, fishing, rowing, driving chariots, and even busying themselves in mechanical labor.

Perhaps no myth is more charming and interesting than that of Eros and Psyche, which is as follows: Psyche, the youngest of three princesses, was so **transcendently**③ beautiful that Aphrodite herself became jealous of her, and no mortal dared to aspire to the honor of her hand. As her sisters, who were by no means equal to her in attractions, were married, but Psyche still remained unwedded. Her father consulted the oracle of Delphi, and, in obedience to the divine response, caused her to be dressed as though for the grave, and conducted to the edge of a yawning precipice. No sooner was she alone than she felt herself lifted up, and wafted away by the gentle west wind Zephyrus, who transported her to a **verdant**④ meadow, in the midst of which stood a stately palace, surrounded by groves and fountains.

Here dwelt Eros, the god of Love, in whose arms Zephyrus deposited his

---

① playfellow ['pleɪfeləʊ] n. 玩耍的同伴
② Anteros ['æntəˌrɒs] n. 安忒洛斯（相爱之神）
③ transcendently [træn'sendəntli] adv. 卓然地
④ verdant ['vɜːdnt] adj. 青翠的

lovely burden. Eros, himself unseen, wooed her in the softest accents of affection; but warned her, as she valued his love, not to endeavor to behold his form. For some time Psyche was obedient to the **injunction**① of her immortal spouse, and made no effort to gratify her natural curiosity; but, unfortunately, in the midst of her happiness she was seized with an unconquerable longing for the society of her sisters, and, in accordance with her desire, they were conducted by Zephyrus to her fairy-like abode. Filled with envy at the sight of her **felicity**②, they poisoned her mind against her husband, telling her that her unseen lover was a frightful monster, and gave her a sharp dagger, which they persuaded her to use for the purpose of delivering herself from his power.

After the departure of her sisters, Psyche resolved to take the first opportunity of following their malicious **counsel**③. She accordingly rose in the dead of night, and taking a lamp in one hand and a dagger in the other, stealthily approached the couch where Eros was reposing, when, instead of the frightful monster she had expected to see, the beauteous form of the god of Love greeted her view. Overcome with surprise and admiration, Psyche stooped down to gaze more closely on his lovely features, when, from the lamp which she held in her trembling hand, there fell a drop of burning oil upon the shoulder of the sleeping god, who instantly awoke, and seeing Psyche standing over him with the instrument of death in her hand, sorrowfully reproached her for her **treacherous**④ designs, and, spreading out his wings, flew away.

In despair at having lost her lover, the heartsore Psyche endeavored to put an end to her existence by throwing herself into the nearest river; but instead of closing over her, the waters bore her gently to the opposite bank, where Pan

---

① injunction [ɪnˈdʒʌŋkʃn] n. 禁令
② felicity [fəˈlɪsəti] n. 幸福
③ counsel [ˈkaʊnsl] n. 建议
④ treacherous [ˈtretʃərəs] adj. 背叛的

(the god of shepherds) received her, and consoled her with the hope of becoming eventually reconciled to her husband.

Meanwhile her wicked sisters, in expectation of meeting with the same good fortune which had befallen Psyche, placed themselves on the edge of the rock, but were both **precipitated**① into the chasm below.

Psyche herself, filled with a restless yearning for her lost love, wandered all over the world in search of him. Casting her eyes on a lofty mountain having on its brow a magnificent temple, she sighed and said to herself, "Perhaps my love, my lord, inhabits there," and directed her steps thither.②

She had no sooner entered than she saw heaps of corn, some in loose ears and some in **sheaves**③, with mingled ears of barley. Scattered about, lay **sickles**④ and **rakes**⑤, and all the instruments of harvest, without order, as if thrown carelessly out of the weary reapers' hands in the **sultry**⑥ hours of the day.

This unseemly confusion the pious Psyche put an end to, by separating and sorting everything to its proper place and kind, believing that she ought to neglect none of the gods, but endeavor by her piety to engage them all in her behalf. The holy Demeter, whose temple it was, finding her so religiously employed, thus spoke to her, "O Psyche, truly worthy of our pity, though I cannot shield you from the frowns of Aphrodite, yet I can teach you how best to **allay**⑦ her displeasure. Go, then, and voluntarily surrender yourself to your lady and sovereign, and try by modesty and submission to win her forgiveness,

---

① precipitate [prɪˈsɪpɪteɪt] vi. 猛地落下
② E. M. Berens, *The Myths and Legends of Ancient Greece and Rome*, pp. 150–154.
③ sheaf [ʃiːf] n. 捆
④ sickle [ˈsɪkl] n. 镰刀
⑤ rake [reɪk] n. 耙子
⑥ sultry [ˈsʌltri] adj. 闷热的
⑦ allay [əˈleɪ] vt. 减轻

and perhaps her favor will restore you the husband you have lost."

Psyche obeyed the commands of Demeter and took her way to the temple of Aphrodite, striving to fortify her mind and **ruminating**① on what she should say and how best **propitiate**② the angry goddess, feeling that the issue was doubtful and perhaps fatal.

Aphrodite received her with sullen countenance. "Most undutiful and faithless of servants," said she, "do you at last remember that you really have a mistress? Or have you rather come to see your sick husband, yet laid up of the wound given him by his loving wife? You are so ill-favored and disagreeable that the only way you can merit your lover must be by **dint**③ of industry and diligence. I will make trial of your housewifery." Then she ordered Psyche to be led to the storehouse of her temple, where was laid up a great quantity of wheat, barley, millet, **vetches**④, beans, and **lentils**⑤ prepared for food for her pigeons, and said, "Take and separate all these grains, putting all of the same kind in a parcel by themselves, and see that you get it done before evening." Then Aphrodite departed and left her to the task.

But Psyche, in a perfect **consternation**⑥ at the enormous work, was at her wit's end, and did not even move a finger to the inextricable heap.

While she sat despairing, Eros stirred up the little ant, a native of the fields, to take compassion on her. The leader of the ant-hill, followed by whole hosts of his six-legged subjects, approached the heap, and with the utmost diligence taking grain by grain, they separated the pile, sorting each kind to its parcel; and when it was all done, they vanished out of sight in a moment.

---

① ruminate ['ruːmɪneɪt] vi. 反复思考
② propitiate [prə'pɪʃieɪt] vt. 安抚
③ dint [dɪnt] n. (by dint of) 借助
④ vetch [vetʃ] n. 野豌豆
⑤ lentils ['lentl] n. 小扁豆
⑥ consternation [ˌkɒnstə'neɪʃn] n. 惊愕

Aphrodite at the approach of twilight returned from the banquet of the gods, breathing odors and crowned with roses. Seeing the task done, she exclaimed, "This is no work of yours, wicked one, but his, whom to your own and his misfortune you have **enticed**①." So saying, she threw her a piece of black bread for her supper and went away.

Next morning Aphrodite ordered Psyche to be called and said to her, "Behold yonder grove which stretches along the margin of the water. There you will find sheep feeding without a shepherd, with golden-shining fleeces on their backs. Go, fetch me a sample of that precious wool gathered from every one of their fleeces."

Psyche obediently went to the riverside, prepared to do her best to execute the command. But the river god inspired the reeds with harmonious murmurs, which seemed to say, "O maiden, severely tried, tempt not the dangerous flood, nor venture among the formidable rams on the other side, for as long as they are under the influence of the rising sun, they burn with a cruel rage to destroy mortals with their sharp horns or rude teeth. But when the **noontide**② sun has driven the cattle to the shade, and the serene spirit of the flood has lulled them to rest, you may then cross in safety, and you will find the woolly gold sticking to the bushes and the trunks of the trees."

Thus the compassionate river god gave Psyche instructions how to accomplish her task, and by observing his directions she soon returned to Aphrodite with her arms full of the golden fleece; but she received not the **approbation**③ of her **implacable**④ mistress, who said, "I know very well it is by none of your own doings that you have succeeded in this task, and I am not satisfied yet that you

---

① entice [ɪnˈtaɪs] vt. 诱使
② noontide [ˈnuːntaɪd] adj. 正午的
③ approbation [ˌæprəˈbeɪʃn] n. 认可
④ implacable [ɪmˈplækəbl] adj. 难和解的

have any capacity to make yourself useful. But I have another task for you. Here, take this box and go your way to the infernal shades, and give this box to Persephone and say, 'My mistress Aphrodite desires you to send her a little of your beauty; for in tending her sick son she has lost some of her own.' Be not too long on your errand, for I must paint myself with it to appear at the circle of the gods and goddesses this evening."

Psyche was now satisfied that her destruction was at hand, being obliged to go with her own feet directly down to Erebus. Wherefore, to make no delay of what was not to be avoided, she went to the top of a high tower to precipitate herself headlong, thus to descend the shortest way to the shades below. But a voice from the tower said to her, "Why, poor unlucky girl, dost thou design to put an end to thy days in so dreadful a manner? And what cowardice makes thee sink under this last danger who hast been so miraculously supported in all thy former?" Then the voice told her how by a certain cave she might reach the realms of Hades, and how to avoid all the dangers of the road, to pass by Cerberus, the three-headed dog, and prevail on Charon, the ferryman, to take her across the black river and bring her back again. But the voice added, "When Persephone has given you the box filled with her beauty, of all things this is chiefly to be observed by you, that you never once open or look into the box nor allow your curiosity to pry into the treasure of the beauty of the goddesses."

Psyche, encouraged by this advice, obeyed it in all things, and taking heed to her ways traveled safely to the kingdom of Hades. She was admitted to the palace of Persephone, and without accepting the delicate seat or delicious banquet that was offered to her, but contented with coarse bread for her food, she delivered her message from Aphrodite. Presently the box was returned to her, shut and filled with the precious commodity. Then she returned the way she came, and glad was she to come out once more into the light of day.

But having got so far successfully through her dangerous task a burning desire seized her to examine the contents of the box, "What," said she, "shall I, the carrier of this divine beauty, not take the least bit to put on my cheeks to appear to more advantage in the eyes of my beloved husband!" So she carefully opened the box, but found nothing there of any beauty at all, but an infernal and truly **Stygian**① sleep, which being thus set free from its prison, took possession of her, and she fell down in the midst of the road, became a sleepy corpse without sense or motion.

But Eros, being now recovered from his wound, and not able longer to bear the absence of his beloved Psyche, slipping through the smallest crack of the window of his chamber which happened to be left open, flew to the spot where Psyche lay, gathering up the sleep from her body, closed it again in the box, and waked Psyche with a light touch of one of his arrows. "Again," said he, "hast thou almost perished by the same curiosity. But now perform exactly the task imposed on you by my mother, and I will take care of the rest."

Then Eros, as swift as lightning penetrating the heights of heaven, presented himself before Zeus with his supplication. Zeus lent a favoring ear, and pleaded the cause of the lovers so earnestly with Aphrodite that he won her consent. On this he sent Hermes to bring Psyche up to the heavenly assembly, and when she arrived, handing her a cup of ambrosia, he said, "Drink this, Psyche, and be immortal; nor shall Eros ever break away from the knot in which he is tied, but these nuptials shall be perpetual."②

Their reunion was celebrated amidst the rejoicings of all the Olympian deities. The Graces shed perfume on their path; the **Horae**③, goddesses of the hours and seasons, sprinkled roses over the sky; Apollo added the music of his lyre; and the Muses united their voices in a glad chorus of delight.

---

① Stygian [ˈstɪdʒiən] adj. 地狱的
② 王磊:《希腊罗马神话赏析》, 第77—80页。
③ Horae [ˈhɔːriː] n. 霍莉 (时序女神)

This myth would appear to be an allegory, which signifies that the soul, before it can be reunited to its original divine essence, must be purified by the chastening sorrows and sufferings of its earthly career.

Questions for Discussion:

1. How was Eros usually represented?

2. Why did Aphrodite become jealous of Psyche?

3. What did Eros warn Psyche not to do?

4. Following the malicious counsel, what did Psyche do?

5. What three missions did Psyche have to accomplish in order to find Eros?

6. How did Eros help her in each mission?

7. What lesson does the story of Eros and Psyche teach us?

Part 3 Reflections

1. Vocabulary Expansion

1) Yue Lao: _____

2) the Weaving maiden: _____

3) Aphrodite: _____

4) Eros: _____

5) Psyche: _____

6) Hephaestus: _____

7) Hermaphroditus: _____

2. Appreciation

1) 媒氏掌万民之判。凡男女自成名以上，皆书年月日名焉。令男三十而娶，女二十而嫁。凡娶判妻子者皆书之。中春之月，令会男女，于是时也，奔者不禁；若无故而不用令者，罚之。司男女之无夫家者而会之。凡嫁子娶妻，入币纯帛毋过五两。

《周礼》

2）杜陵韦固，少孤，思早娶妇，多岐求婚，必无成而罢。元和二年，将游清河，旅次宋城南店。客有以前清河司马潘昉女见议者。来日先明，期于店西龙兴寺门。固以求之意切，旦往焉。斜月尚明，有老人倚布囊坐于阶上，向月检书。固步觇之，不识其字，既非虫篆八分科斗之势，又非梵书，因问曰："老父所寻者何书？固少小苦学，世间之字，自谓无不识者，西国梵字，亦能读之，唯此书目所未觌，如何？"老人笑曰："此非世间书，君因何得见？"固曰："非世间书，则何也？"曰："幽冥之书。"固曰："幽冥之人，何以到此？"曰："君行自早，非某不当来也。凡幽吏皆掌人生之事，掌人可不行冥中乎？今道途之行，人鬼各半，自不辨尔。"固曰："然则君又何掌？"曰："天下之婚牍耳。"固喜曰："固少孤，常愿早娶以广胤嗣。尔来十年，多方求之，竟不遂意。今者，人有期此，与议潘司马女，可以成乎？"曰："未也。命苟未合，虽降衣缨而求屠博，尚不可得，况郡佐乎？君之妇适三岁矣，年十七当入君门。"因问："囊中何物？"曰："赤绳子耳，以系夫妻之足。及其生则潜用相系，虽仇敌之家，贵贱悬隔，天涯从宦，吴楚异乡，此绳一系，终不可逭。君之脚已系于彼矣。他求何益。"曰："固妻安在？其家何为？"曰："此店北卖菜陈婆女耳。"固曰："可见乎？"曰："陈尝抱来鬻菜于市，能随我行，当即示君。"及明，所期不至。老人卷书揭囊而行，固逐之入菜市，有眇妪抱三岁女来，弊陋亦甚。老人指曰，"此君之妻也。"固怒曰："煞之可乎？"老人曰："此人命当食天禄，因子而食邑，庸可杀乎？"老人遂隐。固骂曰："老鬼妖妄如此！吾士大夫之家，娶妇必敌，苟不能娶，即声妓之美者，或援立之，奈何婚眇妪之陋女。"磨一小刀子，付其奴曰，"汝素干事，能为我杀彼女，赐予万钱。"奴曰："诺。"明日，袖刀入菜行中，于众中刺之而走。一市纷扰，固与奴奔走获免。问奴曰："所刺中否？"曰："初刺其心，不幸才中眉间尔。"后固屡求婚，终无所遂。又十四年，以父荫参相州军。刺史王泰俾摄司户掾，专鞫词狱，以为能，因妻以其女。可年十六七，容色华丽，固称惬之极。然其眉间常帖一花子，虽沐浴间处，未尝暂去。岁余，固讶之，忽忆昔日奴刀中眉间之说，因逼问之。妻潸然曰："妾郡守之犹子也，非其女也。畴昔父曾宰宋城，终其官时，妾在襁褓，母兄次没，唯一庄在宋城南，与乳母陈氏居，去店近，鬻蔬以给朝夕。陈氏怜小，不忍暂弃。三岁时，抱行市中，为狂贼所刺，刀痕尚在，故以花子覆之。七八年前，叔从事卢龙，遂得在左右，仁念以为女嫁君耳。"固曰："陈氏眇乎？"曰："然。何以知之？"固曰："所刺者固也。"乃曰："奇也！命也！"因尽言之，相敬愈极。后生男鲲，为雁门太守，封太原郡太夫人。乃知阴骘之定，不可变也。宋城宰闻之，题其店曰："定婚店"。

《续玄怪录》

3）天河之东有织女，天帝之女也，年年机杼劳役，织成云锦天衣。天帝怜其独处，许嫁河西牵牛郎，嫁后遂废织衽。天帝怒，责令归河东，许一年一度相会。

《月令广义·七月令》

4) Then, turning his sweet chords, Demodocus
A jocund strain began, his theme, the loves
Of Mars and Cytherea chaplet-crown'd;
How first, clandestine, they embraced beneath
The roof of Vulcan, her, by many a gift
Seduced, Mars won, and with adult'rous lust
The bed dishonour'd of the King of fire.
The sun, a witness of their amorous sport,
Bore swift the tale to Vulcan; he, apprized
Of that foul deed, at once his smithy sought,
In secret darkness of his inmost soul
Contriving vengeance; to the stock he heav'd
His anvil huge, on which he forged a snare

Of bands indissoluble, by no art

To be united, durance for ever firm.

The net prepared, he bore it, fiery-wroth,

To his own chamber and his nuptial couch,

Where, stretching them from post to post, he wrapp'd

With those fine meshes all his bed abound,

And hung them num'rous from the roof, diffused

Like spiders' filaments, which not the Gods

Themselves could see, so subtle were the toils.

Homer's *The Odyssey*

3. Discussion

1) Draw a conclusion of the features of love gods in Chinese and Greek mythology.

2) What kind of views on love and marriage are reflected in Chinese and Greek mythology?

Unit 10

Myths about Heroes

Introduction

Heroes, despite their exceptional build or unique talent, are not omnipotent or immortal beings. They represent the best of what it means to be human—great strength, courage, wisdom, cleverness, and devotion. But not all heroes possess all these qualities. Through the ages diverse cultures have produced various kinds of legends with heroes, each with a particular emphasis on a wide range of virtues. The male-dominated civilization of ancient Greece, for example, admired strong warrior heroes. By contrast, in the mythology of ancient Egypt, where religion played a central role at all levels of society, the heroes were often priest-magicians. In many cultures women became heroes by using their intelligence or forceful personalities to outwit a foe. Some heroes of myth and legend are wholly fictional. Others are historical figures who have achieved greatness or who have been given such status by writers or by the public. The mythical and legendary heroes in different mythologies usually perform acts of heroism inspired by such diverse motives as revenge, **hubris**[①], military courage, idealism, nobility of spirit, and patriotism.

In Chinese mythology, the hero can be a savior, culture bearer, warrior,

---

① hubris [ˈhjuːbrɪs] n. 傲慢

and founder of a new race, tribe, or dynasty. The Yellow Emperor, who combines both military and civil roles of warrior and culture bearer, is one of the great heroes in the **pantheon**①. Of the demigods Yao, Shun and Yu in the Golden Age, the mythical qualities of the hero are most fully realized in the narratives of Yu, who overcame a multiplicity of heroic tasks while confronting the overwhelming disaster of the flood. While the failed hero, which is another aspect of the hero type, a god, demigod, or human who struggles in a fair contest for supremacy but loses against a more formidable contender complements the dynamic and positive function of the invincible, successful, and dominant mythical hero. Ordinarily, whoever failed is not projected as a monster or villain but always treated sympathetically, which is the case of myths of Chiyou, Xingtian, Yi the Archer, Jingwei, etc. They all show the nobility of failure.

Greek mythology mainly consists of stories of gods and the legends of heroes. The former involve the origin of the universe and mankind, the emergence of God and its **pedigree**②. The latter are originated from the worship of ancestors. It is an artistic review of ancient Greek's struggle against nature. The protagonists in such legends are mostly descendants of gods and human beings—the demi-gods. They are enormously strong in stature, reflecting the heroic spirit and **indomitable**③ will of human beings to conquer nature, and have become the embodiment of the collective strength and wisdom of the ancient people. The heroes of immense popularity in Greek mythology include Perseus, Heracles, Odysseus, Achilles, Jason and many others.

---

① pantheon ['pænθiən] n. 万神殿
② pedigree ['pedɪɡriː] n. 血统
③ indomitable [ɪn'dɒmɪtəbl] adj. 不屈不挠的

Part 1　Heroes in Chinese Mythology

Stories of Saviors

Yi Shooting the Suns to Avert① Disaster

The central myth of Yi the Archer revolves around his heroic feat of saving the world from being destroyed by a solar **conflagration**②. Depicted in "Tianwen," *The Analects of Confucius*, *Mencius*, *Zhuangzi*, *Guanzi*, *Mozi*, *Xunzi*, *Hanfeizi*, and *Lüshi Chunqiu*, or *The Spring and Autumn Annals of Master Lü*, this myth belongs to a **nexus**③ of solar myths including **Xihe**④, the sacred tree called Fu Sang (mulberry), and the pool where the suns were **rinsed**⑤ after each day's journey, especially the ten suns born of Xihe. The Yi myth narrates how the ten suns all came out together and threatened to **annihilate**⑥ the world. ⑦

The story goes like this: in a time when the earth was still very young and the mythical Emperor Yao ruled China, there were ten suns that took turns illuminating the planet. The Jade Emperor told them that only one of them could play in the sky at a time, lest they destroy the earth. Being young children, however, they decided that going out together would be much more fun than going out alone.

---

① avert [ə'vɜːt] vt. 防止
② conflagration [ˌkɒnfləˈɡreɪʃn] n. 大火
③ nexus ['neksəs] n. 关系
④ 羲和是帝俊之妻，是十日之母。《山海经》云："东海之外，甘泉之间，有羲和之国。有女子名羲和，为帝俊之妻，是生十日，常浴日于甘渊"，编者注。
⑤ rinse [rɪns] vt. (用清水) 冲洗
⑥ annihilate [ə'naɪəleɪt] vt. 歼灭
⑦ Anne Birrell, *Chinese Mythology: An Introduction*, p. 77.

When all ten suns appeared in the sky, the temperature on earth became unbearably high. Mass chaos ensued. Crops **shriveled**① up and people fainted in the streets as the earth began to burn. Seeing an opportunity, wild monsters emerged from the shadows and began to prey on human beings.

Hou Yi saw the destruction the suns were causing and immediately went to the Jade Emperor. He told the Emperor that if the suns would not behave themselves, he would have to shoot them down in order to save the planet.

Fearing for the lives of his grandchildren, the Jade Emperor scolded them and begged them to return home. The suns were having so much fun, however, that they could not hear the Emperor over the sound of their own laughter. Though the Jade Emperor loved his grandchildren, he could see that there was no reasoning with them. At long last, he gave Hou Yi permission to do what must be done.

Armed with a massive bow made of tiger bones and arrows made of dragon **tendons**②, Hou Yi set about slaying the monsters terrorizing the countryside. After that, he climbed to the top of a tall mountain to confront the suns directly.

Before shooting, Hou Yi gave the children a final warning and pleaded for them to return to the Emperor's palace. Upon hearing this warning, the suns simply stuck their tongues out at Hou Yi and told him to mind his own business. **Steeling**③ himself, Hou Yi drew back his bow and loosed nine arrows upon the suns. Almost instantly, nine of them fell from the sky. The tenth sun was so scared that he ran away and hid in a cave.

The earth was now plunged into unbearable darkness and cold. Every living thing on the planet begged the last sun to come out, but he was so scared of Hou Yi that he covered his ears and ignored them. After everyone else had tried to

---

① shrivel ['ʃrɪvl] vi. 枯萎
② tendon ['tendən] n. 腱
③ steel [stiːl] vt. 使准备应对（不愉快之事）

coax the sun out, the rooster climbed to the top of his **roost**① and shouted, "Gēgē! Gēgē!" (meaning "Brother!") The rooster's loud, shrill voice was able to reach the sun, and he finally decided to emerge from his cave. Now, whenever roosters crow "brother" in the morning, the sun rises to greet them.②

The following are two readings related to Hou Yi. The first reading, from *The Classic of Mountains and Seas*, relates that Yi was given a sacred bow and arrows by the god Di Jun to shoot the suns down, rescuing humans from disaster. Thus Di Jun is incorporated into solar myths, as his consort, Xihe, is the mother of the suns. The second reading, from *Huainanzi*, gives a slightly different version of this myth. Here Yi was a courtier under the demigod Yao, who ordered him to kill six monsters and to shoot down the ten suns. Yao's success in doing so was rewarded with the title of Son of Heaven, or supreme ruler. Other versions state that it was Mo himself, not Yi, who shot the suns. The Yao tradition did not, however, survive in mythography, and it was Yi the Archer who came to be identified with the act of deliverance.

Di Jun endowed Yi with a red bow and arrows with white feathers so that he would bring relief to the people down on earth. Hence Yi was the first to show pity for people and rid them of a hundred evils.③

When it came to Yao's time, there used to be ten suns appearing at the same time in the sky. As a result, all types of crops were scorched, various plants were killed, and the people did not have anything to eat. To make things even worse, formidable wild animals④,

---

① roost [ruːst] n. 栖息处
② https://mythopedia.com/topics/hou-yi
③ *The Classic of Mountains and Seas*, p. 321.
④ 后羿射杀六个怪物，分别为猰貐、凿齿（居住在南部沼泽地带的怪兽，长有像凿子一样的长牙，手中持有矛和盾）、九婴（为水火之怪，能喷水吐火，叫声如婴儿啼哭，有九头）、大风（一种凶恶的鸷鸟）、封豨（传说中的大兽）和修蛇（也叫巴蛇），编者注。

such as Yayu, Zao Chi, Jiu Ying, Da Feng, Feng Xi and Xiu She also posed severe threats to the people. Then Yao ordered Yi to kill Zao Chi in the fields of Chou Hua, slaughtered Jiu Ying at the bank of Xiong River, shoot Da Feng in the swamp of Qing Qiu, shoot down nine of the ten suns from the sky as well as beheaded Ya Yu on the ground. Yi also chopped down Xiu She in the Dongting Lake, and captured Feng Xi in Sang Lin. Tens of thousands of people were so pleased with such achievements, they enthroned Yao to be the Son of Heaven. At that time in the world, every place, large or small, dangerous or safe, far or near, started to have roads. ①

Questions for Discussion:

1. What kind of myth does "Yi Shooting the Suns to Avert Disaster" belong to?

2. Who ordered Yi to shoot the suns?

3. Apart from the suns, what wild animals did Yi kill?

Hou Ji② Saving Humans from Starvation

The mythic narrative of Hou Ji, the lord of **millet**③ and god of agriculture, illustrates the agricultural function of the grain god who taught humans how to cultivate plants. The text here also underscores the god's role as a savior. This side of the god is expressed within the special mythological context of the Golden Age of Antiquity ruled by the demigods Yao and Shun which the Han historian,

---

① Liu An, *Huainanzi* (Ⅱ), translated into modern Chinese by Zhai Jiangyue, translated into English by Zhai Jiangyue and Mou Aipeng, pp. 457-459.

② 后稷（周始祖），姬姓，名弃，其母有邰氏女，曰姜嫄，生于稷山（今山西省稷山县），被尊为稷王（也称作稷神）、农神、耕神、谷神，农耕始祖，编者注。

③ millet ['mɪlɪt] n. 粟

author of the passage cited here, borrowed from *The Classic of History*. The identity of Hou Ji as the savior, is developed through Shun's instruction to rescue the people from starvation. In this passage, the Han historian Sima Qian presents Hou Ji as a minister of agriculture rather than a primeval god, a humanized hero rather than a savior deity.

  Hou Ji of the Zhou Dynasty was named Qi, meaning "the Abandoned."... When Qi was a child, he looked imposing, as if he had the bold spirit of a giant. When he went out to play, he liked planting hemp and beans, and his hemp and beans were very fine. When he became an adult, he also grew very skilled at plowing and farming. He would study the proper use of the land, and where valleys were suitable he planted and he reaped. Everyone went out and imitated him. Emperor Yao heard about him and promoted Qi to master of agriculture, so that the whole world would benefit from him and have the same success. Emperor Shun said, "Qi, the black-haired people are beginning to starve. You are the Lord Millet (Hou Ji). Plant the **seedlings**① in equal measure throughout the hundred valleys." He gave Qi the **fiefdom**② of **Tai**③ with the title of Lord Millet, and he took another surname from the Ji clan. (*Shi Ji*)④

Questions for Discussion:

1. How did Hou Ji get his name "Qi"?

2. What did Hou Ji like to do?

---

① seedling ['siːdlɪŋ] n. 秧苗
② fiefdom ['fiːfdəm] n. 封地
③ 邰，今陕西乾州武功县西南地区，编者注。
④ Anne Birrell, *Chinese Mythology: An Introduction*, p. 72.

3. What did Emperor Shun ask Hou Ji to do?

4. What title was given to Hou Ji?

Stories of Culture Bearers

The Story of Shennong

Shennong, a popular culture hero who started bazaar, agriculture, medicine and **the Zhaji Sacrificial Rite**①, and who also invented an assortment of farm tools and musical instruments, is one of the Three Divine Sovereigns along with Fuxi and the Yellow Emperor (names may differ with texts; some version also includes the goddess Nüwa on the list). With regard to the meaning of name, "shen" means "divine" or "sacred," and "nong" means "farmer", implying the "Divine Husbandman."

China is a large agricultural country, with a long and rich history of agriculture and farming. As a result, gods of agriculture abound in Chinese mythology, including Hou Ji, Hou Tu, Shennong, and Shujun, among whom Shennong is the most well-known.

Shennong's merits can be easily found in ancient writings since the Spring and Autumn period, including *Zhuangzi*, *Hanfeizi*, and *Guanzi* which give him much fame and respect. Numerous myths, spreading both in various written accounts and in oral tradition, describe his miraculous birth, unique features, and great contributions to humans.

Shennong, like most gods in Chinese mythology, has miraculous birth stories. One myth states that Shennong's mother **Andeng**② was Shaodian's wife.

---

① 蜡（zhà）祭，中国传统祭祀仪式，历史悠久。岁末十二月由于处在新旧交接时段，是祭祀比较频繁的月份。又因该月有"腊月""腊冬"等别称，故在这个月举行的祭祀称为"腊祭"（蜡祭），编者注。

② 安登，古代传说中神农母亲的名字，编者注。

One day, she was playing in Huayang when a divine dragon appeared and copulated with her at the place. Afterwards she became pregnant and later gave birth to Shennong, who had a human's face and a dragon's head. He liked to farm very much, so he was called the "Divine Farmer." Some versions relate that when Shennong was born, nine connecting wells were suddenly **excavated**①. If one drew water from one of them, the water in the other eight wells would ripple. Tales of his youth say that he spoke after three days, walked within five, fully grew teeth in a week and knew everything about sowing and reaping at age three.

Devoted to agriculture Shennong made great achievements. He is said to have first taught people to sow grain, and for this reason he was respectfully addressed as the Divine Farmer. For example, one version of his myth appearing in *Guanzi* (chapter 64) records that Shennong taught people to sow and to grow grain. By this way he reputedly established a stable agricultural society in China. Another version in the same book (chapter 84) maintains that Shennong planted grain to the south of Mount Qi. From then on, men began to understand the uses of grain and relied on it for **subsistence**②. The whole world was changed by his contribution. According to a text from *Huainanzi*, in prehistoric times people ate plants and drank from rivers. They gathered fruit from trees and scratched **wasps**③ and worms for their meat. They suffered from sickness, poison, and pain. Such a primitive form of life did not end until Shennong taught people to sow the five grains (rice, two kinds of millet, wheat, and beans). He also taught people to examine the land and to cultivate it according to the land's quality (dry or wet, fertile or barren, high or low, etc.).

---

① excavate [ˈekskəveɪt] vt. 开凿
② subsistence [səbˈsɪstəns] n. 维持生计
③ wasp [wɒsp] n. 黄蜂

Another story recorded in ***Xinyu***① (literally meaning "new discourse") in the early Han dynasty states that in ancient times people took flesh and blood as their food and drink, and raw animal fur as their clothes. When it came to Shennong's time, things began to change. Shennong felt that it was very hard for humans to live on reptiles and beasts, so he went out to look for better food. He tasted the fruits of hundreds of plants and grasses and recognized their sour or bitter flavors. After this process, he then taught people to take the five grains as their food.

Shennong's great contributions to agriculture are also shown in his multiple inventions related to farming. For example, he invented some of the important farm tools such as the axe, hoe, and leisi, a plowlike farm tool used in ancient China. He cut wood to make the **plowshare**②, and bent a piece of wood to make the handle of the plow. By using these tools, he taught people to cultivate wastelands and **hoe**③ weeds. He also imparted knowledge on excavation of wells and irrigation of land. Moreover, he invented the age-old Chinese way of storing grain seeds: dipping the seeds in boiled horse urine to protect them against being eaten by worms. He also invented the calendar and jieqi. (According to the Chinese lunar calendar, the solar year can be divided into twenty-four seasonal divisions, referred to as solar terms, or jieqi in Chinese, which indicate the change of climate and timing for agricultural activities. They are of great significance to agriculture and are still widely used in rural areas in China nowadays.)

Another of Shennong's main contributions, which clearly derives from his agricultural achievements, is the creation of Chinese medicine. He tasted, or as

---

① 《新语》是西汉时期陆贾的政论散文集，全书共计十二个章节，编者注。
② plowshare [ˈplaʊʃeə] n. 犁头
③ hoe [həʊ] vt. 用锄头锄地（或除草）

it is variously said, he **thrashed**① with a reddish-brown whip hundreds of herbs in order to figure out their medicinal characteristics and functions. Recordings about this are quite abundant in ancient accounts. The text cited above from *Huainanzi* further holds that Shennong tasted the flavors of hundreds of herbs and the sweetness or bitterness of the waters from rivers and wells. Then he told people what they should eat and drink, and what they should avoid. This work sometimes put him in peril. He once consumed seventy poisonous plants in one day. According to a text from *Sou Shen Ji* (*In Search of the Supernatural*, written by Gan Bao, ca. 300 C. E., chapter 1), Shennong thrashed hundreds of herbs with a reddish-brown whip. Then he completely knew their flavors and properties of coldness, warmness, mildness, and **toxicity**②. Some versions say that Shennong tasted the flavors of herbs and plants to find out their medicinal qualities, and then used them to cure diseases. Additionally, he wrote an important ancient medical book, *Shennong Bencao Jing* (*Classic of Shennong's Materia Medica*, one of the earliest Chinese medical books). Some sources even suggest the sites where Shennong tasted or thrashed the herbs.

Besides these mythical achievements in agriculture and medicine, Shennong also gained fame for inventing many other cultural items. For example, he made the pestle, mortar, bowl, pan, pot, rice steamer, well, and kitchen range. People could then use these innovations to **steep**③ and steam rice.

Shennong is also credited with inventing the Zhaji Sacrificial Rite (later it was called the Laji Rite), which was held at the end of each year in order to thank all the gods for enabling the harvest and to pray for another good harvest in the coming year.

In another source, Shennong asked one of his subordinates to draw pictures

---

① thrash [θræʃ] vt. 打
② toxicity [tɒkˈsɪsəti] n. 毒性
③ steep [stiːp] vt. 浸泡（食物）

of water routes in order to prevent rivers from blocking up. He began to measure lands and seas to set up **hypsography**① (the study of elevation and topography). He also taught people to plant mulberry and **hemp**② trees. Since then men could make clothes from cloth and silk. The invention of bow and arrow amazed his contemporaries even more. Additionally, Shennong invented some of the most important ancient Chinese musical instruments, such as qin (a seven-stringed plucked instrument) and se (a twenty-five-stringed plucked instrument). He made them for mood-lifting and self-cultivation, helping to keep people's childlike innocence from turning evil. He also composed a piece of music named "Fuchi" or "Xiamou."③ He created the sixty-four diagrams for divination. He also started the fair tradition—by telling all people to come to a certain place at midday with items that they could exchange for others.

In some ancient writings Shennong was heavily rationalized into a brilliant and accomplished sage king. "The time of Shennong" even became a symbol of the ideal dynasty and golden era of happiness, peace, stability and self-sufficiency in mythical ancient Chinese history. ④

Questions for Discussion:

1. What was the symbolic meaning of Shennong's name?
2. How was Shennong portrayed?
3. How was Shennong born?
4. What was special about Shennong when he was young?
5. What contributions did Shennong make to agriculture?
6. How did he create Chinese medicine?

---

① hypsography [hɪpˈsɒgrəfi] n. 测高学
② hemp [hemp] n. 麻类植物
③ 《通典·乐一》:"神农乐名《扶持》,亦曰《下谋》",编者注。
④ Yang Lihui, An Deming and Jessica Anderson Turner, *Handbook of Chinese Mythology*, pp. 190-194.

7. What musical instruments did Shennong invent?

8. What did "the time of Shennong" symbolize?

The Story of Cangjie

Cangjie is the famous culture hero who invented Chinese characters. He is said to be an official **historiographer**① of the Yellow Emperor in mythical history.

The records about Cangjie's invention can be found in texts of the Warring States period which are progressively elaborated in the Han era. These accounts, like many other mythological recordings, are incomplete and sometimes in conflict with each other. Cangjie is described in these writings as having remarkable vision and ability. He had four eyes and was able to write when he was born. He examined the constellations, observed the footprints of birds and beasts, and studied the signs visible on turtles' shells, birds' feathers, mountains and rivers, and fingers and palms. From these observations he came to understand that natural phenomena could be differentiated and marked by **pictographic**② signs. Relying on these signs, he created Chinese characters. This invention was such a great event that afterward millet fell down like rain from heaven, and ghosts cried during the night. Some scholars interpret that such miraculous phenomena show the magical power of writing. But **Gao You**③ (third century C. E.), a scholar who annotated many of the classics, explained that along with the invention of writing, deceit appeared too. Humans began to neglect farming, their essential work, and attended to trifle benefits. The deity in heaven anticipated they would starve, so rained millet. And the ghosts were afraid that they would be accused by man's writing, so they cried.

---

① historiographer [hɪˌstɔːrɪˈɒɡrəfə] n. 史料编纂者
② pictographic [ˌpɪktəˈɡræfɪk] adj. 象形文字的
③ 高诱，东汉涿郡涿县（今河北涿州市）人。注："仓颉始视鸟迹之文造书契，则诈伪萌生；诈伪萌生，则去本趋末，弃耕作之业，而务锥刀之利。天知其将饿，故为雨粟；鬼恐为书文所劾，故夜哭也。鬼或作兔，兔恐见取豪（毫）作笔，害及其躯，故夜哭"，编者注。

The Cangjie myth continues to be told in contemporary China. A story collected in Shaanxi Province describes the mythic process of how Cangjie invented the characters. The story goes like this: Cangjie, an official of the Yellow Emperor, was tasked with creating a way to record things that happened. He used knotted ropes of various sizes and colors to memorize different events and experiences. But it eventually became difficult to recall what each knot meant. Cangjie then decided to find an easier way to record history and thoughts. He visited many thoughtful people for inspiration. Then he lived in seclusion in a cave and created signs based upon pictographs. The word "日" (the sun) was created according to the round shape of the sun, the word "月" (the moon) the shape of the **crescent**①; the word "人" (human) imitated the profile of a man, and the word "爪" (claw) the footprint of birds and beasts. He called these words "字" (characters). After this invention he began to teach people throughout the country to write. Since the written characters he invented were "as many in number as ten liters of rape seed," people found it hard to learn and remember. Even Confucius, the founder of Confucianism and one of the greatest educators in ancient China, only learned 70 percent of the original amount. Cangjie felt very disappointed and annoyed, so he threw the other 30 percent away to foreign countries.

Another modern myth spread in Sichuan Province associates Cangjie's invention with Nüwa, the goddess and creator of humans. Looking down upon women, Cangjie used "女" (referring to "woman") as a character element and combined it with other components, then the type of words with negative meanings were born, such as "奸" ("wicked") and "妖" ("demon"). Nüwa was very upset about this. She accused Cangjie of prejudice and asked him to create some good words with "女." At last, Cangjie invented the words "好"

---

① crescent ['kresnt] n. 新月形

("good") and "娘"("mother").

As most deities of Chinese mythology, Cangjie is part of a religion of a large population and is respected and worshiped in rituals. During the Song Dynasty he was worshiped as the ancestor who founded the professions of the **Xu Li**[①] group of people, petty officials taking charge of documents and paperwork in government who therefore handled words every day. He was called "King Cang." According to **Shilin Yanyu**[②] (*Records of History and Anecdotes*, written by a Song Dynasty writer, Ye Mengde, 1077 C. E. – 1148 C. E.), every autumn, a party of Xu Li in the capital would put their money together and hold a festival to worship King Cang. They often drank all day during the festival. Today, one can also find evidence of similar worship in Shandong, Henan, Hebei, Shaanxi, and other provinces, where Cangjie's Tombs, Temples and Platforms are set up in memory of his invention of characters. These relics illustrate people's great respect for and remembrance of Cangjie. [③]

Questions for Discussion:

1. What was Cangjie like when he was born?

2. How did he understand that natural phenomena could be differentiated and marked by pictographic signs?

3. Which way did Cangjie use to record human history and thoughts instead of knotting ropes?

4. How was Cangjie's story related to Nüwa?

5. How did Xu Li worship Cangjie in the Song Dynasty?

---

① 胥吏，旧时官府中办理文书的小官吏。"胥，什长也"，"吏，治人者也"，编者注。

② 《石林燕语》，宋朝叶梦得撰，为宋代史料笔记丛书之一种，共计十卷，记叙朝章国典、旧闻时事，朝野故事足以资考，补史缺。书中内容还涉及诗文、词章、奏议、考释、笔记等，编者注。

③ Yang Lihui, An Deming and Jessica Anderson Turner, *Handbook of Chinese Mythology*, pp. 84 – 86.

Hero as Warrior: Chiyou

Being the offspring of Yan Di, or the Flame Emperor, Chiyou was the god of war, and the inventor of military weapons. He rebelled against the Yellow Emperor but failed in the war and was killed. His shackles turned into a maple tree.

Different versions of the Chiyou myth can be found scattered throughout various ancient texts. In these narratives, Chiyou is depicted as the descendant of the Flame Emperor. He invented military weapons such as the spear, **dagger-axe**①, sword, and **halberd**②. In one version, he had eighty brothers (seventy-one brothers in another version), each of them with an animal body, bronze head, and iron forehead, who spoke in a human language and fed on sand and stone. Other versions state that Chiyou took iron and stone as food and that he had a human body, horned head, ox hooves, four eyes, six hands, and ears and temples like swords and spears. The main event of his life story is recorded in *The Classic of Mountains and Seas*. It is said that Chiyou made weapons and attacked the Yellow Emperor. Thus, the Emperor commanded Yinglong to launch an attack against him in the wilderness of the central plain. Yinglong took the vengeance by preventing all the water in heaven from flowing down. But Chiyou asked Feng Bo, the god of wind, and Yu Shi, the god of rain, to release a **cloudburst**③ in response. Then the Yellow Emperor asked the drought goddess Ba to descend from heaven to stop the rain. Upon the arrival of Ba the rain and wind retreated, which eventually led to the defeat of Chiyou.

The war between Chiyou and the Yellow Emperor is one of the fiercest battles among gods in Chinese mythology, since the two sides were neck and

---

① dragger-axe [ˈdæɡər æks] n. 戈（一种武器）
② halberd [ˈhælbɜːd] n. 戟（一种武器）
③ cloudburst [ˈklaʊdbɜːst] n.（突然的）大暴雨

neck. Many stories in record describe the process and circumstances of the war. One states that when Chiyou attacked the Yellow Emperor, no one was able to defend himself against his **butting**① with his horns. In another version Chiyou was said to be able to soar into the sky and surmount all the dangerous and difficult **obstructions**②. But the Yellow Emperor kept on beating the drum he made from the hide of Kui, a one-legged mythical beast. The deafening sound it made prevented Chiyou from flying away. So he was caught and killed by the Emperor. Still another version states that Chiyou led many ferocious mythical animals to attack the Yellow Emperor at the Zhuolu plain. So the Emperor ordered his subjects to blow horns sounding like dragons to threaten them. In another source, Chiyou was alleged to be able to stir up clouds and mist. When in fight with the Emperor, he made heavy fog for three days. The Emperor's army was caught in it and got lost. But the Emperor then invented the compass and guided his army out of the fog. Finally, the Emperor defeated Chiyou and killed him. When Chiyou was executed, his head and body were cut off and buried in different places, and his shackles turned into a maple tree.

Even after his death, Chiyou was still considered a powerful and awful god. One version of the myth said that many years after Chiyou's loss of the battle against the Yellow Emperor, the world was in chaos. In order to **deter**③ his people from revolting, the Emperor drew Chiyou's picture and showed it to them, after which peace reigned again. During the Qin and Han dynasties, Chiyou was worshiped as the god of war by the army leader and even the First Emperor of Qin.

In addition to myths, Chiyou also survives in customs and beliefs.

---

① butt [bʌt] vt. 撞
② obstruction [əbˈstrʌkʃn] n. 障碍
③ deter [dɪˈtɜː] vt. 防止

According to *Shuyiji* (*A Record of Accounts of Marvels*, written by **Ren Fang**[①] in the Six Dynasties era), there was a kind of drama called "Chiyou's Game" in Ji Province. When dancing it, the local people formed into groups of twos or threes. They wore horns on their heads and butted each other, from which possibly originated the horn-butting game in the Han period. In the villages of Taiyuan, people did not use ox heads when offering sacrifices to Chiyou, for Chiyou was ox-headed himself.

Chiyou is also worshiped as the remote ancestor of the Miao ethnic group. Nowadays beliefs about him can still be found in aspects of Miao's daily life. For example, Miao people developed a worship for oxen and maple trees. Oxen are thought to be a symbol of luck, heroism, safety and prosperity in their tradition. Designs of ox horns are embroidered on their clothes or carved on their silver decorations. In Miao mythology, Jiangyang, an ancestor of the Miao people, was delivered from the egg of a goddess who was born in a maple tree. In Chenbu, Hunan Province, Miao people believe that the maple god can expel evils. In Wenshan, Maguan, and other Miao areas in Yunnan Province, a traditional festival called Trembling the Flower Mountain is annually held. It is said that this festival originated from the Chiyou myth. The legend has it that after being defeated by the Yellow Emperor, Chiyou led his tribes back into the thickly forested mountains. In order to call together the scattered people over the mountains, he planted a long trunk with a colorful red waistband on the mountain and asked the young to dance and blow reed pipes around it. On hearing the sound, the people came from all directions. Having been gathered, they continued to fight against the Yellow Emperor. The custom of dancing and blowing reed pipes around a flower-wreathed pole lasted for generations and has

---

① 任昉（公元460年—公元508年），字彦升，小字阿堆，乐安郡博昌（今山东省寿光市）人。南梁著名文学家、方志学家、藏书家、竟陵八友之一，编者注。

become a traditional festival for the Miao people. The colorful cloth tied to the pole was said to be "Chiyou's flag." A song is sung when the pole is planted, which narrates how Chiyou, the Miao ancestor, fought with the Yellow Emperor, the Han ancestor, and how he was defeated and killed in the end, providing an explanation why the Miao people had to flee from the Central Plain toward the southern mountains. [1]

Questions for Discussion:

1. What did Chiyou look like?

2. What did he invent?

3. How was Chiyou killed by the Yellow Emperor?

4. What did his shackles turn into after his death?

5. How is Chiyou related to the customs and beliefs of the Miao ethnic group?

Heroes with Fighting Spirit

Jingwei

Jingwei is a mythical bird that metamorphosed from the daughter of Yan Di, the Flame Emperor and **indomitably**[2] strived to fill up the sea with pebbles.

The Flame Emperor had a young daughter named Nil Wa (different from the great mother and cosmic repairer Nüwa; "nil" means "female," "wa" means "child"). Nil Wa was playing in the East Sea but was drowned and never returned. She then turned into a bird called Jingwei. Jingwei lived on Fajiu Mountain, located in the north. It looked like a crow but had a colorful head,

---

[1] Yang Lihui, An Deming and Jessica Anderson Turner, *Handbook of Chinese Mythology*, pp. 92-94.

[2] indomitably [ɪnˈdɑmətəbli] adv. 不屈服地

white beak, and red claws. Its name is derived from the sound of its call, which sounds like "Jingwei." It constantly carried a pebble or a **twig**① in its mouth and dropped it into the East Sea, where Nü Wa lost her young life. Jingwei kept filling up the sea year after year, never stopping.

In one version Jingwei was said to have mated with a sea swallow and give birth to several children, who had much resemblance to their parents in appearance. Jingwei has an assortment of alias names. She was called Oath Bird for her swearing not to drink the water of the East Sea where she was drowned; Grudge Bird for its perseverance in revenge for the merciless sea; Resolve Bird for her dogged determination and persistence in the face of seemingly impossible odds; and sometimes the Daughter of the Emperor for her former identity as the Flame Emperor's Daughter.

The myth of Jingwei is well-known to most Han Chinese people. Many feel sympathetic to Jingwei's misfortune and admire the bird for its bravery, toughness, and unyieldingness. This myth continues to appear in many poems, novels, and dramas, combining the diverse themes of **pathos**②, courage, and gameness. "Jingwei Filling the Sea" has become an idiom utilized to encourage people to be more diligent and consistent in work. ③

Questions for Discussion:

1. How did Jingwei die?
2. What did she turn into after death?
3. What do people admire Jingwei for?

---

① twig [twɪg] n. 嫩枝
② pathos ['peɪθɒs] n. 同情
③ Yang Lihui, An Deming and Jessica Anderson Turner, *Handbook of Chinese Mythology*, pp. 154-155.

The Foolish Old Man Removes the Mountains

Yugong, or the Foolish Old Man, is recorded in the classic *Liezi* in the fourth-century A. D. , which indicates that the myth is late in the tradition, confirmed by the absence of early classical texts referring to or narrating this myth. The myth shares with the folktale of Jingwei the theme of seemingly **futile**① effort. Different from the earlier myth of the goddess metamorphosed into a bird, the narrative about Yugong in *Liezi* contains assorted motifs and themes. To the basic theme of futility are harnessed those of commitment to an ideal or faith. The thematic framework is based on Taoist concepts and philosophical attitudes paralleling that of *Zhuangzi*, such as the relativity of values and role reversals, under the principle of which the Foolish Old Man proves to be wise while the Wise Old Man in the story the other way. While the myth has enduring appeal due to the theme of adherence to a noble ideal, it lacks the **poignancy**② and individual heroism the myths of Jingwei is rich in. The reason is that the philosophical thrust of the narrative requires the success of the hero in his struggle, and in this case Yugong's eventual triumph is achieved by the device of **deus ex machina**③. ④ The following is an excerpt from *Liezi*:

> The Taihang and Wangwu Mountains, which had a periphery of seven hundred li and were a hundred thousand feet high, originally lay south of Jizhou and North of Heyang.
>
> The Foolish Old Man of the North Mountain, nearly ninety years of age, lived behind these mountains. He was unhappy about the fact

---

① futile ['fju:taɪl] adj. 徒劳的
② poignancy ['pɔɪnjənsi] n. 尖锐
③ deus ex machina [ˌdeɪʊs eks'mækɪnə] n. 解围的人或事件（小说、戏剧情节中牵强扯入的）
④ Anne Birrell, *Chinese Mythology: An Introduction*, p. 218.

that the mountains blocked his way to the south and he had to walk round them whenever he went out or came back, so he called the whole family together to talk about the matter. "What would you say," he said to them, "if I suggest that all of us work hard to level the two mountains, so as to open a way to places south of Yu **Prefecture**① and the Han River?" Many voices said they agreed to the idea.

But his wife had her doubts. "With your strength," she said, "you could hardly remove a small hill like Kuifu. What could you do with the Taihang and Wangwu Mountains? Besides, where could you deposit the earth and rocks?"

"Carry them to the shores of the Bohai Sea and north of Yintu," said several people.

The old man, helped by his son and grandson who could carry things, began to break rocks and dig earth, which they carried in baskets and dustbins to the shores of the Bohai Sea. The seven-year-old son of a widow named Jingcheng, one of the old man's neighbors, came running up to offer his help. One trip to the sea took them a long time: they left in winter and came back in summer.

The Wise Old Man at the River Bend stopped the old man. He laughed and said, "How unwise you are! At your age, old and feeble as you are, you cannot even remove one hair on the mountain, let alone so much earth and so many rocks!"

The Foolish Old Man of the North Mountain heaved a long sigh and said, "You are so conceited that you are blind to reason. Even a widow and a child know better than you. When I die, there will be

---

① prefecture ['priːfektʃə] n. 地区

my sons, who will have their sons and grandsons. Those grandsons will have their sons and grandsons, and so on to infinity. But the mountains will not grow. Why is it impossible to level them?" The Wise Old Man at the River Bend could not answer him.

The old man's words were heard by a god with snakes in his hands. He was afraid that the old man would really level the two mountains, and reported the whole thing to the Heavenly God. Moved by the old man's determination, the Heavenly God ordered the two sons of Kua'ershi to carry the two mountains on their backs and put one east of Shuo and the other south of Yong. After this, there were no more mountains between Jizhou and the Han River.[①]

Questions for Discussion:

1. What did Yugong decide to do?

2. How did Yugong plead against the Wise Old Man of the River Bend?

3. What motifs and themes are contained in "The Foolish Old Man Removes the Mountains"?

4. What are the similarities and differences between the stories of Yugong and Jingwei?

Part 2 Heroes in Greek Mythology

The Story of Perseus

Perseus, one of the most renowned of the legendary heroes of antiquity,

---

① 丁往道:《中国神话及志怪小说一百篇》,第31—33页。

was the son of Zeus and Danae, daughter of **Acrisius**①, king of Argos.

An oracle having foretold to Acrisius that a son of Danae would be the cause of his death, he imprisoned her in a tower of brass in order to keep her secluded from the world. Zeus, however, descended through the roof of the tower in the form of a shower of gold, and the lovely Danae became his bride.

For four years Acrisius remained in ignorance of this union, but one evening as he chanced to pass by the brazen chamber, he heard the cry of a young child proceeding from within, which led to the discovery of his daughter's marriage with Zeus. Enraged at finding all his precautions **unavailing**②, Acrisius commanded the mother and child to be placed in a chest and thrown into the sea.

But it was not the will of Zeus that they should perish. He directed Poseidon to calm the troubled waters, and caused the chest to float safely to the island of Seriphus. Dictys, brother of Polydectes, king of the island, was fishing on the sea-shore when he saw the chest **stranded**③ on the beach; and pitying the helpless condition of its unhappy occupants, he conducted them to the palace of the king, where they were treated with the greatest kindness.

Polydectes eventually became united to Danae, and **bestowed**④ upon Perseus an education befitting a hero. When he saw his stepson develop into a noble and manly youth, he endeavored to instill into his mind a desire to **signalize**⑤ himself by the achievement of some great and heroic deed, and after mature deliberation it was decided that the slaying of the Gorgon, Medusa, would bring him the greatest renown.

For the successful accomplishment of his object, it was necessary for him to be provided with a pair of winged sandals, a magic wallet, and the helmet of

---

① Acrisius [ə'krisiəs] n. 阿克里西俄斯（古希腊神话中阿尔戈斯的国王）
② unavailing [ˌʌnə'veɪlɪŋ] adj. 无效的
③ stranded ['strændɪd] adj. 搁浅的
④ bestow [bɪ'stəʊ] vt. 授予
⑤ signalize ['sɪgnəˌlaɪz] vt. 表明

Hades, which rendered the wearer invisible, all of which were in the keeping of the Nymphs, the place of whose abode was known only to the **Graeae**①. Perseus started on his expedition, and, guided by Hermes and Athene, arrived, after a long journey, in the far-off region, on the borders of Oceanus, where dwelt the Graeae, daughters of Phorcys and Ceto. He at once applied to them for the necessary information, and on their refusing to grant it he deprived them of their single eye and tooth, which he only restored to them when they gave him full directions with regard to his route. He then proceeded to the abode of the Nymphs, from whom he obtained the objects indispensable for his purpose.

Equipped with the magic helmet and wallet, and armed with a sickle, the gift of Hermes, he attached to his feet the winged sandals, and flew to the abode of the Gorgons, whom he found fast asleep. Now as Perseus had been warned by his **celestial**② guides that whoever looked upon these weird sisters would be transformed into stone, he stood with **averted**③ face before the sleepers, and caught on his bright metal shield their triple image. Then, guided by Athene, he cut off the head of the Medusa, which he placed in his wallet. No sooner had he done so than from the headless trunk there sprang forth the winged steed Pegasus, and Chrysaor, the father of the winged giant Geryon. He now hastened to **elude**④ the pursuit of the two surviving sisters, who, aroused from their slumbers, eagerly rushed to avenge the death of their sister.

His invisible helmet and winged sandals here **stood** him **in good stead**⑤; for the former concealed him from the view of the Gorgons, whilst the latter bore him swiftly over land and sea, far beyond the reach of pursuit. In passing over

---

① Graeae [ˈgriːi] n. 格里伊三姐妹（希腊神话中海神福耳库斯和刻托的三个女儿）
② celestial [səˈlestiəl] adj. 天国的
③ averted [əˈvɜːtɪd] adj. 移开的
④ elude [ɪˈluːd] vt. （尤指机智地，巧妙地）避开
⑤ stand sb. in good stead 对某人有用

the burning plains of Libya the drops of blood from the head of the Medusa **oozed**① through the wallet, fell on the hot sands below and produced a brood of many-colored snakes, which spread all over the country.

Perseus continued his flight until he reached the kingdom of Atlas, of whom he begged rest and shelter. But as this king possessed a valuable orchard, in which every tree bore golden fruit, he was fearful lest the slayer of the Medusa might destroy the dragon which guarded it, and then rob him of his treasures. He therefore refused to grant the hospitality which the hero demanded, whereupon Perseus, **exasperated**② at the **churlish**③ repulse, produced from his wallet the head of the Medusa, and holding it towards the king, transformed him into a stony mountain. Henceforth his beard and hair erected themselves into forests; shoulders, hands, and limbs became huge rocks, and the head grew up into a craggy peak which reached into the clouds.

Perseus then resumed his travels. His winged sandals bore him over deserts and mountains, until he arrived at Ethiopia, the kingdom of King **Cepheus**④. Here he found the country **inundated**⑤ with disastrous floods, towns and villages destroyed, and everywhere signs of desolation and ruin. On a projecting cliff close to the shore, he beheld a lovely maiden chained to a rock. This was Andromeda, the king's daughter. Her mother Cassiopea, having boasted that her beauty surpassed that of the Nereides, the angry sea-nymphs appealed to Poseidon to avenge their wrongs, whereupon the sea-god devastated the country with a terrible inundation, which brought with it a huge monster who devoured all that came in his way.

In their distress the unfortunate Ethiopians applied to the oracle in the

---

① ooze [uːz] vi. 渗出漏
② exasperated [ɪɡˈzæspəreɪtɪd] adj. 恼怒的
③ churlish [ˈtʃɜːlɪʃ] adj. 没有礼貌的
④ Cepheus [ˈsiːfjuːs] n. 克普斯（希腊神话中埃塞俄比亚国王安德洛默达之父）
⑤ inundated [ˈɪnəndeɪtɪd] adj. 洪泛的

Libyan desert, and obtained the response, that only by the sacrifice of the king's daughter to the monster could the country and people be saved.

Cepheus, who was tenderly attached to his child, at first refused to listen to this dreadful proposal; but overcome at length by the prayers and **solicitations**① of his desperate subjects, the heart-broken father gave up his child for the welfare of his country. Andromeda was accordingly chained to a rock on the seashore to serve as a prey to the monster, whilst her parents in distress bewailed her sad fate on the beach below.

On being informed of the cause and effect of this tragic scene, Perseus proposed to Cepheus to slay the dragon, on condition that the lovely victim should become his bride. Overjoyed at the prospect of Andromeda's release, the king gladly **acceded**② to the **stipulation**③, and Perseus hastened to the rock, to breathe words of hope and comfort to the trembling maiden. Then assuming once more the helmet of Hades, he mounted into the air, and awaited the approach of the monster.

Presently the sea opened, and the shark's head of the gigantic beast of the deep raised itself above the waves. **Lashing**④ his tail furiously from side to side, he leaped forward to seize his victim; but the gallant hero, watching his opportunity, suddenly darted down, and producing the head of the Medusa from his wallet, held it before the eyes of the dragon, whose hideous body became gradually transformed into a huge black rock, which remained forever a silent witness of the miraculous deliverance of Andromeda. Perseus then led the maiden to her parents now in a **euphoric**⑤ mood, who, anxious to evince their

---

① solicitation [səˌlɪsɪˈteɪʃn] n. 恳求
② accede [əkˈsiːd] vi. 同意
③ stipulation [ˌstɪpjuˈleɪʃn] n. 约定（规定）的条件
④ lash [læʃ] vt.（动物）用力甩动（尾巴）
⑤ euphoric [juːˈfɒrɪk] adj. 极度兴奋的

gratitude to her deliverer ordered immediate preparations to be made for the **nuptial**① feast. But the young hero was not to bear away his lovely bride uncontested; for in the midst of the banquet, Phineus, the king's brother, to whom Andromeda had previously been betrothed, returned to claim his bride. Followed by a band of armed warriors he forced his way into the hall, and a desperate encounter took place between the rivals, which might have terminated fatally for Perseus, had he not suddenly bethought himself of the Medusa's head. Calling to his friends to avert their faces, he drew it from his wallet, and held it before Phineus and his formidable body-guard, whereupon they all stiffened into stone.

Perseus now took leave of the Ethiopian king, and, accompanied by his beautiful bride, returned to Seriphus, where a joyful meeting took place between Danae and her son. He then sent a messenger to his grandfather, informing him that he intended returning to Argos; but Acrisius, fearing the fulfilment of the oracular prediction, fled for protection to his friend Teutemias, king of Larissa. Anxious to induce the aged monarch to return to Argos, Perseus followed him thither. But here a strange fatality occurred. Whilst taking part in some **funereal**② games, celebrated in honor of the king's father, Perseus, by an unfortunate throw of the discus, accidentally struck his grandfather, and thereby was the innocent cause of his death.

After celebrating the funeral rites of Acrisius with due solemnity, Perseus returned to Argos; but feeling **loath**③ to occupy the throne of one whose death he had caused, he exchanged kingdoms with Megapenthes, king of Tiryns, and in course of time founded the cities of Mycenae and Midea.

The head of the Medusa he presented to his divine patroness, Athene, who

---

① nuptial [ˈnʌpʃl] adj. 婚礼的
② funereal [fjuːˈnɪərɪəl] adj. 适于葬礼的
③ loath [ləʊθ] adj. 不情愿的

placed it in the center of her shield.

Many great heroes were descended from the legend of Perseus and Andromeda, foremost among whom was Heracles, whose mother, **Alcmene**①, was their granddaughter.

For the greatness he achieved, heroic honors were paid to Perseus, not only throughout Argos, but also at Athens and in the island of Seriphus. ②

Questions for discussion:

1. How was Perseus born?

2. What brought Perseus the greatest renown?

3. What were provided for Perseus for his accomplishment?

4. How did Perseus kill Medusa?

5. What did Perseus do when the king of Atlas refused to grant the hospitality which he demanded?

6. What did Cepheus agreed to do if Perseus saved his daughter Andromeda?

7. Why did Perseus feel loath to occupy the throne of his grandfather?

The Story of Heracles

Heracles, one of the most renowned heroes of antiquity, was the son of Zeus and Alcmene, and the great grandson of Perseus.

At the time of his birth Alcmene was living at Thebes with her husband **Amphitryon**③, and thus the infant Heracles was born in the palace of his stepfather.

---

① Alcmene [ælk'mi:ni] n. 阿尔克墨涅（珀尔修斯的孙女，与宙斯生下了赫拉克勒斯）

② E. M. Berens, *The Myths and Legends of Ancient Greece and Rome*, pp. 205 – 210.

③ Amphitryon [æm'fitriən] n. 安菲特律翁（珀尔修斯的孙子）

Aware of the **animosity**① with which Hera persecuted all those who rivalled her in the affections of Zeus, Alcmene, fearful lest this hatred should be visited on her innocent child, entrusted him, soon after his birth, to the care of a faithful servant, with instructions to expose him in a certain field, and there leave him, feeling assured that the divine offspring of Zeus would not long remain without the protection of the gods.

Soon after the child had been thus abandoned, Hera and Athene happened to pass by the field, and were attracted by its cries. Athene pityingly took up the infant in her arms, and **prevailed**② upon the queen of heaven to put it to her breast; but no sooner had she done so, than the child, causing her pain, she angrily threw him to the ground, and left the spot. Athene, moved with compassion, carried him to Alcmene, and entreated her kind offices on behalf of the poor little **foundling**③. Alcmene at once recognized her child, and joyfully accepted the charge.

Soon afterwards Hera, to her extreme annoyance, discovered whom she had nursed, and became filled with jealous rage. She now sent two **venomous**④ snakes into the chamber of Alcmene, which crept, unperceived by the nurses, to the cradle of the sleeping child. However, he awoke with a cry, and grasping a snake in each hand, strangled them both. Alcmene and her attendants, whom the cry of the child had awakened, rushed to the cradle, where, to their astonishment and terror, they beheld the two reptiles dead in the hands of the infant Heracles. Amphitryon was also attracted to the chamber by the **commotion**⑤, and when he caught sight of this astounding proof of supernatural strength, he declared that the child must have been sent to him as a special gift

---

① animosity [ˌænɪˈmɒsəti] n. 憎恶
② prevail [prɪˈveɪl] vi. (prevail on/upon) 说服
③ foundling [ˈfaʊndlɪŋ] n. 弃婴
④ venomous [ˈvenəməs] adj. 有毒的
⑤ commotion [kəˈməʊʃn] n. 骚动

from Zeus. He accordingly consulted the famous seer **Tiresias**①, who now informed him of the divine origin of his stepson, and **prognosticated**② for him a great and distinguished future.

When Amphitryon heard the noble destiny which awaited the child entrusted to his care, he resolved to educate him in a manner worthy of his future career. At a suitable age he himself taught him how to guide a chariot; Eurytus, how to handle the bow; Autolycus, dexterity in wrestling and boxing; and Castor, the art of armed warfare; whilst Linus, the son of Apollo, instructed him in music and letters.

Heracles was an apt pupil; but **undue**③ harshness was intolerable to his high spirit, and old Linus, who was not the gentlest of teachers, one day corrected him with blows, whereupon the boy, flying into a fury, took up his lyre, and, with one stroke of his powerful arm, killed his tutor on the spot.

Apprehensive④ lest the ungovernable temper of the youth might again involve him in similar acts of violence, Amphitryon sent him into the country, where he placed him under the charge of one of his most trusted herdsmen. Here, as he grew up to manhood, his extraordinary stature and strength became the wonder and admiration of all beholders. His aim, whether with spear, lance, or bow, was unerring, and at the age of eighteen he was considered to be the strongest as well as the most **captivating**⑤ youth in all Greece.

Heracles felt that the time had now arrived when it became necessary to decide for himself how to make use of the extraordinary powers with which he had been endowed by the gods; and in order to meditate in solitude on this all-important subject, he repaired to a lonely and secluded spot in the heart of the

---

① Tiresias [tai'ri:siəs] n. 泰利西厄斯（底比斯的一位盲人先知）
② prognosticate [prɔg'nɔsti‚keit] vt. 预言
③ undue [‚ʌn'dju:] adj. 过度的
④ apprehensive [‚æpri'hensiv] adj. 忧虑的
⑤ captivating ['kæptiveitiŋ] adj. 有魅力的

forest.

Here two females of great glamour appeared to him. One was Vice, the other Virtue. The former was full of artificial **wiles**① and fascinating arts, her face painted and her dress **gaudy**② and attractive; whilst the latter was of noble bearing and modest **mien**③, her robes of spotless purity.

Vice stepped forward and thus addressed him: "If you will walk in my paths, and make me your friend, your life shall be one round of pleasure and enjoyment. You shall taste of every delight which can be procured on earth; the choicest **viands**④, the most delicious wines, the most luxuriant of couches shall be ever at your disposal; and all this without any exertion on your part, either physical or mental."

Virtue now spoke in her turn: "If you will follow me and be my friend, I promise you the reward of a good conscience, and the love and respect of your fellowmen. I cannot undertake to smooth your path with roses, or to give you a life of idleness and pleasure; for you must know that the gods grant no good and desirable thing that is not earned by labor; and as you sow, so must you reap."

Heracles listened patiently and attentively to both speakers, and then, after mature **deliberation**⑤, decided to follow in the paths of virtue, and henceforth to honor the gods, and to devote his life to the service of his country.

And now it will be necessary to retrace our steps. Just before the birth of Heracles, Zeus, in an assembly of the gods, **exultingly**⑥ declared that the child who should be born on that day to the house of Perseus should rule over all his race. When Hera heard her lord's boastful announcement, she knew well

---

① wile [waɪl] n. 诡计
② gaudy [ˈɡɔːdi] adj. 俗丽的
③ mien [miːn] n. 风采
④ viand [ˈvaɪənd] n. 食物
⑤ deliberation [dɪˌlɪbəˈreɪʃn] n. 考虑
⑥ exultingly [ɪɡˈzʌltɪŋli] adv. 兴高采烈地

that it was for the child of the hated Alcmene that this brilliant destiny was designed; and in order to rob the son of her rival of his rights, she called to her aid the goddess **Eilithyia**①, who **retarded**② the birth of Heracles, and caused his cousin **Eurystheus**③ (another grandson of Perseus) to precede him into the world. And thus, as the word of the mighty Zeus was irrevocable, Heracles became the subject and servant of his cousin Eurystheus.

When, after his splendid victory over Erginus, the fame of Heracles spread throughout Greece. Eurystheus, jealous of the reputation of the young hero, asserted his rights, and commanded him to undertake for him various difficult tasks. But the proud spirit of the hero rebelled against this humiliation, and he was about to refuse **compliance**④, when Zeus appeared to him and desired him not to rebel against the Fates. Heracles now repaired to Delphi in order to consult the oracle, and received the answer that after performing ten tasks for his cousin Eurystheus his servitude would be at an end.

Soon afterwards Heracles fell into a state of the deepest melancholy, and through the influence of his **inveterate**⑤ enemy, the goddess Hera, this **despondency**⑥ developed into raving madness, in which condition he killed his own children. When he at length regained his reason, he was so horrified and grieved at what he had done, that he shut himself up in his chamber and avoided all intercourse with men. But in his loneliness and seclusion the conviction that work would be the best means of procuring oblivion of the past decided him to enter, without delay, upon the tasks appointed to him by Eurystheus.

---

① Eilithyia [ai'laiθiə] n. 厄勒梯亚（希腊神话中的分娩女神）
② retard [rɪ'tɑːd] vt. 减慢
③ Eurystheus [juə'risθiəs] n. 欧律斯透斯（希腊神话中迈锡尼国王，斯忒涅罗斯和尼喀珀之子，珀耳斯之孙）
④ compliance [kəm'plaɪəns] n. 顺从
⑤ inveterate [ɪn'vetərət] adj. 根深的
⑥ despondency [dɪ'spɒndənsi] n. 泄气

His first task was to bring to Eurystheus the skin of the much-dreaded Nemean lion, which **ravaged**① the territory between Cleone and Nemea, and whose hide was invulnerable against any mortal weapon.

Heracles proceeded to the forest of Nemea, where, having discovered the lion's **lair**②, he attempted to pierce him with his arrows; but finding these of no avail he felled him to the ground with his club, and before the animal had time to recover from the terrible blow, Heracles seized him by the neck and, with a mighty effort, succeeded in strangling him. He then made himself a coat of mail of the skin, and a new helmet of the head of the animal. Thus attired, he so alarmed Eurystheus by appearing suddenly before him, that the king concealed himself in his palace, and henceforth forbade Heracles to enter his presence, but commanded him to receive his **behests**③, for the future, through his messenger Copreus.

His second task was to slay the Hydra, a monster serpent, bristling with nine heads, one of which was immortal. This monster **infested**④ the neighborhood of Lerna, where she committed great **depredations**⑤ among the herds.

Heracles, accompanied by his nephew Iolaus, set out in a chariot for the marsh of Lerna, in the **slimy**⑥ waters of which he found her. He commenced the attack by assailing her with his fierce arrows, in order to force her to leave her lair, from which she ultimately emerged, and sought refuge in a wood on a neighboring hill. Heracles now rushed forward and endeavored to crush her heads by means of well-directed blows from his tremendous club; but no sooner

---

① ravage ['rævɪdʒ] vt. 毁坏
② lair [leə] n. (野兽的) [动] 巢穴
③ behest [bɪ'hest] n. 命令
④ infest [ɪn'fest] vt. 骚扰
⑤ depredation [ˌdeprə'deɪʃn] n. 破坏
⑥ slimy ['slaɪmi] adj. 泥泞的

was one head destroyed than it was immediately replaced by two others. He next seized the monster in his powerful grasp; but at this juncture a giant crab came to the assistance of the Hydra and commenced biting the feet of her **assailant**①. Heracles destroyed this new adversary with his club, and now called upon his nephew to come to his aid. At his command Iolaus set fire to the neighboring trees, and, with a burning branch, **seared**② the necks of the monster as Heracles cut them off, thus effectually preventing the growth of more. Heracles next struck off the immortal head, which he buried by the road-side, and placed over it a heavy stone. Into the poisonous blood of the monster he then dipped his arrows, which ever afterwards rendered wounds inflicted by them incurable.

The third labor of Heracles was to bring the horned **hind**③ Cerunitis alive to Mycenae. This animal, which was sacred to Artemis, had golden antlers and hoofs of brass.

Not wishing to wound the hind Heracles patiently pursued her through many countries for a whole year, and overtook her at last on the banks of the river Ladon; but even there he was compelled, in order to secure her, to wound her with one of his arrows, after which he lifted her on his shoulders and carried her through Arcadia. On his way he met Artemis with her brother Apollo, when the goddess reproved him for wounding her favorite hind with indignation; but Heracles succeeded in appeasing her displeasure, whereupon she permitted him to take the animal alive to Mycenae.

The fourth task imposed upon Heracles by Eurystheus was to bring alive to Mycenae the Erymantian **boar**④, which had laid waste the region of Erymantia, and was also the scourge of the surrounding neighborhood.

---

① assailant [əˈseɪlənt] n. 攻击者
② sear [sɪə] vt. 烤焦
③ hind [haɪnd] n. 雌鹿
④ boar [bɔː] n. 野猪

On his way thither Heracles craved food and shelter of a **Centaur**① named Pholus, who received him with generous hospitality, setting before him a good and plentiful **repast**②. When Heracles expressed his surprise that at such a well-furnished board wine should be wanting, his host explained that the wine-cellar was the common property of all the Centaurs, and that it was against the rules for a cask to be **broached**③, except all were present to partake of it. By dint of persuasion, however, Heracles prevailed on his kind host to make an exception in his favor; but the powerful, **luscious**④ odor of the mellow old wine soon spread over the mountains, bringing large numbers of Centaurs to the spot, all armed with huge rocks and fir-trees. Heracles drove them back with fire-brands, and then, following up his victory, pursued them with his arrows as far as Malea, where they took refuge in the cave of the kind old Centaur Chiron. Unfortunately, however, as Heracles was shooting at them with his poisoned darts, one of these pierced the knee of Chiron. When Heracles discovered that it was the friend of his early days that he had wounded, he was overcome with sorrow and regret. He at once extracted the arrow, and anointed the wound with a **salve**⑤, the virtue of which had been taught to him by Chiron himself. But all his efforts were unavailing. The wound, **imbued**⑥ with the deadly poison of the Hydra, was incurable, and so great was the agony of Chiron that, at the intercession of Heracles, death was sent to him by the gods; for otherwise, being immortal, he would have been doomed to endless suffering.

Pholus, who had so kindly entertained Heracles, also perished on account

---

① Centaur ['sentɔː] n. 希腊神话中半人半马的怪物
② repast [rɪ'pɑːst] n. 饮食
③ broach [brəʊtʃ] vt. 钻孔
④ luscious ['lʌʃəs] adj. 甘美的
⑤ salve [sælv] n. 药膏
⑥ imbue [ɪm'bjuː] vt. 使感染

of one of these arrows, which he had **extracted**① from the body of a dead Centaur. While he was quietly examining it, astonished that so small and insignificant an object should be productive of such serious results, the arrow fell upon his foot and fatally wounded him. Full of grief at this **untoward**② event, Heracles buried him with due honors, and then set out to chase the boar.

With loud shouts and terrible cries, he first drove him out of the **thickets**③ into the deep snow-drifts which covered the summit of the mountain, and then, having at length wearied him with his incessant pursuit, he captured the exhausted animal, bound him with a rope, and brought him alive to Mycenae.

After slaying the Erymantian boar Eurystheus commanded Heracles to cleanse in one day the stables of Augeas.

Augeas was a king of Elis who possessed a large quantity of herds. Three thousand of his cattle he kept near the royal palace in an **enclosure**④ where the refuse had accumulated for many years. When Heracles presented himself before the king, and offered to cleanse his stables in one day, provided he should receive in return a tenth part of the herds, Augeas, thinking the feat impossible, accepted his offer in the presence of his son Phyleus.

Near the palace were the two rivers Peneus and Alpheus, the streams of which Heracles conducted into the stables by means of a trench which he dug for this purpose, and as the waters rushed through the shed, they swept away with them the whole mass of accumulated filth.

But when Augeas heard that this was one of the labors imposed by Eurystheus, he refused the promised **guerdon**⑤. Heracles brought the matter before a court, and called Phyleus as a witness to the justice of his claim,

---

① extract [ˈekstrækt] vt. 提取
② untoward [ˌʌntəˈwɔːd] adj. 不幸的
③ thicket [ˈθɪkɪt] n. 灌木丛
④ enclosure [ɪnˈkləʊʒə] n. 围场
⑤ guerdon [ˈɡɜːdən] n. 报酬

whereupon Augeas, without waiting for the delivery of the **verdict**①, angrily banished Heracles and his son from his dominions.

The sixth task was to chase away the **Stymphalides**②, which were immense birds of prey who, as we have seen (in the legend of the Argonauts), shot from their wings feathers sharp as arrows. The home of these birds was on the shore of the lake Stymphalis, in Arcadia, where they caused great destruction among men and cattle.

On approaching the lake, Heracles observed great numbers of them; and, while hesitating how to launch the attack, he suddenly felt a hand on his shoulder. Looking round he beheld the majestic form of Athene, who held in her hand a gigantic pair of brazen **clappers**③ made by Hephaestus, with which she presented him; whereupon he ascended to the summit of a neighboring hill, and commenced to rattle them violently. The shrill noise of these instruments was so intolerable to the birds that they rose into the air in terror, upon which he aimed at them with his arrows, destroying them in great numbers, whilst such as escaped his darts flew away, never to return.

The seventh labor of Heracles was to capture the Cretan bull. Minos, king of Crete, having vowed to sacrifice to Poseidon any animal which should first appear out of the sea, the god caused a magnificent bull to emerge from the waves in order to test the sincerity of the Cretan king, who, in making this vow, had alleged that he possessed no animal, among his own herds, worthy the acceptance of the mighty sea god. Charmed with the splendid animal sent by Poseidon, and eager to possess it, Minos placed it among his herds, and substituted as a sacrifice one of his own bulls. Hereupon Poseidon, in order to

---

① verdict ['vɜːdɪkt] n. 结论
② stymphalide ['stimfəlaid] n. 希腊神话中群居在斯廷法利斯湖畔（位于阿耳卡狄亚地区）的奇鸟
③ clapper ['klæpə] n. 响板

punish the **cupidity**① of Minos, caused the animal to become mad, and commit such great **havoc**② in the island as to endanger the safety of the inhabitants. When Heracles, therefore, arrived in Crete for the purpose of capturing the bull, Minos, far from opposing his design, gladly gave him permission to do so.

The hero not only succeeded in securing the animal, but tamed him so effectually that he rode on his back right across the sea as far as the Peloponnesus. He now delivered him up to Eurystheus, who at once set him at liberty, after which he became as ferocious and wild as before, roamed all over Greece into Arcadia, and was eventually killed by Theseus on the plains of Marathon.

The eighth labor of Heracles was to bring to Eurystheus the mares of **Diomedes**③, a son of Ares, and king of the Bistonians, a warlike Thracian tribe. This king possessed a breed of wild horses of tremendous size and strength, whose food consisted of human flesh, and all strangers who had the misfortune to enter the country were made prisoners and flung before the horses, who devoured them eventually.

When Heracles arrived, he first captured the cruel Diomedes himself, and then threw him before his own mares, who, after devouring their master, became perfectly tame and tractable. They were then led by Heracles to the seashore, when the Bistonians, enraged at the loss of their king, rushed after the hero and attacked him. He now gave the animals in charge of his friend Abderus, and made such a furious onslaught on his assailants that they turned and fled.

But on his return from this encounter he found, to his great grief, that the

---

① cupidity [kjuːˈpɪdəti] n. 贪婪
② havoc [ˈhævək] n. 大破坏
③ Diomedes [ˌdaɪəˈmiːdiːz] n. 狄俄墨得斯（阿耳戈斯国王，海伦的求婚者，特洛伊之战中与希腊人一同作战）

mares had torn his friend in pieces and devoured him. After celebrating due funereal rites to the unfortunate Abderus, Heracles built a city in his honor, which he named after him. He then returned to Tiryns, where he delivered up the mares to Eurystheus, who set them loose on Mount Olympus, where they became the prey of wild beasts.

It was after the performance of this task that Heracles joined the Argonauts in their expedition to gain possession of the Golden Fleece, and was left behind at Chios. During his wanderings he undertook his ninth labor, which was to bring to Eurystheus the girdle of **Hippolyte**①, queen of the Amazons.

The Amazons, who dwelt on the shores of the Black Sea, near the river Thermodon, were a nation of warlike women, renowned for their strength, courage, and great skill in horsemanship. Their queen, Hippolyte, had received from her father, Ares, a beautiful girdle, which she always wore as a sign of her royal power and authority, and it was this girdle which Heracles was required to place in the hands of Eurystheus, who designed it as a gift for his daughter Admete.

Foreseeing that this would be a task of no ordinary difficulty the hero called to his aid a select band of brave companions, with whom he embarked for the Amazonian town Themiscyra. Here they were met by queen Hippolyte, who was so impressed by the extraordinary stature and noble bearing of Heracles that, on learning his errand, she at once consented to present him with the **coveted**② girdle. But Hera, his implacable enemy, assuming the form of an Amazon, spread the report in the town that a stranger was about to carry off their queen. The Amazons at once flew to arms and mounted their horses, whereupon a battle ensued, in which many of their bravest warriors were killed or wounded. Among

---

① Hippolyte [hiˈpɔlitiː] n. 希波吕武（亚马孙族的女皇）
② coveted [ˈkʌvətɪd] adj. 梦寐以求的

the latter was their most skillful leader, Melanippe, whom Heracles afterwards restored to Hippolyte, receiving the girdle in exchange.

On his voyage home the hero stopped at Troy, where a new adventure awaited him. During the time that Apollo and Poseidon were condemned by Zeus to a temporary **servitude**① on earth, where they built for king Laomedon the famous walls of Troy, afterwards so renowned in history; but when their work was completed the king treacherously refused to give them the reward due to them. The incensed deities now combined to punish the offender. Apollo sent a pestilence which **decimated**② the people, and Poseidon a flood, which bore with it a marine monster, who swallowed in his huge jaws all that came within his reach.

In his distress Laomedon consulted an oracle, and was informed that only by the sacrifice of his own daughter Hesione could the anger of the gods be appeased. Yielding at length to the urgent appeals of his people he consented to make the sacrifice, and on the arrival of Heracles the maiden was already chained to a rock in readiness to be devoured by the monster.

When Laomedon beheld the renowned hero, whose marvelous feats of strength and courage had become the wonder and admiration of all mankind, he earnestly implored him to save his daughter from her impending fate, and to rid the country of the monster, holding out to him as a reward the horses which Zeus had presented to his grandfather Tros in compensation for robbing him of his son Ganymede.

Heracles unhesitatingly accepted the offer, and when the monster appeared, opening his terrible jaws to receive his prey, the hero, sword in hand, attacked and slew him. But the **perfidious**③ monarch once more broke faith, and

---

① servitude [ˈsɜːvɪtjuːd] n. 劳役
② decimate [ˈdesɪmeɪt] vt. 大批杀害
③ perfidious [pəˈfɪdɪəs] adj. 背信弃义的

Heracles, vowing future vengeance, departed for Mycenae, where he presented the girdle to Eurystheus.

The tenth labor of Heracles was the capture of the magnificent oxen belonging to the giant **Geryon**①, who dwelt on the island of Erythia in the bay of Gadria (Cadiz). This giant, who was the son of Chrysaor, had three bodies with three heads, six hands, and six feet. He possessed a herd of splendid cattle, which were famous for their size, beauty, and rich red color. They were guarded by another giant named Eurytion, and a two-headed dog called **Orthrus**②, the offspring of Typhon and Echidna.

In choosing for him a task so replete with danger, Eurystheus was in hopes that he might rid himself forever of his hated cousin. But the **indomitable**③ courage of the hero rose with the prospect of this difficult and dangerous undertaking.

After a long and wearisome journey, he at last arrived at the western coast of Africa, where, as a monument of his perilous expedition, he erected the famous "Pillars of Heracles," one of which he placed on each side of the Straits of Gibraltar. Here he found the intense heat so insufferable that he was outraged, raising his bow towards heaven, and threatening to shoot the sun-god. But Helios, far from being incensed at his **audacity**④, was so struck with admiration at his daring that he lent to him the golden boat with which he accomplished his **nocturnal**⑤ transit from West to East, and thus Heracles crossed over safely to the island of Erythia.

No sooner had he landed than Eurytion, accompanied by his savage dog Orthrus, fiercely attacked him; but Heracles, with a superhuman effort, slew

---

① Geryon ['gɛrɪən] n. 革律翁（希腊神话中的三休四翼巨人）
② Orthus ['ɔːθrəs] n. 俄耳托洛斯（希腊神话中的双头犬）
③ indomitable [ɪn'dɒmɪtəbl] adj. 不屈不挠的
④ audacity [ɔː'dæsəti] n. 大胆
⑤ nocturnal [nɒk'tɜːnəl] adj.（动物）夜间活动的

the dog and then his master. Hereupon he collected the herd, and was proceeding to the sea-shore when Geryones himself met him, and a desperate encounter took place, in which the giant perished.

Heracles then drove the cattle into the sea, and seizing one of the oxen by the horns, swam with them over to the opposite coast of Iberia (Spain). Then driving his magnificent prize before him through Gaul, Italy, Illyria, and Thrace, he at length arrived, after many perilous adventures and hair-breadth escapes, at Mycenae, where he delivered them up to Eurystheus, who sacrificed them to Hera.

Heracles had now executed his ten tasks, which had been accomplished in the space of eight years; but Eurystheus refused to include the slaying of the Hydra and the cleansing of the stables of Augeas among the number, alleging as a reason that the one had been performed by the assistance of Iolaus, and that the other had been executed for hire. He therefore insisted on Heracles substituting two more labors in their place.

The eleventh task imposed by Eurystheus was to bring him the golden apples of the **Hesperides**[①], which grew on a tree presented by Gaea to Hera, on the occasion of her marriage with Zeus. This sacred tree was guarded by the Hesperides, the four nymphs of evening and golden light of sunsets, who were assisted in their task by a ferocious hundred-headed dragon. This dragon never slept, and out of its hundred throats came a constant hissing sound, which effectually warned off all intruders. But what rendered the undertaking still more difficult was the complete ignorance of the hero as to the locality of the garden, and he was forced, in consequence, to make many fruitless journeys and to undergo many trials before he could find it.

He first travelled through Thessaly and arrived at the river Echedorus,

---

① Hesperides [heˈsperɪˌdiːz] n. 赫斯珀里得斯（守护金苹果树的仙女）

where he met the giant Cycnus, the son of Ares and Pyrene, who challenged him to single combat. In this encounter Heracles completely vanquished his opponent and killed him. But now a mightier adversary appeared on the scene, for the war-god, Ares himself came to avenge his son. An intense struggle ensued, which had lasted some time, when Zeus interfered between the brothers, and put an end to the strife by hurling a thunderbolt between them. Heracles proceeded on his journey, and reached the banks of the river Eridanus, where dwelt the Nymphs, daughters of Zeus and Themis. On seeking advice from them as to his route, they directed him to the old sea-god Nereus, who alone knew the way to the Garden of the Hesperides. Thither Heracles found him asleep, and seizing the opportunity, held him so firmly in his powerful grasp that Nereus could not possibly escape, so that notwithstanding his various metamorphoses he was at last compelled to give the information required. The hero then crossed over to Libya, where he engaged in a wrestling-match with king Anteos, son of Poseidon and Gaea, which terminated fatally for his antagonist.

From thence he proceeded to Egypt, where reigned Busiris, another son of Poseidon, who sacrificed all strangers to Zeus. When Heracles arrived he was seized and dragged to the altar; but the powerful demi-god burst asunder his bonds, and then slew Busiris and his son.

Resuming his journey he now wandered on through Arabia until he arrived at Mount Caucasus, where Prometheus groaned in unceasing agony. It was at this time that Heracles shot the eagle which had so long tortured the noble and devoted friend of mankind. Full of gratitude for his deliverance, Prometheus instructed him how to find his way to that remote region in the far West where Atlas supported the heavens on his shoulders, near which lay the Garden of the Hesperides. He also warned Heracles not to attempt to secure the precious fruit himself, but to assume for a time the duties of Atlas, and to dispatch him for the apples.

On arriving at his destination Heracles followed the advice of Prometheus. Atlas, who willingly entered into the arrangement, contrived to put the dragon to sleep, and then, having cunningly outwitted the Hesperides, carried off three of the golden apples, which he now brought to Heracles. But when the latter was prepared to **relinquish**① his burden, Atlas, having once tasted the delights of freedom, declined to resume his post, and announced his intention of being himself the bearer of the apples to Eurystheus, leaving Heracles to fill his place. To this proposal the hero feigned assent, merely begging that Atlas would be kind enough to support the heavens for a few moments whilst he contrived a pad for his head. Atlas good-naturedly threw down the apples and once more resumed his load, upon which Heracles bade him adieu, and departed.

When Heracles conveyed the golden apples to Eurystheus the latter presented them to the hero, whereupon Heracles placed the sacred fruit on the altar of Pallas-Athene, who restored them to the garden of the Hesperides.

The twelfth and last labor which Eurystheus imposed on Heracles was to bring up Cerberus from the lower world, believing that all his heroic powers would be unavailing in the Realm of Shades, and that in this, his last and most perilous undertaking, the hero must ultimately succumb and perish.

Cerberus was a monster dog with three heads, out of whose awful jaws dripped poison; the hair of his head and back was formed of venomous snakes, and his body terminated in the tail of a dragon.

After being initiated into the Eleusinian Mysteries, and obtaining from the priest's certain information necessary for the accomplishment of his task, Heracles set out for **Laconia**②, where there was an opening which led to the

---

① relinquish [rɪˈlɪŋkwɪʃ] vt. 放弃
② Laconia [ləˈkəʊnɪə] n. 拉科尼亚（希腊伯罗奔尼撒半岛东南部分的区域）

underworld. Conducted by Hermes, he commenced his descent into the awful gulf, where **myriads**① of shades soon began to appear, all of whom fled in terror at his approach, **Meleager**② and Medusa alone excepted. About to strike the latter with his sword, Hermes interfered and stayed his hand, reminding him that she was but a shadow, and that consequently no weapon could avail against her.

Arriving before the gates of Hades he found Theseus and **Pirithous**③, who had been fixed to an enchanted rock by Hades for their presumption in endeavoring to carry off Persephone. When they saw Heracles they implored him to set them free. The hero succeeded in delivering Theseus, but when he endeavored to liberate Pirithous, the earth shook so violently beneath him that he was compelled to relinquish his task.

Proceeding further Heracles recognized **Ascalaphus**④, who, as we have seen in the history of Demeter, had revealed the fact that Persephone had swallowed the seeds of a pomegranate offered to her by her husband, which bound her to Hades forever. Ascalaphus was groaning beneath a huge rock which Demeter in her anger had hurled upon him, and which Heracles now removed, releasing the sufferer.

Before the gates of his palace stood Hades the mighty ruler of the lower world, barring his entrance; but Heracles, aiming at him with one of his unerring darts, shot him in the shoulder, so that for the first time the god experienced the agony of mortal suffering. Heracles then demanded of his permission to take Cerberus to the upper-world, and to this Hades consented on condition that he should secure him unarmed. Protected by his **breastplate**⑤ and

---

① myriad [ˈmɪriəd] n. 无数
② Meleager [ˌmeliˈeigə] n. 梅利埃格（阿尔戈诸英雄，斩除了卡莱敦的野猪怪）
③ Pirithous [ˈpiriθəs] n. 皮瑞苏斯（伊克西翁之子，拉庇泰人之王，忒修斯之密友）
④ Ascalaphus [əsˈkeiləfəs] n. 阿斯卡拉福斯（河神阿克戎之子）
⑤ breastplate [ˈbrestpleɪt] n. 护胸甲

lion's skin Heracles went in search of the monster, whom he found at the mouth of the river Acheron. Undismayed by the hideous barking which proceeded from his three heads, he seized the throat with one hand and the legs with the other, and although the dragon which served him as a tail bit him severely, he did not relinquish his grasp. In this manner he conducted him to the upper-world, through an opening near Troezenin Argolia.

When Eurystheus beheld Cerberus he stood aghast, and despairing of ever getting rid of his hated rival, he returned the hell-hound to the hero, who restored him to Hades, and with this last task the subjection of Heracles to Eurystheus terminated.

Through all kinds of adventures, Heracles became admitted among the immortals; and Hera, in token of her reconciliation, bestowed upon him the hand of her daughter of irresistible beauty, Hebe, the goddess of eternal youth.[①]

Questions for Discussion:

1. What did Heracles's mother Alcmene do to him?

2. What did Hera do after knowing the identity of the baby?

3. What did Heracles do to the two serpents?

4. Who appeared to Heracles? Whose path did he decide to choose?

5. What did Eurystheus command Heracles to do to put an end to his servitude?

6. How many tasks did Heracles finish? What were they?

Part 3　Reflections

1. Vocabulary Expansion

1) Yi the archer: _____

---

① E. M. Berens, *The Myths and Legends of Ancient Greece and Rome*, pp. 234 – 251.

2) Jingwei: _____

3) Chiyou: _____

4) Shennong: _____

5) Cangjie: _____

6) Hou Ji: _____

7) Perseus: _____

8) Heracles: _____

9) the Hesperides: _____

10) the twelve tasks of Heracles: _____

2. Appreciation

1) 逮至尧之时，十日并出。焦禾稼，杀草木，而民无所食。猰貐、凿齿、九婴、大风、封豨、修蛇皆为民害。尧乃使羿诛凿齿于畴华之野，杀九婴于凶水之上，缴大风于青邱之泽，上射十日而下杀猰貐，断修蛇于洞庭，擒封豨于桑林。万民皆喜，置尧以为天子。

《淮南子》

2) 又北二百里，曰发鸠之山，其上多柘木。有鸟焉，其状如乌，文首、白喙、赤足，名曰精卫，其鸣自詨。是炎帝之少女，名曰女娃，女娃游于东海，溺而不返，故为精卫，常衔西山之木石以堙于东海。漳水出焉，东流注于河。

《山海经·北山经》

3) 夸父不量力，欲追日影，逐之于隅谷之际。渴欲得饮，赴饮河、渭。河、渭不足，将走北饮大泽。未至，道渴而死。弃其杖，尸膏肉所浸，生邓林。邓林弥广数千里焉。

《列子》

4) 奚仲作车，仓颉作书，后稷作稼，皋陶作刑，昆吾作陶，夏鲧作城，此六人者，所作当矣。

《吕氏春秋》

5) Those rocks the billow-cleaving bark alone

The Argo, further'd by the vows of all,

Pass'd safely, sailing from Aeata's isle;

Nor she had pass'd, but surely dash'd had been

On those huge rocks, but that, propitious still

To Jason, Hera sped her safe along.

These rocks are two; one lifts his summit sharp

High as the spacious heav'ns, wrapt in dun clouds

Perpetual, which nor autumn sees dispers'd

Nor summer, for the sun shines never there;

No mortal man might climb it or descend,

Though twice ten hands and twice ten feet he own'd,

For it is levigated as by art.

Homer's *The Odyssey*

3. Discussion

1) Compare the images of heroes in Chinese and Greek mythology and draw a conclusion of their features.

2) What cultural connotations are presented through the hero images in Chinese and Greek mythology?

3) What influence do the myths of heroes exert upon people's personality, the creation of artistic works and the politics in China and western countries?

Unit 11

Myths about Women

Introduction

Women have played significant roles in mythology of various cultures throughout human history. Some women have possessed magical powers, ranging from the ability to predict a person's fate to determining the fate themselves. Ordinary women often accompany male heroes; others are heroic figures in their own right. All in all, whether positive or negative roles, women in mythology display strength, tolerance, calmness, divinity, and many other fascinating and complex qualities.

Although male deities predominate in Chinese mythology, female ones are no less significant in terms of their functions and roles. Nüwa, for example, is both the creator of human beings and the savior of the threatened cosmos; Changxi is the mother of the moons; Xihe is the **charioteer**[①] and the mother of the suns; Xiwangmu, the ruler of the western paradise and a punishing goddess, is also the deity who grants mortals the gift of immortality; Woman Chou (Nü Chou) and Drought Fury (Nü Ba) are the **baneful**[②] demons of drought; Fu Fei is the goddess of the Luo River; Jingwei is a doomed goddess, as is the Weaving Maiden; the Tushan girl gave birth to the demigod Qi; Jiang Yuan and Jian Di

---

① charioteer [ˌtʃæriəˈtɪə] n. 驾双轮马车的人
② baneful [ˈbeɪnfl] adj. 有害的

were the ancestors of the Zhou and Shang peoples. As it is shown, the functions and roles of these female deities are diverse and significant, including creation, the motion of celestial bodies, nature spirit, local **tutelary**① spirit, mother of a god, consort of a demigod or a god, harbinger of disaster, donor of immortality, bringer of punishment, and dynastic foundation. Meanwhile, women who led to the downfall of men or a nation are also depicted. A typical example is Su Daji who was portrayed as a **malevolent**② fox spirit and led to the fall of the Shang Dynasty.

Greek mythology places as much emphasis on male gods and heroes as their female counterparts. Quantities of divine and brave female heroes are celebrated for their notable exploits. Athena, the goddess of wisdom, the practical arts, and warfare, Aphrodite, the goddess of love and beauty, and Demeter, the goddess of the harvest are female deities that bless humans. Ariadne is the famous female hero who guided Theseus through the Labyrinth by giving him **twine**③ and a sword to defeat the Minotaur. More often, women are shown as deceitful and manipulative, and the downfall of men in Greek myths. Pandora, the first woman to be created, exemplified the ancient Greek view of women as "weak, fickle and opportunistic." After being abandoned, Medea took revenge upon Jason by murdering their children. Helen, being abducted by Parris, stirred up the Trojan War. Clytemnestra plotted against her husband Agamemnon and finally killed him. Along with this, men came to be known for their strength and women for trickery. The divergence has been shown by Homer in *The Odyssey* in order to distinguish one gender from the other.

---

① tutelary ['tjuːtɪləri] adj. 监护的
② malevolent [mə'levələnt] adj. 恶毒的
③ twine [twaɪn] n. (两股或多股的) 线

Part 1 Women in Chinese Mythology

Xiwangmu

Xiwangmu, the Queen Mother of the West, one of the most popular goddesses in Chinese mythology and folk belief, was originally a wild beastlike goddess (or god) who evolved into the ruler of punishment, calamity, disease, and a refined queen to date. She was the owner of the elixir of immortality and the divine peaches that can endow longevity. She also was the leader of the goddesses in the Taoist pantheon. As late as the Ming Dynasty she was commonly referred to as Wangmu Niangniang ("wangmu" literally means "queen mother," and "niangniang" is a respectful title for a goddess).

Depicted as a wild and fearsome spirit, Xiwangmu first appeared in *The Classic of Mountains and Seas*. Many Chinese scholars maintain that Xiwangmu's image in *The Classic of Mountains and Seas* illustrates that she possessed both female and male features. One account describes Xiwangmu as a deity of disaster, disease, and punishment. She dwelled on the Jade Mountain, which was very close to Kunlun Mountain, the earthly residence of the Supreme Divinity and a paradise for deities and immortals. She looked like a human but had a **panther's**[①] tail and tiger's teeth. She was good at roaring, and wore a jade **sheng**[②] on her head.

Another text from *The Classic of Mountains and Seas* relates that Xiwangmu

---

① panther [pænθə] n. 黑豹
② "胜",指西王母佩戴的发饰,最早出现于《山海经》:"西王母其状如人,豹尾虎齿而善啸,蓬发戴胜。""有人,戴胜,虎齿,有豹尾,穴处,名曰西王母。"汉司马相如的《大人赋》里也有记载:"吾乃今日睹西王母,暠然白首戴胜而穴处兮",编者注。

leaned against a small table, wearing a jade sheng on her head. To the south of her, three green birds were fetching food for her (in some versions a three-legged crow fetched her food). They were all situated north of Kunlun Mountain. Still another text of the same book states that Kunlun Mountain was located south of the West Sea, on the shore of the Liusha, behind the Chishui River and in front of the Black River. There was a god who had human face, a tiger's body with stripes and a long tail. Underneath where he lived, there was the Ruoshui River (whose water was so weak that it could not float even a feather) circling the mountain. Beyond it, there was Mount of Burning Fire into which anything thrown would immediately burn up. Xiwangmu lived in a cave here. She wore a jade sheng, had a tiger's teeth and a leopard's tail.

From the Warring States era to the Han Dynasty, Xiwangmu's image changed greatly, from a wild and ferocious monsterlike deity to a cultivated queen. In a book named *Biography of Mu Tianzi* (*The Chronicle of Emperor Mu*, traditionally said to have been written in the Western Zhou Dynasty or the Warring States period), Xiwangmu is described as a polite princess who hosted for Emperor Mu of Zhou a banquet. She not only **improvised**[①] poems to communicate with Emperor Mu but also provided elegant singing, though she still lived with wild animals and birds according to her own poems. Additionally in this period, her functions increased rapidly. She was believed to have the ability to control various aspects of human life including wealth, health, fertility, and calamity, and was endowed with even more power and influence than in *The Classic of Mountains and Seas*. She came to be popularly known as the keeper of the elixir of immortality, which had the magic power of keeping one's life and vitality and preventing death. In the early Han book *Huainanzi*, when the hero Yi asked for the elixir of immortality from Xiwangmu, she gave it to him. But

---

① improvise ['ɪmprəvaɪz] vt. 即兴创作

his wife Chang'e stole it, then flew to the moon and became the spirit of it.

In the Han Dynasty, Xiwangmu was popularly depicted to have a **consort**[①] named Dongwanggong, King Father of the East. There are quite a few stories about him in ancient documents. According to a text in *Shenyijing* (*The Classic of Spirits and Strange Things*, allegedly written by a Han writer, Dongfang Shuo, 154 B. C. – 93 B. C., but seemingly compiled later by an anonymous author), there was an immense bronze pillar on Kunlun Mountain, rearing high into the sky. It was, in fact, the pillar which supported the Heaven. On top of it there was a huge bird named Xiyou (literally meaning "rare"). Opening its left wing, it covered Dongwanggong; opening the right one, it covered Xiwangmu. When a meeting was wanted, Xiwangmu had to climb onto the other wing to meet Dongwanggong. In another account, Dongwanggong lived in a big stone house on the East Wild Mountain. He was about ten feet high, with hair as white as snow. He looked like a man but had a bird's face and a tiger's tail. He rode a black bear. With a Jade Maiden he often played the game of throwing chips into a pot. When he scored, heaven sighed; when he missed, heaven laughed.

Since the Han Dynasty, Xiwangmu's and Dongwanggong's names frequently appeared together in inscriptions on bronze mirrors. In most cases, they were described as long-lived immortals who guarded the secret of immortality. Yet people also prayed to them for wealth, safety, honor, and children. Nevertheless, it is seen from funerary stones and brick **bas-reliefs**[②] found in Henan, Shaanxi, Hebei, Jiangsu, Shandong, Hunan, Zhejiang, Sichuan, and many other provinces that the presence of Xiwangmu was not always accompanied by Dongwanggong. She was typically shown as a respectable

---

① consort [ˈkɒnsɔːt] n. 配偶
② bas-relief [ˌbæs rɪˈliːf] n. 浅浮雕

goddess, sitting on a cloud or a seat made of a dragon and a tiger. Much of the time she was surrounded by a Jade Rabbit, a toad, birds, or sometimes a three-legged crow, a deer, a dragon, a nine-tailed fox, and immortal servants with wings. The rabbit (sometimes the immortal servants also) usually was pounding the elixir in a mortar in front of Xiwangmu and Dongwanggong.

During the Wei (220 A. D. – 265 A. D.) and Jin (265 A. D. – 420 A. D.) dynasties, with the flourishing of Taoism, Xiwangmu was further immortalized and became a leader of the female immortals. She also was widely known as the owner of the divine saucer peach, a fruit that had the magic power of endowing longevity. In a book written in this period, **Hanwudi Neizhuan**①, or *The Biography of Emperor Wu of Han*, Xiwangmu is depicted as a beautiful and graceful female immortal dressed up in Taoist style. Thousands of immortals accompanied her, and even her two serving maidens were extremely beautiful. She gave four saucer peaches to the Emperor Wu in the Han Dynasty (who reigned from 156 A. D. to 87 A. D.). Since the peaches tasted so good, the emperor kept the pits, hoping to plant them when he came back to the central land. But Xiwangmu told him that this kind of peach needed to be harvested for 3,000 years before yielding ripe peaches. So the emperor felt disappointed and gave up. In some other Taoist books in this period, Xiwangmu is given a more honorable origin as the daughter of the highest god in Taoism, **Yuanshi Tianzun**②.

After the Tang and Song dynasties, Xiwangmu became more common in folk tradition. She often appeared in a later-formed pantheon (with disordered system) as the consort of Yu Di, the Jade Emperor, the highest ruler of heaven

---

① 《汉武帝内传》又名《汉武内传》《汉武帝传》，中国神话志怪小说。明清人有云为汉班固或晋葛洪撰者，皆无确据，疑为后人伪托，编者注。

② 元始天尊，全称"玉清元始天尊"，也称元始天王，是道教"三清"尊神之一，在"三清"之中位为最尊，编者注。

and gods. In the renowned mythic novel *Xiyouji* (*Journey to the West*, written by Wu Cheng'en, ca. 1500 A. D. – 1582 A. D.), which found many of its sources in folk tradition, Xiwangmu is addressed as Wangmu Niangniang, the bearer of peaches that gave immortality to whoever ate them. She often invited other immortals and gods to the Saucer Peach Banquet. The peaches she used for the banquet were classified into three sorts: the first one ripened every 3,000 years and could make the person who ate it healthy; the second one ripened every 6,000 years and could bring the one who ate it a long life; the third one ripened every 9,000 years and could make the one who ate it as long-lived as heaven and the earth. In the novel, the Monkey King ate many of the best peaches and disturbed the banquet because he was not invited.

Today, the wild and ferocious Xiwangmu can hardly be found in Chinese mythology. Compared to those of Nüwa, Fuxi, Pangu, and many other ancient gods and goddesses in mythology, modern myths about Wangmu Niangniang are not rich in detail. She usually appears in the stories as a minor character, such as a divine predictor, an adviser, a helper, an intervener, and so on. This may be due to the roughness of her original mythological behaviors in record. [1]

Questions for Discussion:

1. In Chinese mythology and folk belief, what kind of goddess is Xiwangmu?

2. According to *The Classic of Mountains and Seas*, where did Xiwangmu inhabit and what did she look like?

3. From the Warring States era to the Han Dynasty, what kind of image of Xiwangmu was shown?

4. What aspects of human life were believed to be controlled by Xiwangmu

---

[1] Yang Lihui, An Deming and Jessica Anderson Turner, *Handbook of Chinese Mythology*, pp. 218–222.

from the Warring States era to the Han Dynasty?

5. Who was said to be the consort of Xiwangmu in the Han Dynasty?

6. How was Xiwangmu depicted during the Wei and Jin dynasties?

7. After the Tang and Song dynasties, who was said to be the consort of Xiwangmu?

Ba[①]

Ba, also called Nüba or Hanba ("nü" means "female" and "han" means "drought"), is the deity who can bring severe drought to the world by withholding water and rain.

Ba is one of the most ancient goddesses in the written tradition, because her name and function are mentioned in *Shijing* (*The Classic of Poetry*, compiled in or before 500 B.C.) though rather simple and concise.

Ba's main function is described with more detail in *The Classic of Mountains and Seas*. She is said to be the daughter of the Yellow Emperor and lived on the Terrace of Gonggong, which was located on Xikun Mountain in the north. She was bald and dressed in green. Wherever she lived there would always be a drought. When at war with the Yellow Emperor, Chiyou asked Feng Bo (the God of Wind) and Yu Shi (the God of Rain) to release a storm. Seeing this, the Yellow Emperor sent down Ba from heaven to stop the rain. Ba killed Chiyou and stopped the rain, but she was unable to go back to heaven and the place where she stayed always suffered from a drought. **Shujun**[②], the Cultivation God, reported it to the God of Heaven. Later the emperor instructed Ba to live north of the Chishui River. But Ba was unwilling to be confined; she often fled

---

[①] 魃,《山海经·大荒北经》:"有人衣青衣,名曰黄帝女魃。蚩尤作兵伐黄帝,黄帝乃令应龙攻之冀州之野",编者注。

[②] 叔均是帝喾之孙、台玺之子,周部族的杰出首领,与父亲一起被周王尊为先祖,编者注。

from this area and wandered to other places, bringing drought with her. Therefore, if people wanted to avoid the happening of drought, they needed to drive the goddess away. The way they did it was to **dredge**① the canals in advance, and then prayed to her, "Goddess, go north to where you should stay!" It is said that it would rain after Ba was gone.

The image and character of Ba, as well as the custom of "driving Ba away" are also described in *Shenyijing* (*The Classic of Spirits and Strange Things*, which by tradition has been written in the Han period or the Six Dynasties era, 386 A. D. – 589 A. D.). Ba was reportedly two or three chi (three chi equals one meter, or 3.3 feet) in height, with two eyes on her head, and she wore no clothes. She looked like a human but walked fast like the wind. Where she appeared, there was a drought. But if she was captured and plunged into **excrement**②, the drought would be stopped.

The custom of "driving Ba away" was common in numerous variations before 1949 in some regions of Henan, Shandong, Sichuan, and other provinces. In the northern part of Henan Province, for instance, Ba was thought to be the corpse of a newly buried person. If it did not rain for a long time, the anxious farmers would open the new grave with fresh earth on top, dig the corpse out, and whip it for they believed Ba would water the grave during the night. They called this "beating Drought Ba." In their belief, it would rain soon after this rite. However, in Sichuan Province in southwest China the ritual was quite different. One man would disguise himself as the Drought Ba and four men would act as warriors. Ba would escape hither and thither, and the warriors would run after "her" while the audience helped them by shouting or beating the drums. The ritual would last for several hours until Ba was driven away from this area. ③

---

① dredge [dredʒ] vt. 疏浚
② excrement ['ekskrɪmənt] n. 粪便
③ Yang Lihui, An Deming and Jessica Anderson Turner, *Handbook of Chinese Mythology*, pp. 79 – 80.

Questions for Discussion:

1. What does the name of Ba mean?

2. How is Ba described in *The Classic of Mountains and Seas*?

3. How is Ba described in *Shen yijing*?

4. What would Ba bring with her?

4. What customs of "driving Ba away" were there in Henan and Sichuan?

Xihe①

Xihe is the mother of the ten suns and one of Di Jun's wives.

The motif of "creation of the sun" is found in many ethnic groups in China. The sun is usually depicted as having been created by gods, transformed from a divine corpse, or born from its parents. For example, a myth in the Buyi ethnic group holds that the god **Wengga**② gave birth to the sky, the earth, day and night, and the sun and the moon. In the **Luoba**③ ethnic group in Tibet, the parents of the sun are the sky and the earth.

The sun in Chinese mythological tradition is commonly said to have been born by its mother Xihe and father Di Jun. However, similar to the myth of Changxi, who is the mother of the twelve moons and another wife of Di Jun, the Xihe myth is quite scarce in mythological texts in spite of her high status. Her accomplishment can mainly be found in *The Classic of Mountains and Seas*. A text from that book states that beyond the Southeast Sea and on the Ganshui River area was the Xihe kingdom. A lady named Xihe, wife of Di Jun, gave birth to

---

① 羲和，太阳女神。《山海经·大荒南经》："东南海之外，甘水之间，有羲和之国。有女子名曰羲和，方日浴于甘渊。羲和者，帝俊之妻，生十日"，编者注。

② 翁嘎，布依族神话中聪明机智、制服旱精和孽龙的神，编者注。

③ 珞巴族，信奉所有的神，他们认为天地、日月、星辰、树木、小草都依附神灵，编者注。

ten suns. She used to bathe the ten suns in the Ganyuan Pool.

Another text from the same book further describes how the ten suns work in the sky. They lived on the Fusang tree, which grew in the water of the Tang Valley. The ten suns stayed in the Fusang tree and bathed in the water there. Nine of the suns stayed on the tree's lower branches while the one that was going to rise stayed on its top branch. The ten suns rose from the Fusang tree one by one. As soon as one sun returned from crossing the sky, another sun went up. Each sun was carried by a crow. In another version in that book, Xihe is portrayed as the driver who steered a cart pulled by six dragons to send her children out into the sky.

As in the Changxi myth about her bathing the twelve moons, the reason Xihe bathed the suns is unclear in these texts. Some myths spread in the Miao, Buyi, and Yi ethnic groups explain that the sun and the moon need to be washed in order to cleanse them from the dust they accumulate during their work to be bright again. These versions may provide some help in understanding the myths about bathing the suns and the moons told among Han people.

Xihe is also variously said to be the deity who takes charge of the seasons and calendar. But the gender seems vague in this case. [1]

Questions for Discussion:

1. According to *The Classics of Mountains and Seas*, where was Xihe's kingdom? What did she used to do there?

2. According to the myths in the Miao, Buyi, and Yi ethnic groups, why the sun and the moon need to be washed?

3. What is the connection between Xihe and the Worship of the Sun?

---

[1] Yang Lihui, An Deming and Jessica Anderson Turner, *Handbook of Chinese Mythology*, pp. 215-216.

Jiang Yuan[①]

The earliest accounts of the virgin birth of Hou Ji occur in lines from two hymns in *Shijing*, or *The Classic of Poetry*, with the latest date of compilation circa 600 B. C. Poem 245, "She Who First Gave Birth to Our People," and poem 300, "The Sealed Palace," relate the myth in slightly differing versions. The latter is briefer, poem 300 being a poetic chronology of the Zhou noble house of the prince of Lu, said to have been descended from Hou Ji and the founding rulers of the Zhou, King Wen and King Wu. Poem 245 gives a fuller version of the myth and focuses more closely on the birth and life of the god Hou Ji. The first half of poem 245, which narrates the birth myth and the three trials of the divinely born infant-hero, is presented, as is the case in the prose version of the myth by Sima Qian.

It is worth enumerating the mythic motifs in these accounts: the ancestry of Jiang Yuan, her relation to the god Di Ku, her erotic experience in the fields (in the prose version), the fertility of God's footprint, the miraculous birth without pain or injury, the three trials of the child god, signs of the protective presence of God in the people living close to nature and in the creatures of nature, and the mythic name Qi, the Abandoned.

It is always rewarding to compare two versions of a myth, whether they are of the same date or, as in this case, separated by five hundred years. Sima Qian clearly rationalizes the mythic narrative of poem 245, in which he must have based his own account, and inserts explanatory data, such as names and Jiang Yuan's motivation for **infanticide**[②], but the historian excludes the fertility rite and Jiang Yuan's barrenness and the inauguration of the new temple rite to

---

① 姜嫄，有邰氏部落人。上古时期历史人物，帝喾元妃，周族始祖后稷之母。编者注。
② infanticide [ɪnˈfæntɪsaɪd] n. 杀婴

Hou Ji with its **paean**① of praise to the glorious line of the Zhou. With the advent of the Han empire, the mythic account, told by the court historian, has shifted away from a belief in the divine descent of the god Hou Ji and his people, the Zhou, to a historicizing and humanizing biographical mode that subverts the mythic themes.

The following are excerpts from *Shi Jing* and *Shi Ji*:

> She who first gave birth to our people
> Was Jiang Yuan.
> And how did she give birth to our people?
> She performed the Yin and Si sacrifices well
> So that she might not be without child.
> She trod in the big toe of God's footprint
> And was filled with joy and was enriched;
> She felt a movement and it soon came to pass
> That she gave birth and suckled
> The one who was Hou Ji.
> She fulfilled her due months
> And her firstborn came forth,
> With no rending or tearing,
> Without injury or harm.
> And this revealed the miraculous,
> For did not God give her an easy birth,
> Was he not well pleased with her sacrifice?
> And so she bore her child with comfort.
> She laid it in a narrow alley

---

① paean ['piːən] n. 赞美歌

But ox and sheep suckled it.

She laid it in a wood on the plain

But it was found by woodcutters on the plain.

She laid it on chill ice

But birds covered it with their wings.

Then the birds went away

And Hou Ji wailed,

Really loud and strong;

The sound was truly great.

Then he crawled in truth;

He straddled and strode upright

To look for food for his mouth.

He planted large beans,

And the large beans grew thick on the vine;

His ears of grain were heavy, heavy,

His hemp and wheat grew thick;

The gourd stems were laden with fruit.

(*Shi Jing*)

Hou Ji of the Zhou was named Qi, the Abandoned. His mother, the daughter of the You-tai clan, was called Jiang Yuan. Jiang Yuan was Di Ku's first consort. Jiang Yuan went out to the wild fields and she saw the footprints of a giant. Her heart was full of joy and pleasure, and she felt the desire to tread in the footprints. As she trod in them there was a movement in her body as if she were with child. She went on until her due time and gave birth to a baby boy. Because she thought he was unlucky, she abandoned him in a narrow alley. All the horses and cattle that passed by avoided treading on him. She moved him into woods, but she happened to meet too many people in the mountain woods. She moved him away and abandoned him on the ice of a ditch, but flying birds protected him with their wings and cushioned him. Jiang Yuan thought he might be a god, so she took him up at once and brought him up until he was fully grown. Because she had wanted to abandon him at first, his name was Qi. (*Shi Ji*)[1]

Questions for Discussion:
1. How did Jiang Yuan give birth to Hou Ji?
2. What did she do to her baby boy?

Su Daji

The legend about Su Daji was made known by the popular *Fengshen Yanyi* (*Historical Romance of Apotheosis*). The novel described Daji as the incarnation of a silvery fox that assumed a human form after a thousand years of self-cultivation. She was summoned by Nüwa, the celestial sovereign, to corrupt the Di Xin, the tyrant of the powerful state of Shang so that his people would rise and overthrow him. Incidentally, Di Xin is known historically as Zhou. Before Daji's departure, Nüwa promised her an immortal status after her mission was accomplished.

According to historical record, however, Daji was the beautiful daughter of a noble family named Su in the state of You Su. In 1047 B. C. , Zhou, the tyrant of Shang, conquered the state of Su and took Daji as his trophy. By then, the king was in his sixties and had been in his throne for forty years. He had been known as strong, heroic, oratory and well-versed in music. Under his

---

[1] Anne Birrell, *Chinese Mythology: An Introduction*, pp. 116 – 118.

reign, Shang had become a powerful and prosperous state. He certainly had his Achilles' heel, namely, his infatuated love for women. Ever since King Zhou had Daji as his concubine, things began to change, for the worse.

Zhou liked Daji so much that he tried every means to **ingratiate**① himself with her. Daji liked animals, so he built her a zoological Xanadu with a large collection of rare birds and animals. She liked dancing and singing, so he ordered artists to compose lewd music and **choreograph**② bawdy dances. Forgetting about state affairs all together, King Zhou began to spend all his time with Daji. He would gather three thousand guests at one party to enjoy his "pond of wine" and "forest of meat," which was cooked meat strips hanging from a wood of trees. King Zhou would allow the guests to play a cat and mouse game in the nude among the trees so that Daji could be amused. When a maid of honor, daughter of Lord Jiu, could not bear the sight of such **debauchery**③ and protested, King Zhou had her slain, her father grounded, and his flesh fed to the tyrant's **vassals**④.

Eventually Daji became a brute herself. It was said that her greatest joy was to hear people cry in physical sufferings. Once, as she saw a farmer walking barefoot on the ice, she ordered his feet be cut off so that she could study it and figure out the cause of its resistance to cold temperature. On another occasion, she had a pregnant woman's belly cut open so that she could satisfy her curiosity of finding out what happened therein. To verify the old saying that "a good man's heart had seven openings," she had the heart of Bi Gan, an honest minister, cut out and subjected it to her fertile scrutiny.

On top of all those atrocities, Daji was best known for her invention of a

---

① ingratiate [ɪnˈgreɪʃieɪt] vt. 使迎合
② choreograph [ˈkɒriəgrɑːf] vt. 设计舞蹈动作
③ debauchery [dɪˈbɔːtʃəri] n. 纵情酒色
④ vassal [ˈvæsl] n. 诸侯

device of torture called Paolao: a bronze cylinder heated like a furnace with charcoal until the sides were extremely hot. Then the victim would be bound on the cylinder and baked to death. Daji would take great delight in the painful cries of the condemned.

While the tyrant Zhou was occupied with making himself and Daji happy, a Zhou tribe began to grow increasingly stronger. Its hatred towards the tyrant was deep-rooted. When Boyi Kao, eldest son of Ji Chang, leader of the Zhou tribe, visited Chao Ge, capital of Shang, he had a love affair with Daji. In his wrath, the tyrant Zhou had Kao killed and his body grounded. As if it were not enough, Zhou made Ji Chang drink the soup of his son's flesh before jailing him. Only after many rescue efforts including intensive bribery was Ji Chang finally released two years later. Twelve years after Ji Chang's death, his youngest son Ji Fa launched an attack against Shang to revenge his family.

The anger and hatred created by the brutality of tyrant Zhou and Daji among their own people made it easier for Ji Fa to achieve his goal. In the face of the Zhou tribe's onslaught, the better armed and once invincible army of Shang suddenly gave in and many soldiers even turned their weapons against their tyrannical ruler. Seeing his dynasty doomed, tyrant Zhou committed suicide by setting fire upon himself. Daji was later put to death by Ji Fa, king of the new Dynasty of Zhou.

According to *Fengshen Yanyi*, however, after the fall of the Shang Dynasty, Nüwa sentenced Daji, the incarnation of a fox, to death instead of making her an immortal as she had promised because she found her overzealous in doing what she had been asked to do. Daji had made her people so mad that it left Nüwa no alternative. [1]

---

[1] https://people.wku.edu/haiwang.yuan/China/tales/daji_b.htm

Questions for Discussion:

1. According to *Fengshen Yanyi*, what did Nüwa summon Daji to do?

2. How did King Zhou ingratiate himself with Daji?

3. What kind of atrocities was Daji well-known for?

4. How did King Zhou and Daji die?

Part 2　Women in Greek Mythology

The Story of Medea[①]

Medea, one of the most fascinating and complex characters in the whole of Greek mythology, is the ultimate heroine, villain and victim, all rolled into one.

Medea was a high priestess, skilled in the art of witchcraft. Her father, King Aeetes, ruled over the land of Colchis, a strange and faraway land at the end of the world to the Greeks.

The Greek god of war, Ares had placed a golden fleece in a grove in Colchis and charged Aeetes with protecting it. The fleece was guarded by a fearsome dragon. Ares had decreed that as long as the fleece stayed in Colchis, the land would prosper and its people would have good fortune.

One day, a Greek ship landed on the shores of Colchis. Aboard this ship, the Argo, was a Greek prince called Jason. On seeing Jason for the first time, Medea fell head over heels in love with him.

When Jason arrived at the palace, he asked Aeetes to give him the golden

---

① Medea [mi'diə] n. 美狄亚（希腊神话中科尔喀斯国王之女，以巫术著称）

fleece. Aeetes had no intention of giving up the fleece, so he set Jason an impossible task, promising that Jason could take the fleece away with him if he could yoke two fire breathing bulls to plough a field and sow it with the magical teeth of a serpent that had been slain long ago by another Greek hero called Cadmus.

Knowing that Jason would not be able to complete these tasks on his own, Medea offered him a bargain. If he agreed to marry her, she would help him win the fleece. Jason agreed. Medea gave Jason a **lotion**① (a magical ointment) to rub on his skin that would protect him from the fiery breath of the bulls. With Medea's help, Jason managed to yoke the ferocious bulls to the plough and planted the serpent's teeth. The teeth instantly grew into an army of men who fought each other until every one of them was dead. When King Aeetes saw that Jason had successfully completed the task, he was furious. He broke his promise, refusing to give up the golden fleece, and even threatened to burn Jason's ship and massacre his crew.

Medea quickly led Jason and his men to the grove where the golden fleece hung. She **soothed**② the fearsome dragon with her spells and potions. Jason unfastened the fleece from the tree. Afterwards he ran back to his ship with Medea and her younger brother Apsyrtus. Together they all set sail at top speed for Greece.

Aeetes, however, was not prepared to let the fleece go so easily. He sent his ships after Jason and Medea. Aeetes' ships were faster than Jason's and he soon caught up with the couple. Medea knew she had to do something drastic to stop her father to save her beloved Jason. So she took hold of her brother Apsyrtus, hacked him to death and cut him up into pieces. She then strewed the

---

① lotion ['ləʊʃn] n. 护肤乳
② soothe [suːð] vt. 安抚

bloody pieces of his corpse about the sea, knowing that her father, stricken with grief, would have to stop to fish them out.

Medea and Jason were married on Corcyra with huge celebrations and over their wedding bed they spread the golden fleece. Together they sailed home to Greece.

When they arrived in Jason's home town of Iolcus, Jason discovered that the king, Pelias, had murdered his parents and his brother. Furious with grief, Jason wanted to launch an immediate armed assault on the city. Medea, however, had a better idea. She told Jason that she could take the city single-handed. She instructed Jason's crew to hide their boat, while she went to the city alone. When Jason and his crew saw a torch waved on the palace roof, they would know she had succeeded and the town would be theirs for the taking.

As Medea approached the city gates, she transformed herself into an old woman. She carried a statue of the goddess of the hunt, Artemis, with her. When she reached the gates, she announced that the goddess Artemis had come to reward Pelias for his piety. Pelias was a very old man and had no heirs. Artemis, Medea told him, had taken pity on him and would make him young again so that he could have more sons.

Pelias was a suspicious man. He didn't believe Medea. So Medea said that she would prove the truth of the goddess's promise to him. She transformed herself back into a young woman, right before Pelias's very eyes. Next, she took an old ram and cut it up into thirteen pieces. She threw the pieces of ram into a boiling cauldron. Then, she plunged her hand into the boiling cauldron and drew out a live lamb.

Pelias was convinced. He lay down on a couch and Medea charmed him to sleep. She gave his three daughters knives and commanded them to cut him up into thirteen pieces like the ram. Then, she told the three girls to take torches up onto the palace roof and invoke the power of the moon to help the cauldron boil. When Jason and his men saw the torches, they rushed into Iolcus and took the town for their own.

Medea's father had once been king of Corinth and it was to Corinth that Jason and Medea went next. Medea claimed the throne for herself and the people of Corinth eagerly welcomed Jason as their king. Medea and Jason decided to settle there. Medea bore Jason seven sons and seven daughters, and they all should have lived happily ever after.

Ten years passed, and Jason's eye began to wander. He fell in love with Glauce, the young and beautiful daughter of king Creon of Thebes. He decided to divorce Medea and marry Glauce instead. Medea was furious. She still loved Jason deeply. She reminded Jason that the throne of Corinth was rightfully hers, not his. Jason laughed at her saying that the people of Corinth had more respect for him than for her, so he should be king still. Medea pretended to give in to Jason and agreed to leave the town without causing any trouble, but she had other plans.

On their wedding day, Medea sent Jason's bride a gift of a poison dress and a poison crown. When Glauce put them on, they burnt into her skin. Her father Creon attempted to **rip**① the dress and crown off Glauce in order to save her, but he too became tangled up in the poisoned dress and they died together in each other's arms. As a second form of revenge on Jason, Medea murdered all their children. Jason went **berserk**② and attempted to hunt down Medea. Medea's grandfather Helius, the god of the sun, saved her. Medea climbed into his winged chariot and escaped. Jason was left behind, brideless and childless.

Medea fled to Athens. The king of Athens, Aegeus, agreed to give her shelter and in return Medea offered to give him a son. Later Aegeus and Medea

---

① rip [rɪp] vt. (使) 撕裂
② berserk [bəˈzɜːk] adj. 狂怒的

were married and they had a son called Medus. One day, however, Medea discovered that Aegeus had already had a son, Theseus, with another woman. Medea wanted her son Medus to be Aegeus's only rightful heir. She invited Theseus to a banquet and put a deadly poison in his cup of wine. Aegeus discovered Medea's plan and when Theseus raised his cup to make a toast, Aegeus dashed the poisoned wine from his hands.

Medea fled the city of Athens and sailed home to Colchis. Her father's throne had been taken from him by his brother Perses. Medea won her father's throne back for him and they were reconciled. Some people say that Jason then arrived in Colchis and was reunited with Medea, however, the truth is that Jason was punished by the gods for breaking his promise to Medea. He was doomed to wander homeless from city to city, hated by everyone. One day, he came across his old ship, the Argo. He sat down in its shadow to remember his past glories and mourn all the disasters that had befallen him. Being so upset, he decided to hang himself from the ship's prow, but instead the ship's prow suddenly fell off and killed him. Medea never died. She was made immortal and went to live forever in the happiness of the Elysian fields.[①]

Questions for Discussion:

1. How did Medea help Jason get the golden fleece?

2. How did she help Jason win Iolcus?

3. What did Medea do when she got to know Jason decided to divorce her and marry Glauce instead?

4. What did Medea do when she got to know Aegeus had already had a son?

5. What kind of woman do you think Medea is?

---

① https://www.citz.co.uk/images/uploads/files/MEDEA_-_LEARN_MORE.pdf

The Story of Helen

A long time ago, in the age of heroes, when gods and goddesses still took a close interest in human affairs, a great wedding was planned between a famous warrior called Peleus and a lovely sea nymph whose name was Thetis. All the kings and queens of the day were invited to the wedding feast, as well as all the immortal ones who lived on Mount Olympus—all that is, except for one, for no invitation was sent to **Eris**①, the goddess of Strife. Now that Eris was personification of strife, it was generally thought a bad idea to invite her to a wedding party, in case she caused the happy couple to quarrel. Extremely annoyed about being overlooked, Eris decided to play a spiteful trick on the wedding guests as revenge. Just as the celebrations were at their height, she appeared in the banqueting hall dressed as a serving girl. A silver plate was in her hands, and on it was an apple on which she had written the words, "For the fairest of them all." This she placed on the table where the three loveliest goddesses were sitting; their names were Hera, Athene and Aphrodite. Immediately as they saw the words on the apple, a quarrel broke out among the three goddesses.

Hera said to the others, "I am the queen of all the immortal gods, and it follows that I must be far fairer than either of you two, therefore the apple belongs to me."

"My dear Hera," said Athene, "You might be queen, but I am the goddess of wisdom, therefore I know absolutely everything that is worth knowing. You must believe me when I say that you are quite mistaken. Wisdom is beauty, and beauty is wisdom. They are one and the same thing, therefore the apple belongs to me."

---

① Eris ['erɪs] n. 厄里斯（不和女神，战神阿瑞斯的姊妹）

"Darlings," **purred**① Aphrodite, "It's quite obvious that the apple belongs to me. I possess the power of love because, to put it quite simply, I am so much more beautiful than anybody else."

The goddesses carried on arguing continuously for years after the wedding was over—for time means nothing to the immortal ones. The king of all the gods, mighty and thundering Zeus, became quite fed up with listening to their **bickering**②. At length, he was at his wits' end, and suggested to the three lovely goddesses that they resolve the question once and for all with a beauty contest. And that is exactly what they did.

The three goddesses agreed on one thing: that the most handsome and fashionably dressed mortal who walked on the face of the earth was Paris, Prince of Troy. They decided to surprise him. One day when Paris was out hunting on the foothills of Mount Ida, he discovered three lovely goddesses standing beneath a tree. In all his life he had never seen such dazzling beauty. For a moment he stood amazed, then Hermes, the winged messenger of the gods, flew up to Paris and spoke to him as follows, "Hail Paris, prince of magnificent Troy. Lord Zeus, the king of all the gods, sends you his greetings. He wishes to bestow upon you a great honor. He asks that you give this apple to the fairest goddess of them all."

Paris, who normally had a keen eye for beauty, found it hard to choose. Each goddess was so beautiful. Hera had the loveliest milky white skin ever seen. Athene had the most dazzling, dancing eyes. And Aphrodite had the most charming smile. Which should he pick?

At length, seeing that he was at a loss, Hera said to him, "Prince Paris, give the apple to me and I will give you the gift of great power."

---

① pur ['pɜ] vi. 发出喉音
② bickering ['bɪkərɪŋ] n. 争吵

Athene, not to be outdone by this offer, said, "Prince Paris, give the apple to me and I will give you the gift of great wisdom."

But Aphrodite laughed and said, "Paris my dear, don't you listen to those two silly goddesses. What fun would you have with power or wisdom? Give the apple to me and I will give you a gift that is much more to your liking. I shall give you the love of the most beautiful woman on earth."

Now Paris no longer found the choice so hard to make. He had long been in love with the most beautiful woman on earth, whose name was Helen. It so happened that Helen was married to King Menelaus, and Paris had thought up until that moment that the possibility of his winning her love was beyond all hope, but now he understood that his chances could be greatly improved—and so Paris gave the apple to Aphrodite. She giggled with delight, but the other two goddesses were furious and flew directly back to Mount Olympus in a great **huff**①, where they complained long and bitterly to Zeus about the unfairness of the competition. Zeus had a dark feeling that there was trouble in store for humankind.

Paris set sail for the land of Sparta, where Menelaus was king and lived with his beautiful Queen Helen. Menelaus welcomed the famous prince into his palace, and while the two sat talking about the affairs of the world, Queen Helen came down from her perfumed room, looking as lovely as a goddess. The maid-servants brought her a seat and covered it with a soft **lambswool**② rug, and she sat before her silver work box, but before she began to embroider, she glanced over at the visiting prince and questioned her husband, "Shall I guess the name of this prince who has come to visit us? Let us see if I am right or wrong? I have heard tell of a prince from far off Troy who is famous the world over

---

① huff [hʌf] n. 发怒
② lambswool ['læmzwʊl] n. 羔羊毛

for his looks and fashionable style. Is it he, Paris, prince of Troy who has come to stay with us?"

"My dear wife," said Menelaus, "As always, you are quite right. It is indeed, Paris, prince of Troy who is paying us the honor of his visit." Paris acknowledged Queen Helen with a nod of his head.

At dinner that night, Helen added a special potion into the wine, so that anyone who drank it would forget all his cares, and be happy for the rest of the evening. They feasted and made merry and while Menelaus was busy laughing and joking with one of his generals, Paris spoke softly to Helen.

"Most beautiful queen," he said, "I beg you, meet me tonight in the orchard beneath the palace walls and we shall sail away together in my ship, and head directly for Troy, the most magnificent city in all the world."

And because the goddess of love, Aphrodite, had wished it so, Helen could not help herself, and agreed to his suggestion.

When King Menelaus awoke in the morning, discovering that his guest and his wife had run away together, he flew into a rage, kicking the furniture and punching the walls of his chamber. He swore before all the gods that his revenge would be truly terrible so he went to see his elder brother, King Agamemnon of Argos, and said to him, "My dear brother, the honor of our family has been **besmirched**① by this foreign peacock, this perfumed playboy, this **prancing**② Prince of Troy. Let us gather together all the kings of Greece and combine our armies into the greatest force that has ever been seen since the dawn of history, and let us sail to the far-off city of Troy, and teach Prince Paris some manners."

Agamemnon was wise and he knew that it would always be a terrible mistake to rush headlong into conflict. He suggested first, that they send an ambassador

---

① besmirch [bɪˈsmɜːtʃ] vt. 弄脏
② prancing [ˈprɑːnsɪŋ] adj. 欢腾的

to Troy to request the return of Queen Helen, whom he was sure had been **abducted**① against her will. He knew that Paris's father, King Priam of Troy was a good man, and he was sure that he would order his son to release her, and so they sent a message to Troy in the name of peace and reconciliation, but Helen did not wish to go home, and Prince Paris refused to return the lovely queen to her husband, saying that they had been brought together by the Goddess of Love, Aphrodite herself; hence the attempt to negotiate failed. King Agamemnon, the brother of the wronged Menelaus, summoned all the kings of Greece and prepared a navy of a thousand ships, the greatest military force to ever set sail. ②

Questions for Discussion:

1. Who was not invited to the wedding feast?
2. What did the three goddesses, Hera, Athena and Aphrodite argue for?
3. What did they promise to give Paris?
4. What did Paris do in Sparta?
5. What did the abduction of Helen lead to?

Clytemnestra③

Clytemnestra, the daughter of King Tyndareus and Queen Leda of Sparta, married King Agamemnon of Mycenae and bore four children: Iphigenia, Electra, Orestes, and Chrysothemis.

When Helen, Clytemnestra's sister, left her husband, King Menelaus of Sparta, and ran away with Paris of Troy, Clytemnestra's husband Agamemnon

---

① abduct [æb'dʌkt] vt. 诱拐
② https://www.storynory.com/helen-of-troy/
③ Clytemnestra [ˌklaitəm'nestrə] n. 克吕泰墨斯特拉

agreed to help his brother retrieve his **wayward**① wife. When the Greek army, led by Agamemnon, gathered at the coast to sail to Troy, the winds refused to blow. The Greeks remained **stalled**② on the coast for weeks, until finally the prophet **Calchas**③ announced that the goddess Artemis would only allow their army to sail when Agamemnon sacrificed his most beautiful daughter to the goddess, whom he had previously offended by killing one of her sacred **stags**④.

Agamemnon knew that his wife would never willingly allow the sacrifice of her beloved daughter, and so he sent a false message with the hero Odysseus that their daughter Iphigenia would marry the great hero Achilles and needed to be sent to the coast for the wedding. The convinced Clytemnestra sent her daughter to her father. When the young woman arrived, Agamemnon had her sacrificed at the altar of Artemis. Unbeknownst to Agamemnon, the goddess **whisked**⑤ the young woman away and so she was not actually killed.

When Clytemnestra discovered the true purpose her husband had in mind for her daughter, she never forgave Agamemnon. While the Greeks set sail soon after the "sacrifice," Clytemnestra took her husband's treacherous cousin, Aegisthus, as her lover. When Agamemnon and his brother were young, Aegisthus and his father, Thyestes had forced them out of their kingdom. After Menelaus married Helen and became the king of Sparta, he and Agamemnon had in turn defeated Aegisthus and his father and removed them from Mycenae. With Agamemnon away at war with Troy, Aegisthus ruled Mycenae again with the help of Clytemnestra. By the time Agamemnon arrived at his palace, Clytemnestra's plans were well advanced.

---

① wayward [ˈweɪwəd] adj. 任性的
② stall [stɔːl] vi. 暂缓
③ Calchas [ˈkælkæs] n. 卡尔克斯（特洛伊战争中希腊军队的阿波罗奉祀祭司和随军占卜师）
④ stag [stæg] n. 牡鹿
⑤ whisk [wɪsk] vt. 拂

Meeting her husband in front of the entrance, she insisted that he should trample over the purple textiles she spread out before him, in a triumphal entrance into his hall. Agamemnon was reluctant to commit such an act of **insolence**① and impiety for it was an honor reserved only for gods. But eventually he gave in, and so ensured his doom. Following him indoors, Clytemnestra attacked him as he lay defenseless in the bath, first **ensnaring**② him in a net, before murdering him most brutally with an axe. Her motives for this savage killing were complex, but it would seem that it was not so much her guilty passion for Aegisthus and her desire to see him avenged for the wrong done to his father and brothers, as her hatred of Agamemnon that drove her to his murder. He had brutally murdered her first husband and child before her eyes; he had sacrificed their daughter Iphigeneia at Aulis. She wanted vengeance. Thus, emerging from the crime scene, Clytemnestra rested on her blood-stained weapon at the door, triumphantly proud and contented over her role as heaven's instrument of justice.

The curse of Atreus did not die with Agamemnon, for he and Clytemnestra had two more children eager to avenge their father's death, Orestes and Electra. Orestes, when a baby, had been sent away by his sister from Mycenae to his uncle Strophius, King of Phocis to preserve him from their scheming mother. In the palace of Strophius, Orestes grew up with the king's son **Pylades**③, and formed with him that ardent friendship. Electra herself remained at home and was very badly treated by Clytemnestra and Aegisthus; according to some versions of the story they married her off to a peasant so that the royal line would end in **ignominy**④. When he grew up, Orestes secretly returned home,

---

① insolence [ˈɪnsələns] n. 傲慢
② ensnare [ɪnˈsneə] vt. 诱捕
③ Pylades [ˈpailədiːz] n. 皮拉得斯（希腊神话中福喀斯国王斯特洛菲俄斯和阿那西比亚的儿子，阿那西比亚是阿伽门农和墨涅劳斯的妹妹）
④ ignominy [ˈɪgnəmɪni] n. 耻辱

accompanied by his friend Pylades. Arriving at the tomb of his father, he laid locks of his hair on the mound, where they were recognized by Electra, who approached to offer a **placatory**① sacrifice on half of her mother; Clytemnestra had had a dream of ill-omen, that she had given birth to a snake which had suckled at her breast and drained away her blood. Orestes quite reasonably saw this as auspicious for himself and after much agonized discussion of the horrors of **matricide**②, Electra persuaded Orestes to murder both his mother and Aegisthus. For this terrible deed he was driven insane by the Furies from land to land. Pylades accompanied him in his wanderings, watching over him. At length, in answer to a second appeal to the oracle, he was directed to go to Tauris in Scythia, and to bring thence a statue of Diana which was believed to have fallen from heaven. Accordingly, Orestes and Pylades went to Tauris, where the barbarous people were accustomed to sacrificing to the goddess all strangers who fell into their hands. The two friends were seized and carried bound to the temple to be made victims. But the priestess of Artemis was no other than Iphigenia, the sister of Orestes, who was snatched away by Artemis at the moment when she was about to be sacrificed. Ascertaining from the prisoners who they were, Iphigenia disclosed herself to them, and the three made their escape with the statue of the goddess, and returned to Mycenae.

But Orestes was not yet relieved from the vengeance of the Erinyes. At length he took refuge with Athena at Athens. The goddess afforded him protection, and appointed the court of **Areopagus**③ to decide his fate. The Erinyes brought forward their accusation, and Orestes made the command of the Delphic oracle his excuse. When the court voted and the voices were equally

---

① placatory [pləˈkeɪtəri] adj. 抚慰的
② matricide [ˈmætrɪsaɪd] n. 弑母
③ Areopagus [ˌæriˈɒpəgəs] n. 阿勒奥珀格斯山（希腊雅典一小丘）

divided, Orestes was **acquitted**① by the command of Athena. ②

Questions for Discussion:

1. How did Agamemnon offend Artemis?

2. What did Agamemnon do to appease Artemis?

3. What false message did Agamemnon send to Clytemnestra?

4. How did Clytemnestra take a revenge on Agamemnon when she got to know her daughter's sacrifice?

5. What did Orestes do? Who acquitted Orestes?

Ariadne③

Ariadne, the daughter of King Minos of Crete and his wife Pasiphae in Greek mythology, was the granddaughter of the sun god Helios by her mother. She was best known for her pivotal role in the myth of Theseus and the Minotaur.

According to the myth, Minos's son died during some games that were organized in Athens. In retribution, the king of Crete attacked Athens and won. He then imposed a heavy burden on the city, demanding that seven young men and seven young women be sent to Crete every year for the sacrifice into the Labyrinth underneath Minos's palace, where the Minotaur dwelt. The Minotaur was a half-bull, half-human creature that was born from the union of Pasiphae with a bull.

When Theseus heard the story of the Minotaur and its wonderful labyrinth, he determined that it should no longer **exact**④ its yearly tribute of human lives,

---

① acquit [əˈkwɪt] vt. 无罪释放
② 王磊:《希腊罗马神话赏析》,第160—161 页。
③ Ariadne [ˌærɪˈædnɪ] n. 阿里阿德涅 (国王米诺斯与皇后帕西法的女儿,曾给情人西修斯一个线团,帮助他走出迷宫)
④ exact [ɪɡˈzækt] vt. 强取

for he would offer himself as one of the victims and end the terrible sacrifice by slaying the monster. When he announced this intention to his father, the king sought to persuade him to remain at home; but Theseus joined the youths and maidens who had been chosen by lot to go to Crete and set sail for the country of the Minotaur. According to the custom, the ship **hoisted**① only black sails, which Theseus promised to change for white ones when he returned unharmed, having slain the monster.

Nothing befell the voyagers until they reached the coast of Crete, but here the ship was stopped by the giant Talus, whose body was made of brass and was always so red hot that if he held any one in his embrace, the victim was burnt to **cinders**②. This giant was a very effective guardian of the island, keeping off the strangers who had no business along that coast. As he knew that the black-sailed ship brought to his master, King Minos, the yearly tribute from the Athenians, he let the vessel pass; and the voyagers, having landed, were led before the king. The cruel mouth of Minos relaxed into a smile when he saw the youths and maidens, for they were all young and beautiful, the very flower of the Athenians, and it gave him special satisfaction to **consign**③ such a chosen company to death. Beside Minos stood his daughter Ariadne, who looked compassionately at those who were destined for the sacrifice, and when she saw Theseus, she pitied him above all the rest, and wished she might save him from his loathsome fate.

When the young hero asked whether he might go first into the labyrinth, and alone, King Minos smiled at what he considered a child's boast—for he had heard that Theseus hoped to slay the Minotaur; but when he learned that the bold youth was his enemy's only son, he gladly allowed him to do as he wished,

---

① hoist [hɔɪst] vt. 升起
② cinder ['sɪndə] n. 灰烬
③ consign [kən'saɪn] vt. 把……置于（令人不快的境地）

although it was contrary to all custom. Theseus was therefore placed alone in a cell of the prison, where he soon did not feel quite so bold or so eager to face the Minotaur as he had when he talked over the adventure at his father's court. His sword had been taken away, and he had no other weapon with which to fight the monster, so his confidence was somewhat shaken; and as he watched the night deepening, he felt disheartened and almost **unnerved**① for his coming battle. Just then the door of the prison opened softly, and Ariadne, the king's daughter, entered. To Theseus's great surprise she gave him a sharp sword and a ball of thread—two things that she assured him were necessary for him to have if he hoped to come alive out of the labyrinth. She bade him fasten one end of the thread to the entrance of the cave, and keep the ball tight in his hand, so that it might lead him out of the labyrinth.

Theseus was very grateful to Ariadne for her assistance, without which he would never have been able to encounter the monster or to escape from its wonderful labyrinth. He assured the maiden that his father would send her a generous reward of gold and jewels; but she refused to accept any return for her kindness until Theseus ventured to suggest that if she would become his wife, he would be proud to take her back with him to Athens. To this Ariadne gladly agreed, and they **plighted**② their troth in the murky darkness of the prison. When at dawn of the following day the hero, now full of courage and sure of success, was led to the labyrinth, he fastened one end of the thread to the entrance. Then, with his hand on his sword, which was hidden under his long cloak, he stepped boldly into the cave from which no human being had ever come out alive. The passage was narrow and dark, and strewn everywhere with whitening bones, so Theseus stepped very cautiously, with his ball of thread

---

① unnerved [ʌn'nɜːvd] adj. 气馁的
② plight [plaɪt] vt. 宣誓

held fast and his hand ever ready on his sword. Suddenly the Minotaur rushed upon him at an **unlooked-for**① turn in the road, and though the hero had no warning of its presence he met it boldly. A terrible battle ensued, in which Theseus struck fiercely at the Minotaur, wounding it mortally, while the pain-maddened brute tore gashes in his flesh and almost suffocated him with its deadly breath. At last, the hero gave a swift thrust with his sword that cut through the monster's great head, and in a moment the Minotaur lay dead among the bones of its former victims.

With the help of the thread, which he had never lost, even in the thick of the fight, Theseus was able to retrace his steps and to reach the entrance to the labyrinth, where he found Ariadne anxiously awaiting him. At the sight of the blood-stained sword, she knew that her lover had slain the Minotaur, and together they hurried to the black-sailed ship, to which Ariadne had already conveyed the youths and maidens who had been Theseus's companions on the voyage. As quickly as possible the ship sped out of the harbor; but before they could clear the Cretan shores, the giant Talus came upon them, and, seeing that some of his master's prisoners were escaping, he tried to catch hold of the vessel by its rigging. As he leaned forward to do this, Theseus dealt him such a mighty blow that he **toppled**② over into the sea and was drowned. At this spot there were later discovered some thermal springs, which gave evidence of the terrible heat in the giant's brazen body.

Only once did the vessel stop on its swift voyage homeward, and this was at the island of Naxos. Here the whole company landed to explore the beauties of the island, and to find some spring from which to get a supply of fresh water. Ariadne wandered apart from the gay company, and being weary, threw herself

---

① unlooked-for [ʌnˈlʊkt fɔː] adj. 没有预料到的
② topple [tɒpl] vi. 不稳而缓慢倒下

down on the bank of a stream to rest. Here she fell fast asleep, and when Theseus later found her there, he at once conceived the treacherous idea of deserting her. So he summoned all his companions, and went stealthily down to the ship, where he embarked, leaving Ariadne alone on the island. For some days the deserted maiden sat on the seashore watching in vain for the Athenian ship to return; but she did not mourn her faithless lover long, for the gods sent her a greater happiness than she could ever have had with the fickle Theseus. The island of Naxos was the favorite spot of Dionysus, god of wine, who landed one day with a merry company of followers, and found the weeping Ariadne. In a short time he won the maiden's confidence that he persuaded her to become his wife. Ariadne was quite content to stay on the island with such a merry company, and if she ever felt any regret over the faithless Theseus, it was soon forgotten in the joy of the wedding celebrations, which lasted for several days. As a marriage gift, Dionysus placed on Ariadne's white forehead a crown adorned with seven glittering stars; but wonderful as it was, it did not eclipse the beauty of the wearer. The happiness of the newly-wedded pair did not last long, however, for in a few months Ariadne sickened and died. After her death Dionysus left the island, and did not return there for many years; but before he set sail, he took Ariadne's crown and threw it up into the sky, where it formed a brilliant constellation known as Corona. ①

Questions for Discussion:

1. Why did Theseus join the youths and maidens who had been chosen by lot to go to Crete?

2. How did Ariadne help Theseus?

3. How did Theseus reward Ariadne?

---

① Emilie Kip Baker, *Stories of Old Greece and Rome*, pp. 295–300.

4. How did Theseus abandon Ariadne?

5. What marriage gift did Dionysus give to Ariadne?

6. What did Ariadne's crown form after being thrown up into the sky?

Part 3　Reflections

1. Vocabulary Expansion

1）Xiwangmu：_____

2）Ba：_____

3）Su Daji：_____

4）Xihe：_____

5）Jiang Yuan：_____

6）Helen：_____

7）Clytemnestra：_____

8）Medea：_____

9）Ariadne：_____

2. Appreciation

1）东南海之外，甘水之间，有羲和之国。有女子名曰羲和，方日浴于甘渊。羲和者，帝俊之妻，生十日。

《山海经·大荒南经》

2）女丑之尸，生而十日炙杀之。在丈夫北。以右手鄣其面。十日居上，女丑居山之上。

《山海经·海外西经》

3）太昊伏羲氏，成纪人也。其母华胥氏，居于华胥之渚。一日间嬉游入山中，见一巨人足迹，羲母以脚步履之，自觉意有所动，忽然红光罩身，遂因而有娠，怀十六个月，生帝于成纪。

《精编廿六史》

4) 黄帝居轩辕之丘，而娶于西陵之女，是为嫘祖。嫘祖为黄帝正妃，生二子，其后皆有天下：其一曰玄嚣，是为青阳，青阳降居江水。其二曰昌意，降居若水。昌意娶蜀山氏女，曰昌仆，生高阳。高阳有圣德焉。

《史记·五帝本记》

5) Of all things upon earth that bleed and grow,

  A herb most bruised is woman. We must pay

  Our store of gold, hoarded for that one day,

  To buy us some man's love; and lo, they bring

  A master of our flesh! There comes the sting

  Of the whole shame. And then the jeopardy,

  For good or ill, what shall that master be;

  Reject she cannot: and if he but stays

  His suit, 'tis shame on all that woman's days.

  So thrown amid new laws, new places, why,

  'Tis magic she must have, or prophecy—

  Home never taught her that—how best to guide

  Toward peace this thing that sleepeth at her side.

  And she who, labouring long, shall find some way

  Whereby her lord may bear with her, nor fray

  His yoke too fiercely, blessed is the breath

  That woman draws! Else, let her pray for death.

Euripides's *Medea*

6) Helen, thy beauty is to me

  Like those Nicean barks of yore,

   That gently, o'er a perfumed sea,

   The weary, wayworn wanderer bore

  To his own native shore.

On desperate seas long wont to roam,

Thy hyacinth hair, thy classic face,

Thy Naiad airs have brought me home

To the glory that was Greece

And the grandeur that was Rome.

Lo! in yon brilliant window-niche

How statue-like I see thee stand,

The agate lamp within thy hand!

Ah, Psyche, from the regions which

Are Holy Land!

Edgar Allan Poe's "To Helen"

3. Discussion

1) Draw a conclusion of the differences and similarities of women in Chinese and Greek mythology.

2) What views on women are shown through the myths?

Bibliography

丁往道. 1991. 中国神话及志怪小说一百篇. 北京：商务印书馆.

茅盾. 2009. 中国神话研究初探. 南京：江苏文艺出版社.

陶洁等. 2007. 希腊罗马神话. 北京：中国对外翻译出版公司.

王磊. 2008. 希腊罗马神话赏析. 上海：上海外语教育出版社.

谢六逸. 2017. 神话学 ABC. 北京：知识产权出版社.

叶舒宪. 1997. 高唐神女与维纳斯. 北京：中国社会科学出版社.

袁珂. 2013. 中国古代神话. 北京：华夏出版社.

袁珂. 1988. 中国神化史. 上海：上海文艺出版社.

袁珂. 1980. 中国神话选译百题. 上海：上海古籍出版社.

[古罗马] 奥维德. 2000. 变形记. 杨周翰译. 北京：人民文学出版社.

[古希腊] 赫西俄德. 1991. 工作与时日·神谱. 张竹明、蒋平译. 北京：商务印书馆.

[美] 雷·韦勒克、奥·沃伦. 1984. 文学理论. 刘象愚、邢培明、陈圣生、李哲明译. 北京：生活·读书·新知三联书店.

Anonymous. 1999. *The Classic of Mountains and Seas*. Anne Birrell (Trans.). London：Penguins Books.

Anonymous. 2010. *The Classic of Mountains and Seas*. Wang Hong and Zhao Zheng (Trans.). Changsha：Hunan People's Publishing House.

Baker, Emilie Kip. 1913. *Stories of Old Greece and Rome*. New York：The Macmillan Company.

Berens, E. M. 2007. *The Myths and Legends of Ancient Greece and Rome*. New

York: Maynard, Nerrill, & Co.

Birrell, Anne. 1993. *Chinese Mythology: An Introduction.* Baltimore and London: The Johns Hopkins University Press.

Birrell, Anne. 2000. *Chinese Myths.* London: The British Museum Press.

Bulfinch, Thomas. 1990. *The Illustrated Age of Fable—Myths of Greece and Rome.* London: Frances Lincoln Ltd.

Christie, Anthony. 1985. *Chinese Mythology.* New York: Peter Bedrick Books.

Collier, Irene Dea. 2001. *Chinese Mythology.* Alershot: Enslow Publishers.

Euripides. 1912. *The Medea.* Gilbert Murray (Trans.). New York: Oxford University Press.

Frye, Northrop. 2000. *Anatomy of Criticism: Four Essays.* Princeton and Oxford: Princeton University Press.

Hesiod. 2006. *Theogony and Works and Days.* Catherine M. Schlegel and Henry Weinfield (Trans.). Ann Arbor: The University of Michigan Press.

Homer. 2003. *The Illiad.* George Chapman (Trans.). Hertfordshire: Wordsworth Edition Ltd.

Homer. 2002. *The Odyssey.* George Chapman (Trans.). Hertfordshire: Wordsworth Edition Ltd.

Liezi. 2005. *Liezi.* Liang Xiaopeng (Trans.). Beijing: Zhonghua Book Company.

Liu, An. 2010. *Huainanzi.* Zhai Jiangyue and Mou Aipeng (Trans.). Guilin: Guangxi Normal University Press.

Lu, Hsun. 2009. *A Brief History of Chinese Fiction.* Yang Xianyi and Gladys Yang (Trans.). Beijing: Foreign Languages Press.

Marx, Karl. 1904. *A Contribution to the Critique of Political Economy.* N. I. Stone (Trans.). Chicago: Charles H. Kerr & Company.

Ovid. 1958. *The Metamorphoses.* Horace Gregory (Ed.) New York: The Viking Press.

Poe, Edgar Allan. 2008. *The Complete Poetry of Edgar Allan Poe.* Berkley: Signet Classics.

Qu, Yuan. 2009. *Elegies of the South*. Xu Yuan－zhong (Trans.). Beijing: China Translation & Publishing Corporation.

Segal, Robert A. 2004. *Myth: A Very Short Introduction*. Oxford: Oxford University Press.

Spence, Lewis. 1921. *An Introduction to Mythology*, New York: Moffat Yard and Company.

Strassberg, Richard F. 2002. *A Chinese Bestiary—Strange Creatures from the Guideways through Mountains and Seas*. Berkley: University of California Press.

Virgil. 2005. *The Georgics*. James Rhoades (Trans.). New York: Dover Publications.

Walls, Jan and Yvonne Walls. 1984. *Classical Chinese Myths*. Hong Kong: Joint Publishing Co.

Werner, Edward. T. C. 1922. *Myths and Legends of China*. London: George G. Harrap & Co. Ltd.

White, Catherine A. 1889. *The Student's Mythology*. New York: A. C. Armstrong & Son.

Yang, Lihui, An Deming and Jessica Anderson Turner. 2005. *Handbook of Chinese Mythology*. Santa Barbara: ABC–CLIO, Inc.

Zhuangzi. 2012. *Chuang Tzu*. Feng Youlan (Trans.). Beijing: Foreign Language Teaching and Research Press.

Zhuangzi. 1968. *The Complete Works of Chuang Tzu*. Burton Waston (Trans.). New York: Columbia University Press.